PRA

"It's YA, but it's sm
so conservative it's a thermonuclear Red Pill." Yonder Bob

"Think of this as a Heinlein juvie for the 21st Century." John L

"I had to laugh out loud at all the points in the story where a poor sensitivity reader's head would gratifyingly explode. Schantz keeps a completely straight face about it all, which only makes it funnier."
Joseph Moore

"A fun read, redolent of both Ayn Rand and Neal Stephenson at times. Engaging, full of conspiracy bits to suck you in, with an oh-too plausible societal backdrop." Brian J. Schnack

"This is a masterpiece of alternative history techno-thriller science fiction. It is rich in detail, full of interesting characters who interact and develop as the story unfolds, sound in the technical details which intersect with our world, insightful about science, technology, economics, government and the agenda of the "progressive" movement, and plausible in its presentation of the vast, ruthless, and shadowy conspiracy which lies under the surface of its world. And, above all, it is charming—these are characters you'd like to meet, even some of the villains because you want understand what motivates them."
John Walker

Let this book warn this generation of the dangers of our day; deep state corruption, fake news, public school political indoctrination, and the panopticon surveillance state; just as George Orwell's Nineteen Eighty Four was warned his generation of the dangers of socialism and political correctness in his day. John C. Wright

"What an enjoyable read! Hans's story pulls you in and won't let you go until the end. I was already familiar with his expertise in electro-magnetics, which is sprinkled throughout the book. But I had no idea he knew so much about computer hacking and the art of picking up girls!

"All fun aside, this book has a more serious purpose – it is an impassioned plea in support of libertarian principles. In this respect, Hans updates the classical arguments of Heinlein and Rand for a more modern and younger audience...

"Hans's technical books have already made him famous in electro-magnetics. It seems likely that his fiction will extend his notoriety outside that narrow area. Bravo for this first effort! I look forward to many more." Amazon Customer

Books by Hans G. Schantz

The Art and Science of Ultrawideband Antennas,
2nd edition, Artech House, 2015
1st edition, Artech House, 2005

The Biographies of John Charles Fremont,
Kindle Direct Publishing, 2015

The Hidden Truth:
A Science-Fiction Techno-Thriller,
Kindle Direct Publishing, 2016

A Rambling Wreck:
Book 2 of The Hidden Truth,
Kindle Direct Publishing, 2017

The Brave and the Bold:
Book 3 of The Hidden Truth,
Kindle Direct Publishing, 2018

THE HIDDEN TRUTH
A SCIENCE FICTION TECHNO-THRILLER

HANS G. SCHANTZ

2016

www.aetherczar.com

The Hidden Truth
A Science Fiction Techno-Thriller

by Hans G. Schantz

ISBN-13: 978-1532712937
ISBN-10: 1532712936

All rights reserved.

This book or parts thereof may not be reproduced in any form, stored in a retrieval system, or transmitted in any form by any means – electronic, mechanical, photocopy, recording, major blockbuster film, epic Broadway musical, or otherwise – without prior written permission from the author, except as provided under fair use provisions of copyright law.

This is a work of fiction. Names, characters, places, and incidents are products of the author's imagination or are used in a fictitious manner. Any similarity to actual people, organizations, and/or events is purely coincidental.

Copyright © 2016 Hans G. Schantz
All rights reserved

Cover Design by Steve Beaulieu at Beaulistic Book Services

10 9 8 7 6 5 4

To my parents, Ray and Hilda

Contents:

- Chapter 1: The Nexus 1
- Chapter 2: The Discovery 9
- Chapter 3: The Preparation 33
- Chapter 4: The Execution 51
- Chapter 5: Independence Day 70
- Chapter 6: A Vacation 87
- Chapter 7: Summers' End 121
- Chapter 8: Back to School 149
- Chapter 9: It Takes a Tolliver to Beat a Tolliver 177
- Chapter 10: Finale 223
- Chapter 11: The Enemy Reports 257
- Chapter 12: My Manifesto 267
- About *The Hidden Truth* 271
- About the Author 274
- Acknowledgements 279

Chapter 1: The Nexus

When two paths diverge, we must choose. One may lead to disaster. The other may lead to new vistas and novel opportunities. Having chosen, we cannot go back and see what might have been. Worse, we might not get to choose our own path, but instead experience the consequences of someone else's choices. A Nexus, or moment of transition, contains elements of both creation and destruction. The creation of a new future implies a corresponding destruction of what might have been. From that moment on, nothing is the same any more.

Grandma recalled hearing about the Pearl Harbor attack on the radio. Then, she listened to the radio broadcast piped through loudspeakers at her school the next day as President Roosevelt declared war. My father remembered as a boy in elementary school hearing that President Kennedy was assassinated. For my generation, I suppose the equivalent moment was that terrible day, September 11, 2001, sitting in class and watching the images of the jet plane crashing into the Capitol building, with the pillar of smoke from the still burning White House in the background. Everyone wondered what it all meant. Then a few days later, everyone was watching as newly sworn in President Lieberman vowed "never again," pledged to wipe out the terrorists' Afghan training camps, and promised to bring their Saudi backers to justice.

The most significant moments of transition in our lives are not necessarily so abrupt nor of such global significance, however. I remember one moment with particular clarity: a moment that shaped my destiny and guided all that was to follow. When I was 16 years old, I wanted to see a hypnotist perform. He was the featured guest at our high school assembly in March of my junior year. The hypnotist regressed one girl to five years old and had her singing "Itsy Bitsy Spider." Another hypnotized guy became as rigid as a board. These and more were just samples of the show he promised us, if only we came back that evening for the deluxe performance, for only a modest admission fee. Everyone in my debate class buzzed with excitement afterwards. I was absolutely sold. I wanted to go with a passion I had previously reserved only for making good grades and clever arguments.

My parents did not share my fervor. When I explained the hypnotist had pledged to "unleash untapped mental powers," Mom was adamant that my mental faculties were just fine as they were and did not require unleashing by an itinerant entertainer. Dad was similarly skeptical about the idea. He thought it was a complete waste of my time, and that stage hypnotism was little better than a confidence game disguised as entertainment. My irresistible enthusiasm crashed headlong into their immoveable disapproval.

Defeat was inevitable. Sure, I could change my parents' minds on trivialities – what I should order at a restaurant or which T-shirt met their standards of propriety. But when they laid down the law, the best I could hope for was for them to deign to give me a reasoned explanation of why I was simply not going to get what I wanted. Still, I had to try. My informal approach was not working, so I imposed structure on my argumentation.

I led off with a classical thesis-antithesis-synthesis. I noted that hypnotism was a technique widely accepted in both psychology and forensics and of great potential value in dialectic and rhetoric. Skeptics might argue that presentation in a traveling show cast doubt on the technique's validity, yet traveling lectures and demonstrations were critical in building awareness of emerging fields of study. Even Dad's own field of electrical engineering could trace its historical roots back to electrical performers giving informative lectures and spectacular demonstrations to enthusiastic audiences. No particular dangers from hypnosis were evident in the scientific literature. Therefore, the potential value clearly outweighed any potential harm.

My parents were unmoved. Turning Dad was my best hope. When I was a kid, there was a time I wanted to go on an overnight camping trip. Mom insisted I carry a nutritious lunch and extra food in case I was out longer than expected. Dad, on the other hand, noted that a pound of body fat is the equivalent of 3500 calories and that I was probably good for several days of starvation without significant impairment. "It's painful as your body adjusts to starvation and starts burning your own tissues for fuel, but once you adapt I understand the discomfort is minimized. It's good that you're taking risks and stretching your limits. Builds character." When he started talking like that, I knew I'd better shut up and bring the extra food. He'd be just as happy to let me suffer the consequences of my poor judgment - at least to a point. There was the time my big sister, Kira, didn't want to wear a coat on a Christmas trip to Atlanta. Sure enough, we got a flat tire and Dad insisted we all get out of the car and stand off the road while he changed the tire. When Mom started to offer Kira her coat, "No," Dad said. "When we make poor decisions we must be prepared to accept the consequences." She wasn't out long enough to get too cold, but I don't recall her second guessing Mom's or Dad's judgment on clothing again. If I could convince Dad that the consequences would be good for me, he might yield.

I applied Rogerian argument: I explained my parents' position back to them so they knew I understood it. I noted the validity of their position in the context of an ill-educated, weak-willed son unable to properly judge the performance and incapable of withstanding the blandishments of a potentially deceptive presentation. I pointed out they had done such a good job raising me, molding my character, and setting me on the right path that they – and I – had nothing to fear from the hypnotist. I further argued that the experience would advance our mutual goals in developing and strengthening my character by giving me practical experience in evaluating the methods employed by the hypnotist.

Dad seemed more amused than persuaded. "I see your debate coach introduced you to Rogerian argumentation. But I thought the point was to establish a common ground with your opponent before you antagonize him with your overly strident advocacy. You should try leading off with the Rogerian approach instead of using it as a last resort." Nothing is more demoralizing than an opponent who ignores your strongest blows and instead critiques your style. I'd have to remember to use that technique sometime.

I was out of brilliant dialectic contortions. I knew better than to try rhetorical tricks. They wouldn't move my parents in the least. Fortunately, my efforts had proved enough to wear Dad down. Not that his opinion of the hypnotist changed at all, but I think he saw how much I wanted to go. He turned to Mom with a half-smile and said, "Sometimes there's no telling someone the truth. You have to show them. Mind if I go with him?"

Under assault from both sides, Mom relented. "If that's what you both want to do, dear," she acquiesced to Dad. Nevertheless, I saw her shoot him a look that both clearly disavowed any responsibility for the consequences and promised further words with Dad once we got back.

The performance that night was an extended version of the daytime show. Finally, the hypnotist called for anyone in the audience who wanted to be hypnotized to come up on stage. I turned to Dad with an unspoken plea, and he frowned in disapproval. Finally, he said, "OK, you can go."

As I was standing up, he grabbed my arm and said, "One more thing. Whatever you do up there, I want you to remember: be honest with yourself."

"Sure thing, Dad," I said casually as I eased past him to the aisle.

There must have been nearly fifty people on the stage. I joined them, as the hypnotist spoke. "I'd like everyone to listen very carefully to what I'm saying and focus on my voice," the hypnotist began. "As I am talking to you, I will be moving around the stage. If I tap you on the shoulder, please step down from the stage and take your seat. Not everyone makes a good subject, so please don't feel bad if you aren't among the elite few left on stage at the end." I was positive I was going to be among the elite few.

"Close your eyes," he commanded with his smooth and confident voice.

I complied.

"Relax. Focus only on the sound of my voice. Now I want you to clasp your left hand with your right hand and pretend they are stuck together. Try to pull your hands apart, but it is as if they are glued one to the other."

I enthusiastically pretended to pull apart my hands as I heard the hypnotist winnowing down his field of subjects. He continued with similar commands, relax, focus, suppose this, imagine that, relax some more. I focused on his voice, tuning out everything else. Finally, there was a subtle change in his patter.

"Now, I want you to imagine your eyelids are stuck shut. If I told you right now to open your eyelids, you would be able to. In a moment, however, I will be asking you to open your eyelids and you will find that you cannot. If you tried right now, you could. But I am going to count slowly to ten, and when I have finished counting to ten you will find that you cannot open your eyes."

He counted to ten.

"Now, you will find that you are so relaxed that you cannot open your eyes."

I remembered what Dad told me – be honest with yourself. I opened my eyes. I was one of only a dozen or so people left on the stage. The hypnotist was looking at me. I didn't need a tap on the shoulder to know that I was certifiably hypnotically deficient. I returned to my seat next to Dad. There was a strange look on his face. I couldn't decipher it. The show continued without my active participation.

The hypnotist led his subjects through a phase in which their hands were stuck together, for real instead of pretend. One by one, he continued rejecting the least enthusiastic hypnotic candidates. He progressed through successive maneuvers, each one just slightly more elaborate than the last. By the time he was done, he was left with one girl quacking like a duck, a guy barking like a dog, another guy with his arms up like a tree swaying back and forth in the wind, and another girl who had become a washing machine spinning back and forth. I would have felt embarrassed for them, except the hypnotist's progression was so gradual that their behavior seemed almost natural under the circumstances. I felt not quite right, but I couldn't explain why. I was not the elite subject I had so desperately aspired to be, and I wasn't sure whether to be disappointed or relieved.

On the drive back home, Dad spun one of his fatherly yarns. To my regret now, I often tended to tune out what he had to say. That night though, I listened attentively. "You know, son," he began, "they say that if you throw a frog in a pot of boiling water, he'll recoil at the heat and jump out, but if you put the frog in a pot of cold water and slowly turn the heat up, he'll stay in until he boils to death. Your character is a lot like that frog. People make little compromises all the time, slowly chipping away at their sense of right and wrong, slowly expanding the bounds of what they consider acceptable behavior. Finally, they'll do things that they never would have done if they hadn't let their standards and morals slip away from them."

"Are you saying my friends on the stage were immoral for barking or quacking?" I asked.

"Not actively immoral," he said. "Call it immorality by negligence: willing to let themselves be nudged and talked, wheedled and cajoled into something that they wouldn't ordinarily do. If the hypnotist had asked them when they first got up on the stage to believe they were a dog or a duck or a tree or a washing machine, do you think they would have complied?"

"No," I agreed. "He started us with pretending and acting. When he said my eyes were stuck and I couldn't open them, I remembered what you said about being honest with myself, and I opened my eyes."

"That's right," Dad said. "But your friends wanted so much to be part of the show, so much to be the mental marvels that the hypnotist was looking for that they were willing to lie to themselves just a little bit and pretend that their eyes actually were stuck shut. Having lied once, the hypnotist was able to get them to lie to themselves just a little further with his next command, slightly further still with his next command, and so on. By the time he was done with them, those boys and girls on stage would have done almost anything he asked of them. They became hypnotic subjects through their willingness to comply with the hypnotist. I'm proud of you for setting a line between acting and pretending on the one side and self-deception on the other, and then refusing to step over it."

"Thanks, Dad." I said. I really meant it. He could be distant at times or consumed in his work. But every once in a while when we were together, my old man would take things that were a confusing jumble, then he'd impose order on the chaos with a keen insight that left me aspiring to be as wise as he appeared.

Be honest with yourself.

"So, how do you figure out stuff like that?" I asked him.

"Observation," he said. "Years of experience dealing with people. Lots of reading about techniques of persuasion."

For months, I'd been thinking hard about what I wanted to study in school and what I wanted to do with my life. "If I want a career where I get to figure stuff out, what would I do?"

"Stuff? Like that hypnotist's act? Probably psychology. Maybe marketing. You might get the practical aspects in studying interrogation techniques in criminology or in military training like your Uncle Rob's. Any job that's worth anything, though, is going to involve lots of figuring 'stuff' out. You just have to decide what kind of 'stuff' you most want to figure out."

"What if I want to figure out how things work at the most fundamental level?" I asked.

"Then, you should take a look at science in general and probably physics in particular."

"Can you help me get started?" I asked.

"Absolutely," Dad said.

Resolving to figure out fundamental stuff, and deciding always to be honest with myself: that is how I decided to become a scientist. Looking back now with the benefit of hindsight, I can see how fateful that decision was. The first steps to becoming a scientist took an enormous amount of time and effort. I had to overcome my youth and my inexperience. However, I had the advantage of boundless energy, burning curiosity, fierce determination, and most of all an open mind.

That's probably why just a few months later I was able to spot the subtle clue that countless others had overlooked. Enormous effort had been spent to hide all the traces and cover up the hidden truth. If you looked hard enough though, the hints were right there, in plain sight, seen by many, yet understood by very few. My experience with the hypnotist left me primed and ready. Having found the clue, I wouldn't let it go until I'd puzzled out what it meant and followed where it led. But, I'm getting ahead of myself.

Chapter 2: The Discovery

It turned out Dad's idea of becoming a scientist involved an incredible amount of reading. Somehow, I had anticipated building electronics at his workbench, working through equations, or bouncing radio signals around with the radio hardware in his study. Dad explained that I was not going to touch his radio equipment until I finally got around to taking and passing my Amateur Radio License exam. He said that if I wanted to be a scientist, I had to think like a scientist. If I wanted to think like a scientist, I had to learn what and how scientists thought, and the best way to do that was to read what they wrote. "Michael Faraday started out as an apprentice to a bookbinder," my father explained. "He taught himself science by reading the books he bound. You could do much worse than to follow his example."

Mom actually was a scientist. She'd studied chemistry and was working on her Ph.D. when she dropped out of school to have Kira and marry Dad. She was a great help when I took chemistry last year, but she expected me to just know all the atomic weights and ionic states and such. All of them. Perfectly. Right away. Trying to learn chemistry from her was an exercise in frustration on both sides.

Dad, on the other hand, was a patient teacher. One of my earliest memories was sitting in his lap while he read Barenstein Bears books to me. He was a great reader and had an excellent library. His books ranged from technical books to works of history, philosophy, and politics. His answer to many of my questions was to hand me the appropriate book to read, and stand ready to rectify my confusions. When I took an introduction to calculus at the community college the previous autumn, he handed me a beat up copy of *Calculus Made Easy* by Silvanus Thompson.

Dad was a great help on my calculus homework. He'd earned a degree in electrical engineering from Georgia Tech, worked for a while, and met my Mom while he was back in school working on a master's. They were married and returned to Sherman, Tennessee, where he got a job in electrical contracting just before my big sister was born. He didn't use all the math he studied in school, but he remembered plenty. His work was feast or famine. He'd land a big industrial job and work sixteen hours a day or even more, including a round trip to Johnson City, Knoxville, or as far away as Chattanooga. He usually had enough work to keep a couple other contractors and apprentices busy. Then, he'd have a few months at a slower pace doing mostly residential construction work before the next big job came up. That spring, he'd finished work at a new auto plant and was back to a more sedate pace.

So when I set out to be a scientist, he handed me a well-worn copy of *Matter and Motion* by James Clerk Maxwell. "He's one of the smartest and most successful scientists that ever lived," Dad explained. "When you read his book you're learning exactly how a brilliant scientist thinks about the most basic concepts. You're learning straight from the guy who figured out how electromagnetics works, instead of suffering through the cleaned-up and dumbed-down version you get from your teachers and textbooks."

I was surprised how interesting and readable the book was. Dad would answer my questions and help me with some of the math when I got home from school. Debate season was over for me since I hadn't qualified for Nationals. I had plenty of spare time to study. Some of the math went completely over my head, particularly the section on what Maxwell called "Least Action." Most of it was merely difficult. I'd grind through, get stuck, Dad would get me going again, and I'd grind some more. I was glad I'd taken calculus already. By the time the school year was almost over, I'd worked my way through *Matter and Motion*.

Dad asked, "Have you given a thought to what you want to do this summer?"

The previous summer I'd tagged along with him doing electrical work as an apprentice. The time wouldn't count toward becoming a journeyman electrician since I didn't have a high school diploma, but the experience would be helpful if I wanted to try working as an electrician while I was in school, like Dad did. The money was good too! "Are you busy enough that I can help you out like last summer?"

"I'm taking some time to help out your Uncle Rob, but it's nothing you need to help on. I'm also working a small residential job near Knoxville, but it's strictly part time. I may want you to help here and there if I get in a crunch. Mom and I want to take the family on a weeklong vacation in August. I want to stop in at a trade show in Houston and visit the Huntsville Hamfest on the way back. On the way out, we'll pick up Kira and visit some of the familiar sights in Nashville and Memphis – just a road trip, nothing elaborate. It may be one of our last opportunities for a family road trip, what with you heading off to college next year and Kira graduating. You'll need to find something to do with the rest of your summer. I have a proposition for you. You keep up with your studies and take a college-level physics class at the community college – the calculus-based one, so you can apply it to a degree in physics or engineering. Ace the class, and I'll pay you for the hours. Same rate as last summer."

That seemed uncharacteristically generous of Dad. Last summer, he had me logging hours on a timesheet for working in the heat and humidity of construction sites all summer long. Getting paid for studying? He must be feeling prosperous after finishing that auto plant job. "Sounds like a good deal," I replied, before Dad had a chance to regret his largess. "I also want to do research for next year's debate topic. Would you let me count that?"

Dad was always supportive of my debate research. "Reading makes a full man, Meditation a profound man, and Discourse a clear man," he was fond of quoting.

"What's the topic for next year?" Dad asked.

I knew this was going to be trouble: "Resolved that the U.S. federal government should substantially increase alternative energy incentives in the United States."

He glared. "You realize the Gore Tax has done more to destroy the country's economy than even 9/11. Coal towns up and down Appalachia have been devastated. Taxing carbon was bad enough. But subsidizing uneconomical forms of energy only adds foolishness to folly."

Yes, my father was a climate denier.

President Lieberman got Congress to pass the Preserving our Planet's Future Act as a monument to the late President Gore. A key part of the plan to decrease greenhouse gas emissions and rein in global warming involved a carbon tax that opponents, like Dad, called the "Gore Tax." Global temperatures had stopped rising and in fact levelled off in the years since the plan passed. A strong consensus of scientists all agreed that the President's action had averted global disaster, yet some extremists denied there was a connection between the law and the climate. It was all just a coincidence and natural variation, they claimed. Dad followed climate-denier websites like wattsupwiththat.com where skeptics argued that because carbon dioxide levels had continued to rise while temperatures levelled off, the Gore Tax was ineffective. But any number of climate scientists had models proving just how much worse greenhouse gases and temperatures both would have been without the law. I'd tried discussing the scientific consensus and the importance of saving the planet from climate change with Dad, but he was just too stubborn to listen to me.

"Of course, I have to be able argue both sides of the topic," I pointed out. "And I'd appreciate whatever evidence, insights, and arguments you could share."

I doubt I fooled him, but he smiled. "I suppose so. But mind you, I'll expect you to keep filling out your timesheet and account to me for the work you do."

I agreed, glad to have averted that potential conflict.

* * *

My summer days fell into a routine. I got up, grabbed a bite to eat, and headed on over to Kudzu Joe's coffeehouse. It was slow in the mornings. The local Masons met there Wednesdays for breakfast, and there were some retired gentlemen who tended to hang out and shoot the breeze. There were a couple of truckers who'd stop in now and then to grumble to each other about how the Gore Tax put them out of business. But most of the customers were lawyers from the Lee County Courthouse across the square, business people with offices nearby, or truckers or working folk who came in, grabbed a cup and left. Joe didn't mind my nursing a cup of coffee and working at one of the tables. Sometimes, my best friend and debate partner, Amit Patel, would join me if we were working on debate prep. Usually though, I spent the time studying physics. By the time the lunch crowd started in, I headed home for lunch.

Then I went off to the community college for my physics class, which was held Monday through Thursday. Friday was a study and review session, which I usually skipped. After class, my schedule was less fixed. Sometimes I'd head back to Joe's. Sometimes I'd head home if Dad were in, and if I thought I'd need his help on the latest homework. Sometimes I'd head over to the Berkshire Inn. It was a national hotel chain, but the Patels owned the local franchise. They had a small lounge where they served breakfast in the morning, and I could work there with Amit, when he didn't have to get behind the desk to check in a customer or run an errand for his folks. His folks didn't mind if we used the exercise equipment in the weight room, so sometimes we'd work out or swim before I headed home for dinner. Moreover, I'd been to the hotel weekly during the school year watching the science fiction-western, *Firefly*, with Amit on the big screen TV in the lounge. By then, the show was in its second season, and we caught every episode.

Amit started joining me at Kudzu Joe's more often when our mutual friend from the debate team, Emma, started working a morning shift as a barista. Lately, he'd been studying up on something called game theory. I'd heard of game theory, but the kind of game theory Amit was studying involved trying to manipulate girls into going out with him. Naturally, I found the concept fascinating, having developed quite an interest in girls, myself. Near as I could figure from Amit's description, it involved "negging" or putting down a girl's self-esteem to the point where she'd go out with you. It didn't make much sense to me why you'd want to date a girl with poor self-esteem who could be so easily manipulated.

One morning, my obnoxious cousin Abby Tolliver came into Kudzu Joe's with a gaggle of her friends. As they were ordering and picking up their drinks, Amit smirked. "Witness my game," he said softly as he got up and walked confidently over to Abby and her friends. "Hi, Abby," he said.

"What do you want, loser?" Abby said contemptuously. I marveled at how effectively she communicated her scorn, making her "you" sound like "eeyoo." Her nose crinkled in disgust at Amit's effrontery in thinking he was worthy to speak with her. Abby's friends giggled at what they perceived to be Amit's humiliation.

Amit looked impassively at Abby for a moment before continuing. "I just wanted to let you know how very sorry I am," he said with seemingly sincere regret, "but I won't be asking you out to the Fall Ball in September."

One of Abby's friends almost choked on her iced, sugar-free, vanilla latte with soymilk. Abby was so outraged at Amit's presumption she couldn't speak for a moment. Amit just stared at her with a concerned and sympathetic look on his face. He was fortunate to have timed his approach before she got her drink or he might have ended up with a face full of scalding hot decaf soy latte. Finally, Abby exclaimed, "What makes you think I'd even consider going out with you?!?"

A look of relief swept over Amit's face. "Oh, I'm so glad you feel the same way. Thanks for taking it so well." He nodded gravely at the girls and said, "Ladies," by way of a goodbye. Then he turned his back to them dismissively, strode confidently over to the table, and sat down facing me. "Do warn me if your dear cousin is about to smack me on the back of the head," he said softly.

Abby's exclamation as she stormed out the coffee shop was unworthy of a proper young lady. Her friends followed in her wake. "You certainly pissed her off," I observed. "If that was an example of your 'game,' I'd say 'you lost.' Abby is even less likely now to ever go out with you than she was before. Of course that's an accomplishment in itself."

"You still don't get it." Amit sighed. "I wasn't gaming Abby."

"Huh?" I was confused.

"Look, Abby may be bitchy, but she's cute, her family is loaded, and she's probably the single most popular girl in school. She thinks she's way too good for the likes of me. Only the top guys in her little clique's pecking order have a chance with her, right?"

"Yeah…" I still didn't get it.

"So where does that leave the guy who apparently just turned her down?"

I began to see what he was getting at, but it still didn't make sense. "It's not like you're going to be, oh, homecoming king just because you preemptively turned down Abby when you had no shot with her in the first place."

He grinned "No, of course not. But Abby just got rejected by someone her clique rates as a zero. That's blood in the water for the sharks she swims with."

"All I see is you came up with a clever and convoluted way to cut down and infuriate Abby. Not that she doesn't deserve it. But I don't see what it buys you."

"Ah, but not every girl is a part of her clique, and the ones Abby and her gang snub and put down will jump at the chance to perceive themselves as better than Abby – to go out with the guy who turned down Abby Tolliver."

Realization was beginning to dawn. "You're 'gaming' Emma."

He got that cocky grin again. "Not necessarily. Can't tie yourself down to one girl, dude. Gotta play it cool, have the attitude that you're in demand; you don't need any particular girl. 'Gotta fake it 'til you make it.'" He dropped the attitude and stopped regurgitating his pick-up artist slogans. "But if all this lands me a date with Emma, I'll start there. You pick up any vibes from Emma?" His back was to her, and she was serving another customer.

"She did seem awfully amused when Abby and her gang stormed off. And she's been looking over this way. Are you going to ask her out?"

"'Indications of interest,'" he said proudly, as if he were a doctor providing a professional diagnosis. "I'm not going to ask her out right now. Too obvious. She's no dummy. But, soon." He took a sip of his coffee. "See, you need to understand game. I have the Indian thing to overcome, so I have to have good game just to break even, at least with girls around here. You could clean up if you put your mind to it. And you've got the whole bad-boy mystique going for you, what with your dad marrying a Tolliver."

I never ceased to be amazed how everyone in town seemed to know everyone else's business. I'd certainly never mentioned my parents' story to him, what little I actually knew of it.

It must have been fifteen minutes later when Sheriff Gunn walked into Kudzu Joe's. He came through the door and stopped. Seeing us, he came straight over to our table with a slow and commanding authority. He was a big and imposing man, and he also had some trick of posture and body language that made him seem even more imposing. I took a deep breath and studied how he walked and held himself. It helped me distance myself from his intimidating influence. I still had to will myself to remain calm as he spoke.

"Boys, a very respectable young lady filed a complaint with me just now that she was verbally assaulted in this establishment not long ago," The sheriff towered above Amit. "Either of you two have any comment?"

"Well, sir," I preempted Amit, "if there were any abuse I'm afraid it was directed by my cousin, Abby, at Amit, here. He very politely declined to go with her to a dance, and unfortunately, Abby took it rather poorly."

"You expect me to believe that Abby Tolliver," the sheriff was so incredulous he said her name twice, "Abby Tolliver wanted to go to a dance with Amit Patel?"

"Oh, I don't know, sir. I didn't think so either at first, but Abby got so upset when Amit turned her down that, well, I have to wonder if maybe she truly did have a crush on him. But, anyway, Amit was polite and courteous throughout the entire exchange. A perfect gentleman." I said all that just loud enough that Emma could hear and, hopefully, take the hint. Sure enough, Sheriff Gunn called her over. Emma was no great friend of Abby. She explained it to the sheriff more or less the same way.

I think Sheriff Gunn could see this was going nowhere, but he felt he had to put us in our place. "Boys, this is a quiet town and I aim to keep it that way. If I hear any more complaints from Miss Tolliver, so help me I will run you both in for disturbing the peace and I'll let your fathers tan your hides when they pick you up, you hear me?"

"Yes, sir," we both said.

The sheriff looked straight at me. "I understand there's been heavy traffic up by the Cove Creek Plant. Lots of trucks off the old highway near your Uncle Rob's place. You know anything about that?"

Dad had mentioned something about a project up at Uncle Rob's but he'd lectured me strongly never to mention his business around town. "No, sir. I haven't been up to see Uncle Rob in months," I said truthfully.

Sheriff Gunn grunted and left.

"Thanks guys," Amit said to both me and Emma, "I owe you." He turned to Emma and casually laid his hand on her forearm. "How about I treat you to a movie and ice cream when you get off, by way of thanks?"

Damn if she didn't take him up on it. They exchanged numbers.

"What happened to waiting and asking her out later," I asked after Emma was out of earshot, back behind the counter serving her next customer.

"It was the right time. Mutual shared danger. Excitement. And now all those tingles are linked in her mind with me asking her out. Twenty bucks says we make out on the first date."

After what I'd seen, I wasn't going to take him up on the offer. "So you're doing her the favor by allowing her the privilege of a date with you?" I was still a bit incredulous at it all.

"Gotta maintain the right frame," he said. "Establish your superior value and follow through." He dropped the cocky attitude for a moment. "That did work out better – and faster – than I expected. And thanks for the save with the sheriff. Like Abby got so upset because she secretly yearns for me." He was loving it. "I can't wait for that one to get around. I owe you, dude."

"Yeah, the next family get-together is going to be pretty interesting, but it was worth it to see her taken down a peg," I assured him. By then, it was lunchtime. Amit nonchalantly blew Emma a kiss as we left. She giggled. Girls.

The Lee County sheriff interrogating someone about a teenage squabble speaks volumes about how the Tollivers owned the county. And yes, my mom actually was one of those Tollivers. My Great-Great-Great-Grandpa Jake Tolliver started off in coal but the family wisely diversified into lumber, chemicals, natural gas, and other businesses long before the great coal crash. When Mom fell for Dad at school, her parents forbade the match. They saw Dad as an uncouth adventurer trying to marry his way into money. The Tollivers disowned Mom and it was years before they spoke again. More recently, Grandma Tolliver insisted on inviting us over for Thanksgiving. Grandma was always gracious, but she was the exception. With Abby's father, my Uncle Larry, around, we spent most of the meal pretending not to notice that the Tollivers were pretending not to look down on us. Mom's other brother, my Uncle Mike, was just as bad. The social structure of the community was simple. The Tollivers were on top. The lawyers, doctors, and senior Tolliver executives were in the next tier. There was a decent middle class of Tolliver managers, engineers, teachers, and county workers. A number of nuclear workers, engineers and managers who worked at TVA's Cove Creek Plant the other side of the ridge from my Uncle's place. Some Oak Ridge or other TVA workers who didn't mind the long commute. Blue-collar workers, like Dad, were not as well respected. Social status at school was strongly influenced by social status of one's parents.

That afternoon Amit was going out with Emma, so I didn't go over to his folks' hotel after my physics class. I went to the Tolliver Library instead. The place had a fascinating history. Before Great-Great Grandpa Tolliver died over a hundred years ago, he decided to endow a university: Tolliver Technical Institute. By the time of the Great Depression, Tolliver Tech rivaled places like Vanderbilt, Georgia Tech, and Auburn as a regional engineering powerhouse. However, the Tollivers failed to keep a tight grasp on their namesake. They lost control of the Board of Directors during World War II when the school reorganized as a military training institute. Dad claimed that in the 1950s and 1960s, the school became "a hot bed of experimental and progressive foolishness." Even I'd heard stories about how it was a real party school. Quality suffered. In any event, by the 1970s, the Tolliver Corporation stopped hiring Tolliver Tech graduates. The school blew through its endowment, and went bankrupt. The State of Tennessee acquired the campus and integrated the facility into the community college system. Now the place only offered two-year technology degrees and basic classes. Through all the turmoil, however, the Tolliver Library remained intact and funded under a separate endowment run by whichever Mrs. Tolliver fancied herself as a patron of knowledge. The technical books were dated, and the library had long since stopped keeping up with the leading edge of scientific and technical development, but it was a beautiful and little-used facility perfect for some quiet study.

When I finished my homework on waves, I decided to see if I could find a good book, so I could learn more. I was browsing the shelves when I found it. In faded gold letters, the cover said "*Electric Waves*. Franklin. The Macmillan Company." Of course, I knew about Benjamin Franklin and that he flew his kite and developed lightning rods, but waves? I thought electric waves were much later. Intrigued, I picked up the book. "*Electric Waves – An Advanced Treatise on Alternating-Current Theory* by William Suddards Franklin, Professor of Physics in Lehigh University." The book was printed in 1909. I almost put it back when I realized it wasn't written by *that* Franklin. I started leafing through it, and I found it was full of wonderful and simple drawings of waves: water waves, sound waves, and electric waves. Just what I needed. I found a comfortable chair, settled in, and started reading. I was on page 115 when I saw the words that forever changed the course of my life:

> *"The theory of wave distortion in transmission lines and cables was first developed by Heaviside. The second half, pages 306-454, of Heaviside's Electromagnetic Theory, Vol. 1 (London, 1893), is an extremely simple and interesting discussion of this subject. In his forthcoming third volume, Heaviside will elaborate on his remarkable theory of wave interference whereby electric waves bounce off each other.*

This ingenious discovery promises to unlock similar valuable insights."

That confused me. "Wave distortion theory" seemed esoteric enough. Electric waves bouncing off each other? That just didn't seem right. But, it was time for me to be heading home. I replaced the book on the shelf and resolved to ask my dad about it.

* * *

"Radio waves do not bounce off each other," Dad said matter-of-factly. "They pass right through each other. They only bounce off material things, particularly conductors."

I told him what I'd read.

"'Electric waves' is just an old fashioned way of describing a radio wave, or more generally, an electromagnetic wave," Dad explained. "Whatever you want to call it, that's either a mistake or you're misremembering it," he insisted.

I took offense at the implied slight on my powers of recollection. I asked Dad if I could borrow his computer. I went to his study and fired up the web browser. By that time, many books that were out of copyright were available online. I searched for "electric waves franklin" and had no trouble finding it. I navigated through to page 115 as Dad watched over my shoulder.

"The theory of wave distortion in transmission lines and cables was first developed by Heaviside. The second half, pages 306-454, of Heaviside's Electromagnetic Theory, Vol. 1 (London, 1893), is an extremely simple and interesting discussion of this subject."

That was it. A blank void loomed below that text. There was no further discussion of a forthcoming volume three nor a mention of bouncing waves.

"You must be studying too hard," Dad said with a chuckle.

Now I wasn't merely offended. I was mad. I knew I wasn't imagining things, and I wouldn't have made a stupid mistake like that. I controlled my temper, and printed out a copy of the page to keep for reference. Further discussion wasn't going to help, so I decided to bide my time and change the subject.

"What's the project you're working on with Uncle Rob?" I asked.

"I'm just helping him clear some land and pour a foundation for a new barn."

"The reason I asked is Sheriff Gunn asked me this morning if I knew anything about a lot of truck traffic at Uncle Rob's place."

Dad was normally very expressive. He froze for a moment. He checked the time on his watch. With an obviously feigned casualness that belied his too-long dramatic pause he asked, "So, what did you tell him?"

"I said I hadn't been up there in months and I didn't know."

Dad looked at me gravely.

"Anything else?"

"That was the end of it," I assured him. "So, why would Uncle Rob's barn require so many trucks?"

"I called in some favors and borrowed a back hoe and a bulldozer for the excavation." I saw Dad glance down at his watch. "And we had a cement mixer up to pour in the foundation and a pad." That sure didn't sound like enough truck traffic for the sheriff to find noteworthy. I could tell he was hiding something, but if he didn't want to discuss it, it wasn't any of my business.

Just then, Mom called us both to dinner. Dad said Grace, and we ate. He ate quickly, checked his watch again, excused himself, and told Mom, "I need to head back to Rob's tonight. I'll be up late. Don't wait up for me. You can call me at Rob's, but only if you really have to." He forestalled any questions by looking at me and saying: "Do clear the table and wash the dishes for your mother, please."

"Yes, sir." I could tell a direct order when I heard one.

I could see Mom was deep in her "I'm worried but can't discuss it in front of the children" mode. "OK, dear."

Dad popped back into his study. I could hear him power up his radio. A staccato burst of Morse code punctuated the air. A few moments later, came a reply with a slightly offset tone. I was wishing I'd mastered Morse code back when he first started trying to teach me.

Once Dad left, I asked Mom if she knew what was going on. "I'm sure your father will tell you what you need to know about his business when you need to know it. In the meantime, you should remember not to discuss family business outside of the house."

"Yes ma'am," I said, and I cleared the table for her. She said she'd wash the dishes.

Knowing Uncle Rob, it might be a still. Dad had let slip that Uncle Rob was prone to condense some of the corn he grew into more marketable form without benefit of government sanction. Dad did not approve. Not that he didn't imbibe some of Uncle Rob's product now and then, but he didn't think the risk Uncle Rob ran was worth it. I couldn't see Uncle Rob building a meth lab or marijuana grow house, let alone Dad helping him with either project. And frankly, I couldn't see how any construction project would involve enough trucks for the sheriff to notice or care. When I went to bed, I plugged in my phone and noted that Dad's phone was charging on the counter. Was he back already and I hadn't noticed? I stepped into Mom's sewing room. Dad had installed a four-camera security system that recorded to a computer there. I checked the camera that covered the driveway. His truck was still gone.

He wasn't back the next morning. "He probably stayed up at Rob's last night," Mom assured me. Probably? She didn't know? My, Dad was playing whatever it was close to the vest if he wasn't telling Mom.

I texted Amit: "Can't Joe this am. How'd it go?" I had time to get a lunch mostly pulled together when I got his reply: "You'd owe me 20." Heh. "Berkshire after class?" I asked. "Come on over," he replied.

I asked Mom to let me know if she got any updates from Dad and drove to the community college. I walked to the Tolliver Library, bounded up the stairs to the third floor, and found *Electric Waves* right where I left it on the shelf. I turned to page 115. It was still there:

> *"In his forthcoming third volume, Heaviside will elaborate on his remarkable theory of wave interference whereby electric waves bounce off each other. This ingenious discovery promises to unlock similar valuable insights."*

I knew I hadn't been imagining things. But, why would two copies of what looked like the same book have such a discrepancy?

I carefully compared the Tolliver Library copy in my hand to the printout of the Omnitia scan I made last night. They looked identical, except for the extra sentence about bouncing waves in the footnote. I made a photocopy of the page to take home and show Dad. Then, I went to the catalog terminal and searched for Heaviside's *Electromagnetic Theory*. Up came Volume 1 published in 1893, Volume 2 published in 1899, and Volume 3 published in 1912. They were all listed at 538.3 H44, right near where *Electric Waves* had been shelved. I found Volume 3. It was dedicated to the memory of someone named George Francis FitzGerald.

I began reading Heaviside's idiosyncratic prose. In the first section of the book, he talked about waves and reflections. If there was anything in his dense prose about electric waves bouncing off each other, my head was too wooden to find it. I didn't have the physics or the math skills at that point to actually understand electric waves, let alone electromagnetic waves. It was tough going; maybe Dad could help. By this point, I was becoming suspicious of online books. I went back to the Omnitia scan of the Franklin book. I pulled it up on my laptop, and I compared the scans in the Omnitia pdf file to the physical book from the Tolliver Library in front of me. Same title page. Same 1909 copyright date. Both copies even said "Published October 1909." I started reading, comparing each page, paper versus screen. No differences. This was taking too long. I turned to the index of the physical book and looked up Heaviside: "Heaviside's Electromagnetic Theory, 113, 115." Page 113? I checked. Yes, there was a mention of Heaviside on page 113 and both books had identical versions of that page. I looked at the index in the scanned file. "Heaviside's Electromagnetic Theory, 113." There was no mention of page 115 in the scanned index. But, both the scan and my physical copy had a mention of Heaviside on page 115!

This puzzled me. Was the Omnitia scan the original version? Then, did someone add the "bouncing waves" verbiage and the extra reference in the index of the Tolliver Library copy somehow? But, if that were the case, there was already a reference to Heaviside on page 115 that should have been indexed but wasn't. Or, was the Tolliver Library hardcopy the original? Then, did someone delete the bouncing wave verbiage and the index reference, forgetting that there was still another reference to Heaviside on that page? Which was the original version?

I thought about this. Suppose someone, for whatever reason, wanted to delete the reference to Heaviside and the bouncing waves text on page 115. Suppose they wanted to hide the fact that it was ever there. They might then delete the mention from the index, forgetting that there was another mention of Heaviside left behind on that page. Perhaps. But, why go to such trouble?

Maybe these bouncing waves were nonsense, like Dad had said. Maybe not. I'd read nearly half of the Franklin book. He was a good writer – easy to follow and clear in his descriptions and analogies. If he vouched for it, that made it potentially credible. I certainly didn't have the physics expertise to debate the facts. As my debate coach, Mr. Stinson, was fond of saying, though, "If you can't debate the facts, then debate the personalities." If there was one thing a couple years of high school debate training made me good at, it was research. I set out to understand the personalities involved to see if some kind of motive or explanation might become evident.

James Clerk Maxwell developed the theory of electromagnetics in the 1860s and published his *Treatise on Electricity and Magnetism* in 1873. He was dead six years later at age 48 of stomach cancer. Heinrich Hertz discovered and characterized radio waves in the 1880s. He published his great work, *Electric Waves*, in 1893. He died the following year – technically – on January 1, 1894. A couple references I found spoke of a "bone malignancy" in his jaw. Others ascribed it to "granulomatosis with polyangiitis" whatever that was. Heaviside died at age seventy-five in 1925, but his final years were unproductive. His behavior became increasingly paranoid and erratic as he complained of being constantly harassed and distracted by the neighbors and their children. Heaviside had dedicated his book to FitzGerald. I looked him up. An electromagnetic pioneer, his work apparently anticipated Einstein's relativity theory. He died in 1901 at age 49 of some kind of indigestion. Another stomach cancer?

Three top electromagnetic pioneers died prematurely in what should have been the primes of their lives. It could just be coincidence. Medical science wasn't that advanced and folks died early of ailments we could cure today. It was certainly curious. I had more questions than answers to show for my morning of research. After class, I headed over to the Berkshire Inn to see Amit.

I explained what I'd found to him. "Coincidence?" Amit's eyes lit up. "That many deaths? No way. Don't you know the expression? The first time is happenstance, the second, coincidence, and the third time is enemy action. Some enemy had it in for the discoverers of electromagnetics."

Amit became more convinced when I explained the discrepancy between the book from the Tolliver Library and the scanned version from Omnitia."

"Dude," he said almost condescendingly. "The scan is clearly bogus."

"Why?" I asked.

"You can't trust Omnitia to tell you the truth," he insisted. "They're in bed with the government." Ah, yes. Amit and his Omnitia phobia. I recalled he'd done a report for civics class about the company. Now he was repeating the highlights of his conclusions. Again. "It's all right there in the name," he insisted. "Omnitia is Omni – T – I – A: Total Information Awareness. That's a secret government program to capture and store all emails, all phone calls, and all data transmitted over the Internet for the National Security Agency to search. The government has always wanted comprehensive control over communications. During the First World War, the Navy took over radio completely. After the war, they were forced to return radio to the private sector, but the government colluded to force all the radio companies to sell out to a single company they could monitor and control, the 'Radio Corporation of America' or RCA."

We'd had this conversation before, if you could characterize my listening patiently to Amit describing the many ways Big Brother was out to get us as a conversation. Amit had even analyzed photos from the December 2001 press conference held on top of the World Trade Center announcing the formation of Omnitia from a consolidation of leading search engines like Yahoo, Alta Vista, and an obscure little start up with a name something like Googol. He examined press photos of the event, and he was convinced some of the bystanders at the press conference were principals at a CIA-backed venture company called In-Q-Tel. I tried to tell him it was ridiculous to think that tens of thousands of people could possibly keep secret the wholesale violation of everyone's civil rights, but he insisted that's exactly what they were up to, in the name of national security.

"The politicians were scared shitless some terrorists were able to drop a plane on top of the Capitol and the White House and kill so many of them, let alone President Gore. They demanded that the government make sure nothing like that ever happens again. They're allowing wholesale surveillance of every communication to try to catch terrorists before they can act. And they're sweeping up everything else at the same time. Just in case."

This was not helpful. "So do you think the folks at Omnitia developed a time machine to send their assassins back to take out the discoverers of electromagnetics?" I asked.

He took my question seriously. "'He, who controls the past, controls the future. And he who controls the present controls the past.' That's Orwell. Omnitia controls the present. You can see, before too much longer, there won't be any more libraries with actual physical books. It will be too easy to look up and read scans on a computer. And if there's some truth that the powers-that-be find inconvenient, they can edit our collective memory of it in Omnitia's database. Besides, the digital copy is trivially easy to modify. No one would go to the trouble of carefully modifying a physical book and then scanning it, when they could make the modifications so much more easily in the scanned images."

I began to think he might actually be on to something. "I stumbled across this one tiny discrepancy between a physical book and Omnitia's online database of book scans. How many more discrepancies are out there? If someone has been editing history, there are probably more edits out there waiting for us to find."

"Us?" He looked amused. Then he turned more thoughtful. "We could systematically compare texts in the Tolliver Library to the online scanned versions."

"That would take a long time. I spent the better part of an hour reviewing a hundred pages in one book," I pointed out. "If we both worked full time, we might manage a half dozen books in a day. We need to narrow down the search."

"Only books in the public domain are going to be available for free online, because of copyright issues." Amit launched into another diatribe. "Did you know that the duration of a copyright used to be the same as the term for a patent? About twenty years. But, authors and publishers and now media companies kept lobbying Congress to the point where it can be nearly a century before anything gets into the public domain. It's the Mickey Mouse rule of copyright. Mickey Mouse will never go into public domain, because they keep changing the rules every time it gets close. Since Disney created Mickey in 1928, only works created before 1923 are in the public domain."

"That's a five year difference," I pointed out to him.

"Yeah," he countered, "they built in a margin of error in case they have any trouble getting the term extended – and by remarkable coincidence the margin is just long enough that they will have at least one chance to elect a pliable President."

"So we only look at books older than 1923," I got us back on track. "That's still an awful lot of books."

"I wonder if we could automate the process?" Amit speculated. "What if we scanned the Tolliver Library books page by page and let a computer compare our scans to Omnitia archived scans?"

I did a quick mental calculation. A couple dozen books per individual shelf, so maybe a hundred books per stack, and a thousand or so per row. There must be dozens of shelves. Maybe as many as fifty to a hundred thousand books. I couldn't think of a way to estimate the pre-1923 fraction of books, but it still had to be huge. "Even if we could compare one book per minute, it would still take us years." I started to search for "book scanners."

"Stop!" Amit shoved my hands off the keyboard. "You think maybe Omnitia is messing with your books and you want to trust them with your search?"

Now he definitely had a point.

"Look. You remember how we set up the wireless network at the hotel?" He began.

"Sure."

Amit's father installed a wireless network throughout the hotel for the guests to use. I picked up some extra money after school my sophomore year helping Amit and his father run Ethernet cable and set up wireless nodes. Amit and I had impressed his father by figuring out we could get better coverage installing the wireless access points inside rooms, instead of along the hallways as the instructions from the corporate IT team had suggested.

"Every once in a while, we'll get Sheriff Gunn or some Tennessee state troopers out here because we have a guest downloading or sharing kiddie porn. They trace it back to the IP address of the hotel. Then they give my dad the MAC address of the guest's computer and ask my dad to identify which guest used that MAC address to log into the hotel network. We tell them which door the troopers need to knock on."

"What's that got to do with Omnitia?"

"The cops could only do that if they were watching everything. I wrote up a screening application for the hotel so my dad monitors all the Internet traffic from the hotel. Unfortunately, he went back and reset the filters. He decided he didn't like the game and pick-up artist websites I was visiting. And he caught me looking at porn and chewed me out. I could have hard-coded a work-around in the app, but then he'd be wondering why I was giving him a new executable. So I figured out how to anonymize my Internet traffic. I use Tor – The Onion Router." He explained. "Tor routes all your Internet traffic through a network of relays to conceal where it came from and where it's going. It's too slow for video, but I can download pictures just fine. But, my point is if Omnitia is hiding something and you start looking for it, they're going to trace it right back to you and your computer. Look – you're even logged into your OmniMail account. They know exactly who downloaded that old book, for instance." I must have looked worried, because he added, "Don't worry. There's too much going on the Internet for anyone to pay attention to one search and one download. But if you make a pattern of these kinds of searches, and if it truly is something they're actively hiding, they're going to notice, eventually."

"You think I should use this Tor when I do any online searching regarding this mystery?"

"That's a start, but it's not good enough. If you actually attract interest, they can link you anyway to your computer and any non-anonymized Internet usage. I think we need to be careful and take every precaution. Let's think about how to protect us."

We brainstormed for a bit. The solution we came up with seemed robust. We knew a pawnshop in Knoxville that recycled computers from Oak Ridge and other businesses around Knoxville. Between us, we'd chip in to buy a couple of used laptops and pay cash so they couldn't easily be traced to us.

Amit would figure out how to get online without a trace and install Tor. We'd use the first machine for preliminary research. I'd look into building a book scanner and Amit would research and download the software to take the scans, perform character recognition, and compare the scans of the physical books to the versions downloaded from Omnitia. Then, we'd disable the Ethernet connection on the first machine.

Amit would use the second laptop to search Omnitia for the online book scans. He'd download the specific ones I wanted and a bunch of other ones besides just to confuse the trail. Then, he'd burn them to a CD and transfer them to the first laptop. He called it "air gapping." The first computer was air gapped from the Internet so no one could possibly plant computer malware to spy on what we were doing and report it back over the Internet. The computer that searched for information on book scanning and performed comparisons between our scans and Omnitia's scans was a completely different computer than the one that downloaded the specific Omnitia scans we'd use. That way no one could make a connection between the fact that someone was scanning physical books and comparing them to particular scans of books online.

We'd only communicate about the project in person. Amit insisted that calls and texts were monitored and the location data could be used to trace us. I thought he was being paranoid again, but it made an interesting game to follow all the procedures he insisted upon.

By the time I had to go home for dinner, we had our plan. I would take the lead on identifying our target list of books: ones older than 1923 so they would be in the public domain and likely available online. That was easy. They were already organized by subject thanks to the Dewey Decimal system, so I planned to start at Franklin's Electric Waves and Heaviside's Electromagnetic Theory, and work out from there. I'd compile a list and pass it on to Amit. I'd also take the lead on getting us to Knoxville to buy the computers. Meanwhile, Amit said he wanted to work out the details of how to get online without a trace. We agreed to meet back at Kudzu Joe's the next morning to compare notes and see where we stood. I was eager to go home and see what was up with Dad and his secretive project with Uncle Rob.

Chapter 3: The Preparation

Dad was home when I got there. Mom said he'd gotten back around noon, showered, and went to sleep. When I pressed her for information about what was going on, she acknowledged she didn't know either. Dad told her he'd explain over dinner. "It will be ready in a few minutes, so why don't you wake up your father and ask him to come down to the table?"

Mom had dinner ready by the time Dad came to the table. Dad said Grace, and we ate. "I'm sorry to worry you both running off like I did last night," he began. "But there was no time to explain. When I heard the sheriff had been asking about the activity, I knew I had to head up to Rob's and help him finish up our project, before the sheriff decided to stop by and poke around in person."

"What's this project?" I could refrain from asking no longer.

"I'm helping Uncle Rob with his barn," Dad said matter-of-factly. "We got his slab poured and we'll be starting on the construction next month. Rob's invited us all up to his place for a bonfire and barbecue to celebrate the Fourth. We'll bring the guns, and do some shooting, too. You'll get a chance to see it all then."

I wasn't buying it. Dad and Rob wouldn't be worried about the sheriff seeing a barn under construction. Dad read the skepticism on my face. I was going to have to learn to do a better job hiding it.

"Yes, there is more to it than that. And no, I'm afraid I can't go into details just yet. But I do need to be able to trust you to keep your suspicions to yourself. You can't tell anyone there's anything out of the ordinary at Uncle Rob's. Not a hint. Not to your friend Amit or anyone else." He looked at me. "Get it?"

"Got it," I replied.

"Good. So how are your studies coming along?"

I explained what I'd found out about the difference between the physical version of Franklin's *Electric Waves* and the online version.

"I thought you were supposed to be studying science, not concocting conspiracy theories," Dad said dryly. He looked at the photocopy I made and acknowledged that I had correctly recalled the bouncing electric waves language. He compared the copy from the Tolliver Library book to the printout of the Omnitia scan. Dad allowed it was curious that two apparently identical editions of the book differed in the footnote and index. "But minor tweaks like that happen all the time in publishing. The publisher sells out of a first printing and makes minor corrections for a second printing. Given that bouncing electric waves make no sense, the mention was probably deleted from subsequent printings including the one that was scanned online. The discrepancy in the index is hardly proof of a deliberate omission. Accidents and omissions happen all the time. I'd believe some poor student overlooked a reference in an index he was compiling for his professor, before I'd believe some deliberate deletion."

"Isn't it possible," I asked, "that Heaviside did write something about bouncing waves? His book is full of discussion on electromagnetic waves, even though I couldn't follow much of it."

"The idea doesn't make any sense," Dad insisted. "Sure, waves bounce off objects. That's why cell phone coverage can be spotty – find a location where the radio waves happen to bounce and interfere the wrong way and you can lose the signal and drop the call. But bounce off each other? No." Dad looked thoughtful. "If Heaviside ever did describe anything like waves bouncing off each other, Jim Burleson might know something about it. He's a real Heaviside fanboy and likes digging into EM history. I can ask him about it when I see him again."

I told Dad about Maxwell, Hertz, and FitzGerald all dying in their prime.

"I knew about Maxwell and Hertz," he said. "I wasn't aware FitzGerald died so young. While those deaths might be a statistical anomaly, I think part of it is selection bias. Plenty of other scientists participated in the discovery or extended upon Maxwell's ideas in one way or another. Off the top of my head, I believe Faraday and Kelvin lived to ripe old ages. I'm not sure about Lodge, Larmor, and Lorentz. I'm probably overlooking other. The only reason you included FitzGerald was the Heaviside dedication, and the only reason Heaviside dedicated his book to FitzGerald was because of his premature death. So I think you're just back to just two – Maxwell and Hertz – not three." He smiled. "You have a coincidence, not enemy action.

"Besides," he added. "How does your hypothetical enemy kill someone with cancer? No one had the least clue how cancer worked back then. If an assassin wanted to kill someone and make it look like natural causes, they'd have probably used poison and no one would have been the wiser."

I also told Dad about my plan to work with Amit looking for other discrepancies between old physics books in the Tolliver Library and the versions available online.

"I don't think your project with Amit will turn up much of interest. But I think Amit is right about Omnitia. Developing the skill to use the Internet anonymously is worthwhile and I'll count that as billable study time. The book scanner sounds useful, also. If it works out, I may ask you to scan our books as well." Dad paused in thought again. "In fact, I need to go to Knoxville to help Jim Burleson on the auto plant job. If you have Friday off, I could take you and Amit along to speak with him about Heaviside. I'd also like to get set up with an untraceable laptop myself, if Amit wouldn't mind configuring it for me. And I think you and Amit might like to work with me handling the IT side of one of my jobs."

* * *

"That'd be great!" Amit said the next morning at Kudzu Joe's. "I'm sure my folks won't mind if I go with you and your dad to Knoxville. And I'll be happy to configure Tor for your Dad, too." I couldn't tell him anything else about Dad's project because Dad hadn't shared the details with me, but Amit was eager for another chance to exercise his IT skills.

Amit had apparently spent most of the previous evening scheming about online access. "The problem with Tor is that someone who's determined to track you down can eventually figure out your IP address. They send you some kind of exploit that pings their server outside the secure Tor channel and they've got you. So you have to find a way to get online through an IP address that can't be traced backed to you."

"So we only connect through public places like the Wi-Fi at Kudzu Joe's," I offered.

"OK," Amit acknowledged, "but what happens when someone starts asking Joe who hangs out here in the mornings? You and I would be on a very short list of suspects. The trick is to use public Wi-Fi, but not in a way that can be linked back to you."

"So we sit down the street from Joe's in our car, only it's probably a good idea to avoid using the Wi-Fi at any place that can be directly associated with us," I suggested.

"Exactly," Amit said. "They call it 'wardriving.' You drive around looking for open Wi-Fi connections or ones with old routers and weak encryption. We find a few prospects and we mix it up, never using any particular connection more than a few times."

"Someone's going to get suspicious if we park in front of their house and surf the web for an hour," I pointed out.

"We need a high gain antenna for our Wi-Fi to extend the range," Amit explained. You can make one from a Pringles can. Your dad's an amateur radio operator, right? Think he'd help?"

"A Pringles can?" That sounded improbable. But Amit actually seemed serious. "I'll ask him," I agreed. "He'll at least help me figure it out. He's been trying to get me to take the exam to become a ham radio operator."

"What we actually need, though," Amit continued, "is a good, busy, public place where we can get online using the Wi-Fi at another nearby busy public place. One of the truck stops along the interstate, for instance."

"What about your hotel?" I asked. "You have up to a hundred different guests at a time. That's a lot of anonymity."

"All our guests have to log on to the Wi-Fi, and then we log their traffic, remember? Sure I could spoof the login of a real guest but if I make a habit of doing it and anyone started digging, they'd know someone at the hotel was up to something."

"Hotels are great for anonymity. Can you get information for guests at a different Berkshire hotel? Like in Oak Ridge or Knoxville? There's one not far from my dad's office."

"I should have thought of that," Amit said ruefully. "I do have a login on the corporate network. The problem is they log queries. If anything is traced back to a bunch of random guests, they'll quickly discover that what they had in common was that I'd looked them up. They do that all the time when someone tries to skim guests' credit card numbers, for instance."

Clearly, avoiding the scrutiny of Big Brother while online was no easy task.

"On the other hand," Amit began. I could see a dawning realization on his face. "The only reason my dad's hotel is so well buttoned-down is because I worked through all the network security details for him. I'll bet a lot of other hotels never changed the default settings on their routers, or their network admin passwords, or their management systems passwords. And I know all the default passwords."

"So you think you can get logged on to get their guest information?"

"I think I won't even need to, because I can convince most any Berkshire Hotel network gateway to let all our traffic through and then forget about it." Amit was getting smug again. "I'll have to work through the details."

After class, I swung by the library to compile an initial list of books for Amit to download, and I bought a half dozen cans of Pringles on the way home. Dad agreed to help build some antennas, but he exacted a payment from me. For years, he'd been trying to get me to take the ham radio exam and get licensed. He insisted both Amit and I take the license test at the Knoxville Hamfest that Saturday. I called Amit to give him a heads up and he agreed. Dad got to work assembling the antennas, and I started cramming for the test. The technical side was easy. The only real challenge was learning all the frequency bands, operating modes, and the rules and regulations. I took some practice tests and passed, although it was close. I'd have to study some more to guarantee success.

* * *

The next morning, Dad drove Amit and me to Knoxville. Our first stop was the big auto plant outside town where Dad had been working. He showed his ID to the guard at the gate and drove back to an area where there were half a dozen trailers set up in a parking lot surrounded by pickup trucks and contractors' vans. We walked into one of the trailers. A lady got up from her computer.

"Good morning, sir!" she said brightly to my Dad as she stood up. "You're here to see the boss?"

"We're a bit early, but he's expecting me. We can wait until he's free."

"I'll just let him know you're here." She made a call.

Jim Burleson walked in the door a couple of minutes later and greeted my Dad. Dad introduced him to Amit. I'd met him when I was working for Dad the previous summer. Mr. Burleson was a young guy. Not too long ago, he'd been one of

Dad's apprentices. He'd struck out on his own and been successful in his own right. I think he still looked up to Dad as a mentor, and Dad was always eager to include him in jobs that were too big to handle by himself. A couple of hard hats had miraculously appeared on the table while I wasn't paying attention – Dad had his own. Mr. Burleson signed me and Amit in as Dad's "apprentices" so we could tag along.

"How's the job going, Jim?" Dad asked.

"We're running our asses off getting that special inverter you spec'd out for us installed," Mr. Burleson was telling Dad. He turned to us. "The Germans just love their super-special welding robots that only drink 50 cycle current. Only no one bothered to spec that out in the plans. So now we're playing catch up."

He and Dad launched into a technical discussion. Apparently, they were installing a huge inverter to meet the requirements of the German industrial equipment. The inverter was causing radio interference to a real-time location system and Dad was helping with some kind of grounding and filtering arrangement. It took them a half hour or so to work it through. It seemed Mr. Burleson was pleased with Dad's help. As we were walking back out, he said, "It's like you're always telling me – an hour of the maestro's time is worth more than days of an amateur's. That's still true at the rate you're charging now!"

"As with any good idea, it's 1% inspiration and 99% perspiration," Dad observed.

"Yeah," Mr. Burleson countered, "but the perspiration ain't worth nothing unless the inspiration puts it where it's needed. Are you still sure you don't want a piece of the job? There's lots to do and we're making a great margin on the expedite fees. Faster we get done, the bigger the bonus. I could cut you in for a lot of hours if you'd lower your rate some. I still owe you for including me in your bid."

"No, I'm trying to retire," Dad told him. "Feel free to call me in if you need me to skim your cream again with an hour or two of my high-priced consulting. I do have a favor to ask of you, though. May we step into your office a minute?"

"Sure thing," he said leading us in and closing the door behind us. "What do you need?"

"My boy here ran across something in the library the other day." Dad handed the print out from the Tolliver Library's copy of Franklin's *Electric Waves* to Mr. Burleson.

He studied it. "Electric waves bouncing off each other? Makes no sense," he declared. "Waves on wires or in the air – they just pass through each other."

"That's what I thought," Dad confirmed. "Can you think of anything Heaviside might have done that this might be describing?"

"When was this written?" he asked.

"It was published in October 1909," I answered.

"That was later in his life," Mr. Burleson noted. "He was slowing down, but still compiling the third volume of *Electromagnetic Theory*. It makes sense that he'd have put this bouncing waves result there."

"I did take a look," I offered, "but it was awfully complicated. And Heaviside's writing seemed a bit..."

"Offbeat?" Mr. Burleson asked with a smile. "Yes Heaviside was quite a character. Something of a hermit. Odd. Absolutely brilliant, though. He's the man who took Maxwell's clunky, poorly expressed ideas about electromagnetics and made them into the beautiful theory we all use today. What we call Maxwell's Equations used to be called the Heaviside-Maxwell Equations, because Heaviside came up with them, and they're so much better and clearer than Maxwell's own work."

"Standing on the shoulders of giants," Dad observed.

"Indeed," Mr. Burleson acknowledged. "But a giant in his own right. He was a self-taught telegrapher who studied Maxwell's books in a library in Newcastle where he worked. He took Maxwell's ideas and worked out what are called the Telegrapher's Equations that describe how waves behave on transmission lines. He showed that when you have a balance of electric and magnetic energy, you get distortionless transmission of signals. You have to have the right ratio of inductance to capacitance to make long distance telephone lines work. Michael Pupin patented Heaviside's idea and sold it to AT&T for a mint. Heaviside never saw a dime of it, and he lived – and died – in poverty." Mr. Burleson was very passionate about Heaviside and the injustice done to him.

"Many of the basic concepts we electricians use – impedance, inductance, conductance – they were all defined and named by Heaviside," Mr. Burleson continued. "Heaviside and Oliver Lodge between them did most of the basic work in AC or alternating circuit theory that we electricians use today.

"Heaviside spent the last years of his life in a cottage near the sea. He complained of being harassed by the neighbors' boys. He was trying to compile a fourth volume of Electromagnetic Theory. The manuscript was never completed, although some folks claim to have found bits and pieces of it here and there."

"So you don't think there's much to this bouncing waves business?" Dad brought Mr. Burleson back on track.

"Hard to say," Mr. Burleson acknowledged thoughtfully. I could tell Dad was a bit surprised he was taking it so seriously. "In the 1960's, it turned out that Heaviside had worked out a result for radiation from moving charges that was re-derived by the famous physicist, Richard Feynman. Only everyone had overlooked and forgotten it. Heaviside's work was far ahead of its time in many ways. It wouldn't be at all surprising if there were some more forgotten or overlooked insights sprinkled here and there in his writing.

"You have me curious about this business now," Mr. Burleson confessed with a grin. "I'll take a look through Heaviside and see if I can find your bouncing waves and figure out what it all means."

We thanked him and were on our way out. "Hold on a sec," he said to Dad. Mr. Burleson reached into his desk drawer and pulled out a credit card. "Here's a $100 gift card."

He handed it to Dad. "A personal gift from me – not the business. A little more immediate thanks for saving our bacon here this morning."

Dad seemed a bit embarrassed by it. "The check you'll be cutting me is thanks enough," he assured Mr. Burleson. "Don't worry – I'll be getting my invoice in later today. And since when did you start dealing in credit cards? I thought you usually paid cash for your personal expenses."

"By the time your check gets cut you might forget the link between what you did for us and the money," Mr. Burleson explained. "Call it insurance. I just want to be sure, when I need you again, you'll get right down here and help us out. It's a prepaid credit card with $100 on the tab. Treat yourself. And let me know when you're ready to get off your lazy rear and get back to it. There's plenty of work here to do!"

As we were driving out, I asked Dad why he wasn't taking Mr. Burleson up on his offer. "You know," Dad reminded me, "I stayed in contracting when I married your mom instead of getting an office job as an electrical engineer. In a professional job, you're paid a good salary for a 40-hour week, but you're usually expected to work more than that. As a contractor, you get paid 50% more for your hours past forty. With the extra hours and overtime, I actually made more money in contracting than I would as an electrical engineer that first year. As a young family, we needed the income. I considered going back to engineering. You can make a good living selling your labor by the hours whether you're an engineer or a contractor, but there are only so many hours in the day," Dad explained.

"I quickly figured that out, and I started shifting my business toward making connections, arranging deals, and taking a percentage. I started by finding some apprentices to let me tackle larger jobs. Now, I pull together a consortium of contractors I trust to handle big jobs like this one, and I manage them to keep everything on track. If I succeed, I take away much more than if I'd merely sold my labor as either an engineer or a contractor. The reward is commensurate with the risk. This plant was a very successful job for me, so I'm in a position to retire and pursue other interests. To land the job, I had to get all my contractors to bid the main job at near cost and just make sure they at least break even. On a big job like this, though, even a narrow margin is a lot of money if everything goes well – which it did. Better yet, there are always last minute changes and complications and rush projects that need to be done, and can't be put out for bid because an outsider couldn't get up to speed fast enough to get the job done at a reasonable cost. My team gets a chance to make good money on all the change orders. I still get a piece of that action, though it's smaller because I'm not directly managing everything."

Our next stop was in a fancy gated community not far from the plant. We stopped by a big open lot that had just been cleared. "I wasn't planning on taking any more residential work," Dad explained, "but the manager of the auto plant insisted on having me design and supervise a project for him. It's an interesting job. He wants a solar installation, battery storage, and a backup generator. He's making it worth my while to design and manage the project, although I'm not doing most of the actual work. I want to remind you both that this is a confidential project and you're not to talk about it with anyone." Amit and I pledged our secrecy.

Dad took us to the back of the lot where a square hole about 75 feet on a side and more than twenty feet deep lay before us. The bed was covered in gravel, and concrete pilings popped up arranged in rectangular patterns. Capped plumbing and conduit sprouted up here and there like weeds. Dad had Amit and me take turns with a long tape measure guiding us to this piling and that piling while he took measurements and checked them against a plan. We climbed back out of the hole and watched as Dad scribbled notes and calculations. Before long, a sleek German sedan pulled up and a distinguished looking man stepped out and walked up to us. Dad met him half way. "Guten Morgen Herr Doktor Kreuger." Dad introduced Amit and me to the German.

"Hello y'all," Dr. Kreuger said with a heavy accent and a broad smile. Dr. Krueger and Dad walked to the edge of the big hole. "I like very much the cargo container concept," Dr. Krueger was saying to Dad. "They will be here in few days. Some welding to cut und join und then we pour all around with the concrete. Very good was this idea. Much less expensive than building the plywood forms. Did not think so fine a place was in my budget. Very sturdy. And the built-in shielding."

"The grounding and power isolation will keep you running even with a nuclear or solar EMP," Dad assured him. "The generator and reserve fuel tank go over there," Dad pointed out a smaller hole connected by a trench to the larger hole. "The solar inverter and battery bank are on the other side. The septic system looks good, and the pilings for the reserve water tank and all the containers look to be aligned properly."

"Very good," Dr. Kreuger beamed like a big kid on Christmas morning. Then, he became more serious. "I read something very smart from that professor you tell me of at the law school here. Instapundit. He say, 'Something that can't go on forever, won't. Debts that can't be repaid won't be. Promises that can't be kept won't be.'"

Dad nodded ruefully, "The folks in Washington keep on spending and racking up deficits. They've created a vast class of bureaucrats whose livelihood depends on distributing the largess and an even vaster class of folks dependent on government handouts. The bureaucrats craft regulations so their masters can get political contributions from the affected industries trying to game the system to their advantage."

"Is worse in Germany," Dr. Krueger said. "Eventually, the system will collapse. Maybe take a decade. Maybe longer. You and I may not see it. But our Kinder," he looked at me and Amit, "they will. I want a safe place for my family."

"A secret refuge doesn't have much value if outsiders know about it," my Dad observed. "I'm spreading the work around a couple of trusted contractors, and none of them have the complete picture of what you're building here. I brought my son and his friend here because they will be helping me with the IT infrastructure, the video surveillance, and the sensors and alarms."

"You bring his friend?" Dr. Krueger seemed a bit skeptical about Amit.

"I've known him and his family for years," Dad assured him. "Good people. And Amit and my son know better than to talk about this."

"Good," Dr. Krueger seemed reassured. "Is good for young people to see how the world works," he said.

"Call me when the containers start to arrive so I can confirm the placement and anchoring," Dad said. "Then, I'll turn the welder loose to cut and connect the containers before the pour."

"Ja," said Dr. Krueger smiling. "Oh, and thank you for your good advice."

"Which advice?" Dad asked.

"You say tell all my folk building houses here not to pay their general contractor up front, but to insist on progress payments to the subcontractors as work is completed. The general contractor they were all using here pulled out, bankrupt. Would have been big mess with money paid and work not done. They found another contractor who's finishing the project. Not much delays."

"Yes, I heard about that." Dad acknowledged. "It gets tough in a down market for home builders. You think you've sold a house but the buyers back out. Meanwhile, you have half-built spec homes that you can't afford to complete, but you have to get them finished somehow to stand a chance of selling them and recouping your investment. It gets tempting to take the latest customer's money to pay off the subs you owe on the earlier jobs. Not the builders' fault. Juggling the cash flow to make ends meet is part of the job, but when you cut it too close to the edge, it's easy to get caught short, and then your customers and subs pay the price."

Dad and Dr. Krueger talked more about business, politics, and the economy. They seemed to share similar "the sky is falling and the big evil government is pulling it down around us" views. Dad could get quite apocalyptic at times. Nevertheless, it was a fascinating visit – definitely one of the most interesting construction sites Dad had taken me to. And helping to run and set up the electrical and IT wiring would be a nice project. We finished up at Dr. Krueger's lot and accompanied Dad to see his lawyer in downtown Knoxville.

We parked and walked into a big bank building and up an elevator. The elevator opened to a beautiful lobby. The law firm occupied the whole floor. "I'm here to see Greg Parsons," Dad handed the receptionist his card. Mr. Parsons came out to meet Dad. Dad introduced us, but he left Amit and me in the lobby while he went back to talk with Mr. Parsons.

"I had no idea your dad did anything but just electrical contracting and construction jobs," Amit said. "He's got a lot going on."

"He likes to keep a low profile," I acknowledged. "Grandpa Jack Tolliver hated Dad for stealing Mom away. Dad's existence was a daily reminder that the Tollivers don't control everything and everyone. I don't know if he just wants to avoid their attention, but he's always been very private about his work."

"Maybe he just thinks it's none of their or anyone else's business," Amit pointed out. He walked confidently over to the receptionist. "Hi, I'm Amit." He held out his hand and took hers almost like he was going to kiss it. "Do you have Wi-Fi access here?" He proceeded to chat with her. I wondered if it was as obvious to her as it was to me that Amit was hitting on her. Sure enough, he asked her for her number.

"I have a boyfriend," she said coolly.

"Wow," Amit replied, "I mean... that's absolutely amazing!"

She looked confused. "It's amazing that I have a boyfriend?"

"No," Amit corrected her. "It's amazing that I've barely known you a couple of minutes and already you're telling me all about your problems."

"You were hitting on me," she insisted indignantly.

"What?" Amit looked genuinely surprised. "You thought I was hitting on you? We're just talking here. No worries, you're not my type. Thanks for the Wi-Fi help though." She looked equal parts bewildered and amused as he returned and sat down.

"Let me guess," I said quietly so as not to be heard over the ambient noise of the office. "You turned her rejection of you around into you rejecting her to reestablish your dominant frame."

"You're getting better at this," Amit conceded, "but understanding the theory is no substitute for getting out and practicing it."

"I'm not going to get much practice hanging out with you when you jump on all the likely prospects."

"Seriously, dude," Amit said, "had it even crossed your mind to try?"

"No," I admitted. "She's way too old. Must be in her late twenties. She's way out of our league."

"The only way to guarantee you're out of her league is to be too timid to even try. Attitude makes up for a lot," Amit counseled. "You'll never know until you try."

"I thought you and Emma were an item, now," I said.

"True," Amit acknowledged. "If I get lazy and complacent, though, I'll lose Emma. I have to take the opportunities to practice my flirting when I find them. I can't flirt aggressively with all the girls at school because it's such a small crowd. Word would get around, and then I'd be the creepy guy who hits on everyone and is always getting turned down. Bad for the image. I can't wait to get to college next year."

"If this is any example," I noted, "you're setting yourself up for a lot of failures."

"Failure?" Amit smirked. "You have to set a goal and follow through. Sure, you'll get shot down, but with every attempt, you get better and more experienced until you succeed. Like I did just now." He looked me in the eye, daring me to dispute him.

I called his bluff. "But, you didn't succeed," I pointed out. "She shot you down."

"Ah," he said. "There you go operating under an erroneous assumption again. Yes, I took a shot, though I knew I probably wasn't going out with her. It was good practice to try, though. And while I was chatting with her she pulled out her password sheet, so now I have the password for both their guest and secure Wi-Fi." He showed me a Post-It note where the receptionist had written down the guest Wi-Fi information. Amit wrote the SSID and password for the main office Wi-Fi below it. "Don't log in. Let's just add it to our growing list of credentials."

Watching his moves was certainly... educational.

By that time, Dad had finished, and we went over to the pawnshop for some used computers. On the way over he said, "No sense us all going in. That will just make us more memorable. Tell me what specs I should be looking for, and I'll buy the computers." Amit made some suggestions. Dad left us in his truck parked a block away from the store. He returned with six laptops. "They had a good deal," he said, "so I bought us each an extra. Let's go to my office and get them set up.

Dad's office was in a building just west of town. The folks who ran the office collected his mail, took messages for him, and had offices and conference rooms available. Sometimes he'd lease an office or two for the duration of a job. Like right now, he and Jim Burleson were still sharing a single, though rarely used, office. Other times, he'd just pay a flat rate for the phone and mail service, and an hourly rate for a furnished office or conference room as needed to entertain guests. He only had to pay by the use, which made sense because he did his design work at home and the rest of the time, he was out in the field at a job site. I suspect he chose the office because it gave him a Knoxville address, so he could keep all his business out of the county. It was far enough away from Sherman to avoid scrutiny by the Tollivers and the rest of the Lee County local establishment.

We set up in the back conference room of the office complex, and Amit got to work. He wiped the computers clean and installed Linux. He disabled the onboard Wi-Fi so the laptop had to use a USB connected Wi-Fi to get online. "That way, we can be sure the Wi-Fi is only on when we plug in the USB Wi-Fi dongle," he explained. As the installation completed, he installed Tor and Open Office. We had an assembly line going, so by the time the last computer was getting wiped, the first one was completing installation. Dad opened up a box and handed out three Pringles cans he'd adapted to use as antennas. He connected them to the USB Wi-Fi modules. Amit tried one out. Dozens of Wi-Fi networks popped up on the screen. One of the three antennas didn't work, so Dad took it back, and said he'd build another one for us when he got home.

Amit gave us a quick tutorial. "Don't use your secure machine to log into your email or Facebook or any social media or any other site that can be linked back to you. Don't even frequent the same web sites. Make sure there's no cross over between your regular online presence and your secure online presence."

Amit asked Dad, "How much do I owe you for the computers?"

"Consider it an even trade," Dad said. "The computer in exchange for setting up these two and continuing to help us both out as needed. Let's head out and get started." We packed up our computers and took everything out to Dad's truck. Amit and I set up in back with one of the machines.

We stopped at a truck stop along the interstate. Sure enough, the setup allowed us to tap into the free wireless at a fast food place on the other side of the highway. While Dad filled up with gas, I searched for information on building a book scanner. I found and downloaded information about a variety of promising-looking options. Amit then took over and downloaded a couple of optical character recognition programs and some text comparison programs. By that time, Dad had finished buying gas. He'd paid cash inside and bought a few more items to slow down the process further. Dad walked slowly out and hopped in. "Need more time?"

"I think we're all set," Amit said. "Now we just have to study what we've captured."

"You both could stand to study for the ham radio license test tomorrow," Dad reminded us.

Chapter 4: The Execution

Somehow, I was doing more reading, studying, and test taking during the summer than I ever did at school. Amit and I both became proud holders of Technician Class amateur radio licenses. On the way back from the Knoxville Hamfest, I popped into a couple of stores, picking up some webcams in one place, and materials to build the frame for the scanner in another. I paid cash. Dad stopped at a different truck stop, and Amit downloaded the first batch of scanned books from Omnitia. That weekend, I built and tested the book scanner. Once I got into a rhythm, I could scan a good-sized book in as little as five to ten minutes. Dad had me start on some of his technical books. Amit also asked if we had a printer he could set up to use with our air-gapped laptop. Dad donated an old color inkjet from the office that he'd given up on because of the cost of the toner. Dad ordered a fresh set of toner cartridges and gave Amit the printer to use.

Monday morning arose. Amit and I were ready to begin scanning. The library didn't open until 10am, so we decided to start scanning at the library after my class. We'd been so busy that we had yet to get started on our preparation for debate. The goal for our morning at Kudzu Joe's was to do something about that.

We'd have to be ready to argue the affirmative, in favor of alternative energy incentives, or take the negative, against them. Toward the end of the summer, our high school debate class would have a round robin tournament. We were paired up in four teams and we'd have a chance to argue once in the affirmative and once in the negative with each of the other three teams for a total of six rounds.

I always preferred taking the affirmative, because we'd get the initiative. The affirmative gets to pick the specific implementation of the topic to be debated, so the other team has to scramble to keep up. We were sure many teams would pick conventional aspects of alternate energy like wind, solar, hydrogen, or maybe nuclear, and of course we'd have to be prepared to argue against any of those when it was our turn to be on the negative. Amit and I planned to develop a case for Radioisotope Thermoelectric Generation (RTG). The idea is to use the heat from a radioactive decay to generate electricity. It's a very safe and proven technology with a great track record: everything from interplanetary probes to pacemakers. We figured it was obscure enough that most of our opponents would have little research on it, until word got around about our case and other teams started digging. They'd oppose it with generic anti-nuclear power arguments and we'd be ready to cut them to shreds, because RTG wasn't the same thing as conventional nuclear power.

Preparing to debate on the negative was more challenging because you had to be ready to take whatever specifics the affirmative came up with and counter them. Occasionally of course, we'd run into an affirmative case that we weren't comfortable arguing against, either because the opposition was too well prepared or because they'd come up with something too obscure for us to have thought about – in effect exactly what we hoped to do to the other teams. When that happened to us on the negative side, we had to be ready with a "counterplan:" agree with the affirmative case but offer a better plan to implement their program. Amit called it "agree and amplify." He wanted to do a free market counterplan – yes, the affirmative notion is a good idea, but it should be implemented in the free market, not by government action, funding, or subsidy.

We get a lot of free-market and libertarian types here in Tennessee as judges, particularly at tournaments with lots of amateurs, instead of professional debate judges. Read the judge right and a free market counterplan can be very effective. Unfortunately, it was also an obvious counterplan, so the affirmative would likely be ready to argue why government action was essential.

In any event, we split up the debate research responsibilities and got to work. I took the lead on the RTG affirmative case; Amit took the lead on the free market counterplan. We divvied up the remaining alternate energy concepts we thought might come up and got to work. We broke for lunch and got back together at the library after my class.

The scanner was harder to use than I thought. I'd built it so it could be disassembled and put back together easily. Amit and I split up the pieces and carried it into the library in our backpacks. Up in the stacks there was a row of a half dozen study rooms. Each room had a table and chairs. We could close the door so conversation wouldn't carry, but a big window allowed passersby to look in on what we were doing. The scanner had a 90-degree bed for the book and two cameras, one for each page. Many of the books were old and fragile, so the scanner allowed us to copy each page without having to stress the bindings by laying the books flat. I wasn't quite able to flip the pages once a second but it was close to 50 flips or 100 pages scanned a minute.

The difficulty lay, not in the scanner, but in avoiding detection. We had a couple of close calls when a librarian or a student walked right past us, but fortunately didn't notice what we were doing. Amit volunteered to serve as a lookout. That slowed down the scanning some, because I had to turn the pages and tell the laptop to capture the scans by myself. That afternoon, we scanned a dozen books. I focused on books from the same period, 1905–1915, that were in the vicinity on the shelves – Dewey decimal 537–538. It was a good start. Then, Amit took the laptop home to compare our scans to the online scans.

The next morning I got a text from Amit: "Busy. No Joe this AM. Come by after class." I studied physics at Kudzu Joe's for a while. As I got up to get a refill from Emma, I noticed one of the truck drivers who used to hang around the place walk in. Come to think of it, I hadn't seen any of them in a while. The truck driver bought a coffee from Emma and was heading for the door when he noticed me behind him. He froze a second, and then said enthusiastically, "You're Rob's nephew, ain't ya?"

"Yes, sir?" I confirmed tentatively, confused about what was going on.

He stuck out a hand. "Bud Garrety," he introduced himself, shaking my hand vigorously. He had quite a grip. "That uncle o' yours, he's a godsend he is. Not a load to haul for months, and now more work than I can hardly keep up with. Lemme buy you your coffee," he insisted, slapping a five-dollar bill on the counter.

"Thank you, sir," I acknowledged gratefully, but no less confused, "however, it's actually free refills."

"Well then, yer next one's on me, and the young lady can keep the change," he insisted, undaunted.

Emma took his money, "Yes, sir. Thank you, sir."

He beamed proudly. "Well I need to be...," he cut himself off and added quietly, "but I know your uncle don't want no loose talk, now does he, son?"

"No, sir." It appeared Mr. Garrety and I were keeping Uncle Rob's secrets so well that I was still completely clueless what this was all about.

"You thank him for me when you see him again, you hear?"

"Yes, sir," I replied. "And thank you, Mr. Garrety, for the coffee."

"See you over yonder," he said, gesturing to the hills in the direction of Uncle Rob's place.

Mr. Garrety had to be involved in whatever it was Uncle Rob was doing that involved lots of trucks, but I was no closer to understanding the mystery. At least Mr. Garrety had just given me a great excuse to ask Uncle Rob about the trucks when I saw him next. I got back to work on physics.

When I finished my homework and got tired of physics, I got online and researched alternate energy sources for my debate preparation. Finally, it was home for lunch, off to class, and then to the Berkshire Inn to see how Amit was doing.

"I had trouble getting the optical character recognition to work," he told me. "I finally set up the computer to flash the scans side-by-side so I could eyeball them manually. And, I got one!" He triumphantly handed me a couple of printouts. On one he had written "Omnitia" and on the other he'd written "Tolliver." "I also got your old printer working," he added, "so now I can print hard copy from a dedicated printer that's not connected to the network."

The discrepancy Amit had found was on page 640 of *The Principles of Electric Wave Telegraphy* by J.A. Fleming in 1906. I remembered scanning that book. It had been a real pain, because it had a bunch of pullout or foldout pages. The Tolliver copy listed "HEAVISIDE, O., On the Interactions of Electromagnetic Waves, 1905" in the bibliography of papers. The Omnitia copy, however, had no mention of Heaviside, and two entries down, a listing of a paper by Sir Oliver Lodge was stretched way out so "p. 72" fell on a new line by itself, just enough to fill in the space from the missing Heaviside entry.

"When Franklin was talking about Heaviside's work on the interference of waves and how it described bouncing electric waves, he may have been talking about this paper that Fleming had listed in his bibliography," I concluded.

"Seems likely to me," Amit agreed. "There's no indication the paper was ever published in a journal. Franklin must somehow have corresponded with Heaviside to know it was supposed to end up in Heaviside's third volume of *Electromagnetic Theory*."

"Or some mutual friend shared the paper and the news," I pointed out. "Heaviside's process was to serialize his work in papers, then compile them in a book." I pulled up my scan of *Electromagnetic Theory* Volume 3 and reviewed the table of contents. "That process was breaking down in 1905. He couldn't find a journal to keep up with him, judging by the table of contents. Franklin might have just assumed Heaviside's intention was to include the paper in volume three. But he didn't."

Amit looked over my shoulder at the table of contents for volume three of Heaviside's *Electromagnetic Theory*. "There's no 'Interactions of Electromagnetic Waves' in Heaviside's table of contents."

"Heaviside does talk a lot about electromagnetic waves," I noted, "but I couldn't find anything about electric waves bouncing off each other. Maybe Mr. Burleson will have better luck figuring it out." It wasn't spectacular, but it was progress: an obvious example of history having been rewritten, if only in a small way. We had a second clear discrepancy between an old book and a modern Omnitia scan. Our discovery confirmed that the Franklin edit was a deliberate attempt to hide information about Heaviside's work. Amit and I transitioned to the exercise room to continue our discussion and speculations. Amit was convinced we were looking at a digitally altered copy of a scan of the same text that was in the physical book. I wasn't so sure. Looking carefully at the scan, I could see hints of the texture in the paper in the borders of the type. No letter was exactly the same. I didn't buy it. Would someone actually go to all that trouble? Someone meticulous enough to fuzz letters just right so as to simulate the soaking in of the ink? That would be almost as easy to do with real ink and paper. And these were the same electromagnetic villains sloppy enough to delete a page reference to Heaviside from the index of Franklin's *Electric Waves* despite there being a mention of Heaviside on the page.

Amit countered that modifying the physical printed copy would be even more difficult than modifying the scan. But he allowed it was curious anyone would go to the extreme difficulty of concocting such a convincing scan.

In the end, neither of us was certain whether what we had discovered was a recent change made in a scan of an old book, or an accurate scan of a book modified long ago. If it was an old modification, then there were some old books with omissions and edits and others, like the copies we'd found in the Tolliver library, without the edits. We made little progress resolving the question before I headed home.

* * *

Every so often, Dad would sip from a small shot glass of bourbon after dinner, as he sat in his favorite chair in the living room. At the time, I found it a noxious drink – it would be years before I developed a taste for bourbon, myself. Somehow the interaction of time and temperature with wood and liquor turns raw ethanol into a complex mix of flavors. Something similar happens to old books after a century or so. They acquire a subtle yet distinctive odor with hints of vanilla and musty grass. Even today, when I smell old books, it reminds me of the Tolliver Library and scanning books with Amit.

"Interesting," Dad said, thoughtfully, savoring a sip of bourbon, as he examined the two versions of the Fleming bibliography. "This does tend to support your theory that the edit was deliberate, but both of these edits are so minor, so subtle. I can't imagine why anyone would go to the trouble. That's why I tend to favor the notion that these are edits in the scans, not in the original hard copies of the books themselves."

"Why?" I asked.

"Amit is right. It's easy to alter a digital copy," Dad explained. "Altering a physical copy? You'd have a real problem matching the paper and ink, unstitching the binding, and replacing a substitute page. It would almost be easier to reprint the entire book. Modifying a line or a page here and there and to do so in a way that a casual observer wouldn't notice something off in the paper, ink, or font — that's a real challenge."

Dad made good sense. "You don't think it's possible?"

"It's certainly possible," Dad argued. "A skilled forger with sufficient time and motivation could pull it off. Get hold of period paper, maybe from other books of the era printed by the same publisher. Recreate the ink recipe, being careful not to include any modern chemicals or trace elements that might give the game away. Digitally match the font. Etch a plate. Reprint the page. It would take a real craftsman to pull it off, but it could be done.

"There was a guy I heard about, Mark Hofmann, who made a career out of forging old historical documents. He posed as a collector of rare old books and papers, and he concocted some plausible but embarrassing forgeries that cast doubt on the origins and history of the Mormon church. He found period paper by cutting out blank pages in old books, so it passed carbon dating tests. He perfected a recipe for old ink. He'd hand write letters. He had a printing plate photographically engraved so he could reproduce some lost early colonial document that would be worth millions. Experts authenticated his forgeries. Church officials, prominent Mormons, and other collectors of historic documents bought them, paying lots of money.

"But Hofmann lived lavishly and spent even more than he earned. In desperation, he planted some bombs to distract his creditors, killing a couple of people. He almost blew himself up, too. An amazingly persistent forensics examiner went back and found subtle clues. Hofmann's ink cracked differently than real period ink, supposedly different letter writers shared common quirks, stuff like that.

"So, yes, old documents can potentially be forged and will pass all but the most scrupulous and careful authentication. If you don't leave pipe bombs with your associates and draw attention to yourself, you may very well avoid detection. Still, it would still be much easier to do the forgery digitally."

"It would be easier if the change were made right at the time of the printing," I pointed out. "Maybe someone persuaded the printer to modify the book? Change the original type – just a line or two on a couple of pages – and print new copies. Perhaps they tried to recall the original printing and remove copies of the books from circulation, but they missed some. A few copies from the initial printing were missed and one ended up at the library here. But most of the copies in circulation have the change."

"That's an easier to imagine scenario than a later forgery," Dad acknowledged. "But the Franklin book was printed in New York. The Fleming book – he was British, right? Unless it was an American printing?"

I checked my scans. Both the Tolliver copy and the Omnitia scan said the book was printed by Longmans, Green, and Co., 39 Paternoster Row, London. The title plate also listed offices in New York and Bombay. "Probably printed in London."

"That complicates matters," Dad said thoughtfully. "If it were government coercion, it was two different governments in cahoots. Whoever it was would need a presence in New York and in London."

"So," I summarized, "we have three scenarios: first a modern digital cover-up likely with collusion from Omnitia, second a more recent elaborate forgery, or third, someone coerced the printer to make the changes and missed some of the copies already in circulation."

"I still think the first is more likely," Dad opined. "a modern digital change. Next most likely is a change right at the time of printing like you suggest. A modern forgery is extremely unlikely. It wouldn't stand up to any scrutiny without enormous effort. And there must be hundreds of those books around in various university library collections. The best way to test the modern digital change hypothesis is to find other old copies of *Electric Waves* and *Principles of*

Wireless Telegraphy. If the old books all match the Tolliver copies, then you are probably looking at a modern digital alteration. If you find altered books, then you'll have to do some detailed testing to try to identify whether they are alterations from the original printer or more recent forgeries."

"I can visit libraries, and check for copies," I pointed out. "I don't even have to use an online catalog since I know right where they ought to be shelved."

"Avoiding any sort of electronic trail is a good idea," Dad agreed. "let's continue this conversation with your mother over dinner."

I wasn't sure this was a good idea. "Should we be adding Mom to the discussion?"

"Son, you have to assume when you tell a man something he's going to tell his wife. Your mother is one of the most trustworthy and level-headed women I've ever known, which is a big part of why I married her in the first place. You would be wise to take her into your confidence as well, and you should seek out her opinions."

I agreed that Dad should tell Mom, but I had a good notion she wasn't going to like it.

At the dinner table, Dad brought Mom up to speed on what we'd found. It took most of the meal. Mom's counsel was for caution. "You and your father are running around playing secret agent investigating this mystery of yours. If you're right, the folks with whom you're tangling are ruthless experts willing to kill to keep a secret."

"I don't think his suspicion of a conspiracy to kill electromagnetic scientists is at all credible," Dad pointed out to Mom. "He found a coincidence. Many people, even prominent people in the nineteenth century died at what we'd consider to be young ages due to diseases or cancers we could cure today."

"The only suggestion we have of foul play is over a hundred years old, Mom," I pointed out. "We're taking the risks very seriously which is exactly why we're being so careful and 'running around playing secret agent.'"

She was not convinced. "'The most exquisite folly is made of wisdom spun too fine,'" she chided us as Dad and I cleared the table. "Go ahead," she said. "I'll take care of the dishes and leave you boys to playing with your fire – mind you don't get burnt." Mothers.

"I wish we could just order used books," I noted to Dad as we settled back into the living room. "But even if we placed the order anonymously online, the books have to be delivered to a real world physical address."

"That's a problem," Dad acknowledged. "Why don't you and Amit search online anonymously and see what you can find? Try eBay, Alibiris, and ABEBooks. Be a bit vague in your search terms so it's harder for a third party to figure out exactly what you're looking for. You could search on "electric waves" and "wireless telegraphy" then manually sort through the results. Add a bunch of other searches to hide the significance of the ones that really count. Something might pop up at McKay's here locally. Unfortunately, most of the top used-book dealers are too far away for us to just stop by and purchase a book – like Powell's in Portland, Oregon; Cat's Curiosities in Las Vegas, Zubal Books, in Cleveland, Ohio; or Books-on-Benefit in Providence, Rhode Island. Depending on the location, Rob or I might have an acquaintance we could trust to swing by, purchase a book in cash, and then ship it to us. If you find any leads from book sellers or dealers in Memphis, Houston, Birmingham, or anywhere along the route of our road trip in August, we could swing by and pay cash for what they have. But that's the only safe way to make an anonymous purchase."

* * *

At Kudzu Joe's the next morning, I shared the previous night's brainstorming with Amit. He liked the idea of searching for other copies of the books to try to figure out whether we were looking at an old or a recent conspiracy. He and I worked out a used book search strategy, and he agreed to spend some time searching during his next wardrive. Amit also pointed out that many libraries had online listings of books, and he proposed to look into it. Once we had our plans laid out, we worked on debate research until lunchtime.

Amit joined me after class at the library for more book scanning. There weren't all that many physics books older than 1923, so we decided on a strategy of scanning them without reference to availability of an online scan. We began working our way through the 537-538 section, but it was slow going with Amit having to serve as lookout in case one of the librarians came by. I think the librarian was getting suspicious because the visits seemed to be getting more frequent. It was a frustrating and not terribly productive experience. There had to be a better solution. We gave up for the day.

Amit's father had him running errands for the hotel. He could wardrive on his trips, find an open Wi-Fi connection, download a book or two and continue driving on. When he had a break, he'd stop and do some serious searching while downloading a book or two in the background. He found some promising results in the online library catalog at the University of Tennessee at Knoxville.

* * *

That Friday, I drove into Knoxville – solo, since Amit was busy at the hotel, and Dad was off with Uncle Rob. My first stop was the John C. Hodges Library on the University of Tennessee, Knoxville, campus. As I was walking through the first floor, an archeological exhibition caught my attention: "Centaur Excavation at Volos." There on display was a half-excavated skeleton of a "centaur," half-man and half-horse. I was amazed at the time and energy it must have taken to create such a convincing looking, yet obviously phony display. How many other less obvious scientific deceptions might be lurking in the library?

Unfortunately, the library didn't have a copy of Franklin's *Electric Waves*. They did have a copy of Fleming's *Principles of Wireless Telegraphy*, however, up on the 6th floor. The library used a more complicated classification scheme from the Library of Congress, rather than the Dewey Decimal system with which I was more familiar. I got off the elevator, hung a right and found Fleming's book at the arcane location TK5741.F6 1910. Wait, 1910? Not quite the same edition. The Tolliver Library had a first printing from 1906. The Hodges Library copy was a "second edition, revised and extended" from September 1910. I looked for the bibliography, but this edition only had books, not papers. I pulled out my digital camera and snapped a few shots of the bibliography just in case, but it looked like a dead end.

My trip wasn't a complete waste, however, because I had a list of books to investigate on electromagnetic history. Just a few shelves away, I found a marvelous book about Heaviside by Paul J. Nahin, *Oliver Heaviside: Sage in Solitude*. I was tempted to scan the whole book, but since it wasn't old enough to be in the public domain, I refrained. I continued my search down on the fifth floor where I tracked down a copy of Bruce J. Hunt's *The Maxwellians* QC670.H84 1991. I didn't have borrowing privileges, nor would I have wanted to leave a trail if I could avoid it. I resolved to figure out a safe way to acquire copies, soon!

On my way home, I found a copy of *The Maxwellians* at McKay's Used Bookstore. I also stopped by Harbor Freight where I found a wonderful wireless motion detector. That would come in handy the next time we scanned some books.

* * *

By the end of June, Amit and I were on a roll. We'd start the day at Kudzu Joe's reviewing the previous day's results. Amit's OCR routine threw so many false positives we still had to manually review each page. At least he had it set to highlight the text, so we could focus on potential discrepancies. We didn't find any actual hits, however. In well over a hundred books, we had a grand total of two suspicious changes, one each in the Franklin and Fleming books. At least it made sense why this rewriting of history had apparently escaped detection. We knew it was there and despite our best efforts it was next to impossible to find the evidence!

After reviewing the previous day's haul, Amit worked on another fascinating project that had just started up. His father had described Amit's network traffic monitoring application to the Berkshire Inn's regional management team, and now Amit was on the hook to make a presentation on it to the company's management at their operations center in Charlotte, NC in August. If it went well, Berkshire Inn might want to roll out Amit's application at other Berkshire Inn locations for a trial. He was coding furiously, trying to clean up the user interface and make the application easy for non-experts to use. Amit was positively gleeful at the possibility of having his code distributed across multiple Berkshire Inns. He assured me he could exploit the company's intranet to disguise our Internet traffic and eliminate the need for wardriving. Even with all this to keep him busy, he still continued flirting shamelessly with Emma.

On my side of the table, I'd either do debate research, work on my physics homework, or study more about the electromagnetic pioneers and the geopolitics of the early 1900s. We hadn't been able to confirm whether the electromagnetic villain whose fingerprints we'd found was working on modern digital copies or had been active only around the time the books were published. I was confident, though, that we'd find the edits in old books and prove it was a century-old conspiracy. That the pioneers of electromagnetics and wireless engineering could be talking seriously about bouncing electric waves sounded crazy. I couldn't believe it wouldn't get a mention in the history books. Unless it had been suppressed almost immediately, word would have spread.

In the back of my mind, I was still amazed at how dangerous it had been to be an electromagnetic pioneer. The originator of modern electromagnetic theory, James Clerk Maxwell died prematurely. Heinrich Hertz proved the validity of Maxwell's theory by discovering radio waves and was dead within a year of publishing his book, *Electric Waves*. Maxwell's ideas were formalized by Hertz and a group of other physicists that historian Bruce J. Hunt had dubbed "the Maxwellians." The Maxwellians worked out the implications of Maxwell's thinking and streamlined it into modern form. These men included George FitzGerald, Oliver Lodge, and Oliver Heaviside. FitzGerald died not long after he'd worked out what would become some of the basic principles of relativity theory, deriving them from a study of electromagnetics. Oliver Lodge became convinced of the reality of psychic phenomena and it looked as though the last half of his life was spent largely writing about spiritualism. The only one of these pioneers who kept working on electromagnetics to the end of his life was Heaviside. But even Heaviside was clearly slowing down by the time his book came out in 1912, and he never finished the fourth volume on which he was working until his death in 1925. Heaviside complained of continual harassment distracting him from his work, of rocks through his windows, and vandalism from the neighborhood boys. His friends thought he was paranoid. But what if someone actually was out to get him, to keep him from productive work?

So three of the five pioneers of electromagnetics died prematurely at the peak of their careers. A 60% mortality rate was scary high. Dad was convinced it had to be natural causes since an assassin would have used poison. Death by cancer was inherently a death by natural causes. But three out of five dead in their prime? I wasn't so sure. The odds against that had to be astronomical. And the remaining two were harassed or distracted away from making significant further progress. It was as if someone realized that killing them all would start to look suspicious and merely sidetracked the remaining two. Between the editing of electromagnetics books and the high mortality rate, I became increasingly convinced Dad was wrong, and there had to be a connection. I had frustrating hints of a much larger picture, but without more pieces of the puzzle, I could do little more than speculate.

After a morning at Kudzu Joe's, I still went home for lunch. Dad was off with Uncle Rob or in Knoxville working on Dr. Kreuger's place. I regretted telling Mom about the 60% mortality rate business, because it just made her more nervous. I avoided discussing my research with her over lunch for fear of sparking more lengthy maternal admonishment to be safe and careful. That didn't work, of course.

"I'm so proud of you, son," Mom told me over one lunch. "You're growing up into a fine young man. You have that same energy, determination, and drive that I dearly love in your father," she added with a maternal smile. Then the smile faded. "But you have your father's faults as well," she added sternly. "You may understand intellectually that there are bad people in the world, but you're so confident in your abilities, that you think you can overcome any obstacle and defeat any adversary. Usually, that's a good thing. But there are powerful forces at work in the world: ruthless people with power and influence who will trample over anyone who gets in their way.

"My grandfather...," she began, "well that's not my story to tell. My family, the Tollivers, have been working for generations to acquire power and influence, to make the right sort of connections to break into the elite. Men like your Uncle Larry, or Uncle Mike, or like Sheriff Gunn only care about preserving and enhancing their power, and they won't hesitate to do whatever it takes to get what they want.

"There are some lions whose tails are best left unpulled," she admonished me.

I promised Mom I'd be really careful. And, I kept right on doing what I was doing. Really carefully, of course.

I remember clearly another Friday from that June. I went to Knoxville with Dad and helped him run the electrical power in Dr. Kreuger's underground refuge. The place had gone from a hole in the ground to a structure in under a month. But then, most of Dad's construction projects were like that. The structure went up quick, the detail work of plumbing, HVAC, and electrical took longer, and the finish work – the dry wall, trim, painting and cabinetry in residential jobs seemed to take forever. Instead of the giant hole that had greeted us a month earlier, there was a raised gravel field maybe five or six feet above grade and topped with low foundation walls. The walls were a giant nine-foot spaced periodic honeycomb with raw rebar stretching up like a Venus flytrap to catch a passing house and anchor it to Earth.

The place was a network of cargo containers sandwiching concrete walls between each one. The bottom level of cargo containers was all supported on concrete piers making about a three-foot-high crawl space. I figured out quickly why Dad brought me along. My job was to run, or more correctly, crawl, the Romex power cable from the power panel where Dad poked it through a hole in the floor over to where he was drilling through the floor to install power outlets. Then, he'd drill another hole and I'd drag the wire from the earlier hole to the newest hole. A half dozen holes later, and it was back to the power panel to start on the next circuit. I couldn't complain though. Last summer I worked on a renovation project in a rental house where the plumbing had leaked sewage all over the crawl space. As the junior apprentice, I got stuck with that job. Fortunately, I had a full body suit. It only took a few hours, and we completed the crawl space part of the work before the day got hot and unpleasant. But that odor was stuck in my hair for days and no amount of scrubbing or washing could completely remove it. Dr. Kreuger's refuge was actually one of the nicest crawl spaces I've ever worked in, because it was so new and clean and cool.

Most of those June afternoons were not nearly so memorable. I went to physics class after lunch. It was fairly easy after all the private tutoring I'd had from James Clerk Maxwell via *Matter and Motion*, supplemented by my father. I had to keep at it to avoid getting complacent, but I was cruising toward an easy A and one more core class for which I was not going to have to pay university tuition, once I'd transferred in the credits.

After class, I was off to the Tolliver Library where I'd meet Amit and scan more books. The wireless motion detector was invaluable – at least hourly a librarian would check to make sure we were behaving ourselves. We had the sensor set up at a choke point and we got a good thirty seconds to a minute of warning whenever anyone was drawing near our study room – plenty of time to secure the scanner under the table and pose earnestly studying over books or homework for the benefit of any passers by. We had a few false alarms as students walked by, but the traffic was low. We were well on our way to exhausting the library's supply of older physics and engineering books, so we'd started scanning journals and periodicals as well, like *Physical Review* and the *Proceedings of the Institute of Radio Engineering*.

When we were tired of scanning and studying, Amit and I would swing by the hotel to work out and swim in the pool. Sometimes Emma would join us. I was still a bit amazed that Amit of all people had attracted her. I had to hand it to Amit – that girl looked hot in a swim suit. Not that Amit could do much of anything about it. The pool area was under video surveillance – which, come to think of it, may have been why Mrs. Patel was working the front desk where she had access to all the live video feeds. Amit did a wonderful impression of being completely nonchalant about Emma. He rarely slipped up. But one afternoon as I was heading out, he asked me if he could borrow the wireless motion sensor.

"Why do you want it?"

"I thought I'd go back to the library after dinner to do some research with Emma. Just generic alternative energy stuff – nothing that would give away our case."

Nice redirection on his part. I held his gaze for a moment or two longer than was comfortable. Then I asked, "So why exactly do you need the motion detector?"

He was squirming a bit. "So we can study without being disturbed," he explained with a poker face that needed some work.

"Learn lots," I said, handing it over.

"Oh, we will," he assured me.

CHAPTER 5: INDEPENDENCE DAY

With June behind me, I went up to Uncle Rob's with my folks for an Independence Day celebration. When I'd first heard we were going to Uncle Rob's place for the Fourth, I had been expecting a small gathering with just immediate family. I'd been waiting patiently for a month now to get the scoop on Dad's project with Uncle Rob. When I heard about my sister Kira and her beau driving in from Nashville, I was unconcerned – there'd be no problem getting a quiet moment with Dad and Uncle Rob and getting the details from them. Then, Dad suggested I invite Amit and his family. Mom said she'd extended an invitation to the Tollivers. I wasn't looking forward to having to hang out with Abby, but fortunately, they didn't deign to attend. And then, I learned Rob had invited all his veteran buddies and the festivities were going to start with shooting. This was clearly not destined to be a quiet and intimate family gathering.

Mom and I picked up Amit and his mother – Mr. Patel had to stay at the hotel, and Dad had gone up early to help Rob set up. We made the dozen-mile drive out of town and up into the hills to Uncle Rob's gate. Usually locked, barred, and punctuated with a couple of "No Trespassing" signs, today it was wide open and even decorated with some red, white, and blue bunting. We drove in about fifty yards to where an arch of welded rebar spanned the gravel road. The sign spelled out "Robber Dell" in twisted rebar with a thin patina of rust. Heh. Below, someone had added a "Welcome!"

sign. More red, white, and blue decorations were threaded though the arch. Just past the arch, the road entered a narrow defile with a steep incline and even steeper sides. The road cut sharply into a scarp just barely wide enough for Mom's car to get through. Mom drove slowly and carefully up the slope. The road opened to a broad clearing, full of corn.

The property had belonged to Great Aunt Molly, my grandmother's sister on my father's side. Back a few years ago, Dad and Uncle Rob inherited the property on the death of their mother. The property had not been lived on in years – merely leased to nearby farmers for hay or corn. A stone chimney and a foundation of rubble were all that were left of an old farmhouse. The gravel road ended by the ruined farmhouse, and a dirt road still damp from an early morning rain shower led back through the cornfield. At the far side of the corn field, backed up almost to the mountain, was a doublewide trailer and a small metal barn. I don't know how Dad and Uncle Rob got the trailer in through that steep cut up the hillside, but Uncle Rob had been living there since he got out of the service, supplementing his military retirement by working the farm.

Mom parked next to a low, flat hill. We climbed up the gentle slope where we met Dad. On top of the mound was a fresh concrete pad surrounded by low concrete walls with rebar fingers sticking in the air like a giant Venus flytrap waiting... Realization dawned. I looked curiously at Dad. He smiled and placed a finger in front of his lips to gesture for silence. I was sure I knew where Dad had prototyped the design for Dr. Kreuger's refuge.

I also saw a low, sloped-wire antenna between the mound and the trailer. It looked a lot like the one Dad had in our backyard. I'd figured Uncle Rob and Dad were communicating using amateur radio, but the similar antenna confirmed it for me. I also saw a few propane tanks on pads distributed around the pad. One I could understand – many folks with trailers would have a propane tank for heating or cooking. But, Uncle Rob had three and what looked like pads for a couple more. I was rapidly adding to my list of questions to ask Dad and Uncle Rob, but for now, I was going to have to be patient.

Uncle Rob put us to work organizing and setting up his shindig. He gave responsibility for the shooting range to Amit and me. We set up targets on hay bales on the field Rob had designated as the range, and we piled a row of double-stacked bales to form a firing line. We stacked up a half-dozen bales at each shooting location to form an impromptu platform for prone or kneeling shooting positions. All that work left us tired and thirsty, so we headed back to the trailer in the Mule.

By then it was clear Dad and Uncle Rob had invited quite a crowd. There were a number of clean-cut men. I pegged them as some of Uncle Rob's veteran friends. I recognized some of Dad's contractor friends and colleagues. All the men seemed to have brought their wives and children or girlfriends. I saw a couple of Mom's friends and their husbands and families, including some kids I knew or recognized from school. I spotted Emma – Amit would be happy. There was even a familiar looking German sedan – I spied Dr. Kreuger accompanied by a woman I assumed to be Frau Kreuger. Following them were an attractive blond girl and a couple of younger boys. I assumed they were the Kreugers' children.

I caught up with Uncle Rob and asked him where and how he'd met so many folks around Sherman. "Folks I worked with, mostly," he explained. "Some from the rifle range. Pity all the deputies are on duty for the holiday or we'd have had most of the sheriff's department over."

"You shoot with the deputies?" I asked. "So how do you score compared to them?"

He chuckled. "My scores are better than any deputy, but that's what you might call a 'loaded question.' On the range, a smart law officer makes his qualification score and not much better. Shoot a perfect or near-perfect score and heaven help you if you ever accidentally shoot a bystander in the line of duty. No one will believe it was truly an accident. My scores are better than any of them – officially. Unofficially, there's a few who're probably on par and maybe a bit better on a good day. Sheriff Gunn runs a tight ship. He makes sure all his deputies know what they're doing."

Before I could get into any further questions, he excused himself, and made an announcement to the throng. "Anyone who'd like to learn how to shoot, come on to the range," Uncle Rob shouted out. "We'll be training and practicing for an hour, and then we'll see who's the best shot here today."

I ran to the truck to get my gun case, but Dad already had it and met me halfway. "Make sure you spend your time teaching others who haven't had your opportunities to learn," he advised me. I was a bit disappointed, but I saw the wisdom of Dad's direction. I could come and shoot whenever I wanted, after all. I taught Amit and the Kreuger boys, Carl and Frank, how to shoot with my .22 rifle. I asked Amit where Emma was, and he told me she wasn't interested. My .22 was a simple single-shot bolt-action rifle. It didn't take long before all three of my students were getting quite good. I saw Dad was teaching Mr. Kreuger how to shoot his .45 pistol. Mom was using her slim .22 pistol to instruct Mrs. Patel and Mrs. Krueger. Another of Mom's pupils was the Kreuger's daughter, who was very cute, and was taking to shooting with a bouncy enthusiasm.

Finally, we cleared the range, secured the weapons, and I replaced the targets. The competition began, first rifle, then pistol. The top three scores from each round advanced to the final. I made it to the final with my .22 rifle, beating out one of Uncle Rob's friends. He was shooting a fancy, tricked-up AR-15, and he was incredulous that I shot better using the iron sights on my simple .22. At that relatively short range, however, my .22 was every bit as accurate as the more expensive weapon. Uncle Rob, Dad, and I were all beat in the final round by another of Uncle Rob's friends. In the pistol competition, my Mom cleaned up. She shot a perfect score in her preliminary round, and then did it all over again in the final. The holes from her shots formed a tight group right in the bullseye ring.

"You still got it," Dad said to Mom. "Shall, I?" He offered to take her gun. "No, go ahead, dear," she said. "I'll clean her up and store her myself." Dad carried our rifle case back toward the truck as Mom quickly and skillfully cleaned her pistol.

"That's some mighty fine shooting, ma'am," one of Rob's friends was saying. He'd been the runner up and shot a near perfect score with his .45, but Mom's grouping had been tighter. "But, that little gun isn't very practical for self-defense, though," he continued. "Those .22 rounds have no real stopping power. You might consider looking into something with more power that shoots a .45 round. A .22 is a lousy gun to take to a real gunfight."

"I've tried other calibers, sir," Mom replied politely, "but the recoil makes those big guns hard for me to handle. I prefer to be accurate with a .22 rather than spray large caliber rounds in the general direction of my target."

"I think you'll find that grouping would be plenty tight to put a magazine of rounds into someone's nose," Rob observed in Mom's defense. "That's gonna be effective. The best gun for a gunfight is the one you're most proficient and effective with. The worst is not to have one at all."

That seemed to settle the debate. I walked with Mom back to Dad's truck to put away our guns. "Where did you learn to shoot like that?" I asked her.

"It was your Uncle Rob who got me and your father started," she explained. "From then on it was just a matter of practice. I've been too busy to shoot regularly of late, so I'm glad we had this opportunity."

"But why did you and Dad spend the time to get so proficient?"

"It was a bit... wild," she explained, "in the early days when your father and I first came back to Sherman. It made sense to be prepared for any... eventualities. And the less said about those days the better." That was all I could get out of her.

After everyone had locked up their weapons and secured them in their vehicles, Dad stepped up on a stump, and held up his hands to silence the crowd. "I want to thank you all for joining us on this fine Independence Day."

"Can't keep me away from your barbeque!" came a cry from the crowd.

"Well, y'all should know there's no such thing as a free lunch!" he exclaimed back, "So quiet down, and listen up! Legend has it that 'Robber Dell' is where the Unionists hid their horses when the Confederate raiders swept through these hills. The place had fallen into some disrepair. I can't imagine a more appropriate proprietor for this spread than my brother." Dad got some chuckles.

"John Adams said that Independence Day should be 'solemnized with pomp and parade, with shows, games, sports, guns, bells, bonfires, and illuminations, from one end of this continent to the other, from this time forward forever more.' We got the games, sports, and guns well underway. Now's the time for the show where we 'solemnize with pomp.' Being a most unpompous sort myself," that drew more good-natured chuckles, "I'm going to turn the stump over to our host to remind us all what we're celebrating here today. Rob?"

Dad stepped down, and Uncle Rob stepped up on the stump. "I want to thank my big brother not just for that introduction, but also for introducing me to Sherman. I haven't been here long, and I'm grateful so many of you have honored me with your friendship. I appreciate y'all spending your valuable time to gather here today.

"Some of us take liberties like these for granted: the right to assemble, the right to speak our minds, the right to have a say in how we're governed. It hasn't always been that way. A couple hundred years ago some folks just like you and me got fed up with being pushed around and oppressed by tyranny. They joined together, and they resolved to send a message to tyrants then, now, and in the future: a message that would never be forgotten, a message that goes like this." Rob pulled out a sheet of paper.

> *"When in the Course of human events, it becomes necessary for one people to dissolve the political bands which have connected them with another, and to assume among the powers of the earth, the separate and equal station to which the Laws of Nature and of Nature's God entitle them, a decent respect to the opinions of mankind requires that they should declare the causes which impel them to the separation."*

It was uncanny how Uncle Rob's voice quieted the rowdy crowd.

> *"We hold these truths to be self-evident, that all men are created equal, that they are endowed by their Creator with certain unalienable Rights, that among these are Life, Liberty and the pursuit of Happiness. – That to secure these rights, Governments are instituted among Men, deriving their just powers from the consent of the governed, –That whenever any Form of Government becomes destructive of these ends, it is the Right of the People to alter or to abolish it, and to institute new Government, laying its foundation on such principles and organizing its powers in such form, as to them shall seem most likely to effect their Safety and Happiness.*

I'd read Jefferson's words before and since, but never did they have more meaning to me than that day, spoken aloud by my uncle. It was easy to imagine a patriot of old standing on a stump in a clearing informing friends and neighbors who'd gathered to hear the latest news from Philadelphia.

> *Prudence, indeed, will dictate that Governments long established should not be changed for light and transient causes; and accordingly all experience hath shewn, that mankind are more disposed to suffer, while evils are sufferable, than to right themselves by abolishing the forms to which they are accustomed. But when a long train of*

> *abuses and usurpations, pursuing invariably the same Object evinces a design to reduce them under absolute Despotism, it is their right, it is their duty, to throw off such Government, and to provide new Guards for their future security."*

The crowd became livelier, punctuating the recitation with boos and hisses as Uncle Rob recited the list of tyrannies, and responding with cheers as he described our rights and independence. Finally, he concluded:

> *"And for the support of this Declaration, with a firm reliance on the protection of divine Providence, we mutually pledge to each other our Lives, our Fortunes, and our sacred Honor!"*

The crowd burst out with sustained cheers and applause. When they quieted down, Uncle Rob continued. "As we're celebrating here this fine day, kindly remember to lift bottle or glass in honor of our founding fathers, our comrades, our friends and family, and all the others who have pledged their Lives, their Fortunes, and their Sacred Honor in the cause of liberty." He took a swig from his bottle, as did many in the crowd. "I am informed," Uncle Rob, continued, "that the barbeque is ready to be served. If you'd like to get an early start, head on up to my new pad. Otherwise, please carry on with the fun and games."

I thought I was finally going to get my chance to corner Uncle Rob, but he was busy talking with a group of men. I recognized Mr. Garrety and some of the other truckers from Kudzu Joe's among them. Before I got a chance to hear what they were discussing, Uncle Rob interrupted the man who was speaking, and drafted me to supervise the ATV rides. Dad and Uncle Rob had carved a mile-long loop trail roughly around the perimeter of the property. Now that the shooting was over, the trail was open for business. Some of Dad's and Uncle Rob's friends had brought some ATVs and dirt bikes. The kids did laps while I served as a pace car, driving the Kawasaki Mule at the head of the pack and making sure none of the kids got too wild. I did several laps over the course of an hour. When the Mule ran low on gas, I stopped to fill it up. I waved over Amit and Emma, letting them take over with traffic control. The Mule had two seats and they liked the idea of being out of sight. By then, I was getting hungry, so I climbed the mound to Uncle Rob's pad to get a helping of barbeque.

I saw Dad and Uncle Rob talking privately. Finally! I grabbed some pulled pork, heaped it on a bun, and went on over to join them. Before I could make it over to them, however, Mr. Burleson stopped me.

"You folks sure know how to throw a party," he said. "Find any other clues about those bouncing waves?"

I told him about the Fleming bibliography and the missing reference to the 1905 paper by Heaviside: 'On the Interactions of Waves.'

"Your father passed that one on to me last week," he acknowledged. "Unfortunately, I haven't made much progress. Heaviside talks plenty about reflections of waves from conductors, but not from each other. If he wrote a paper on electric waves bouncing off each other, he certainly didn't include it in *Electromagnetic Theory*."

"A completed search is progress of a sort, sir," I offered, "even if you don't find what you were looking for. At least now we have fewer places to look."

"That's looking on the bright side!" he acknowledged with a grin. "Sorry I haven't called you earlier, but your father has this notion we should only discuss it in person."

"He's just being careful," I noted. "Dad thinks if there's anything to this at all, it must be a modern cover-up from the folks at Omnitia. I think it's more likely to have been something going on a hundred years ago."

"Hard to say," Mr. Burleson said with a shrug, "but it was interesting to look into. If you do find out anything further, let me know. I'll see what I can do."

"Thank you, sir," I replied. "I appreciate all your help."

Dad and Uncle Rob were still talking off by themselves, sipping from small shot glasses of amber liquid as I approached. Bourbon, I presumed. Maybe Uncle Rob had aged some of his moonshine? I figured they'd respond best to directness. I squared myself in front of them, I looked Uncle Rob in the eye, and I asked, "So, what is this grand scheme you're working on with my father?"

Uncle Rob turned to address Dad, "He sure don't beat around the bush much, does he?"

"He's got a determined streak to him," Dad acknowledged. "Grabs onto something and won't let it go. Must get that from his mother."

"Well, he might have gotten that from our side," Uncle Rob speculated. "But at least he has better sense in his choice of obsessions than Grandpappy. You know…"

"With respect, sir," I cut him off, "I would appreciate it if you'd do me the courtesy of an answer."

Uncle Rob burst out with a laugh. "Real polite, too. Should I tell him?"

"Go ahead," Dad smiled. "I expect you'll have no peace until you satisfy him. And it was your notion got us into this scheme, after all."

"Aren't you the one always saying that the inspiration is only 1%? Well, OK then." He turned to me. "You read up much on your history?"

"Some," I said cautiously, figuring Uncle Rob would have some obscure point on which he'd trip me up.

"Do you recall the Whiskey Rebellion?"

I'd read about that in Paul Johnson's *A History of the American People*. "Sure. Frontier folk in Pennsylvania couldn't get their corn to market because the expense of carting it in bulk across the mountains was too high. So, they distilled it to whiskey, which made it more portable. But then, the federal government started taxing whiskey and they rebelled. Washington sent the Army in to restore control."

"Yeah, that's the gist of it," Uncle Rob agreed. "That's what gave me the idea. Up and down the Appalachians, there are natural gas wells. Not so many in these hills, but more up into Kentucky and West Virginia. Part of the Gore Tax included a heap of new regulations on how to transport natural gas. The regulators carefully designed the rules in collusion with Tolliver Corporation and some of the other large energy companies who were big campaign contributors. They engineered the regulations to make it very difficult for small independents to get their natural gas transported to market at any reasonable expense. So most of their wells are idle and their owners are losing their shirts. It's the same problem as faced those frontiersmen with the bulky corn they couldn't transport. How did they solve it?"

"By distilling it down to a more compact form," I answered. "You mean chilling and liquefying the natural gas?"

"Sharp kid," Uncle Rob said to Dad. "But, not quite there yet," he said to me. "Liquefied natural gas, chilled and compressed to make it more compact is a standard technique. But, the energy companies and their lobbyists thought of that. They forbid shipping liquefied natural gas by tanker truck except for very short distances. And somehow, while it is perfectly safe and acceptable to truck gas from a rail depot or a distributor to a customer, when the gas is being moved the other direction from a gas field to a rail depot or to a distributor or directly to an end user, it suddenly becomes too dangerous to transport on a truck. The upshot of it is, if you don't have a rail spur to your gas field, you can't ship your gas in compact liquefied form which means it just isn't economical to ship."

"So how do you ship it?" I asked.

"You don't," Uncle Rob grinned. "That's the beauty of it. If you can't bring your natural gas to your customer, you bring your customer to your natural gas." I was confused. Uncle Rob continued. "Your Mom and Dad engineered a mobile system in a cargo container for compressing, liquefying, and distilling air. It burns natural gas to drive the compressor and chiller. We truck our rig on up to a natural gas field, and we tap into what would otherwise be an idle well for a few hours. We burn the natural gas and collect the liquefied compressed air into tanker trucks: about four tanker trucks of liquid nitrogen for every tanker truck of liquid oxygen. We have a small tank that collects the residue of argon and heavier gasses. Our production method isn't as efficient as big fixed plants, but our energy costs are much lower. The small independents are happy to get a market for natural gas they otherwise couldn't sell, and we're able to get a steep discount. The rules for trucking compressed liquefied oxygen and nitrogen are still much less stringent than for liquefied natural gas.

"We're building a nice customer list that's happy to get cut rate liquefied gases. Welders use oxygen and argon, for instance. Many folks use nitrogen for cooling. There's a restaurant in Knoxville that uses it to make the creamiest ice cream you ever tasted. We even have a couple distributors we're working with, now that our volumes are getting high enough. They're willing to buy our compressed gas in bulk and sell it to end users."

"So, effectively, you're 'bootlegging' liquid air," I said.

"You could say that," Uncle Rob acknowledged with a smile. "But nothing we're doing is the least bit illegal."

"For now," Dad said ominously. "The point of the regulation was to shut down these small natural gas producers in the name of safety and the environment so they couldn't compete with the politically connected elites. If those elites found out we were providing a legal mechanism for small producers to sell their gas, they'd likely concoct some kind of excuse to shut us down. That's why it's important this not get out."

"Is there any particular safety hazard?" I asked.

"Of course," Uncle Rob offered, "if you splash the stuff on yourself you get freeze burns. That's why doctors will use liquid nitrogen to burn off warts. If you let liquid nitrogen evaporate in a confined space, you could asphyxiate if it replaces too much of the oxygen. Liquid oxygen isn't particularly flammable in and of itself, but pure oxygen gives a much more intense fire than normal air. That's why welders like it. I've been using it in the welding jobs I've been doing for your dad."

Ah-ha. Now I knew where Dad had found a reliable and trustworthy welder for Mr. Kreuger's refuge project. And, I'd already figured out we were standing right on top of the testbed where he and Dad had prototyped the underground refuge concept using buried cargo containers. I kept my epiphany to myself.

Uncle Rob continued, "So there are certainly dangers and things we have to be careful about, but the technology for storing and shipping the stuff is well established."

"What happens if you get shut down?" I inquired. "Won't you take a big loss?"

"The business model is the tricky part," Dad observed. "We have to minimize our capital investment in case we get regulated out of business on short notice. We have to rent all our trucks and gear and only buy used hardware that will retain a decent resale value. Fortunately, there are lots of out-of-work truckers and idle rigs around. We've nearly recouped the initial investment and the margins are solid. We're at a point now where we'd at least break even if we were shut down."

"You always were the inquisitive kid," Uncle Rob noted. "Any more questions?"

"It comes of being in a family with an awful lot of secrets, sir," I replied. "So, Mr. Garrety is working for you? Oh, and that reminds me, he bought me a coffee the other day, by way of thanks. He also asked me to convey his thanks to you in person."

Uncle Rob looked concerned "He didn't say anything about the work, did he?"

"No, sir," I confirmed. "Which was remarkable, because he seemed to think I knew all about it. Only, I was even more confused after we talked than before."

"Good," Uncle Rob said with a smile. "He's not actually an employee. Mr. Garrety and some other truckers work for me part-time as contractors. They haul the stuff to the distributors and customers, but your Dad and I do most of the actual production," Uncle Rob explained. "It's time for some fireworks, so you'll have to settle for one last question."

I pondered what I should ask. I might not get another opportunity like this for a while. "I see you have an antenna just like Dad's, but how do you communicate using amateur radio? Don't you need a line of sight or a repeater to make it work?"

Dad noted, "He just got his Technician Class license."

"Oh, congratulations, kid," Uncle Rob smiled. "Now if you study for your General Class License, you'll learn that lower frequencies, like below 30 megahertz, tend to bounce off a high layer in the atmosphere called the ionosphere. We're using 'Near-Vertical Incidence Skywave' or 'NVIS,'" he explained. "The signals go straight up to the ionosphere and back down over an area as much as a couple hundred miles wide."

This was puzzling to me. "I learned about the ionosphere when I was studying for my exam, but I thought it was only for long distance communication."

"Same phenomenon, different application," Rob explained. "Instead of bouncing signals at an angle so they hop around the world, we bounce them straight up and back down. Your dad can probably explain it better than me. Gotta run." With that, he departed to prepare the fireworks, and Dad followed him, leaving me with yet another admonition to keep family business private.

The fireworks were spectacular – not as big and elaborate as you might get in a professional big-city show – but the proximity and intimacy of the pyrotechnics had a greater emotional impact. I watched the show with my sister Kira and her boyfriend. He seemed like a jerk, and I wondered what Kira saw in him. He wasn't at all interested in hanging out with Kira's kid brother. After the fireworks ended, Dad and Uncle Rob lit a big bonfire. I left Kira in peace.

Uncle Rob had a variety of logs arrayed in a broad circle around the fire. I walked a slow circle around the dancing flames. Uncle Rob had gone over to chat with a couple of his friends. Mom and Dad were sitting together, Mom with her head on Dad's shoulder. I didn't want to interrupt their privacy by joining them.

Amit and Emma were off to the side sitting together on a log. As I approached them, I heard Amit explaining to Emma why Women's Suffrage was such a bad idea. What? Yes, I'd heard him correctly. "Women are too emotional on average to make the hard rational decisions needed to responsibly exercise the vote," he was saying. Emma was clearly not happy with him. Was he deliberately provoking her to make her mad, which would then be evidence in support of his thesis? That would be just like him – always the debater. Or, was this just part of another convoluted tactic on his part? Probably. I made a mental note to ask him about it later, and left him to his "game."

Then I saw the Kruegers and their attractive daughter. She was sitting with her family. I probably would have left well enough alone but Amit's influence had rubbed off on me. I approached the family, "Guten Abend Herr Doktor Krueger und Frau Krueger. Wie geht es Ihnnen?" I think that was more or less correct for "how are you," but I wasn't sure if it was right for formal plural usage.

"Sehr gut meine junge Freund und guten abend zu Ihnnen!" Doktor Krueger said cheerfully. I think I caught the gist, but anything other than the most basic greetings were beyond me. Fortunately, he switched to English. "But we here are the Hessians in this history drama of your father and uncle, ja? You would still speak with us?"

"I understand we got many of our best and hardest working patriots from the Hessians who decided to change sides, bring their families over from Germany, and make a go of it as Americans," I said to Doktor Krueger. "I hope you and your family will decide to stay also."

He cracked a broad smile at that, "I think we will. Please have a seat." The girl had been sitting next to her father and quickly slid down the log to make room for me. I remained studiously focused on her father as I sat down and he continued speaking. "Please thank your father and uncle for the invitation. This has been great experience. Like Oktoberfest but with guns and fireworks!"

"Did you have any experience with guns before, sir?" I asked.

"In the Bundeswehr. I was drafted. Not since. Carl and Frank, they like your teaching," he said.

"They've both got good eyes and steady hands." I noted them both smiling. "They're excellent shots."

"You have met my daughter, Eva?" he asked. He pronounced it "AY-va."

"No I haven't had the pleasure." Finally! I turned to face her, took her hand, and held it as I introduced myself. "You seemed to enjoy learning how to shoot this afternoon."

"Very interesting. We have nothing like that in Germany," she said with only a mild accent. "America is very different."

"This is your first time?" I asked. She looked confused. "You hadn't shot a gun before?" I added.

"Oh. No," she said. "I just came here with my mother and brothers last month."

"Eva will start eighth grade in fall at school," Doktor Kreuger offered. I'd thought she was older. I was feeling a bit awkward. "Carl and Frank are in fourth and sixth grade."

"I hope you all enjoy the rest of your summer vacation." I tried not to sound too lame. "I understand I'll be seeing you again soon, helping my father with your project," I said to Dr. Kreuger.

"Yes, it goes well the work," he replied. "Tell your father and uncle thanks again for us all. We had a wonderful time."

"I'll do that," I said, standing. "A pleasure meeting you all," I added to the family and excused myself. That was a bit uncomfortable, but I survived. I hoped Amit was right that approaching girls got easier with practice.

I stood by myself a way out from the circle of light and watched the happy people. Eventually, the party faded out as folks departed and headed on home. Amit got a ride with Emma's family. Mom, Dad, and I followed the path of light sticks away from the bonfire, our shadows dancing in the dim light ahead of us. It had been a busy day of celebration, a day to recall our history punctuated with guns, barbeque, bourbon, bonfires, and fireworks. I would not see its like again for many years.

CHAPTER 6: A VACATION

"'Is this your first time?' Seriously?" Amit was vastly amused as I recounted my experience with the Kreugers. Leave it to Amit to note the possible sexual connotation. I felt mortified. Hopefully if I'd missed it, the Kreugers would have as well. Amit continued, interrupting my reverie. "That was slick. And right in front of her dad, too. No wonder she was flustered." Argh. He might have a point. Eva may have noticed it, although her English wasn't the best. I hoped that she was just confused, and had missed it like I did. "Way to go," Amit added. "Did you get her number?"

"In front of her father? Are you crazy? And she's only fourteen."

"Hey, lots of the wildest girls have daddy issues," Amit opined as if he were an actual expert instead of a compulsive reader of pick-up artist blogs. "You set yourself up as the bad-boy rival to his authority and she'll swoon for you."

"I seriously doubt she has any 'daddy issues,'" I said. This was getting tiresome. "She seemed like a very well-adjusted girl."

"I bet there will be daddy issues when he finds a sixteen-year-old boy chasing after his fourteen-year-old daughter," Amit observed with excessive enthusiasm. "That's mathematically out of bounds. He'll overreact for sure."

"I am not chasing, merely being friendly," I said insistently. "And you mean to tell me there's a mathematical formula?" Now Amit had to be pulling my leg.

"Half your age plus seven," he assured me. "You're still sixteen, right? So fourteen-year-old girls are out of bounds for you. But when you're seventeen in September and she's turned fifteen, then she's fair game."

Yes, his math worked out but was there actually some exact rule? "That's got to be general social guidance, not a fundamental law of nature," I countered. I'd had enough of his insinuations, so before he could dispute me, I added, "Why have you become an anti-suffragette?"

"Oh you heard that?" he looked smug. "Just keeping Emma off balance."

"You know," I observed, "if you like the girl, you might consider being nice to her."

"Of course," he acknowledged. "But you have to mix it up some. If you're nice all the time, a girl won't respect you."

I didn't get it. Amit had one of the most attractive girls from school as his girlfriend. Emma certainly had other options. I was surprised she put up with his antics. But then, I found Amit annoying at times too, and I put up with him.

Whatever.

Amit and I continued our search throughout July, but progress was scarce. In a couple of additional weeks of searching, we'd only found one more possible omitted mention of Heaviside – this one in Sir Edmund Whittaker's *A History of the Theories of Aether & Electricity*, printed in 1910. It, too, was frustratingly vague. Those couple of sentences from William Suddards Franklin about bouncing waves remained our best hope of understanding what was going on.

With the lack of progress in finding new clues, I spent more effort understanding the history and personalities behind the evolution of Maxwell's theory. I read Hunt's *The Maxwellians* and Nahin's book on Heaviside. Dad had managed to acquire a copy of the Nahin book for me on a visit to McKay's, a used bookstore in Knoxville. Maxwell's premature death, in 1879, left the field in some disarray. Many of his contemporaries doubted there was an electromagnetic basis to light. FitzGerald wrote a paper "On the Impossibility of Electromagnetic Waves," in the early 1880s. He was only barely persuaded at the last minute to strike out the "Im" and retitle his paper "On the Possibility of Electromagnetic Waves." This skepticism deterred many who were following in Maxwell's footsteps.

My physics textbook made everything seem so simple, clean, and inevitable: Maxwell came up with his equations, Hertz discovered radio waves, and then on to atomic theory. Reality was much messier.

While professional physicists skeptically toyed with Maxwell's theories, an unemployed telegrapher put them to immediate practical use. Heaviside applied Maxwell's ideas to telegraphy, deriving the equations that describe how signals propagate on transmission lines. He showed that you have to have a balance of electric and magnetic energy to send a signal without distortion. Most telegraph lines of the period didn't have enough magnetic energy. Heaviside demonstrated that telephone lines needed more inductance – circuit elements to increase the magnetic energy in the right amount to carry signals without distortion. As Mr. Burleson pointed out, AT&T paid Michael Pupin a fortune for his "invention" of this solution, and Heaviside never saw a dime.

Heaviside's contributions aided theory as well as practice. He came up with the compact vector notation that transformed Maxwell's ill-expressed concepts into the simpler and easier-to-use form that scientists and engineers still use today. What we call "Maxwell's Equations" are actually Heaviside's successful attempt to make sense of Maxwell's ideas.

While ivory tower thinkers debated, Heaviside continued demonstrating the worth of Maxwell's ideas by putting them into practice. He joined forces with a professor, Oliver Lodge, to develop much of the theory behind alternating current and high frequency electronics. Establishment figures tried their best to crush them and their ideas. The chief engineer of the British Postal System, William Henry Preece, despised

Heaviside and Lodge, mocking and belittling them. Heaviside returned the favor with some brilliant and vicious sarcasm. When Oliver Heaviside tried to publish a joint paper with his telegrapher brother, Arthur, Preece refused permission for them to publish their results and analysis. I was looking for clues to a conspiracy of some sort to cover up hidden truths in electromagnetics. Was Preece's attempt to silence Heaviside and suppress his ideas a part of the same cover up?

This epic feud was soon overshadowed by reports from Germany that a young and previously unknown physicist, Heinrich Hertz, had succeeded in generating and detecting electromagnetic waves. He demonstrated that electromagnetic waves behaved as Maxwell predicted – propagating at the speed of light and bending, reflecting, and behaving just like light, once allowances were made for the much longer wavelengths.

By then, it appeared to be too late to suppress the truth.

Hertz's premature death in 1894 hardly slowed down the progress of electromagnetics at all. Marconi and others were quick to grasp the commercial implications of Hertz's electric waves. Fundamental research continued. At the turn of the century, Heaviside, FitzGerald, and a Dutch physicist named Hendrik Lorentz were poised on the cusp of some great breakthroughs. Michaelson and Morley had demonstrated that the speed of light appeared constant no matter what the orientation of their experiment or time of day or time of the year. This negative result was strong evidence against the æther theory – the notion that electromagnetic waves were conveyed by undulations in some physical medium that pervades the universe.

Heaviside, FitzGerald, and Lorentz had pieced together various aspects of how this all worked from a bottom-up, fundamental study of electromagnetics. For instance, they showed how apparent length contracts and how the mass of objects increase with velocity. FitzGerald died prematurely in 1901. Lorentz explicitly worked out how electromagnetics required transformations to adjust measured length and time depending on the velocity of an observer.

Just as all these discoveries positioned electromagnetics to go to the next level, along came Albert Einstein: a 26-year-old who had not yet completed his doctorate and was working in a patent office. In 1905, he published five papers, each of which was a profound and fundamental breakthrough in physics. It was as if Einstein had all of a sudden figured out most every outstanding problem in the physics of his day, from atomic to quantum theory, including an explanation of electromagnetics he called "special relativity." They called 1905 his "annus mirabilis," his "miraculous year," with good justification. It certainly looked like a miracle. It seemed too good to be true. Maybe it was.

The bottom-up approach of Heaviside, FitzGerald, and Lorentz was swept away. In its place, Einstein offered a top-down approach starting from two axioms – first that the speed of light must be constant with respect to the observer, and second that physical laws do not depend upon the inertial frame within which one makes a measurement. To me, his axioms looked like conclusions disguised as starting points that begged the question of why these things held true. Lorentz's æther theory agreed with Einstein's special relativity, but the æther concept seemed superfluous, so special relativity came to rule the day. Lorentz continued in physics for a time, but soon he was sucked into administration. He even invested the last part of his life in planning flood control dams that were so critical to the safety of his Dutch homeland. By all accounts, it was great work, but it distracted him from further progress on his æther theory.

Was it the electromagnetic villain at work? Did someone aid or influence Einstein? I found some suggestion that Einstein may have been helped by his wife, Mileva Maric, a fellow student from whom he was soon separated. The suggestions I found, though, were not well supported. Most historians concluded she did not make substantive contributions to his work. There didn't seem to be anyone else close enough to Einstein to have influenced or contributed to his work.

What better way to derail technical progress than to jump to the conclusion and skip over the details of how and why something works? Show someone the answer, but don't explain how it works or where it comes from, and you guarantee they can only calculate and will be unable to make further progress. Hand a first-grader a calculator. Show them how to key in their arithmetic problems. Let them use it exclusively. How likely is it they will ever truly understand what they are doing? Einstein passed out the magic calculator that solved the problem, and the result was that everyone stopped trying to figure out how and why it worked and what it did. Heaviside, FitzGerald, Lorentz, and all their efforts to work out why electromagnetics led to special relativity were largely neglected and forgotten.

I suggested this to Dad, and he pointed out the glaring error with my hypothesis. Suppose Einstein's remarkable discoveries actually were too good to be true. Then, whoever was manipulating Einstein and feeding him results would have to be even further ahead. It simply wasn't credible. He had a point. I put aside my electromagnetic conspiracy theories while I looked for more clues.

Amit and I were both tiring of the search and the lack of results. A big part of the problem was that – contrary to our expectations – a good number of the books simply weren't available online. Or if they were available, it was in an earlier or a later edition so no direct comparison with the Tolliver Library copy could be made. Absent a scan to compare against the book, we'd never be able to tell if there were any suspicious omissions or edits. The fundamental question that still stumped us was, "When were the edits and omissions made?" Were these recent changes implemented as the books were scanned into Omnitia or Project Gutenberg, like Dad thought? Or were these truthful and accurate scans of actual hardcopy books that had already been edited and modified a century ago, long before Omnitia and Project Gutenberg got to them? That was my suspicion. The solution was to seek out more copies of the books and find out.

The University of Tennessee library in Knoxville did not have the editions we needed. Amit found an online listing: a copy of Fleming's *Principles of Wireless Telegraphy* was available at Vanderbilt University. It looked like the right edition, too. I thought of asking Kira to check, but I decided to bide my time until I could check in person, rather than risk a phone call or email. I'd make a point of stopping by the library at Vanderbilt when we were in Nashville on our vacation.

Amit also found a number of leads to used books online. But they tended to be snapped up quickly. Our thought that we could drive to Cleveland or Chicago, let alone Portland or Providence, to buy a book anonymously was simply not workable. The books would be gone by the time we got there. Someone was snapping them up faster than Dad or Uncle Rob could arrange the logistics for a friend to buy them for us. And we could hardly ask one of bookstores to hold the books for cash payment and pick-up, because that would be announcing our presence to whoever was also buying the books. They might be waiting for us when we got there! I know Dad discounted my thinking, but I remained convinced that there was some century-old conspiracy at work. I didn't buy into all of Dad and Amit's paranoia about Omnitia. There was simply no way so many people could keep a secret.

While I researched the history and personalities of electromagnetics, and planned how I was going to get hold of more books, Amit was busy on his software project. His presentation went so well that he'd been invited to install his network administration application at three additional branches of the Berkshire Inn, two in Knoxville and one in Oak Ridge. He'd been busy testing it out and training the managers there how to use it. He'd also convinced Berkshire management that he needed access to the company's guest database, so he could assign the MAC address of the guest's wireless devices to the guest and room number. The side effect of this was that he could impersonate any guest, sending his own Internet traffic and making it appear as though it came from any arbitrary guest. He hadn't exploited the ability yet – explaining that four hotels didn't make a big enough haystack within which to hide his spoofing. Besides, Amit didn't want to tip his hand and jeopardize a large-scale deployment. He wanted to get his network administration utility adopted throughout the Berkshire Inn chain before beginning to exploit it to disguise our traffic.

In whatever spare time we had, we continued researching alternative energy sources for debate. I was confident my case on Radioisotope Thermoelectric Generation was a winner. Amit and I also had a dozen negative rebuttals prepared for the various alternative energy schemes our affirmative opposition might throw at us.

My physics class ended with my acing the final exam. With my reading of Maxwell's *Matter and Motion*, not to mention Dad's patient tutoring, I had a firm grasp of the basics.

* * *

At the end of July, Dad rented a sedan, and we were off on our family road trip. Our first stop was Vanderbilt University in Nashville to pick up Kira. "Damn pricey finishing school," Dad muttered until Mom hushed him up.

When we picked up Kira, I explained that I needed her assistance to examine a book at the library. Visiting a library on a vacation? She thought I was pulling a joke of some kind. Mom and Dad had to assure her that it was no joke. I truly did need to see the book, and it had to be secret. I went into the library with her, only to discover that the Fleming book wasn't there – it was stored in the library annex. Kira was about to whip out her ID, when I preempted her, telling the librarian we forgot our IDs and didn't need to check it out anyway, only check a couple of references in it. Kira noticed my cue and asked pretty please if the nice librarian couldn't recall the book from the annex, so we could just take a look at it tomorrow? That cute and sweet act never worked on Mom and Dad, but the librarian clearly wasn't made of such stern stuff. Or maybe Mom and Dad were immune through repeated exposure, like I was. In any event, the librarian told us we could check with her tomorrow morning and it would be there.

We toured many of the nostalgic destinations we'd all visited when Kira and I were kids, like the Parthenon, the Grassmere Zoo, and the Cumberland Science Museum – although now they were calling it the Adventure Science Center. I persuaded the rest of the family to swing by some of the local bookstores, including McKay's. None of them had any of the old technical books I wanted.

We stayed at Kira's apartment near campus. The next morning we all ate breakfast at the Pancake Pantry across the street from yet another used bookstore near the Vanderbilt campus – BookManBookWoman – a quaint place, but not much of a selection of old technical books. Then Kira and I swung by the library. The librarian handed Kira *The Principles of Electric Wave Telegraphy*. I restrained the urge to rip the book out of her hands and fling it open. Good thing. It was in bad shape. I could see why it was no longer shelved with the regular books. It wasn't aging well. It had an off, musty smell and the binding was starting to separate the cover from the text.

I gently opened the dark green book and looked at page 640. There was no mention of Heaviside, and the Lodge reference had large spaces in it and "p. 72" dropped to the following line. It matched the Omnitia scan exactly. I took a closer look at the paper. Page 640 seemed to be printed on the same paper as any other page. It had the same faint gray fog from a century of the opposing page's ink being rubbed against the page. I made a photocopy of page 640 as well as the title page. Either I was holding a masterful forgery or the alterations to the text had been made in conjunction with the original printing. It looked as though Omnitia had scanned an actual book, not concocted a digital fake. That meant there were two kinds of old books in circulation: some with the Heaviside reference, and some without.

Kira and I returned the book and walked back to her place. As we walked, my mind whirled with the implications. I had to be careful, since this was only one data point, but it looked like an old conspiracy to modify the books not long after they were printed. A more recent forgery? It could be. Even in the case Dad mentioned, though, the forged historic documents were a page or two of old letters or documents, not an entire book, and the forger was selling them for large sums of money, not leaving them to gather dust in a university book storage facility. The forgery theory didn't make sense. Someone must have pressured the printer to withdraw the books probably as soon as the electromagnetic villains noted the disclosure of Heaviside's bouncing waves concept. They must have leaned on the authors and publishers alike to be quiet. Threats? Bribes? Appeals to patriotism? Hard to say. Whatever they did was effective to have kept their secret for so long. Mostly. But, a few copies of the suppressed book escaped into the wild, and Tolliver Library just happened to get some of them.

We continued on to Memphis for more family touring. We visited Mud Island and enjoyed barbeque and blues on Beale Street. Each stop in the tour, I spent at least a couple hours looking through the local booksellers. Finally, in Houston, at Half Price Books near the Rice University campus, I hit the motherlode.

I was browsing the science section and coming up empty again, when I noticed a cute clerk walking by. Amit's influence had been rubbing off on me, and I decided to try an approach. "Hi there."

"Hi," she said, "May I help you find something?"

"I was looking for Franklin's *Electric Waves*," I replied.

"Oh!" She said excitedly. "I think we have that, but it's a special order for another customer." My heart rose and then sank between beats. I followed her to the service desk, where I spotted the plain, blueish book on the shelf behind the desk.

Yes, that was definitely a copy of Franklin's *Electric Waves*. So close, yet the prize was tantalizingly out of reach. My mind raced, trying to figure out how to handle this while she continued looking. Eventually she found the book I'd already spotted. By then, inspiration had struck.

"May I take a look? I'll be careful."

"I suppose so," she said. I picked up *Electric Waves*. She continued, "Please be extra careful. This is a very special book because it has a particular printing flaw."

A what? Really? I struggled to maintain an even tone. "Oh, what kind of printing flaw? I don't see anything wrong with it." I leafed casually through the Franklin text, pausing just a moment to glance at page 115. There was the extra Heaviside text about the bouncing waves, just like the Tolliver Library copy! I casually kept on leafing as if I saw nothing special. There was a packing slip in the back of the book: Xueshu Quan with an address in Arlington, Virginia. I silently repeated the name and address repeatedly, willing it into my memory.

"I'm not sure exactly about the printing flaw," the clerk said. "Our customer had us scan and fax one of the pages to him so he could look at it."

"Oh, which page?" I asked.

"Page 115," she said. Oh my. I casually opened the book to page 115.

> *In his forthcoming third volume, Heaviside will elaborate on his remarkable theory of wave interference whereby electric waves bounce off each other. This ingenious discovery promises to unlock similar valuable insights.*

Yup. There was the 'printing flaw,' all right. "Gee, that's funny," I said. "There doesn't seem to be anything wrong with that page."

"I know," she said, "It's so crazy! Apparently that page makes this a $1000 dollar book!"

"Wow!" I said in honest amazement. I stole another sneak peek at my new friend, Xueshu Quan from Arlington,

Virginia. This time I worked on his cell phone number and e-mail address. "It must be so cool to work in a place where any day, you might uncover a secret treasure!"

"I never thought of it that way," she said with a bright smile, "but I guess you're right. Only, this is the first time I found a book that's so valuable."

I handed the book back to her. I think I had Xueshu Quan's contact information memorized, but I'd need to write it all down soon before I forgot any of it.

"Well surely there are other treasures like this one waiting to be found here," I offered.

"Well, that's true," the clerk said. "There's a whole list of books with printing defects our customer wants." Yee hah! I hadn't felt this giddy since I was a kid on Christmas morning! Calm. Control. Focus.

"You know," I heard myself saying as if from a distance, "I visit lots of other used book stores. I could keep my eyes open for you. If you can give me a copy of that list, and your phone number…"

"You just want my number!" she said with a smile.

"Well," I condensed all the confidence I could muster into a smug grin, "you can't blame me, even if it weren't for the money I could make for us. You know, if I contact you directly, couldn't you just go straight to your customer and pocket the money?" She probably did have a responsibility to take deals like that to her boss here at the store. She looked uncertain – good, she was cute and honest. "You should probably think it over and figure out the right thing to do." I added quickly.

"I suppose so. Hold on a sec." She stepped away from the counter and vanished in the back. She reappeared with the list. The top part was truncated as if she'd folded over the original with the customer's contact information. On the top, she had written her number and "Call me! Nicole." She handed it to me with a grin that just melted me inside. Then, she looked around and said softly, "Don't let anyone see this list, OK? I'm not even supposed to have it myself."

"Glad to meet you Nicole. I'll take good care of it." I felt like a heel. The first time I'd actually "number closed" a girl, to use Amit's phrase, and there was no way I could call her. "My name's Dan," I compounded my sins further with a lie. "Oh, by the way, did any other books come in with the Franklin book? Maybe there's something else I'd like to get."

"I think so, she said. I'll check," she stepped into the back.

While she was away, I casually walked past Dad as if checking out the shelf next to him and said, "Jackpot! Make sure no one buys anything here with credit cards. Leave no trace." He nodded in affirmation. He slowly moved off. By the time Nicole was back, I saw him whispering to Mom and Kira.

"Come with me," Nicole said. I followed her to the science section. I saw Mom and Kira leave the store. Dad continued browsing, but he'd worked his way over to where he had a line of sight to me. Nicole pulled out *Philosophy of Mathematics and Natural Science* by Weyl. Princeton was apparently the publisher, and there was a label that said "Bk-82" on the spine. I opened the cover. Bingo! There was what I presumed to be a former owner's name on what looked like an address label – Kenneth A. Norton, 4623 Kenmore Drive, N.W. WASHINGTON, D.C. Just below it in pencil was scribbled $8 and some illegible text. "That's the only other book," she said.

"Great! You sold me." I handed her a ten-dollar bill. "You can keep the change."

"You want your receipt or a bag for that?" she asked.

"No, thanks," I said.

"Well, you at least need a bag or they're going to think you're shoplifting. Back in a sec."

She brought me back the book in a bag. "Your receipt is in the bag."

"I gotta run." She looked disappointed. "When are you off?" I added.

"My shift ends at eight," she said.

"I'll see if I can make it." That wasn't exactly a lie, but it sure felt like one. I already knew there was no way I'd be back to see her. I'd be checked into my hotel for the night with my family before she got off work. Alas.

I met Mom and Kira at the car.

"What's with all the cloak and dagger, Little Buddy?" Kira asked. She knew I didn't like her calling me Little Buddy, particularly now that I was taller than she was.

"Hold on a sec," I said. "Let's wait for Dad." I pulled it out. There was the list. I had it. It was in my hands. Next to Nicole's name, I began to scribble: "Xueshu Quan." I wrote his address in Arlington, Virginia. I'd ignored the zip since I figured I could work it out later. I added the cell phone and email. Gotcha, Xueshu Quan!

Dad hopped in and we drove off. "Okay, son. Spill it. What did you get?"

For Kira's benefit, I started from the beginning. For months, I had been scratching away with Amit, closely examining straw after straw in search of a few needles. Now instead of a painstaking search for the puzzle pieces, I had them all, or at least a list of them. I reviewed the list aloud.

"This is incredible! Look, here's the Franklin book listed for $1000, 'send p. 115 to confirm.' That's the first reference I found. The list has the Fleming reference for $500, 'send p. 640 to confirm.' It has the Whittaker reference we found a couple of weeks ago also listed at $500. There are several other references at the $500 level. Another $1000 reference. And here's Oliver Lodge, *Modern Views of Electricity*, third edition revised, 1907, 'send pages 302-303 to confirm,' $5000! This really is like a treasure map!"

"So, if you can find this book," Kira asked, "you'll be able to sell it for $5000?"

"Not exactly," I replied. At that point, I decided to explain it all to her. By the time we got to the San Jacinto Monument, Kira was up to speed. "So, we don't know exactly who was responsible," I summarized, "but someone apparently suppressed a discovery by Heaviside – something about wave interaction that got described as electric waves bouncing off each other."

"It can't be the same person as this Xueshu Quan," Kira observed. "He'd... maybe she? ...would have to be a hundred fifty years old."

"This Quan is probably just someone, like us, interested in understanding what happened," Dad offered. "The lesson we learned here today is even if you are discreet, when you go out in the world seeking information, you leave traces."

"I can't believe how lucky I was to stumble across this list," I said.

"'Luck comes to the well-prepared,'" Dad opined. That always was one of his favorite sayings. "You were looking in the same sort of places for the same sort of things as this Quan. Quan had to expose a bit of his secret, putting it at risk in the hope of the greater reward of being the first to identify and secure these old books. Most anyone who came across the list would think nothing of it. Only because you had already identified the significance of some of the items on the list, were you able to work out Quan's secret."

"I think you're missing the implication of your father's point," Mom said to me. "As you've gone out searching for these secrets, you've left traces. Someone who knows the secrets would also realize that you know a part of the same secret, and you're actively looking for more. You and your father are both amateurs at this, yet you're playing a very dangerous game. I think you should stop."

"Even now, I don't see much risk," Dad assured Mom. "Suppose this Quan came asking, wondering why you were so interested in the list. Quan is offering a lot of money for these books, and all you're trying to do is keep your eyes open, find the books, and offer them to Quan. Of course your interest is in the suppressed discovery, but you could explain it away by saying you were only interested in finding and selling potentially valuable books, not in any secrets."

"Still," Mom insisted, "I'd feel much better if we didn't stay the night in Houston. Hotels mean IDs and credit cards and a huge red flag announcing we were there. I'd like to put more distance between us and the bookstore to make it all the less likely anyone could connect us to it if they started looking seriously. We were planning on staying here and driving to Huntsville in the morning. Why don't we just head on up there?"

Dad countered, "I was planning on stopping by the big contractors' tradeshow in the morning, and meeting up with Jim Burleson and some of my other professional colleagues. That lets me treat a big part of the trip as a professional expense."

"You'll be seeing most of them back up around Knoxville, anyway," Mom noted. "It's not as though this trip was so expensive we can't afford to pay for it as a personal expense. I know you don't like having your plans disrupted, but I'd appreciate it if you'd take my concerns seriously and just get us as far away from here as possible."

"I think that's an over-reaction on your part," Dad countered levelly. "Also, I'm tired from driving all day. You're talking about another ten-hour drive. I'm not comfortable trying to pull an all-nighter."

It was rare for Mom and Dad to argue like this in front of Kira and me. I felt bad about it, because I'd been more or less ignoring Mom's concerns from the beginning. "I could drive," I offered.

"I'll drive," Mom said. She turned and looked at me. "You can sit in the front seat, talk to me, and help keep me awake."

Dad clearly didn't want to dispute the issue further. "OK," he acquiesced, "but, at some point, you will need to pull over and check us into a hotel, so we can at least get some sleep in a real bed. Maybe around Tuscaloosa or Birmingham?"

Mom agreed.

We cut short our visit to San Jacinto and skipped our tour of the Battleship Texas. Dad got us to Beaumont, where we topped off our gas and bought dinner at a McDonald's. Dad paid cash. Mom and I got some coffee. Mom took the wheel, and I sat in the passenger seat.

Well after midnight, we pulled in to a truck stop somewhere on I-59 near Hattiesburg. Dad had a wad of cash that he'd been planning to spend at the Huntsville Hamfest – sort of a combination amateur radio convention and flea market. He'd handed it over to Mom for gas and the hotel, saying he'd just visit an ATM in Huntsville. She peeled off a few bills for me. I paid cash inside and pumped the gas for Mom, while she visited the restroom and got us coffee. Then, it was my turn. When I got out, Mom was waiting with the car. I hopped in and we continued.

Before long, Dad and Kira were sound asleep in the back seat. I'd been meaning to ask Mom about the "unpleasantness" she'd mentioned at Robber Dell on Independence Day: the reason why she'd practiced and become such a good shot. I took the opportunity to do so now.

"Why ever do you want to know about all that?" she asked.

"Because you've never told me much about the time when you and Dad got married. I pick up hints and teases about there being big trouble about it here and there around town. How scandalous it all was. Half the town must know the details. I'd rather hear the truth from you, so I don't have to wonder how much of what I hear is exaggerations or lies."

"What have you heard?" Mom asked.

"Frustratingly few actual details," I explained. "I mean I know you and Dad got married in Atlanta, and I know Kira was born six months later. And I understand your family was not happy."

Mom was quiet, thoughtful. "This is very personal."

"I understand," I said. "If you don't want to talk about it, that's fine. I don't want to make you uncomfortable. It's just awkward for me when folks talk about you or Dad and I'm clearly missing the context."

She weighed my words. "The town only has the vaguest idea of what actually happened. What I am about to tell you needs to be a secret. The reason you need to keep this secret is it would be profoundly embarrassing to my family, particularly to my brothers, your Uncle Lawrence and Uncle Michael. Not that they don't deserve whatever measure of embarrassment that might come to them, but we've had a truce for two decades now, and I don't want to give them cause to throw their weight around at the expense of you or your sister. Also, I know your father still feels bad about it. He shouldn't, but he does, and I won't have you bringing this up with him. I suppose, though, if you're old enough to ask, you're probably old enough to know. With this frolic you and your father have undertaken, you're clearly good at keeping secrets. You understand and give me your word that all this is in confidence between you and me?"

I did and I did.

"Very well," Mom began. "I went to Princeton as an undergraduate. I was supposed to be getting my MRS degree while studying art or music or some other major appropriate for my gender and class."

"MRS degree?" I interposed. "Master of what, Rocket Science?"

Her face broke into a bright smile. "No, dear. MRS as in 'missus.' My job was to look pretty, socialize with the most elite scions of the country's aristocracy, and land a suitable husband. My parents expected me to make an appropriate match, to marry up into another elite family. To form a strategic alliance between the Tollivers and another great family, maybe even break the Tollivers into the power elite who run the country, the offspring of someone on the Trilateral Commission, the Council on Foreign Relations, the Bilderbergers, the New York Stock Exchange, the Federal Reserve, or maybe even someone in the Civic Circle."

"I haven't even heard of most of those?"

"Yes, and that's the way they like it. They are associations of the most powerful and influential people in the country. The people who are in charge behind the scenes. Some, like the board members on the Federal Reserve, the Stock Exchange, or major corporations have actual power. The other groups' power lies in the ability of members to network and coordinate among and between the captains of industry and government. It's all about the connections, trading favors among the power brokers, setting and enforcing what will become the accepted wisdom.

"In any event," Mom continued. "I might well have taken the path of least resistance, except that Father, Grandpa Jack, was too pushy. I became resentful. And, art appreciation was boring. I loved chemistry. It was just like cooking – putting together precise recipes, keeping all the glassware spotless to avoid contamination – and the results were endlessly fascinating. It was all directly relevant to the Tolliver Corporation's business, too, of course.

"And then, my senior year when I should have been planning June nuptials with my Prince Charming, instead I was planning my admission to graduate school. Father was furious. He had just come to accept the fact that I was going to come home and work in the family business as a junior chemist, and he was going to have to settle for pairing me with some rising young Tolliver star deserving of marrying the boss's daughter. Instead, I was off for a Ph.D. in chemistry that might take six years or more.

"But, you never finished," I pointed out. "You got married instead. What happened?"

"I started graduate work in chemistry and began working as a research assistant for a professor at Georgia Tech on chemical fertilizers. It's a big part of the Tolliver business, and I liked the idea of putting my chemical knowledge to work figuring out how to feed people.

"You have to understand a bit of what was happening at the time," Mom explained. "A famous biologist, Paul Ehrlich, convinced many people that mass famine was just around the corner and hundreds of millions of people were going to starve. The press had stories every week about hunger in America and how the heartless Reagan administration wasn't feeding the poor. I was idealistic, and I wanted to do what I could to help fend off the pending starvation.

"As I started studying and researching, however, I began to realize that the apocalyptic scenarios were grossly exaggerated, and that we weren't truly on the brink of famine, starvation, and disaster. An economist named Julian Simon wrote a book called *The Ultimate Resource* that explained how shortages in physical resources were overcome historically by human imagination and creativity. When a resource becomes scarce, people go out and find more of it, they recycle and use it more wisely, or they find substitutes.

"Simon and Ehrlich made a bet back in 1980. Ehrlich selected a group of metals: copper, chromium, nickel, tin, and tungsten. He bet Simon that they would become scarcer over the next decade. They bet $1000 with Simon to pay Ehrlich the difference if the metals became less available and more expensive, and Ehrlich to pay Simon the difference if the metals became more available and less expensive."

"What happened?" I asked.

"The $1000 selection of metals from 1980 became something like $400 in 1990. Instead of the metals becoming more rare and expensive due to the shortages Ehrlich predicted, they become more plentiful, like Simon had expected. Ehrlich paid Simon the difference. That was after I already left graduate school, though," Mom explained.

"So, why did you leave then?" I asked her.

"I learned about a man named Norman Borlaug. He did some pioneering work in plant breeding that created amazingly hardy and productive variants of common food crops. At the same time Ehrlich was pontificating about how India would never be able to feed itself, Borlaug was introducing better, more productive varieties of wheat that solved the problem. While Ehrlich was whining about how we were all doomed, Borlaug was already solving the problem.

"Here I'd been thinking the world was in crisis and I had to do my part to fight as hard as I could to keep humanity from starving, and it turned out to simply not be the case. There was no great danger, just a bunch of academics who should have known better who were puffing themselves up to gain notoriety and power through their dire predictions.

"And then I met your father."

"So it was love at first sight?" I asked.

"No," Mom laughed. "I thought he was an arrogant... well, I thought he was arrogant and full of himself."

"Really?"

"Really," Mom assured me. "He came up to me at a club where my friends had dragged me for drinks and dancing, and he asked me what I was drinking. "I told him I wasn't interested in him, and I started to turn my back on him, but he stopped me, saying 'That's not what I asked you. I asked what you were drinking.' I told him I was drinking a fuzzy navel – that's orange juice and peach schnapps. He asked me if it was any good. I told him it was. Then, before I could do anything, he took my drink, took a sip of it, set it back down, and said, 'Your judgment in drinks is every bit as poor as your judgment in men.' Then, he turned his back on me and just walked away!"

That did sound awfully arrogant, although I had to chuckle at his brashness. "How did you two get together, then?"

"I kept my eye on him. He didn't seem to have any particular dance partner. He'd dance with one girl for a while, then another. He was very good at it, too. The more I watched him, the angrier I got at him blowing me off, turning around, and having a good time. It was silly of me, I suppose. I finally got angry enough that I went over to tell him off. I caught him between dances, and I told him he was the rudest man I'd ever met.

"He just laughed and said, 'Now on that subject, your judgement is somewhat better, given your own expertise.'

"I asked him, 'What do you mean?'

"He explained, 'I came over to make small talk and perhaps introduce myself and get to know you better, and all you could do was cut me off and tell me you're not interested? Who was rude to whom?'

"I thought about that a bit, and I realized that he might have a point. What's more, he'd even used 'whom' correctly, so he wasn't your run-of-the mill womanizer. So, I said, 'I'm sorry if I were rude to you.'

"He said, 'No "if" about it. You were. But, we can call it even if you'd like to join me for a late dinner at Waffle House.' That was our first date. He and I went out dancing a lot. He was such a great dancer, and he loved dancing even more than I did." Mom had quite a smile on her face.

"So, you left grad school to marry Dad?" I asked.

"More or less," Mom answered. "Once I realized that humanity wasn't doomed and calamity wasn't just around the corner, I lost most of my motivation. Without a great deal of motivation, it's tough to get through a Ph.D. program. I just wanted to be happy, and being with your Dad made me happy in a way I'd never felt before."

"It wasn't a tough decision to just walk away from a career like that? After all the time and effort you'd invested to get there?"

"Not really," Mom said matter-of-factly. "I had been lured to graduate school under false premises. Not only was I not going to save the world, the world didn't need saving, after all. It wasn't my professors' fault, I suppose, although they ought to have known better. When you've built a career landing grants to figure out how to save the world, it's difficult to be honest with yourself, and realize you've been living a lie and contributing to a fraud. Your whole livelihood becomes bound up in the lie, and you'd overlook almost anything to protect it. But I felt I was being pushed and controlled and used to meet other people's agendas. I'd thrown off my father's control only to fall under the control of professional pessimists and fear mongers, feeding me their lies and trying to use me as a tool to build their own little empires in a phony crusade that wasn't worthy of my time and energy to fight.

"You see by that point, I had a good idea who was actually saving the world. It was men like Borlaug coming up with ways to feed billions and men like Simon pointing out the fallacies of the doomsayers. I saw how I stood in the hierarchy. I was top of my class in high school, and still one of the top students in chemistry at Princeton. But by the time I got to Georgia Tech, I was in with all the other top chemistry students from all the other top schools. Perhaps I was a bit above average – I'd like to think so – but there were other students there who were absolute geniuses. It rubbed my nose in the fact that I was nothing special. That's a hard pill to swallow. Perhaps if I worked very hard, I could carve out a little niche for myself, some small backwater area overlooked by the geniuses, where I could build my own career and make my own mark, but that's not nearly as exciting as saving the world.

"A century from now, the people who know and care about who we are and where we came from will still speak of heroes like Borlaug and Simon with respect and reverence. They'll even remember a great villain like Ehrlich for the harm he caused and laugh at his ridiculous misconceptions. Making a great difference for good or for evil, building a lasting monument out of your career and life and performing work that actually has an impact on the course of humanity for better or worse – that's extraordinarily rare.

"A century from now your grandchildren will be telling their children about you and me and your father and our lives. They will be sharing family tales like this one. If you've raised them right and taught them well, just as your father and I have tried to do with you and your sister, then your grandchildren will have raised their children right and taught them well. And all of them will be going out to make their own marks on the world. That is a monument far more impressive and far more worthwhile than any modest contribution I might have made to the world of chemistry."

We drove in silence for a while, the hum of the road, the wind rushing past the car, the sound of Dad's heavy breathing in the back of the car, and the lights of the reflectors zipping past. I sat doing nothing more and nothing less than just experiencing a moment in life's great journey.

"How did you and Dad decide to settle in Sherman?"

"My father forbade the marriage, so your father and I eloped. I thought it made sense to stay in Atlanta, but your father had family in Sherman – his Aunt Molly had left Robber Dell by that point and was living in town. Your father was already working on a job in Chattanooga by then, so it wasn't much different from commuting from Atlanta. I did want to be near my mother when Kira was born. I had concerns about my father, your Grandpa Jack, but your father insisted we should move to Sherman. It was a mistake. Your Grandpa Jack was used to getting his way. Always. Seeing me there with your father just set him off. Grandpa Jack was used to controlling everything, but he couldn't control me, and he couldn't control your father.

"Your father and I were renting a small house off of Maple Street when the harassment started in earnest. Someone slashed the tires of his truck. A dead animal left in our front yard. A trash can upended in the bed of your father's pick up. A rock through the window. I don't know what Grandpa Jack was thinking. I suppose he thought he could scare off your father and have his daughter back. Somehow, he thought he could make everyone forget that I had defied him. I was pregnant and married to a man he'd forbidden to me. Bringing me back to Sherman – I suppose Grandpa Jack saw that as your father taunting him. Your father had to keep working to support us, but we were both afraid what might happen if the violence escalated further. That's when your father and I both got pistols. When Rob had some leave, he stayed with me while your father was out working. Rob took me out to a range, and we practiced for hours on end. I simply couldn't handle larger guns, but with a .22, I got proficient.

"Then, one night your father and I were at home when we heard a noise on the front porch. We both got our guns. He walked to the door, to look through the peephole when BAM the door was kicked open in his face, knocking him down and sending his gun flying across the floor. Three men burst into the room: my brothers, Larry and Mike, and a big, burly Tolliver foreman. They grabbed your father. And then, in stepped Grandpa Jack. 'You don't seem to take hints very well,' he said to your dad, 'so we're running you out of town. You don't belong here.'

"None of them noticed I was armed – they were too preoccupied with your father. The foreman and Mike held your father while Larry punched him. They discounted an obviously pregnant woman as a threat. I raised my gun and sighted between my father's eyes. 'Get out of my house now and leave my man alone or so help me I will shoot you.'

"'You put that toy...' Grandpa Jack started to say, when I shifted my aim a bit to the side and interrupted him, BANG.

He flinched as I shifted to cover the others. 'Let my husband go.' They did. Your dad retrieved his gun and fell back covering the others while I sighted down the barrel again right between my father's eyes.

"'That last shot was three quarters of an inch from your right ear. This may be a toy, and I know you have a thick skull, Daddy,' I told him, 'but do you truly want to risk a .22 slug between the eyes? Get out now, don't come back, and if you, Larry, Mike, or any of your thugs lay a hand on my man again, I swear I will end you.'"

The look of astonishment and disbelief on my face must have been evident when Mom glanced over at me.

"Well," she said with a modest smile, "or words to that effect."

"So Grandpa Jack, Uncle Larry, Uncle Mike, and the foreman left?"

"Not exactly," Mom clarified. "Because some neighbor must have heard the commotion and the gunshot and called the police. I heard someone bark 'What's going on here?' through the open door behind Grandpa Jack. It was Sheriff Gunn. Only, he was Deputy Gunn back then. It didn't take him long to figure out what happened.

"I told him 'My father and his... associates were just leaving and have no intention of returning.' I assured him there would be no further trouble.

"Gunn looked at my father and asked him, 'Is that so, sir?'

"Grandpa Jack agreed. 'You OK?' he asked your father. 'Our guests have overstayed their welcome,' your father told Gunn, wiping the blood from his nose. 'If they're not coming back, and if they agree there will be no more trouble, I suppose there's no need to press charges.'

"Gunn said, 'Well, if there's no trouble, and if there's not going to be any more trouble, I guess I don't have to report this.' So far as I know, Gunn never breathed a word of it."

"And that was the end of the harassment?" I asked.

"Grandpa Jack, Larry, and Mike had been shamed in front of his foreman, me, your father, and Gunn," Mom explained. "If they made any further trouble, there was Gunn as a witness to the standoff. That was the last time I ever saw my father. Even when he was dying he refused to see me, but he kept the peace. Larry has kept the peace as well. He's not friendly, but he's at least civil, and there's been no other harassment. And Gunn... that man blusters about like some dumb hick. It's an act. He's clever, devious, and ambitious. I swear he parlayed his knowledge of that incident into getting my father's support when he ran for sheriff a few years later."

"You think Sheriff Gunn blackmailed Grandpa Jack?" I asked.

"I doubt he was that explicit," Mom explained. "Grandpa Jack would never have stood for outright blackmail. I'm sure it was a matter of him pointing out how trustworthy he'd been and how Daddy needed a sheriff he could trust to keep his secrets, or something to that effect. I'm confident Larry and Mike don't want to cross Gunn either. Mark my words. Sheriff Gunn knows all the local secrets and uses them to help himself. Never trust the man."

"I still have trouble imagining you staring down anyone with a gun," I noted.

Mom smiled. "You'll find it easier to imagine when you have a family of your own to protect. When I was a girl, I'd hear news stories, like 'Girl drowns at beach as she's swept out to sea, parents try to save her despite not being able to swim, drown as well.' And I thought to myself, 'How stupid. Why would you drown yourself if you know there's nothing you can do?' But that was before I had children of my own.

"You know, your father dragged me down to Alabama for the Huntsville Hamfest when Kira was a little girl. This was before you were born – Kira must have been two years old. They have a nice park there – Big Spring Park – with a sidewalk along the gently flowing water and brightly colored carp swimming in the water. The three of us were walking along side. Kira was fascinated by the fish swimming there. She stopped right on the edge and leaned over to get a better look. I remember your father saying, 'Kira, step back...' I guess that startled her because she lost her balance and went face first over the side. Before Kira could even hit the water, I was in motion, jumping in after her.

"You pulled her out? Was she OK?"

"She was fine, just wet and a little scared. But I didn't pull her out."

"What?" I was confused.

"I landed almost on top of your father," Mom explained. "He'd been paying closer attention, I suppose, and he got in the water just a split second before me. He already had had Kira in one hand and was helping me get my balance with the other before I could do anything. It turned out the water was only waist deep, although it was so murky, I had no idea until my feet had touched bottom. Your father got Kira up on the bank. She just looked at us both, soaked, standing waist deep in the water and started giggling at us. And we joined in, too.

"That's just how it works when you're a parent. You don't stop to think, 'What's going on?', 'Will someone else do something?', or 'How deep is the water?' You don't always plan methodically what you're going to do. You act. You do the best you can right then and right there and you do whatever it takes to save your family. In retrospect, it may not be the smartest thing you could have done. But you act. 'Improvise, adapt, overcome, and drive on,' your Uncle Rob is fond of saying."

By then, we were nearing Birmingham. We stayed the night at a Berkshire Inn, and we got a late start the next morning visiting the McWane Science Center, the Vulcan statue, and other sites around Birmingham. Friday afternoon, we stopped by the U.S. Space and Rocket Center in Huntsville before checking into our hotel. On Saturday, Mom and Kira visited the Huntsville Botanical Garden and Burritt on the Mountain, an outdoor historical museum on a mountain just east of town. Dad and I hung out at the Huntsville Hamfest – browsing the vendor tables and sitting in on some interesting talks. I passed the test to upgrade my Technician Class Amateur Radio license to a General Class ticket. In a slow moment, I asked Dad about meeting Mom, to get his perspective. "So, was it love at first sight?"

"No," he snorted with a chuckle. "I thought she was an arrogant... well, I thought she was arrogant and full of herself."

"Really?"

"Really," he assured me. "I was at this club where a lot of the girls I danced with tended to go. I saw her, not particularly enjoying herself, abandoned by her friends at the bar. I'd had my eye on her for a while, saw her turn away a bunch of guys, and thought I'd give it a try. I went over to hit on her, and she completely blew me off. So I helped myself to her drink – some fruity girly drink – and returned the favor by blowing her off.

"How'd she take it?" I asked.

"I think it wounded her pride a bit," Dad speculated. "Of course, I didn't realize at the time she was some sort of heiress. She was used to boys walking on eggshells around her. The fact I was a man who wouldn't take nonsense from her, well I'm not sure if it bothered her or made me more attractive to her – probably a combination of the two. Then, I made a point of dancing with every cute girl I could, right in front of where she was. Half the girls in that bar I knew from the Dance Club on campus, and they all knew I was good for a whirl around the floor. All the while, I studiously ignored her. Finally, she came over to complain to me about how rude I was. I pointed out she'd started it and suggested we go out to dinner to make amends."

"So, that was your first date?" I asked.

"It was almost our last date," he said with a rueful smile. "I took her to the Varsity for a late dinner. It was only after we ordered that I caught her full name and realized she was one of those Tollivers. I nearly walked out on her. If she'd been a guy, I might have punched her then and there."

"Why?" That didn't make sense to me. "I thought the running feud with the Tollivers came after you defied Grandpa Jack and married her."

There was a long pause as Dad appeared to be mulling something over. "I haven't ever told you the whole story," he began. "By the time you were old enough for me to tell you, Jack Tolliver died. Your mother was eager to try to mend fences with her mother. I didn't want to rock the boat. It's never just been about me marrying Mom. No, our family feud with the Tollivers goes way back – nearly a hundred years – long before I was born. For generations, my father's family carved a farm and a living out of the wilderness up in the Great Smokies. They fought, bled, and died, some of them, to defend it from Cherokee, and later, from Confederate raiders during the Civil War. And then ol'Tom Tolliver and his cronies came along, stole our land, and kicked us off it to starve in the middle of the Great Depression.

"You see, back in the 1920s, folks began to recognize the scenic beauty of the Great Smoky Mountains was in danger. Huge tracts were being deforested or burned out. A movement started up to preserve that natural beauty by creating what would come to be known as Great Smoky Mountain National Park. The backers of the park included the Tollivers and other important Knoxville area business leaders. They thought – correctly – that a tourist destination like the Great Smokies would be a boon to the Knoxville economy. They brought congressmen, senators, and financial backers to lobby them to support the park idea. But, they didn't show them the burned out and deforested slopes owned by the logging companies. No, they brought them right up to the Cove to show them our beautiful farm and the farms of our neighbors with our painstakingly cleared pastures and fields nestled up to the mountains.

"It wasn't just a local effort. Tom Tolliver was joined by outsiders like the Rockefellers and Civic Circle heavyweights who contributed a fortune toward the idea. They lobbied the state of Tennessee to assemble the land needed for the park and donate it to the federal government to manage.

"The backers of the scheme up to and including the governor and our senator all swore up and down that no one's property would be taken away from them. Cove folk were naïve enough to believe them. Then, the state started condemning and seizing farms using eminent domain. They tried to take Pigeon Forge, Gatlinburg, Townsend, all the small towns on the slopes, but there were enough folks there to raise a stink and make them back down. But our Cove? Nestled right in the heart of the most beautiful part of the Smokies with just a few hundred folks living there? Some folks fought as best they could through the courts, but they never stood a chance. The lumber companies like the Tolliver Corporation made out all right. They had the political pull to get paid well for their land. Small farmers and landowners? They got maybe 50 to 75 cents on the dollar. A whole community that had stood together against the worst that man and nature could throw at them was dispersed to the winds, just when a man and his neighbors most needed to help each other out. Because that was right as the Great Depression was starting.

"Soon the rest of the country learned for themselves what it meant to trust the word of the elite. Most of the folks in the Cove banked in Maryville, so when the banks there failed, they lost what little they got for their land. To add insult to injury the federal government forbade "hoarding" of gold. What little real gold money people had stashed away, they were made to turn in under penalty of prison and given $20 in paper money for every ounce. Then, overnight that gold was revalued at $35 an ounce, so effectively, the government stole nearly half of whatever was left.

"Poor folks everywhere suffered, but they could lean on their neighbors, their church, and their community for help. Cove folks had none of that. Many of the older folks who thought they could live out their remaining decades on the rent from their fields simply died under the stress of the eviction. Our family was devastated. Farming was all my grandfather knew and he couldn't so much as find work as a sharecropper. Finally, he got enough together to put a down payment on a small spread west of Knoxville.

"My pa was in school there one day a few years later when the principal called all the students together. 'I just got a call from Senator McKellar,' the principal told my pa and the rest of the students. 'He wants me to tell you to go home and tell your parents: you're all going to need to find a new place to live. The government's going to take your property for the war effort.' The Tollivers and their cronies saw the economic advantage of a huge federal facility in their backyard, so they offered up other people's land to make it happen.

"Sure enough, a few days later pa and his folks came home to find an eviction notice pinned to their door and flapping in the wind. They had three weeks to get off the property – not even enough time to finish harvesting the crops. That was in 1942 when the government seized all the land for the Oak Ridge lab. Grandpa was wiped out a second time. It was months before he saw any money, and when the check arrived, it was just barely enough to pay off the mortgage. It broke the man. Grandpa took to drink.

"My pa was born in the Cove but didn't remember much of it. He had vague memories of playing in the fields in the beautiful mountains. But his childhood was a hardscrabble existence – homeless, never enough food, never a toy or present.

"Pa took me into the Great Smoky Mountain Park once, and up into the Cove. It was springtime. He brought me to the pasture where the family farm once stood. It wasn't one of those historic log cabins, so the park service people had razed his family's home to the ground. There in the open field, where the house once stood was a sprinkling of beautiful jonquils – the last remnants of his mother's flower garden, still hanging on tenaciously, years later. My father was a strong man. But somehow, those flowers broke something inside him. He cried. I think that was the only time I ever saw him cry.

"My father suffered tremendous hardships growing up. He did his best to insulate me and Rob and your Grandnana from it all. He succeeded, mostly. But it came at a cost. He was short in stature because he never got enough food while he was growing. And all the hard work and stress took a huge toll on his health – he never made it to retirement.

"And all that happened because the Tollivers and their Civic Circle buddies bulldozed our family farm to make a playground for hikers and picnickers. And then they wiped out the family a second time to profit from a bomb factory. They are brutal, vicious thugs willing to trample the weak and powerless to achieve their ends. That is why I despise the Tollivers, your mother excepted of course, with a burning passion."

Wow. "How did you and Mom ever get together with all that between you?"

Dad looked a bit guilty. "When I figured out who she was, I decided to get back at her family through her. But, the more I came to know her, the more I came to realize an important truth – just because you are in a family, or any other group for that matter, doesn't mean you agree or endorse everything they do. When I finally confronted her and explained how our family histories were related, she was appalled at what her family had done. She had her own issues with them as well, but my story was what convinced her to break with them entirely. So, ultimately, I did achieve a measure of the revenge I had been seeking, but only because your mother became my ally instead of my enemy."

This was all a bit much for me. I changed the subject. "I'm still having trouble imagining you and Mom out dating and dancing," I explained. "I didn't know you liked to dance so much."

"Dancing's not much of a sport," he said. "Mediocre exercise compared to running or swimming. I only danced because it was such a great way to meet girls. You get into their personal space. You break down inhibitions. I met many attractive women dancing. You should consider getting into it."

"I may at that." My parents' different perspectives were fascinating. "Have you taken Mom dancing any time lately?"

"We haven't been dancing in years," he said. "Too busy with work and family."

"Now that I'm about to leave home and go to college and your business is winding down," I suggested, "you might want to take Mom out dancing somewhere. I bet she'd enjoy it."

He looked at me with one of those strange looks. "That's a good idea," he acknowledged. "Thanks for the suggestion."

My suggestion helped ease my conscience for getting Dad to corroborate Mom's story without either knowing I'd been speaking to the other. Since I'd given my word to Mom, I couldn't go any further with Dad about goings-on in Sherman.

Looking back, I still have trouble thinking of my parents as real human beings with passions and interests, struggles and adventures of their own. Even today, my parents feel like a primal force lurking in the background, still guiding my actions through the force of their teaching and example. They just are. The nature of the relationship dominates my mental picture of them. It's tough to keep in mind the fact that they too were real people with real problems, who did as best they could to do right for themselves and their family. I'm sad now to recall, but that weekend was the first time I began to understand my parents as real people. I saw my mother as a girl rebelling against her over-controlling father, a young woman setting out to save the world, a disillusioned chemist turning her back on fraud and deceit, choosing to break away from her profession and her family and make a new life for herself with my father. I saw my father as a young man dancing his way into girls' hearts, burning to right the wrong committed against his family, allying with my mother to put the Tollivers behind them and make a new life and a new family together. They both worked so hard and overcame so much to give me a good start in life. Soon I would be facing even greater challenges, and I would have to do my best to live up to their example.

Chapter 7: Summers' End

The Monday morning after we got home, I caught up with Amit at Kudzu Joe's. "You know, it would have been much easier to just talk by cell phone," I told Amit.

"You've got to be kidding," Amit insisted. "They're listening, you know." I'd only been away for a week and already I was actually missing Amit's paranoia. He'd been busy, too.

Amit's demonstration to Berkshire management had gone well. Their IT people were pleased with what his network monitoring software did, and the operations team was impressed with how easy it was to use. Amit may not have had much experience with professional software projects, but he had years of experience helping his folks run their business. He knew hotel business processes and procedures cold. He understood exactly how to make a tool that a typical hotel manager would be able to understand and use. The Berkshire executives were happy to throw enough money Amit's way to pay for his first year at college. In return, they were going to get a business tool that would have cost them hundreds of thousands of dollars to develop otherwise.

"I might have been able to charge them more for it," Amit acknowledged, "but the recurring revenue for maintenance and upgrades will be huge if it gets adopted across the company. They've already agreed to roll out my software to an even larger scale pilot – a couple dozen hotels around eastern Tennessee, north Georgia and northern Alabama."

In truth, I had mixed feelings. I was genuinely happy for his success but also a bit jealous that his accomplishments were so far beyond my own. "That's great news," I told him. I did mean it. "Is this going to make it easier to get online anonymously?"

"Absolutely," Amit exclaimed gleefully. "No more wardriving for Internet access. I have to debug and test the software by capturing and sifting through an entire hotel's worth of Internet access at a time. It should be easy to hide a search here or a download there in the data stream. But it's going to take time for me to get everything set up so I can do it smoothly and without leaving a trace. Do you think we need to do more searching?"

"I think once we download scans of everything on this list, we're done with book downloading for the time being." I handed Amit the Xueshu Quan list I got from Nicole, and I brought him up to speed on my encounter at the bookstore in Houston.

"That was smooth, dude," he said, admiringly. "I knew you had it in you. Next time you pump and dump a girl, though, try to do better than just pumping for information and a number." It was hard for me to tell if he was being sincere and serious or if he was just trying to provoke a response out of me, so I ignored him.

"Our top priority should be getting this one – a copy of Lodge's *Modern Views of Electricity*." I suggested. "It's the most expensive book on the Xueshu Quan list, so it's probably the most revealing. We should be looking for more scans as well as physical copies. It's on the list of books we already checked out from the Tolliver Library."

"I thought that title looked familiar," Amit said. "So, did you notice anything on page," he glanced down at the Xueshu Quan list, "302 and 303?"

"Look at this!" I turned the laptop over to him and showed him pages 302-303 from the scan we made of the

Tolliver Library's copy. "See this figure?" In the middle of page 302, there was a collection of graphs labeled "Diagram of the electric and magnetic forces concerned in radiation" drawn by a Mr. Trouton. "This figure is labelled 'Fig. 65,' see? Only, there's no mention at all in the text of Figure 65."

"Interesting," Amit said, thoughtfully. "You compared the Tolliver Library scan to the ones we downloaded off Omnitia?"

"Yes," I confirmed. "The pages look the same. I think this is a case where the Tolliver Library copy was already altered." I explained the discovery from Vanderbilt University where I found a physical copy of Fleming's *Principles of Electric Wave Telegraphy* that differed from the copy in the Tolliver Library but exactly matched the Omnitia scan we downloaded.

I saw the light bulb turn on immediately for Amit. "So, it's not just a modern digital forgery, after all," he said. "Your electromagnetic villains censored some copies of these books, and they missed others. It probably happened right at publication. The book was published, someone noticed, recalled what copies they could, and reissued a 'corrected' or censored version. The Tolliver Library happened to get uncensored versions of the Franklin, Fleming, and Whittaker books. With the Lodge book, though, the one book that's most important to figuring this out, we got stuck with a censored version."

"Exactly," I confirmed. "That's the fundamental problem with our method. We've been comparing scans of Tolliver Library books to Omnitia scans. But, if the Tolliver Library book has already been censored, there's nothing left to find except, perhaps, for some evidence of the censoring."

"Like a mystery figure that conveniently eats up almost a whole page of text but is never mentioned in the text itself," Amit noted.

"Oh, and speaking of evidence of alteration," I scrolled down the scan to the index of the book. "Check out the index entry for Heaviside." The index listed "Heaviside, 153, 233,

325, 391," and then on the following line, "399n., 417." There were broad gaps between the numbers, as if a page number had been deleted. "Our electromagnetic villain got the index right this time, but was too lazy to roll the "399n" up to the earlier line," I hypothesized. "Take a look at the Hertz index entry." Hertz was followed by six numbers. "I measured the text," I explained to Amit. "There's no reason why the '399n' should have been dropped to the bottom line. I'll bet a mention of Heaviside on page 302 or 303 was deleted and the remaining numbers were spaced out."

Amit scrolled back up to pages 302-303. The remaining text on the page ended with a paragraph talking about a quarter-wave acceleration of phase. It seemed fascinating, but neither of us understood it.

"I suspect any library copies are going to be missing the 'printing defects' we're looking for," Amit speculated. "Just like the copy of Fleming's *Principles of Electric Wave Telegraphy* at Vanderbilt."

"If someone's trying to hide what's in these books, you'd think they'd have removed anything easily accessible from a library by now," I agreed.

"It's hard to believe the Tolliver Library was overlooked," Amit said.

"Tolliver Tech was never that significant a university," I pointed out. "In its day, it had a good reputation for engineering, but the place was never more than a regional standout. Tolliver money gave the library here an acquisitions reach on par with the top schools of the day, but even then, I doubt many people outside the region would have heard of it. Now that it's a community college, who would anticipate that the library of some backwoods community college would have a world-class collection of century-old technical books?"

"It wouldn't hurt to check nearby libraries just to be sure," Amit observed. "It's going to be tricky if this Xueshu Quan is looking, too. If he's prepared to pay $5000, you can forget trying to outbid him on eBay."

"I've been thinking about that," I explained. "If we find a copy online from eBay or some other place, we could just contact the seller and get him to send a picture or scan of the appropriate page to an anonymous e-mail. That's all we actually need."

"That's doable," Amit concluded. "I can use an anonymous email account to make the request. The fundamental problem is that the information is time-sensitive. Up until now, I could head out every few days to make an anonymous search and download a few scans. No real time pressure. Now, we have to be able to move quickly on the information and try to act before Xueshu Quan or anyone else can snap the books up before us. I'll have to search every day or set up an automated search. At least it's not a lot of data – not like trying to download an entire book at a time.

"What about that other book you got," Amit asked, "the one that came in to the Houston bookstore?"

"It was *Philosophy of Mathematics and Natural Science* by Hermann Weyl," I explained. "I skimmed through it, but it doesn't seem relevant. We ought to look into the owner, though, someone named Kenneth A. Norton."

"So you think this Norton owned the Franklin waves book that you looked at, too?" Amit asked.

"Maybe," I said. "Nicole said the books had come in together. I'm not positive. Norton stamped his address in the front cover. It didn't have a zip code, which probably means he owned it a long time ago. The book was published in 1949, so this Norton may have been just one of several owners."

"We can try to find out about Norton, but I want to try researching this Xueshu Quan, too," Amit added. "He doesn't seem like someone just investigating this bouncing waves stuff. From that list, it's as if he already knows what's out there, and he's trying to gather up all the copies before anyone else finds them. At least we can download scans of the books on the list."

"I want to call Nicole and apologize for standing her up." I'd felt guilty about lying to the girl and felt I owed her at least that. "Can we do that while we're wardriving?"

Amit looked at me, gently shaking his head. "Girls stand up guys all the time. Turnabout is fair play."

"That's not how I care to play 'the game,'" I insisted.

"If you insist," he acquiesced. "I can set up a VOIP call."

"What?"

"Voice Over IP," Amit explained. "You can make a phone call over the Internet connection. We need a pre-paid credit card number, though. Can you ask your Dad to get a prepaid card on one of his trips to Knoxville? That'd be safer than buying it around here. I'll need the card number to set it up."

Amit agreed we'd complete a wardrive looking into Xueshu Quan and Kenneth Norton. Amit was going to look for more scans of the Lodge book just in case a different source might have scanned the uncensored version. The Tolliver Library had four of the books on the Xueshu Quan list, and we had scans for them all. Amit was going to hunt down scans of the remaining half dozen or so. We'd review the results, and then make one last wardriving expedition to let me make my call, to try to gather data on any open questions.

Our more immediate deadline was the pre-season debate tournament. We had less than a week to go, so Amit and I spent the rest of our morning at Kudzu Joe's running through our debate plans. Amit wasn't happy with the Radioisotope Thermoelectric Generator case I'd come up with. He was concerned that it wouldn't be significant enough – that legalizing RTGs wouldn't have much impact. I needed to work on that. We also agreed we should both be working on some alternate affirmative cases. We spent the rest of the morning brainstorming and researching.

* * *

Finding an open Wi-Fi connection while wardriving was only half the battle. The other half was finding one with enough bandwidth to download book scans. Many of the free public Wi-Fi hot spots were throttled. You could check your email or browse the web, but they put a limit on how much and how fast you could download. Amit had found a number of good locations. And Tor itself tended to be slow, requiring a long time to download large files.

Monday night, we went almost into Knoxville, and we bought dinner at the drive-through of a Zaxby's. I parked in the back of the lot, so we could eat our chicken fingers and do our web browsing. I got the Pringles can antenna out. "Point it at that hotel," Amit said. I aimed it carefully at the hotel across the street. "The hotel manager never changed the default passwords securing the Wi-Fi access system," Amit explained. He used an administrator login to get access to the network, fired up a web browser with Tor, and we were online. Amit liked to use a search engine called DuckDuckGo. The site was directly accessible via Tor, and promised to protect user privacy.

We started searching on Xueshu Quan, himself. We found a very minimalist website with the name and address, but it had no details. There wasn't much else available on him. His address turned out to be a mailbox store in Arlington. His phone number came up as unlisted in a reverse search. The name translated from Chinese to English as something like "Academic Circle." Maybe it was an organization instead of an individual?

We had the opposite problem with Kenneth Norton. There were many Kenneth Nortons, mostly dentists, doctors, and other professionals advertising online. The address in Washington, DC, seemed to be associated with someone else, and the District of Columbia did not have property records for us to search for any details on when a Kenneth Norton might have lived there. The lack of a zip code in his address suggested pre-1963, although Norton might possibly have continued using an older stamp on more recently acquired books after that. My guess was he acquired the book not long after it was published in 1949.

We ran right down the Xueshu Quan list, downloading scans of the books from Omnitia. Then, we tried a couple of other sites – Project Gutenberg, and a few libraries that had scans of old books online. We also searched online card catalogs for libraries with copies of the Xueshu Quan books. We found a few hits at the University of Tennessee and at Georgia Tech. By then, we'd spent nearly an hour searching, and we weren't getting anywhere. We packed up and took our digital booty home for analysis.

* * *

The next morning at Kudzu Joe's, we reviewed what we'd found. The scans we downloaded of the Xueshu Quan books were not terribly helpful. They'd clearly been scrubbed of any relevant mentions of Heaviside or bouncing waves. There were a couple of hints here and there that a deletion had been made, but of course, any relevant information was gone.

On the plus side I was now prepared with an untraceable credit card from Dad. It was the same gift card Dad got from Mr. Burleson. Since Mr. Burleson had paid cash, it should be untraceable. We realized in all our scanning that we hadn't done a good job looking through used bookstores online. The plan for our next, and hopefully final, wardriving excursion would be to complete a search of used bookstores and to make the VOIP call to Nicole to apologize for standing her up. I thought I owed it to her. We headed out again that evening.

* * *

"This is one of my favorite spots for online access," Amit explained. We were in the parking lot of a convenience store overlooking an interstate exit. We had a good line-of-sight to the far side of the highway where there were three truck stops, a restaurant, and a hotel. "They all have Wi-Fi, and with the Pringles Can antenna your father made, I can hit about six different wireless networks from here. I was over at that truck stop for lunch last month, and they gave me the password for the 'secured' wireless they provide for truckers who are overnighting in their lot. Let's see if they've changed the password yet."

He set up the Pringles can antenna on the dash of the car and tweaked the orientation to maximize the signal strength. "Password's good; we're connected." He started up Tor to route our Internet traffic through a complicated network of relays, making it difficult for anyone to trace our traffic back to a physical location. Then, he fired up the VOIP program and handed me a headset. He fired up a web browser with Tor, and we were online. I called Nicole's number through the web interface.

"Hello," a man's voice answered.

"Hello," I said. "I'm calling for Nicole. Do I have the right number?"

Amit had a very concerned look on his face, I saw his hand move to the keyboard and hover.

"This is Nicole's phone," the man said. "May I ask who's calling?"

Amit was frantically shaking his head no.

"I'll call again later, thanks!" I could hear the man begin to bark something as Amit cancelled the connection.

"This is not good, dude," he said.

"Can they trace us?"

"Not likely," Amit assured me. "Even if they did get the number, all it will do is lead them to the credit card. But Mr. Burleson paid cash, so they shouldn't be able to trace it. Let's finish what we came here for."

"Let me try one more call," I insisted.

"To Nicole? You're crazy..." Amit began.

"No, to the bookstore where she worked," I explained.

"Oh," Amit said. "Be ready to hang up quickly if it gets weird." He looked up the number and dialed it for me.

"Thank you for calling Half Price Books," a cheery woman answered.

"Hello," I said. "I was wondering if I could speak with Nicole. I haven't been able to get hold of her on her cell. Is she there?"

There was a long pause.

"Oh, honey," the lady said. "I'm so sorry, but Nicole is dead." Amit and I stared blankly at each other. "Hello?"

"Sorry," I said. "I hadn't heard. Do you know what happened?"

"The police say she was killed by someone she was seeing. Someone named 'Dan.'" Amit looked as dumbfounded as I felt. "Do you know this Dan?" the lady asked.

"No ma'am, sorry. I hardly knew Nicole. I just met her once in the store. You probably knew her much better than I did. I'm sorry for your loss."

"Oh, bless your heart," she said. "My, it's just been so crazy here losing Nicole and Mr. Rodriguez, too."

My jaw was running out of room to drop any further.

"He was her... manager?" I asked.

"Well not actually her manager, no," she explained. "He was our Acquisitions Manager. Handled all our book purchases, things like that."

"And what happened to him?"

"Hit and run accident. Right outside the store. They were gone before anyone saw. It was horrible," she seemed upset.

"I'm so sorry to trouble you," I needed to finish this. "Thanks for your time."

"You're welcome," she said. "Sorry about Nicole."

Amit hung up the phone.

Sorry about Nicole. Yeah. Me, too. I'd good as killed her.

"It wasn't your fault," Amit said. He was getting way too proficient at reading me. "You didn't kill her. Your electromagnetic villains did. It's them. And if it weren't Nicole, it would have been someone else. Maybe you or me."

They were on to me. "They're looking for 'Dan.' They're saying I killed her." I tried to keep calm, but I was feeling overwhelmed by it all.

"They must have interrogated her first," Amit said softly. "She must have told them all about you, including that name you called yourself."

"That's so cold," I was still in shock. "She told them everything she knew, and they killed her, anyway."

Amit searched on "Houston, Nicole, Murder." He turned up some local news reporting. She'd been found strangled in her apartment. Police suspected foul play. They were seeking a boyfriend, Dan, for questioning. There was a sketch. It looked a bit like me, but was off. Anyone with information should call the Houston Police Department.

"They don't have video," Amit said. "They should have had surveillance video of you buying the book."

"I didn't pay at the register. I handed her cash. She took care of it and brought it back to me." This couldn't be allowed to stand. It had to be this Xueshu Quan. Was he the electromagnetic villain?

"You want to call it a night?" Amit asked.

"Let's finish what we came out here to do."

Amit nodded in agreement.

We found and downloaded some more scans of Lodge's *Modern Views of Electricity* from various sources, and then began working our way through online booksellers looking for copies. A helicopter buzzed overhead. That was odd. We don't get many helicopters flying around this far out of the big city. I looked around in time to see a couple of state troopers lined up making a left-hand turn to cross back under the interstate – away from us and toward the truck stop. "Shut it down," I exclaimed, as I yanked the antenna off the dash and pulled the Wi-Fi dongle out of the computer. Amit did a hard power off on the laptop.

"What's going on?" Amit asked.

As I described the helicopter and began explaining about the state troopers to Amit, an explosion of flashing blue lights burst out around the truck stop on the far side of the interstate – the same truck stop whose wireless access we had been using moments before.

"Let's go!" Amit fumbled for his keys.

"No!" I grabbed his hand. "Too obvious. We'd just draw attention to ourselves. It could be a complete coincidence." I thought for a moment. We'd let ourselves get cornered. The roads on this side of the interstate were all dead ends that terminated in a wilderness area. We had to go past the police barricade. But, not just yet. "Let's go into the convenience store, buy some Cokes, and head home."

We got out of Amit's car, and got our Cokes. As we were checking out at the cash register, I had an inspiration. "I'll take a pack of Marlboros."

The clerk eyed me suspiciously. "You got an ID?"

I made a show of searching my pockets. "Nope. Must have left it at home."

"You should stay away from that shit, kid," the clerk advised me. "It'll rot out your lungs."

Amit and I departed. He looked at me incredulously. Then I saw the light bulb flash on. "Oh, I get it. If anyone saw us sitting here for the last hour…"

"…the clerk is going to tell them we're a couple of underage losers stealing a smoke in the parking lot," I finished the thought.

"Better to look like we're guilty of something else than draw attention to what we were really doing," Amit approved. "Slick. Now let's get out of here before they run out of innocent truckers to hassle."

I seconded Amit's motion. Our best bet was to get out now before they spread a wider net. The on ramp to the interstate was blocked by a state trooper. We had to drive right past the truck stop to get home. A couple of sheriff's deputies had the truck stop blocked off, and they weren't letting anyone in or out. We drove up slowly trying our best to remain calm and unconcerned. They waved us on past. I could see some state troopers' vehicles and trucks. We didn't pause to get a better look. As we were driving away, I heard more helicopters flying overhead. It was clearly something major. Perhaps it was all a coincidence – some big drug bust or something else going down? Could they truly be after us? Amit drove me home. It was late, so I didn't wake up my parents to tell them what happened. After all, it could have been a coincidence.

It wasn't.

The next morning, Dad woke me up early to see the news. Homeland Security and the Tennessee State Troopers had "thwarted a cyber-terror attack" that had been underway from the truck stop. According to the reports, the terrorists had been hacking into critical infrastructure at TVA's Cove Creek nuclear plant. Only Homeland Security's quick and decisive action had prevented a potentially dangerous situation. Unfortunately, the terrorists were still at large. The terrorists were likely using directional antennas to exploit unsecured wireless networks and even hacking into secured networks. One morning show host showed a picture of a Pringles can antenna – identical to what we were using. Tennesseans were advised to be on the lookout for any suspicious behavior. I couldn't imagine there actually being "cyber-terrorists" who just happened to be at the same truck stop at the same time. It had to be a cover story for an effort to find Amit and me.

Dad insisted on collecting everyone's cell phone and placing them in the microwave. "It makes a great Faraday cage, so there's no chance anyone can turn them on remotely and listen to us." He called Mom and me to the dining room to discuss the situation. I told them about Nicole and about what happened at the truck stop. He chewed me out for not waking him up last night. "They're after you and Amit," Dad concluded. "It can't be a coincidence, but it makes no sense to me why anything you've done would trigger such an extreme reaction."

"You're always saying actions have consequences," Mom pointed out to Dad. "You two thought you found some kind of dangerous conspiracy and just had to keep poking at it until the conspirators woke up. Well, now, they have. People have already been killed. That's water under the bridge, now. How do we protect ourselves?"

"We go about our daily routine," Dad said. "Don't draw unnecessary attention, but we need to get ready." He turned to me. "Take the DVD burner and back up all the data you and Amit collected. Make six copies – that ought to be plenty.

Put a working copy on a flash drive. We'll risk hiding it here. Gather up any hard copies as well as the laptops, wireless dongles, and antennas. Make sure all your other files are backed up, too."

He turned to Mom. "Backup all your files. I'll be doing the same. Let's get any family records and documents together. I was going to be seeing Rob this morning anyway. I'll run everything up to his place for safekeeping. We need to talk with a lawyer. I'll call Greg Parsons in Knoxville to see if he can connect us with someone appropriate. I'll try to set up a meeting for this afternoon." Finally, Dad asked me, "When will you be seeing Amit?"

"I was supposed to be seeing him at Kudzu Joe's this morning."

"Good. Get Amit to do the same – back everything up and gather all the equipment. I'll probably want to swing by the hotel later this morning. We'll need to speak with him and his folks. You both know not to say anything and not to text or call each other regarding this, get it?"

"Got it," I replied.

"Good," he said.

We all got to work. A few days ago, I thought it ludicrous to think that all communications were being monitored. Now, I wasn't nearly so confident. How could Amit and I have been monitored after all our precautions? I got my backups and equipment to Dad. He cautioned me to leave my cell phone at home so I couldn't be easily traced. Then, he left for Uncle Rob's with our backups and instructed me to get Amit back to the hotel – he'd meet us there. I headed off to Kudzu Joe's just a bit late.

* * *

"I was beginning to think they got you," Amit said softly.

He was already a couple of steps ahead of me. The state troopers had stopped by the hotel late last night looking for suspicious out-of-town characters who might be involved in cyber-terror. He'd been up a good part of the night backing up the data and caching his equipment. He assured me it wouldn't be found. "A hotel is a big place with lots of nooks and crannies." He'd even had time to look at what we'd downloaded. Let's go back to the hotel. I think you'll find it very interesting."

When we got back to the hotel, I asked him if he'd told his folks about last night's events.

"I didn't get back until late, and they've been too busy with the morning rush for me to tell them anything," he explained. "I think I'll wait for your dad to show up. My father sometimes doesn't understand what I do. He's proud of what I've accomplished, but if there's trouble, he's likely to blame me, even if it actually isn't my fault. He's less likely to blow up at me if your father is around. Your father can help explain everything. He'll listen to your father."

Amit's father had finished up with a guest, so Amit headed to the reception desk. I followed along for moral support.

"Dad, I may have gotten into some trouble last night," Amit confided to his father. "I need to talk with you about it. May we take over the Smoky Mountain conference room? It might take an hour or so."

"Sure, the room is open, but what is this trouble?"

"My father will be here in a little bit, Mr. Patel," I explained. "It's a potential legal problem we hadn't realized might be an issue. He needs to check with a lawyer and get some questions answered. He asked me to arrange a meeting with you later this morning to discuss it in private."

Amit's father seemed both concerned and curious. Another guest approached the desk, cutting short his desire to interrogate us further. "Okay, I'll see you back there in a bit."

Amit led me to a storage room off the laundry. He moved some jugs of cleaning supplies and unscrewed an air vent cover. Behind was a small compartment with a laptop and the Pringles can antenna. Amit pulled out a flash drive. "All the scans and data are on here," he explained. "Here's a copy for you." He handed me one of the flash drives. "I have a smaller hidey hole near where I work. I normally keep the flash drive there. For now though, I'm keeping everything in here." He reached in and pulled out a couple of papers – a printout of the crucial pages from Lodge's *Modern Views of Electricity*.

Amit looked thoughtfully at the pages. "Why is this so important that someone wants to kill Nicole and her boss and call our searches 'cyber-terror?'"

"Beats me," I confessed. "We need to figure out what was here on these pages before they altered it. Let's take it up to show our fathers. We can shred it when we're done."

* * *

Amit's father led mine into the conference room. "What's this trouble our boys are in?" Mr. Patel asked. We told him the whole story and showed them both the suspicious pages from the Lodge book.

"This is what all the trouble is about?" Mr. Patel was incredulous. "This old physics book is what they call cyber-terror?"

"It's all a cover story of some kind," my father explained. "Somehow, this Lodge book is a clue to a very important secret: a secret so important that someone high up in the government is willing to go to extreme lengths to suppress it and keep people like our sons from looking into it."

"The state troopers here last night," Mr. Patel began, "they were here looking for my boy, all because of this?"

"I'm sure the state troopers have no idea about the Heaviside paper or the Lodge book or whatever the hidden truth is," my father clarified. "They honestly believe what they've been told – that 'cyber-terrorists' were trying to break into a TVA nuclear plant from the truck stop. If they find our boys, they will be arrested, handed over to the people who do know the score. They might even kill our boys. The girl who gave my son the list with this book on it was murdered. The co-worker from whom she got the list was murdered. Some of the historical evidence the boys found suggests that a number of the famous scientists who worked on this problem a century ago were killed or silenced. I thought it was all a coincidence, but the fact that there could be all this trouble, this extreme reaction, it all makes me think there's really something to it. We need to be very, very careful."

"This can't happen." Now Mr. Patel was angry. "This is supposed to be a free country. We work hard. We build a life here. We raise our boy right. And they want to come after him because of some old physics book?"

"I know some good men, honorable men, men who believe in this country and what it can and ought to be," my father assured him. "I've set up a meeting at their law office this afternoon. I hope you and Amit can come with us."

"No, you don't understand!" Mr. Patel was getting insistent. He spoke with a quiet intensity. "They are here already. They are right here in my hotel, up on the second floor! They checked in late last night. They took a copy of all my surveillance video, and a print out of all the guest information. They are right on top of us!"

Amit looked stunned. Then his eyes narrowed. "What room are they in, Dad?" He began opening his laptop. His father told him the room numbers. "Maybe we're right on top of them." Amit pulled open his software and clicked around a bit. "I have the log files for their internet usage. It looks like a lot of the traffic went over a VPN." His father looked confused. "A Virtual Private Network. It's an encrypted tunnel to try to keep your Internet traffic safe from the kind of poking around I'm about to do."

"Is this a good idea?" Amit's father asked him.

"Is there any way they can detect what you're doing?" my father asked.

"I own this network," Amit said possessively. "They're playing on my turf now, and there's no way for them to know what they're leaving behind in my log files or if I fork their traffic and make a copy of it. If they want to try to frame us for cyber-terror, I want to fight back."

"I think you should let him," my father said. Amit's dad nodded his head in agreement.

"I can't tell exactly what they were looking at last night because all I have right now are the IP headers in the log file – the addresses where all their traffic was going. That's about to change, because I'm setting the server to record all their traffic in the future." He paused a minute, fingers clicking decisively across the keyboard. "Done," he said confidently. He went back and began scrolling through the log file. "Sloppy, sloppy, sloppy. The point of a VPN is to shield all your traffic by encrypting it and routing it to a secure server back at your office. But look at these lags! Their VPN is crap!"

"You think you can read it?" I asked.

"Probably not," Amit acknowledged. "VPNs are always encrypted, or what's the point of having one. But apparently, the VPN these guys use is so slow that they did a bunch of Omnitia searches outside their secure tunnel. They probably got fed up with the lags." He kept scanning the log file. "Oh, and here's something interesting! One of these guys is checking out the Hook Up Landing website. No wonder he doesn't want the main office IT staff to know about this.

"What is this Hook Up Landing website?" Mr. Patel asked his son.

"It's a dating website…," Amit began. Then he realized the trap he was getting into. "I… I understand it's for people interested in… 'short-term' relationships." He looked flustered. "I read about it somewhere," he insisted. "It has a bad reputation."

His father looked at Amit severely.

"In any event," Amit continued, regaining his composure, "all this traffic outside the VPN is protected by a much less powerful default encryption. I might be able to hack into it."

"That's a project for another day," my father cautioned. "We need to get out of here without being seen. You two really do need to accompany us to Knoxville to speak with my lawyer."

"I'll have to come up with something to tell your mom, Amit," his father said. "I'm not sure she'd be able to deal with our guests if she knew the truth." Amit's father led us out the back door. "We'll see you at the lawyers' this afternoon."

* * *

"Hi there!" Amit said cheerfully to the receptionist at the law office.

She looked us over, suspiciously. "May I help you gentlemen?"

"We're here to see Greg Parsons," my father told her.

"Yes, sir," the receptionist responded. "Please have a seat, and he'll be out in just a moment." She called back to tell Mr. Parsons we were waiting. Amit lingered as the rest of us took our seat.

"I still have a boyfriend," the receptionist pre-empted him.

"So does my girlfriend," Amit assured her, confidently, "but I don't have time to compare notes with you just now. I was wondering where the bathroom is?"

Not long after Amit got back, Mr. Parsons and another man came out and led us back to a conference room.

"Bill Burke," the stranger introduced himself to Dad and then shook hands. We all introduced ourselves.

"Greg said this might be a criminal matter," Mr. Burke began. "I usually defend more white-collar crimes like fraud, but I may be able to help you."

"Before we begin," Dad cautioned the lawyers, "this is highly confidential. How confident are you that this room is secure?"

"We take our security very seriously here," Mr. Burke assured us. "We do a weekly sweep for electronic devices, and we have a professional security company that sweeps through every month or so."

"May I ask you to leave your cell phones outside the room?" Dad asked. "We didn't bring any."

Mr. Burke and Mr. Parsons complied with Dad's request although they probably thought they were humoring him.

"You know that big 'cyber-terror' case in the news this morning? These boys are being sought for it." Dad explained how we'd uncovered mysterious edits and omissions in old physics books, and how we'd been wardriving to download scans. He handed over a copy of my note from Nicole with the book list and Xueshu Quan's contact information. He explained how we'd found out about Nicole's murder and the murder of her co-worker. Finally, he handed out copies of the critical page from Lodge's *Modern Views*. They looked dumbfounded. There was a lot of that going around.

"This has to be the craziest story I've ever heard," Mr. Burke said, shaking his head. He looked at Amit and me. "Boys, I'm your lawyer now. Anything you tell me is protected by attorney-client privilege. That means I cannot be forced to disclose anything you might share with me. Whatever secrets you have are safe with me. If I disclose them, I'm likely to get myself disbarred. That means I lose my job. I get some clients who don't want to come clean with me and tell me the whole story. They hold back information that eventually comes out anyway, and it takes me by surprise. If there's anything relevant, you need to tell me about it now. We can take action to avoid worst-case scenarios, and minimize the likelihood of fines or a jail sentence. You're both underage, so you might get off with probation. I can't protect you very well, though, if you let me get surprised when the facts turn up, as they inevitably will.

"Did you hack into any nuclear or TVA computers?"

"No, sir," Amit and I concurred.

"Now I know computers can be complicated and sometimes you end up doing something you didn't truly mean to do," he continued. "So, tell me, did you access them at all, even by mistake or accident?"

"No, sir," we confirmed.

"To the best of your knowledge, this cyber-terror alert is all about these old physics books and this Xueshu Quan person?"

"I suppose, sir," I began, "I mean it's possible that there actually was a cyber-terrorist at the same truck stop at the same time, but I don't think it's likely."

"Neither do I," Mr. Burke agreed. "You have two basic options. Normally, I would make sure I had all the facts and then accompany you to the police or the agency investigating the alleged crime. In this case, I don't see that you have committed any crime. The feds might argue your access to the truck stop wireless network was unauthorized. I don't think they'd be likely to prevail on that theory since the truck stop gave you the password at an earlier visit and the network is set up for their customers' use.

"I'd like to do a little digging first." Mr. Burke offered. "I think this must be some kind of national security issue – something considered classified or otherwise secret. I want to poke around a bit. I have a private investigator I work with in the DC area. He's trustworthy and discreet. I can ask him to investigate Xueshu Quan – see who picks up the mail from Quan's box and where they go."

"It would be unwise for any of this to lead back to you, let alone us," Dad pointed out. "They must know we have their address. They'll be on guard. And I'd hate for your investigator to get in trouble with these folks. These people have been killing to keep their secrets."

"As I said," Mr. Burke assured Dad, "my investigator is very discreet and very careful, particularly if I emphasize the risks."

"Investigators, particularly good ones, are expensive. How much will this cost?" Mr. Patel asked.

"Seeing as how my son got your son into this, I'll be paying for it," Dad offered.

"I appreciate the offer," Mr. Patel said, "but let's discuss it between ourselves later."

"While we're looking into this further," Mr. Burke continued, "I should advise you what to do if you are approached by the police or federal agents. If they want to ask you questions, you should politely decline to answer any questions without your parents present. If they continue to press you, all you have to do is say the magic words, 'I refuse to answer any questions without my attorney.' Then, you should ask 'Am I free to go?' In principle, this requires them to either arrest you or let you go. Either way, you don't talk unless I'm present. In practice, however, they're likely to keep trying to persuade you to talk."

"Don't they have to read us our rights?" Amit asked.

"Only if they arrest you, but, they might not arrest you immediately," Mr. Burke warned us. "Lying to federal officers is a crime, and there's nothing they like better than to engage you in a long rambling conversation. Then, if they can trip you up the least little bit, find the slightest error or misrepresentation in what you said, they can charge you with lying to federal agents and use the case as leverage against you.

"In any given situation, you should use your judgment, and you don't necessarily want to escalate to immediately demanding a lawyer. The general rule is you should never volunteer information to an officer or agent that might in the least way be pertinent to some kind of investigation that might be related to you.

"The Supreme Court Justice, Robert Jackson, who also served as the prosecutor of the Nazis at the Nuremberg trials, said, 'Any lawyer worth his salt will tell the suspect in no uncertain terms to make no statement to the police under any circumstances.'"

"We'll keep that in mind," I assured him.

"It's trickier than just that," Mr. Burke added, smiling at our naïvety. "Police can be ruthless and devious in how they get you to incriminate yourself. They can deceive you, lie to you, pressure you, and trick you in order to get an admission from you, to help the prosecutor build a case.

"They'll leave you alone in a room a long time to soften you up – bright lights, uncomfortable chair, one-way observation mirror. They'll send in a scary, intimidating interrogator to work you over in hope of getting you desperate and scared enough to then confide in a friendlier, more supportive interrogator who'll come along later. That trick is so common it has its own name. It's called the 'good-cop, bad-cop' routine.

"They'll take you and your friend in, interrogate you separately and tell each of you that the other has confessed to everything and your only chance to avoid a long sentence is to admit your guilt. They'll tell you that they already have all the evidence they need to convict you and that it will go easier on you if you take responsibility. They may tell you that they already have your fingerprints or a video of you. They'll ask you to write a letter of apology – and there's little more incriminating than a confession written in your own hand. They'll hand you a cup of coffee, and then take the empty cup when you're done to surreptitiously collect a sample of your DNA.

"They have years of experience breaking down hardened criminals. Don't talk with them. Don't play their game. Just say the magic words, 'I refuse to answer any questions without my attorney.' And, unless they've already arrested you, you should ask, 'Am I free to go?'"

* * *

The next morning, Amit got me up to speed on events at the hotel. He'd compared the IP log from the hotel's current "FBI" guests to the IP activity from some FBI agents who'd stayed at one of the Knoxville locations of the hotel. "Totally inconsistent," he explained. "Different VPN IP address and completely different protocols. I don't think they're actually FBI agents. I told Dad, and he called the sheriff. Dad explained to the sheriff that his new FBI guests seemed a bit suspicious, and would the sheriff please confirm that they were truly FBI agents. So apparently, Sheriff Gunn called the Knoxville office of the FBI, and they had no record of these guys. He told Dad to keep an eye on them and came out with a couple of deputies. They stopped the guys in the lobby as they were coming in and asked them for identification. Sheriff Gunn called the Knoxville office again right in front of them and they said they had no record of them. The sheriff was about to run them in for impersonating Federal agents when they told him to tell the Knoxville office to call the Director of the FBI in Washington. There was a long pause – a couple of minutes or more – and then suddenly the sheriff was apologizing for the misunderstanding.

"After the FBI guys left, my father apologized to the sheriff for getting him in trouble with the false tip, but the sheriff said, 'No, that was a good call on your part. There's something just not right about those guys. The FBI is very territorial. I've never heard of FBI agents operating independent of the local office. They should at least have checked in. The Knoxville office seemed pissed off about it, but apparently, someone in the Director's office told them to mind their own business. Keep an eye open, and don't hesitate to let me know if you pick up on anything else.'"

"That doesn't sound like Sheriff Gunn to be so talkative," I noted.

"He and Dad have a good relationship," Amit explained, "Dad tips him off all the time when he sees suspicious activity. It makes the sheriff look good to the state troopers when he gets an arrest or tips them off. Trust me, you don't want to have to clean up a room after someone has used the bathtub to make meth."

"Who are those guys, really," I wondered.

"Some secret group within the FBI?" Amit speculated. "Some group with the power to pose as FBI agents and make the FBI back them up in a pinch? It's hard to tell."

* * *

With all the anxiety and pressure, neither Amit nor I felt like preparing for the pre-season debate tournament. Both of us had begun the summer with the goal of getting prepped for it, but between all our other projects, we hadn't done as much preparation as we should. The tournament was a full day affair. Our top competition would be Emma and her partner Sharon. They had just missed out on going to the national debate tournament representing Tennessee and were expecting to go all the way in their senior year. They were very good, very creative, and very formidable.

David and my Cousin Shawn and were also contenders. They were slick, smooth, and totally unscrupulous. At a tournament last year, I'd caught David strategically editing quotations, removing key words or phrases and inserting ellipses to change their meaning. We proved it to the judge and they not only lost, but also got a reprimand and a suspension. They'd had it in for us ever since.

The final contenders were Alex and Daniel. They would be sophomores this year and had taken an interest in debate. They didn't have much experience, but I understood that our debate coach, Mr. Stinson, had been working with them over the summer to get them up to speed.

The intraschool debate tournament was something of a tradition with Mr. Stinson, our debate coach and teacher. His notion was to get us thinking early about the debate topic and working to collect research. By having our first tournament experience at the beginning of the school year, and by continuing to practice, review and improve ourselves, we'd be experienced veteran debaters by the time the first interschool tournaments rolled around in late October. Mr. Stinson's insistence on an early start gave the Lee County High debate team a huge advantage, even over the top Knoxville debate programs.

We beat Sharon and Emma in our first match-up, and handily trounced Alex and Daniel, in both our debates with them. We'd also lost one round to Shawn and David. Going into the sixth and final round, we had a rematch with Sharon and Emma that would decide the tournament.

It was not our day. I presented our affirmative case for RTGs as an alternative energy source. In cross-examination, Sharon blindsided me with a bunch of questions about how unpopular nuclear power was with women. Then, Emma sprung their trap. They conceded the need for RTG, but insisted women would never approve of them because of their strong disapproval of nuclear power. Our approach of approving subsidies for RTGs through the regular democratic system, would never work in the face of this feminine opposition, so they offered a counterplan: they proposed repealing women's suffrage.

Emma threw all of Amit's claims and arguments from the Independence Day party right back at him. She and Sharon had done a remarkable job finding facts and statistics to buttress their case. Women do vote differently than men, they argued, citing a study by John R. Lott, Jr. and Larry Kenny. In her speech, Sharon claimed that women were directly responsible for the growth of the welfare state and its crippling effect on economic growth and progress. Writing in *Public Choice*, Burton Abrams and Russell F. Settle concluded that the 1971 extension of suffrage to women in Switzerland led to a 28% increase in social welfare spending and increased the overall size of the Swiss government. She had an impressive array of statistics. Overcoming the irrational objections to RTG was only the beginning of the benefits possible from the negative counterplan. By repealing women's suffrage, we would roll back the oppressive state and launch a new era of growth and prosperity. Sharon almost had me convinced.

Amit and I made a valiant try in our rebuttals. We both argued for the complete infeasibility of expecting women's suffrage to be repealed by any significant number of state legislatures, but we were simply unprepared to do much more than argue vaguely for fair play, equality, and justice. They'd caught us absolutely unprepared for any substantive rebuttal. Amit gave an impassioned closing statement, but I was sure we'd lost.

Mr. Stinson finished scribbling some notes, and finally looked up at the four of us waiting patiently for his pronouncement. "I wish I'd videoed that one," he said, "because it was one of the most improbable and fascinating debates I've ever seen. Where on earth did you get the idea for that counterplan?"

"A good friend of mine suggested it," Emma said coyly.

"You took the Affirmative by complete surprise. They were utterly unprepared for that counterplan and had nothing but cheap rhetorical appeals to equality and justice to offer in opposition. I do agree with the Affirmative's point that your plan is completely unfeasible because no state legislature is going to act to deny women the vote. Their own plan, however, suffers the same shortcoming given the opposition, irrational or not, to nuclear power. I'm awarding this one to the Negative."

We shook hands and congratulated the girls. Despite the loss, I enjoyed spending an entire day thinking about something other than electromagnetic villains and the suppressed Heaviside paper on bouncing waves.

* * *

The following Monday was the first day of school. I'd already taken the core math and science classes I needed, so I'd signed up for shop class, drawing, and electronics to fill the gaps in my schedule. Shop class in particular was a fascinating experience. I had shop just before lunch. I showed up a bit early and found a seat.

"You're not a shop rat," said a big guy sitting down right behind me. "What are you doing here?" I had to think to remember his name – Rick. He was on the football team, but I didn't know much about him, because he wasn't in my usual classes. And he didn't seem very friendly.

"Hi, Rick," I said. "What do you mean by a 'shop rat'?"

"That's what we all call ourselves," he explained. "All the guys who take shop every year. What are you doing here?" His question had an edge of hostility to it.

"Just trying to pick up some useful skills," I explained, evenly. "I worked as an apprentice electrician last summer for my dad. He's a contractor, but I never got a chance to learn my way around wood and metal working tools."

That seemed to mollify him a bit, and our conversation was interrupted by the bell. Coach Warner, who doubled as the shop teacher, got all our attention very quickly by holding up his hand. He was missing a finger.

"This is what happens to you if you don't pay attention in my class," he said slowly and clearly. "There will be no horsing around, no joking, nothing but absolute attention to what you are doing. A momentary lapse in concentration, and something like this can and will happen to you."

The coach had gotten a good way through an introductory safety lecture when there was a loud knock on the classroom door. The shop had Plexiglas panels so folks in the hall could look into the shop and vice versa. As I turned to look, I saw Sheriff Gunn stepping through doorway.

The room was utterly still and completely silent. The sheriff had everyone's attention.

"Please pardon the interruption, coach," the sheriff said, "but I need to speak with one of your students." I tried hard to maintain my poker face, but I had a sinking feeling I knew what this was about.

"Of course, Sheriff," Coach Warner said. "Which one?"

"You," the sheriff said pointing right at me, his eyes boring a hole through mine. "Come. With me." I left my books and calmly stood up and followed the sheriff out into the hallway. I figured he was going to lead me to the principal's office, but no. He closed the door and stood looming over me, uncomfortably close.

"So," the sheriff asked, "when did you start smoking?"

Chapter 8: Back to School

Looking back, I think Sheriff Gunn arranged the surprise interview to try to keep me off balance. In the time it took to walk to the principal's office I'd have had plenty of opportunity to collect my thoughts, figure out what to say, and calm down. Thanks to my discussion with Mr. Burke, though, I was ready, and I knew what I had to do.

I returned the sheriff's gaze and forced myself to remain impassive. "I have no comment."

"It can't have been long ago you started smoking," the sheriff continued. "Your teeth are pearly white, your fingers clear of nicotine stains, and your clothes don't reek of stale smoke. We had a little trouble at the truck stop down by the interstate a couple weeks ago. You may have heard?"

"Yes, sir," I answered.

"You see, son," he began in a patronizing manner, "my deputies saw you and Amit drive right on past the truck stop not long after the feds raided the place. So I poked around a bit. The feds grabbed up all the surveillance video for anywhere around that exit. There was Amit's car arriving just about the time the 'cyber-terror' attack started. The feds spoke with the convenience store clerk. They 'discovered' your underage smoking, and since a couple of kids aren't what they're looking for, they foisted your case off to the locals – that would be me – so they could spend their ever much more valuable time and their ever much more sophisticated professional investigative resources pursuing more credible leads."

He hadn't asked a question, so I continued to exercise my right to remain silent. I looked him in the eye, and did my best to appear completely unconcerned.

"Now, I know your parents," the sheriff said, "and I know Amit's father. Both of you, you and Amit, you were raised right by good folks. You're both of you too damn smart to start in on smoking. You're just not the type. I'd sooner believe you were both cyber-terrorists before I'd believe you were smokers. This 'cyber-terror' crap Homeland Security and the FBI are shoveling is every bit as much bullshit as you and Amit being secret smokers. Which is why you and I are having this little conversation about your disturbing proclivity for juvenile delinquency, and why I'm here counselling you on the evils of tobacco instead of you and Amit having your asses hauled down to Knoxville for the feds to be grilling you about your 'cyber-terror.'"

Sheriff Gunn paused, his eyes boring into mine. I held my poker face, and I willed myself to be calm. I decided now was as good a time to test the waters as any, so after a long and awkward silence, I finally asked, "Am I free to go?"

The sheriff gave me a thin grin. "I got my eye on you, boy. You'll be talking to me, or you'll be talking to the feds. You think on it, now, you hear me?"

"Yes, sir," I answered matter-of-factly. He turned and walked away. I'd bet anything he was heading off to see Amit if that hadn't been his first stop. I quietly opened the door and returned to my seat. Coach Warner handed me an information sheet, then studiously ignored me and continued smoothly with his safety and orientation.

When class was over, I collected my things and began heading to the cafeteria to try to find Amit. "Hey," Rick stopped me. "What was that about with you and the sheriff?" There were a half dozen shop rats all standing around us waiting intently for me to answer.

"Tell you what," I said. "Let's get some lunch, and we'll talk." They agreed, and we all headed to the cafeteria together and got our lunches. Apparently, they had their own special table in the corner where they all sat, and today, I was the guest of honor.

"The sheriff thought I might be smoking," I explained.

"Were you?" Rick asked.

"I'll tell you just what I told the sheriff: I have no comment." They all seemed to get a kick out of that. Sheriff Gunn intimidated everyone, them and me included. From their point of view though, the sheriff had come to work me over. I stood my ground, and I'd made him back down and walk away. In retrospect, the sheriff couldn't have done a better job of securing my status with the shop rats and their crowd if he'd tried.

I relayed the lessons that Mr. Burke had taught me. I covered interrogation techniques, good-cop-bad-cop, all the details I could remember. Don't answer any questions, I told them. If pressed, ask to have your parents and a lawyer present. Pick the right moment and ask, "Am I free to go?"

"That's what I finally did," I concluded. "It was a bit risky. If he actually had something on me, he could have arrested me and taken me away. Of course, he'd have arrested me eventually anyway if he actually had evidence. Clearly he didn't, because he let me go." I had a feeling the sheriff was not going to be pleased when he discovered how well prepared the shop rats were for his next interrogation. He might even figure out who'd tutored them. Tough. I was getting really tired of the sheriff pushing me around and it was time for a little push back in my own way.

They all started sharing their own stories of run-ins with the sheriff. By the time lunch was over, I was in with the shop rat crowd. I was worried, though, that I hadn't seen any sign of Amit. I finally caught up with him in electronics class after lunch.

Amit had a private lunch with Sheriff Gunn in the vice principal's office. I guess since the bad cop routine hadn't worked with me he went all good cop on Amit. He was ever so concerned about Amit running with a bad crowd, i.e., me. Amit's parents would be so extremely disappointed with him if he got in trouble after they'd worked ever so hard to build a life here. If Amit didn't confide in the sheriff, matters would soon be beyond the sheriff's control. The sheriff wouldn't be able to protect him, and he'd be facing years in a federal prison. Hardened criminals and felons would be eager to commit unspeakable acts on his tender young body. "They take terrorism very seriously," the sheriff had assured him. "They might even extradite you to a secret interrogation camp where you'd never be heard of again." Amit had listened politely and no commented his way through all the questions. Finally, he said, "If you'd like to interrogate me, I'll be wanting a lawyer. Otherwise, I'm going to be late to class. Am I free to go?" The sheriff had given him a final admonishment to decide whether he'd like to speak with the sheriff or with the feds and then let him go.

We'd hardly had a chance to get started in electronics when class was interrupted by an announcement that all students were to proceed to the gym for an unscheduled assembly. That was unprecedented in my experience at Sherman High. Mr. Martin, our electronics teacher, seemed similarly surprised, but advised us to go on to the assembly.

The principal introduced an FBI agent who addressed the assembly telling us all about the cyber-terror attack. The terrorists had been trying to hack into TVA's Cove Creek nuclear plant, maybe even try to make it melt down, the agent explained. The whole region could have been covered with fallout and we'd have had to evacuate.

Why the terrorists felt the need to go to a truck stop nearby the Cove Creek plant instead of, oh, use the Internet from some much safer location further away was not explained.

Sheriff Gunn was standing behind the FBI agent. He scanned the crowd until he caught sight of Amit and me. Calm, poker face, no reaction, I told myself. His gaze rested on us as the FBI agent explained how the terrorists used a directional antenna to tap into wireless networks. What was it with Pringles can antennas? The picture the agent showed looked just like our set-up. The agent advised us all to be on the lookout for suspicious activity. Maybe the terrorists were just passing through. Maybe they were among us. We were all told, "If you see something, say something," and then the principal ordered us back to class.

"Just great," Amit was muttering. "I can't wait for more opportunities to explain the difference between Indians and Arabs to more bigots." Then he looked at me directly. "I think my folks and I better come over to your folks' place for dinner. We need to talk."

I agreed, and I took the liberty of extending the invitation on my family's behalf.

* * *

We held our first council of war that evening. Of course, none of us at the time realized that was what it was, let alone exactly what we were up against. Dad thought Uncle Rob's place might offer better privacy. I'd called Amit and casually invited him and his folks to dinner at 7pm up at Robber Dell. Mrs. Patel couldn't make it – someone had to keep an eye on the hotel. In attendance were my folks, Uncle Rob, Amit, Mr. Patel, and of course, me – the six of us. We shared a couple of takeout pizzas in Uncle Rob's double wide and discussed the situation.

Amit and I began by relating the day's events and our run-in with the sheriff. "You boys did good," Dad said. "Exactly what Mr. Burke advised. The question is, do we arrange a meeting with the sheriff?"

"Absolutely not," my mother insisted. "Sheriff Gunn is not to be trusted."

"I'm not so sure about that," Uncle Rob countered. "He clearly understands that the FBI and Homeland Security are lying about this cyber-terror business. He could be an ally in figuring out what's actually going on and who these people are."

"He could also turn our boys over to the FBI, or whoever these people are," Amit's father observed.

"The only interests Sheriff Gunn has are his own," Mom insisted. "He will sit on this secret until such time as it is clearly to his advantage to tell someone. He won't do so until he understands what's going on. I think it's unlikely he'll figure everything out before we do, since we're already several steps ahead of him. Help him by disclosing what we know, and it only gives him more leverage over us. There's no rush to confide in the sheriff. Count on it."

"There's something else you all should know," Amit broke in. "I haven't had a chance to tell anyone, yet." He handed us each a sheet of paper:

Incident Report: Sherman Nexus (Category III), Sherman, TN

Summary: Unknown person or persons investigated online sources relevant to Xueshu Quan technology management project. Incident correlated with detection of a Nexus, potentially as severe as Category III. Incident may be connected with recent unauthorized disclosure of Xueshu Quan technology management project in Houston. Situation now appears under control, however investigation ongoing to identify suspects and potential connection.

Details: Unknown person or persons investigated online sources relevant to Xueshu Quan. Searches correlated to proscribed publication acquisition list for Heaviside wave interaction paper and unauthorized disclosures thereof in period literature. Security compromised suspect's computer with exploit package to relay IP address outside secured Tor channel. Security traced IP address to locations near Sherman, TN. Suspect investigated publications describing fundamental electromagnetics outside safe paradigms. Suspect only secured approved, redacted, and sanitized copies through Omnitia and other sources. However, search pattern closely targeted specific works relevant to suppressed Heaviside analysis on wave interaction. Search *terms and order of search consistent with suspect having access to proscribed publication acquisition list distributed to trusted used book dealers by Xueshu Quan. Timing of Sherman incident correlates to phone call to suppressed person of interest in Houston incident.*

Notified Homeland Security, FBI, state and local law enforcement, and our Quick Response Team, characterizing suspect activity as ongoing cyber-terror attack. Suspect evaded capture and remains at large. Suspect active twice in vicinity, but unknown whether suspect is resident of area or transient. Investigation focusing on local area.

Remote Nexus sensing further detected a Category III Nexus. Proximity to TVA's Cove Creek nuclear facility and Oak Ridge National Lab suggests reading may be a measurement error due to artificially induced neutrino flux. Latest area measurements show negligible levels and no Nexus.

Recommendations:

Review security of proscribed publication acquisition list to prevent future leaks.

Perform a local Nexus sweep of Sherman, TN and surrounding area.

"So there actually is a secret paper by Heaviside on wave interactions," I noted. "We were right about that all along."

"That's obviously just the tip of a much larger iceberg," Dad observed.

"Mighty peculiar way to write a report," Uncle Rob commented.

"What I want to know is how on Earth did you get this?" I asked Amit. "Where is this from?"

"EVIL," Amit explained cryptically, exaggerating the "ee" in evil. "You've been calling them the 'electromagnetic villains.' It's clearly bigger than that, however, so I've dubbed our bad guys: EVIL – the Electromagnetic Villains

International League. And let me tell you, EVIL IT is seriously hosed."

"How do you mean?" Uncle Rob asked.

"Near as I can figure, EVIL IT at EVIL Headquarters makes EVIL minions in the field use their very own EVIL VPN – that's a Virtual Private Network – for all their most secret and EVIL communications. It's not like any other VPN traffic I can find mentioned anywhere. It must be some custom or proprietary stuff. Maybe it's some kind of state of the art ultra-secure decryption-proof tunnel. I don't know, but the lags are obscene. It must be a real pain to use.

"I'm guessing EVIL IT doesn't care at all about a quality user experience for EVIL minions in the field," Amit continued. "They've got some kind of clunky word processing app minions are required to use called EMACS. I don't know what it stands for – probably "EVIL Minion Archaic Construction of Strings" or some such because the EVIL minions can't stop complaining about it. It's obviously clunky and difficult to use, and they're all required to draft their reports using it. And I'll bet it's really, really secure because it's local to their laptops and guaranteed not to leak information anywhere online except through the ultra-secure VPN that is equally clunky.

"Apparently one of our bright, but thoroughly EVIL, minions got a brainstorm and started to use some lower security, but much easier to use, cloud-based application to draft reports – Omnidocs, I think, but I'm not sure exactly. Since this runs right through the VPN tunnel, EVIL IT figured out what was going on and chewed out the EVIL minion for violating security policy. I got a copy of the EVIL minion's acknowledgement to the reprimand. I'm guessing EVIL minions resent being chewed out. What's more, I'll bet it's not much fun relaxing after a hard day's work doing EVIL things when you're trying to stream cat videos, online movies, and porn through the EVIL VPN tunnel that can't possibly keep up with your streaming video. And then if you go to the Hook Up Landing site to try to score some local action, it gets you in even more trouble with those EVIL IT jerks at EVIL HQ who have no idea what it's like being an EVIL minion out in the field, and who insist that your EVIL laptop must only be used for EVIL purposes." Amit was getting animated now in his explanation.

"So our EVIL minions, who actually are quite cunning in their own EVIL way, must have figured out that they can split the EVIL VPN tunnel to send only EVIL communications to EVIL HQ, and the rest of their Internet traffic through the local connection, where they can watch porn and cat videos to their hearts' content through a standard web connection without all the clunky delays of their EVIL VPN. The EVIL minions type in their reports in Omnidocs, then copy the completed Omnidocs text to paste it into EMACS and then submit the report to Evil HQ. Were you aware that Omnidocs auto-saves your document to the cloud? The EVIL minion must really hate losing any work, because he set it to auto-save every five minutes. It's not just an incremental backup – no, his entire document gets sent again and again and again every five minutes while he's drafting it."

"You can read all these messages their computers are sending back and forth?" Mr. Patel asked.

"No, not exactly," Amit clarified. "The web connection is actually encrypted by default, but the encryption is nowhere near as complicated as I bet the fancy EVIL VPN uses. After all, the NSA doesn't want to have to work too hard to decrypt all our web traffic. It's secure enough that someone like me, who doesn't have a supercomputer in my basement, isn't likely, in principle, to crack it. In principle. All that depends on how badly the user abuses the encryption, though.

"Ever hear of Venona? That's the secret operation that became known a while back where the NSA cracked the Soviets' codes and verified that there really were Communists embedded throughout the U.S. government right after WWII. Do you know how they did it? It wasn't because the Soviets' codes were bad. They used one-time pads. In principle, one-time pads are uncrackable because you encrypt a message with a unique random sequence that's only used once. But, some enterprising KGB officer decided it was taking too much time and money to generate unique one-time pads for each use, so they saved money by using the same one-time pads multiple times. Even back then, the NSA was listening. They collected messages using lots of these 'double-time' pads, and that little bit of extra redundancy was enough to decrypt big chunks of many messages.

"That's exactly the vulnerability in how our EVIL minions operate," Amit explained.

"So, you're able to hack all their communications?" I asked. "Sweet!"

"Again, not exactly. It's still way complicated to correlate and decode all the packets correctly, but I found a cracking tool on the dark web."

"Dark web?" Mr. Patel asked.

"Parts of the web that aren't normally accessible. You can use special web addresses to access dark web sites via Tor to find," Amit paused, "well, in this case to find people talking and sharing hacking ideas and software. I found an application that takes encrypted web traffic streams, and if the same text strings pass through often enough, it seems to be able to recover most of the text."

"Wouldn't that mean you'd get the early parts of the messages, but the latter parts that aren't passed back and forth as often would be harder to crack?" Uncle Rob asked.

"You'd think that," Amit said smugly. "Only there's a great new feature in the latest build of Omnibrowser. When people search, sometimes they copy and paste text strings into the search field, so some genius at Omnitia figured he could improve the search speed by automatically sending the contents of the clipboard straight to Omnitia every time you copy something. That way, Omnitia can pre-cache the results for you, instead of waiting to start the search when you actually paste something into your search field. Anything copied from an Omnidocs document is automatically sent to Omnitia over the network, and Omnitia sends the same string right back including the first page of search results to the local computer to enable pre-caching of search results. I think I'm getting most all the latest edits to the EVIL minions reports, because even the final version gets passed back and forth outside the encrypted VPN a couple of times."

Uncle Rob looked up from the message, "I hope you haven't been using that laptop from the truck stop," he told Amit, "because it looks like it's all set to summon the EVIL hordes the moment it connects to the Internet."

"Yeah, I'd figured as much," Amit said. "I've been afraid to turn it on for fear that whatever exploit they used to find us might somehow auto-enable the internal Wi-Fi that I disabled. I've been using my backup laptop, and I've begun routing searches, like for dark web tools, to different hotels here and there."

"Is that safe?" Uncle Rob asked. "Won't they be able to trace it back to you? They clearly have tripwires around Xueshu Quan and other relevant searches."

"The virtual machine I'm using employs Tor. I tuned up the firewall and I'm blocking all cookies and scripts, so I don't think they'll be able to catch me using the same trick," Amit assured him. "Even if they do, a couple of our hotels using my network administration software have conference and meeting centers," Amit explained. "I found one hosting a big engineering technical conference, and I made my virtual machine look like it was a guest at the conference, using the conference Wi-Fi code, to access Tor. It could be any attendee at a conference with nearly a thousand people. Or anyone who got the access code from them. Or anyone at the hotel who happened across the access instructions that might have been lost or misplaced by one of the attendees. And if EVIL does get on my trail, I'll know about it, because the first thing they'll want to do is access the network log files at the hotel. Which will show them precisely what I want them to see."

It did appear he was being very careful.

"What do they mean by a 'Nexus?'" I asked.

"That one was tricky," Amit conceded, "They toss the term around and take the definition for granted. It could mean something like an inflection point, an intersection or divergence, a change or a transition, but it may be something else entirely that we don't understand. Whatever we were doing at the truck stop made this Nexus thing start, and there must be more than one kind because ours was the third type."

"Is that the kind of Nexus, or the intensity of the Nexus, or what?" Dad asked.

"I don't know," Amit acknowledged. "It has something to do with how severe the Nexus is, so it might be intensity, or perhaps there are different types, some worse than others."

"These Nexuses – Nexii? – can be sensed from a distance, and sometimes they get false alarms from nuclear reactors like the ones at Oak Ridge or the TVA plant," Dad speculated.

"That was my guess," Amit confirmed.

"This local 'Nexus sweep' business is puzzling," Dad noted. "So they can be detected from a distance but localizing them precisely requires a sensor to be in closer proximity. We need to figure this out if it's somehow allowing them to trace you online."

"I think I discovered how they did it. They traced us by embedding an exploit of some kind on the Xueshu Quan web page we visited the other day. It infected my laptop and effectively broadcast our IP address to them," Amit clarified. "This Nexus business is something else entirely."

"I think you're all missing the most important point," Mom noted. "EVIL – or whatever you want to call them – they're still actively searching for our boys right here in town. The sheriff already figured out the boys are connected to this business. If EVIL or their Homeland Security or FBI helpers keep investigating here, and keep looking for suspects, eventually some bright minion will take a second look through all the leads they've already dismissed, notice the juvenile smokers, and when they ask around about our boys, most anyone in town will be able to tell them that story doesn't add up."

"We need to divert them," Uncle Rob said. "Give them a false lead to follow. Amit, why don't I borrow your infected laptop and take it on a little road trip?"

"You might want to wait a few days, Rob," Dad advised. "Nothing has happened for a couple of weeks and then the 'suspects' start logging in all over the place the day after the sheriff confronts our boys and they have that assembly at the high school? Someone might connect the dots. The sheriff certainly will."

"Don't wait too long," Mom countered. "A couple of days, maybe, but it needs to be this week, and it needs to be during school hours so the boys have an airtight alibi."

"I don't think a road trip is necessary," Amit said. "I can 'infect' a virtual machine with the same exploit and set it to trigger at any of the couple dozen locations across the southeast where my software has been installed. Some of them are even using the default passwords for the admin page of their wireless access points and I can reconfigure them to log into the wireless network of an adjacent building that offers free Wi-Fi to customers."

"I appreciate the work you've done, Amit," Uncle Rob began, "but I think it would be safer for me to go physically to the location with the actual laptop. Couldn't the exploit relay the Wi-Fi access point signal strengths in the area and use it to localize itself to the hotel? You've opened up a great resource for us to know how 'EVIL' operates and what they're doing. Let's not jeopardize it and you by using your access if we don't have to."

Amit and Uncle Rob arranged for Uncle Rob to pick up the laptop the following evening.

"We also can't keep meeting like this," Uncle Rob observed. "It's too easy to hide a tracker on your car and even a casual surveillance would note if you all keep coming out to my place. We can relay messages by hand and avoid surveillance. It's slower, but more secure. The boys see each other at school and can keep us all connected. But we need a solution for quick communications in an emergency or if something urgent comes up."

"For a while now," Dad explained, "Rob and I have been keeping in touch by amateur radio. We use low-frequency signals that bounce off the ionosphere so we can transmit out of Robber Dell here over the mountains, and back into town. We can get Amit set up at the hotel. You're not supposed to use any encryption on amateur radio transmissions, but we worked out a code based on the frequency and the timing of the transmission so it's not obvious. It rolls over every fifteen minutes. I'll let you borrow an old transceiver and get an antenna set up on the roof of the hotel, if that's OK."

"Sure," Mr. Patel assured him. "Thanks."

"I can get you up to speed on how the code works, Amit," Uncle Rob volunteered, "when I come over to get the laptop from you."

* * *

Uncle Rob's diversion appeared to work. The "cyber-terrorists" struck again, this time in New Orleans. Now we were apparently trying to blow up oilrigs. It was closer to the original Houston incident, so hopefully EVIL would think our activities were centered near Houston. The EVIL minions checked out of the hotel, and Amit lost track of them. He concluded they must have been staying at a different hotel chain or under a different identity. His network admin software would let him know if anyone started using the EVIL VPN at any of the hotels where his software was installed. The tension and anxiety began to recede, and I could get back to enjoying my senior year. After a few weeks, even Mom was willing to let me go out again. I fell into a comfortable routine.

Now that I wasn't taking honors math or science, my classes weren't very time consuming. I was enjoying learning my way around the shop, making things out of wood, or designing and implementing electronic circuits. I actually hung around with the shop rats more than my usual, more academic crowd. They took me out one evening to a favorite hangout of theirs – the steam tunnels under the old Tolliver Tech campus. They used some loose access panels to enter the tunnels. They had designed and constructed a clever tool perfect for grabbing the corner of a panel and lifting it up. They knew which tunnel had a motion sensor that would summon campus security, but even avoiding the alarmed section, there was a lot of interesting infrastructure to explore. There were a couple of big open areas that probably held generators or some other equipment at one point. We explored most of the tunnel system.

With Amit and Emma going to the Fall Ball, I felt left out, so I asked Sharon to go with me. We double-dated with Amit and Emma. For someone who'd agreed to go with me, Sharon sure didn't seem to be enjoying herself. We ended up going back to Amit's hotel and watching *The Princess Bride* on the big screen in the lobby under the watchful eye of Mrs. Patel. It was a quirky movie, but here and there, it had some great heroic lines: "My name is Inigo Montoya. You killed my father. Prepare to die." Of course, nothing in real life could ever be as heroic as that. Or so I thought at the time. The movie was the highlight of the evening. Sharon rebuffed my attempt to kiss her when I dropped her off at her place.

One Saturday morning in early October, we picked up an NVIS signal from Amit. He was calling in Morse code for anyone to answer, but the actual message lay in his choice of frequency and the time stamp. I looked them up in our codebook. "We need to meet. Come here, soonest." Dad replied in Morse code precisely five minutes later and at a frequency offset to indicate we were on our way. Mom insisted on joining us. We headed on over to the Berkshire Inn.

"Should we get started?" Amit asked Dad.

"Rob's out of town," Dad explained. "What have you found?"

Mr. Patel dimmed the lights in the conference room, and Amit connected his laptop to the projector.

"Look at this." Amit showed us all the web page he'd cached on his laptop. It was an eBay listing for the third edition of *Modern Views of Electricity* by Oliver Lodge, published in 1907. "This popped up last night. I asked the seller to email a scan of pages 302 and 303 to my anonymous e-mail account. Remember how the Tolliver copy and the Omnitia scan both had the peculiar figure on page 302? The one that's never mentioned in the text? This is what the seller sent me."

We looked at the scan glowing from the projection screen. The "diagram of the forces of electricity and magnetism" drawn by a "Mr. Trouton" was gone. The text missing from the Tolliver copy and the Omnitia scan but present in the eBay copy read as follows:

> *Energy flows at a right angle to the direction of the electric and magnetic forces. Close to the oscillator, these forces sometimes agree and sometimes disagree in phase, resulting in an ebb and flow of energy. Far from the oscillator, these forces are in phase yielding an inexorable outward flow of energy. Following up on a suggestion by FitzGerald, Heaviside recently demonstrated that when two identical waves are coincident, they may add either constructively or destructively depending upon whether their phases agree or disagree, respectively.[2] When the waves add constructively, their electric forces combine, and their magnetic forces cancel. All the energy is thus electric. When the waves add destructively their electric forces cancel, and their magnetic forces combine. All the energy is thus magnetic. Since the flow of energy requires both electric and magnetic force, the cancellation of either implies that the energy must be momentarily stationary. The energy, which hitherto travelled at the speed of light, comes to a rest and changes direction. The waves trade their energy. In effect, the energy bounces elastically as it is exchanged from one wave to the other.*

The eBay scan also had an extra footnote:

[2] *"Interactions of Electromagnetic Waves,"* Unpublished, 1905.

Dad's brows furrowed as he stood up and slowly walked to the screen. He stood there a while deep in thought. "Heaviside and Poynting came up with the theory of how electromagnetic energy moves from place to place," he explained. "It's called the Poynting vector, since Poynting came up with it a few months before Heaviside published his discovery. The Poynting vector says that 'the flow of energy requires both electric and magnetic force,'" Dad explained, reading from Lodge's text. "When waves interact and interfere, if either the electric or magnetic field gets cancelled out, the energy left in the other field has to stop moving. The waves themselves are travelling at the speed of light." He pondered this. "If the energy stops, that can only mean that it changes direction. The waves have to swap their energy. I suppose in that sense the energy actually does bounce elastically." He still seemed puzzled by it all.

I think I actually followed a bit of that, but it wasn't nearly as clear to me as it apparently was to Dad. Even Dad was still confused. Amit interrupted our contemplation.

"I asked the eBay seller to send a scan of the index also. Check this out," he said. Amit showed us scans of page 510. "In the Tolliver copy and the Omnitia scan, the Heaviside index entries are spaced out. In the eBay copy, there's an added reference to page 303. The minions of EVIL got the index right this time, but were too lazy to roll the "$399n$" up to the earlier line. Take a look at the Hertz index entry for a comparison." The entry for "Hertz" was followed by six numbers. "There's no reason why the '$399n$' should have been dropped to the next line in the 'Heaviside' entry," Amit explained. "It's clear that the 303 was deleted and the remaining numbers were spaced out."

"You have your smoking gun," Mom observed. "It's obvious that someone modified the book to remove that paragraph from nearly all copies of Professor Lodge's book. They also removed the reference from the index. You even have an explanation of Mr. Heaviside's paper, but what does it mean? Why is this so important that someone would kill to keep it secret?" Mom asked.

"I don't know," Dad confessed. "The physics actually seems basic, but it's deeply counterintuitive." I could see Dad disengaging from pondering the physics and gathering his thoughts.

"They say all crimes require means, motive, and opportunity," Dad observed. "We have a good start on the means: censorship of technical ideas, and potentially even the assassination of leading scientists. What's the motive?"

"Fear of technical progress?" Mom speculated. "But this doesn't seem like some run-of-the-mill Luddite. It's too specific. It's the fear of some particular, narrow aspect of technical progress, not technical progress in general."

"We've discussed that idea," Dad acknowledged, nodding in my direction, "but trying to nudge or perturb the course of technical development in a particular direction? You couldn't do that unless you already knew the potential technical destination and you were trying to divert folks off some particular path and force them in a different direction."

"Some personal rivalry?" I suggested. "Someone who made a breakthrough, but kept their progress secret, and then wanted to deter or derail competitors? A company?"

"Possibly," Amit said, "but remember this is international in scope: publishers in New York and London were apparently altering books. Assume Maxwell, Hertz, and FitzGerald were actually murdered, Heaviside was harassed, and Lodge was distracted. Then you're talking about EVIL working in Germany, England, Scotland, and Ireland, too, in additional to the US."

"That's bringing us to the question of opportunity? Who could be responsible? I don't have a clue," Dad admitted. "It could be an international corporation, although those were much rarer a century ago than today. It could also be a government. You've found examples in the writings of American and British writers. If it were today, I'd assume the

US and UK were in cahoots for some reason – that they regarded this as some classified technology with some great military significance. Back then, they were not always friendly rivals. Maybe the US was taking action against Britain or vice versa, but that seems unlikely. The more likely culprit would be Kaiser Bill." Amit looked confused, so he explained. "I mean Kaiser Wilhelm. Imperial Germany. No other major power would have been likely to be starting something with the UK or US. The French were allied with Britain. Japan and Russia were too busy with each other – they fought a war in 1905. China was in turmoil and their last Imperial dynasty was on the verge of collapse. As you research the personalities, you need to also take a look at the geo-political context."

"What about Heinrich Hertz?" Mom insisted. "Why would the Germans kill their own scientist – Heinrich Hertz – at the peak of his powers while he's making such wonderful discoveries?"

"Maybe the Germans killed Maxwell and the British killed Hertz in retaliation?" Amit suggested.

Dueling assassinations of a rival's leading scientists? It didn't make much sense to me. "Maxwell died in 1879," I pointed out. "When did Kaiser Wilhelm appear on the scene?"

Amit grabbed a different laptop, and did a quick search, being careful to route it to one of his virtual machines in another hotel. "Wilhelm II was proclaimed Kaiser of the Imperial German empire in 1888... oh, my..." His jaw dropped as he stared bug-eyed at the screen.

"Well?" Dad asked.

Amit plugged in his laptop to the projector so we could follow along. He continued reading aloud:

"Wilhelm ascended to the throne upon the death of his father, Frederick III, whose 99-day reign ended prematurely due to his death from throat cancer at age 56. The moderate, progressive, Frederick opposed the more conservative and militaristic Chancellor Otto von Bismarck, and spoke out against Bismarck's policy of German reunification by force. Bismarck in turn aimed to instill Prussian militarism and turn the young Wilhelm against his father. Observers in both Germany and Britain had hoped that Frederick's reign would liberalize the German empire and reduce military tensions. His death was widely considered a turning point in German history."

"That sounds almost exactly like how Hertz died, just a few years later," Mr. Patel noted.

We were all silent for a moment. "A turning point," I said quietly. "Like a Nexus?" I felt overwhelmed by the potential implications.

"And EVIL has a way to detect a Nexus." Amit observed. "And then they send someone to investigate and take action to shape history, including killing people who might change history in ways they don't like."

"What's more, they must have been at this a very long time," I noted. "Kaiser Wilhelm couldn't have been the prime mover. He had to have been a tool. A tool in the hands of whoever killed Maxwell in 1879, Frederick in 1888, Hertz in 1894, and FitzGerald in 1901. Heaviside wrote a paper on wave interactions in 1905. It was unpublished but must have circulated among his professional colleagues, because it was mentioned by Franklin in 1909, by Whittaker in 1910, by Fleming in 1906, and here we have Lodge describing it in 1907. EVIL has systematically covered up all the evidence. They removed the original mentions in print, and they forced the publishers to modify their printings. although some copies of the originals still pop up now and then. EVIL seeks them out and buys them through at least one used book dealer – the folks in Houston. Maybe there are other book dealers in their program. Maybe there are other books. Heaviside published the third volume of *Electromagnetic Theory* in 1912, and talked a lot about electromagnetic waves, but he omitted – or was forced to omit – any mention of bouncing waves. And, who can tell what else EVIL was up to?"

"You're both missing the big flaws in this theory," Dad pointed out. "Now EVIL not only induces cancers long before radioactivity was discovered, they also have a high-tech device that uses some kind of nuclear sensor to detect when and where the course of history is being changed – a good fifty or sixty years before the development of nuclear physics? Heck, there's no technology known to this day that could do such a thing."

"Because it's been suppressed?" Amit speculated. "Just like Heaviside's work on electromagnetic waves?"

"I don't know, Dad," I said. "Maybe the technology came first and the science later. Folks were using magnetic compasses for navigation for centuries before magnetism was understood. Maybe someone stumbled across a device of some kind, something like a compass, but instead of pointing north it points to where history is changing."

"An ancient fortune telling device that exploits some kind of nuclear phenomenon and points to the location where history is being made?" Dad was skeptical. I can't say as I blamed him.

"I thought Hertz died of granulomatosis, not cancer," Mom said.

"I don't know about that," I countered. "I found some older books that characterized Hertz's death as due to complications from a surgery for jaw cancer. So, we may have Maxwell's stomach cancer, Frederick's throat cancer, Hertz's jaw cancer, and FitzGerald's perforated ulcer – which might also have been correlated with cancer. I don't think it would take a high tech x-ray machine to pull it off. If someone put a nasty enough concentration of some radioactive material in someone's food, it might account for all these deaths."

"The Radium Girls!" I could see the lightbulb turn on for Mom. "Radium paint was used to make luminescent watches during the First World War," she explained. "The women who did the painting would lick the paint brush to get a sharp point. With each lick, they got a little bit of radium in their mouths. In a few years many of them developed horrible jaw cancers from their exposure."

"Again," Dad said patiently, "radium wasn't isolated until..."

"1910 by Marie Curie and André-Louis Debierne," Mom conceded, promptly. "Although Curie actually discovered it back in the 1890s."

"Even supposing someone had access to radioactive poisons before then," Dad continued, "which is highly questionable, there's still the matter of motive and opportunity. If it wasn't Imperial Germany, but rather some secret cabal acting behind the scenes, it could be anyone: the Illuminati, the Free Masons, the Catholic Church, the Rosicrucians, the Elders of Zion, the British Royal Family, the Knights Templar – pick your favorite conspiracy theory."

"The Deep State," Amit added.

"I'm not familiar with that one," Dad said.

"It's the idea that there is a loose cabal of senior bureaucrats and officials calling the shots and running the show in the government, with the active collusion of the crony capitalists, contractors, and bankers who profit from it all," Amit explained.

"Oh," Dad acknowledged. "I doubt there was much of a Deep State back in the 1870s when you're supposing all this began. Again, there's an international component to it all. We've seen British, German, and now even hints of a Chinese connection with this Xueshu Quan."

"Or the Deep State is just one more modern tool in the hands of EVIL?" I speculated. "I mean, someone is sending FBI agents after us who somehow aren't 'real' FBI agents."

It hardly seemed possible, let alone credible. I could imagine conspiracy and counter-conspiracy everywhere, which was getting us nowhere. And yet, Heaviside's paper was still out there, and someone with enormous resources had not only gone to great trouble to hide it a century ago, but also was actively trying to suppress it today. I kept going around in circles. The only conclusion I could draw was that we needed more evidence to get anywhere.

"Let's see what we have," I summarized. "An organization we've dubbed EVIL, for lack of a better name..."

"You have to admit that's a great name for our villains," Amit interrupted, smugly.

"...has been operating for more than a century," I continued, ignoring his interruption. "They appear to have a means or device for detecting a Nexus. We're not sure what a Nexus is, but it might be considered some kind of turning point in history. EVIL may have been involved in the assassination of political and scientific leaders. They may have worked behind the scenes in nineteenth century Germany, in the UK, and they are definitely active today, perhaps with a Chinese connection as well. They are affiliated with or able to operate as agents of our own government. They are actively covering their tracks and suppressing certain hidden truths, like Heaviside's ideas on wave interaction."

"This science stuff is all well and good," Mr. Patel noted, "but the most important hidden truth is the fact that there is one, and someone is trying very hard to hide it." We pondered Mr. Patel's point.

"That about sums it up," Amit broke the silence. "Someone had the clout to not only suppress Heaviside's paper, but also get all mentions of it removed from books in the US and Britain alike. And all those deaths are awfully suspicious, even if we don't know exactly how they happened."

"That's all awfully speculative," Dad commented, "but I'm increasingly convinced we face an extremely dangerous enemy. They may well have killed before to keep their secrets. They've successfully hidden the truth for more than a century. Moreover, it looks like they're killing people who get too close to their secrets. They must be very, very good at what they do if they've kept this thing a secret for so long. That suggests to me they must be absolutely ruthless. I'm beginning to regret encouraging you boys to run open loop on this."

I could see Mom frown, shooting him an "I told you so" look.

"Perhaps we should just publicize what we know," I suggested. "If we've already told the world, there's no incentive to silence us."

"I'd be tempted," Dad said, "but we're dealing with experts in silencing people and suppressing information. It would have to go viral fast before it got shut down. And this business about bouncing waves sounds absolutely crazy, even before we add the bit about assassinated scientists. You finally have me believing that there's something to it, but even I don't think it makes any sense. No one would believe us. It would make a little splash, it would sound ridiculous, and it would be forgotten. And then, they'd make certain we never had a chance to try anything like that again."

"Amit," Dad continued, "would you print off a copy of that text from Lodge on bouncing waves? Jim Burleson may have some ideas. If you don't mind, I'd like to get a printout of this to share with him. I want to study it further and try to make more sense of it."

"Sure thing," Amit replied. He opened a credenza in the conference room to reveal a printer and connected his computer. The laser printer that Dad donated to the cause hummed and out spat the paper. Dad grabbed the printout.

* * *

The eBay listing for the book was withdrawn before the book sold. The seller wrote back to Amit saying the book was no longer available, but it came with a Heaviside manuscript and would Amit be interested in purchasing it? Amit asked him to send a scan. The seller sent an executable zip file. Spooked, Amit didn't open it. "I'm not logging back into either the email or the eBay account again," he explained. "I'm sure they're doing their best to arrange some kind of a trap if I do."

A few weeks later, Dad took Amit and me to meet Mr. Burleson for breakfast. He'd been puzzling over Lodge's cryptic text for a few weeks, and was finally confident he had the meaning. "Radio waves really do bounce off each other," he explained, "in a certain sense." He drew a couple of pictures for us to help explain what happens when two waves collide or interfere with each other. An electromagnetic wave has an electric wave "**E**" coupled at a right angle to a magnetic wave, "**H**". Both fields operate at a right angle to the direction in which the wave and the energy propagate, "**S**". A collision is called "constructive" if the electric fields point in the same direction, and "destructive" if the electric fields point in opposite directions. But a very interesting thing happens when the two waves interfere with each other.

He drew a couple of pictures for me to help explain what happens when two waves collide or interfere with each other.

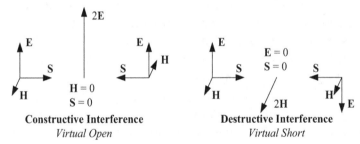

Constructive Interference
Virtual Open

Destructive Interference
Virtual Short

When the electric fields align constructively, the magnetic fields align destructively. When the electric fields align destructively, the magnetic fields align constructively. It's fascinating how the balance of electric and magnetic energy in a wave gets disrupted, with electric energy transforming to magnetic energy or magnetic to electric. The total amount of energy is conserved – it's just one kind changing to another.

Waves must have both electric and magnetic fields in order for energy to move, so all the energy comes to a rest when either field cancels out. But, the waves keep on propagating through each other at the speed of light. The waves exchange energy with each other. In that sense, radio waves – or at least the energy associated with them – really do bounce off each other.

It seemed like a basic concept, once I understood it. "This is stuff that should be in any basic class on electricity and magnetism," Dad acknowledged. "I'm amazed that something this simple and basic could have been overlooked. It all makes perfect sense. At the same time, I don't understand why a fundamental concept like this would be deliberately suppressed. What possible threat could this basic physical concept pose to anyone's interest?" Yet again, we'd peeled back another layer of the puzzle only to be left with more questions.

* * *

November rolled around. President Lieberman and Vice President McCain won re-election on a unity ticket. The first virtually unopposed presidential election since 1820 wasn't nearly as important to me as my continuing concern that EVIL lurked, ready to pop up unannounced. On a more pleasant note, however, Mom and Dad were planning a second honeymoon of sorts to Nashville over the Thanksgiving weekend holiday.

I tried to focus on my schoolwork and debate, but my heart wasn't really in it. Although the debate season was in full swing, by November, Amit and I had both virtually dropped out. Amit's time was consumed with his network administration software development. I was spending all my spare time reading and reviewing history and physics books to try to get a handle on what happened, and why Heaviside's work on bouncing waves had prompted such an extreme reaction. Neither of us had time to prepare properly for debate. We didn't want to let Mr. Stinson down, so we agreed to participate in a Student Congress event held in Knoxville. We introduced resolutions, debated them, and practiced parliamentary procedure. I'd been looking forward to an opportunity to have freewheeling public policy discussions, but it seemed the whole event was an exercise in horse trading, bribery, and vote buying – support our school's candidate for speaker and we'll back your bill – instead of open and objective discussion on the actual pros and cons of the measures we were discussing. I finally complained to Amit how disappointed I was in everyone else's childish behavior – why couldn't my fellow students discuss and analyze the issues like adults? "Dude," he replied shaking his head. "Don't you think this is exactly how the real Congress works?" That observation explained a lot about politics I hadn't understood before.

One Wednesday evening in mid-November, I was at home with Mom and Dad when there was a loud knock on the door.

"FBI!" shouted a voice. "We need to talk with you."

Chapter 9: It Takes a Tolliver to Beat a Tolliver

"FBI!" came the voice again on our front porch. "Open up."

"Son, make sure the video surveillance on the front porch is running on continuous capture," Dad said. Then, he turned to Mom, "Call 911, tell them about our visitors, and ask if the sheriff could drop by," he added, as he grabbed a small tape recorder he sometimes used to dictate notes. He headed for the front door. I went to the sewing room computer that also controlled the video capture for the security system, unclicked the motion capture mode, and set it to record. I heard Mom on the phone talking with the 911 dispatcher, as Dad opened the door.

"Yes, may I help you?" I heard Dad.

"FBI," one of the men claimed. "We need to ask you some questions. May we come in?"

"Have a seat on the porch," Dad offered, "and I'll be happy to talk with you." I heard the door click shut behind him, so apparently that worked. I could see shadows through the front windows. I moved closer, quietly, to listen in on the conversation. "I'm sorry gentlemen," Dad was saying, "but I didn't catch your names."

"Special Agent Wilson. We want to talk with you about the cyber-terror incident a couple of months back," I heard one of them say.

"What brings you here?" Dad asked.

"We're asking the questions," the other one said. "It will go better for you if you cooperate."

"'Cooperate' implies working together, you answer my questions, and I answer yours," Dad said matter-of-factly. "If you're not going to answer my questions, I think the word you mean to use is 'obey,' not 'cooperate.' In any event, I don't care to answer your questions without my lawyer present."

"We're investigating a matter of critical national security," Special Agent Wilson said. "If you don't cooperate you might be charged with obstruction of justice."

"I do not think that word means what you think it means," I could hear a hint of humor in Dad's voice. I doubt the FBI guys, if that's who they were, caught it. "Nevertheless, I'm standing on my constitutional right to have my attorney present for any questioning," Dad insisted. "Shall I call him?"

"We have the authority here, and you'd better cooperate, or you're going to be looking at serious trouble," Wilson contended. "This is a matter of national security. You have no rights."

"No, sir, that's not correct," my father countered. "It is beyond your power to take away my rights for 'national security' or for any other reason." I heard one of the agents start to speak, but Dad cut him off. "You cannot take away my rights; you can only violate them. I trust you perceive the distinction? Now am I free to go, or am I under arrest?"

"Your attitude is going to get you in trouble," Wilson was saying as blue flashing lights illuminated the curtains. I heard a car door slam shut and the sound of creaking footsteps on our porch stairs.

"Good evening, gents." It was Sheriff Gunn. "What brings the Director's favorite special agents back to little ol' Sherman?"

"This is a federal investigation, Sheriff," Wilson replied. "We'll let you know when we require local assistance."

"Sure thing," the sheriff said with an amiable drawl. "Not meanin' to interfere or nothin', but your investigation might could proceed a bit more smoothly if y'all kept us locals informed. Otherwise, we locals might get a report of, say, a public disturbance on this otherwise quiet residential street. Then, of course, since we got nothin' better to do, this being a mighty peaceful little town, out we go for a look-see. And, well, here we all are."

"This situation is under control," Wilson said, an edge growing in his voice, "and we do not require your assistance."

"I surely can tell that," the sheriff said, "so this suspect here has consented to being questioned?"

"No, actually," Dad piped up. "I've exercised my right to an attorney."

"Oh," said the sheriff in what had to be mock surprise, "well then, I suppose these federal agents must have probable cause to arrest you. Funny, we locals tend to cuff 'em when we get us a suspect. Read the miscreant his rights. Guess you feds do things a bit differently?"

"This is outside your jurisdiction, Sheriff," Wilson said coldly. "Unless you'd like the governor to have a call from the Director."

"Now boys, this county is my jurisdiction, every bit as much as yours," Sheriff Gunn said. "If y'all got business here, why, go right on ahead. I ain't stopping you. As I see it, though, if this man don't want to talk with you, you either got to arrest him or let him go. Now, which is it gonna be?"

There was a long pause. "So help me, the governor is going to hear about this," Wilson said.

"He's mighty hard to get hold of these days, busy as he gets down there in Nashville," the sheriff said. "But, if you do manage to catch him, kindly remind him it's his turn to buy the beer next time he comes up here to Lee County lookin' for votes."

The FBI agents – if that's what they truly were – stormed off. I peeked out the window and saw them drive off in a white van.

"So," the sheriff was saying to my dad. "Seems your boy mighta bought himself a heap o' trouble."

"Now, Sheriff," Dad began amiably, "not that I'm ungrateful for your quick response to our little 'public disturbance,' but I just spent the last ten minutes refusing to answer any questions. You interested in an encore performance?"

"I suppose not," the sheriff said. "I can control my curiosity." He paused. "For now," he added. "Still, this has been the most excitement we've had around here in a good ol' while. What could your boy have done to twist their tails into crapping out this cyber-terror bullshit? With the feds poking about, I figure they'll be getting to the bottom of it right soon now, one way or another." There was another long pause. Dad was silent. The sheriff broke first. "You change your mind, you let me know, you hear? Tell that wife of yours I said, 'Hey.'"

"Will do. Thanks again, Sheriff," Dad said. "Good night." Sheriff Gunn left, and Dad came inside.

"Thank goodness for the enemies of my enemies," Dad said to Mom and me. Now that it was over, he looked tired and haggard, noticeably older than I was used to seeing him. "You got that video?" he asked me. We checked. The video wasn't great quality. The audio had some rustling noises from sliding in the fabric of Dad's pocket, but you could certainly hear the conversation clearly. "Let's get these to Mr. Burke." As he started burning the video to a CD, he told Mom, "Thanks for the call. The cavalry arrived in the nick of time."

"More like the other tribe of savages," Mom said.

"Oh, and Sheriff Gunn says 'hey,'" he told Mom.

"One makes hay while the sun shines," Mom observed. "Not in dark of night."

A couple of hours later, Dad's radio started to chatter, waking me. I stumbled sleepily down the stairs to find Mom and Dad in his study. "Amit says they're back. I replied, 'we know.' You can fill him in tomorrow."

* * *

Mr. Stinson let me and Amit use the debate room at lunchtime, so we were able to have a private conversation. I brought him up to speed on last night's visit, and he shared his discoveries.

"They were hunting these Nexus things," Amit explained. "They found some. Here's the report they sent in early this morning." He opened and unscrewed a pen, pulled out a small scroll of paper from one half, and passed it over to me. I read the small print:

Incident Report: Sherman Nexus (Category III)
Sherman, TN

Summary: *Completed Nexus Sweep of Sherman vicinity. Three low-level Nexuses detected. Unable to establish any link to unauthorized disclosure of Xueshu Quan technology management project. Continuing to Houston tomorrow to sweep for Nexuses there.*

Details: *Identified four Nexus locations in vicinity of Sherman, TN as part of continuing investigation of unauthorized disclosure of Xueshu Quan technology management investigation. The following locations show abnormally strong Nexus readings, but not rising to the level of a Category III Nexus.*

Tolliver Library: *the library associated with the local community college showed the strongest readings.*

Kudzu Joe's Coffee Shop: *a coffee shop near the county courthouse showed modest indications of a Nexus. Proprietor unable to provide useful information.*

A Private Residence: *we attempted to interview the owner, but the local sheriff interfered with our investigation. Owner out of state at time of Xueshu Quan incident, but no apparent connection.*

Berkshire Inn: *we stayed in this hotel previously. This is our current local base of operations, so readings are probably due to our own activities.*

Recommendations: *Investigate library for links to Xueshu Quan and other proscribed data.*

"We were thinking those Nexuses were places where things are happening to make a change or a difference in history," Amit noted. "This is consistent. They figured out exactly where we've been working."

"That's not good," I observed. "The EVIL minions were in a white van last night. They must have the Nexus detector in it."

"It's parked at our hotel, or was this morning," Amit clarified.

"Worse, they're totally on to us," I noted. "You might be able to get away, since they think the signature they're seeing at your hotel is due to their own presence. I wish we understood how this Nexus stuff worked."

"I've been thinking about that," Amit said. "A point of transition. A point of change. A Nexus happens when somehow, someone does something that's going to make a big change. It's history coming to a crossroads. But, what I don't get is how that tells them whether it's a change for the better or a change for the worse." He looked as confused as I felt.

"You need to stop doing any work at all at home," he insisted. "Any future work needs to take place at the hotel. Or maybe we can spread it around, work at different places so nothing gets localized. Maybe that will make the Nexus signature at your house fade and keep a new one from appearing."

He rolled up the message and stuck it back in the pen. "Keep it, I have a box of them," he said handing the pen to me. "Pass it on to your dad and uncle."

* * *

When I got home, we went through our usual ritual of closing the cell phones in the microwave. Then I shared Amit's intercept with Mom and Dad. "I'd figured as much," Dad said. "I told Rob about the events of last night, and I'll pass Amit's new information on to him. We need to stop working on this project of yours. It's become too dangerous. Our best bet is to hang tight, and hope everything blows over. I spent a good part of the day with Bob and Greg at their law office. They have the video of last night's encounter. Their investigator has been at work, looking into Xueshu Quan. They want to speak with us about it, so we'll arrange a meeting at their office next week."

"Once you headed off to college, your mom and I had planned on leaving this house and moving up to Robber Dell," Dad said, looking at Mom. She nodded. "Now, we're going to be making the move sooner, instead of later."

"What?" I was aghast. I'd spent my entire life in this house.

Dad smiled. "Yes, I know," he said paternally, "but you should never fall in love with anything that can't love you back – places or possessions. Rob's place is much safer than our house here in town, particularly if no one knows we're there. With Amit keeping an eye on EVIL and their minions, we'll have some warning before they make any move. Nevertheless, I think we're going to need to pull you from school at the end of the semester, if not sooner."

I was too shocked to speak.

"The important thing," Mom said to me, "is to make sure you're safe. And that means we can't have you going to school where they can get to you so easily." She'd been creeped out by the sheriff pulling me out of class. "I think we should take him from school now and not send him back," she was saying to Dad. "He's just coasting anyway – not taking any real classes. He can be working on college level material if we keep him home."

"Let him have his senior year," Dad insisted, "or as much of it as is safe. His shop, and drafting, and electronics classes will all stand him well in the future. A man should know how to build things with his hands. 'He who has a trade, has an estate.'"

"Amit's message said they're heading to Houston," Dad noted. "It's a big place. Lots happening. I figure it will take them a while to check it all out and get back to bother us again here. He can go to school tomorrow," Dad insisted to Mom. "Then we have Thanksgiving and our trip to Nashville."

Mom and Dad had been planning this second honeymoon for months. Now that they'd revealed their plan to go underground in the very near future, and remain there for an unknown length of time, I understood the new importance of this last fling.

"He can stay with Rob while we're gone," Dad observed. "We'll get an update from Amit, and decide whether he can safely go to school on Monday. He has a couple of weeks left. We'll let him finish out the semester and then we'll all vanish together up to Robber Dell."

Talk about a change in the course of history. I was about to lose my future. "But what about the spring semester?" I asked. "What about going off to college next year?"

"Maybe matters will have resolved themselves by then," Dad explained. "We'll see. But it's not safe for you now, living in the open where they can get to you. You're going with your uncle up to his place right after Thanksgiving. Pack what you need for a long stay. We'll be joining you when we get back, and then we'll decide whether you can go back to school Monday or vanish.

"We'll move in with Rob and live off the grid for a while up at his place," he explained. "Rob or one of his buddies can plant a false trail that we're all on the road together somewhere."

"I love your brother dearly for all he's done for us over the years," Mom told Dad, "but we are not moving into his double-wide and sharing his bachelor pad with him until you've built a proper house for us. I thought you planned on another trailer up there for us."

"Rob's place is more spacious than you might think," Dad said with an amused twinkle in his eye. I realized then he hadn't even told Mom anything about the construction project under Rob's new barn. "This is probably a slow week for him with the holidays and all. If he's going to be around tomorrow, you should drop by and see what he's been up to."

Mom could tell Dad was holding back something. "Very well," she yielded. "I suppose I could bake him some cookies," she added dryly. They both smiled far more than they should. Must have been a private joke.

"I figure we have a few days," Dad said. "With Thanksgiving coming up, they're unlikely to move this week. Feds can't hardly accomplish anything around a federal holiday.

"I know Rob will be glad to get you up there full time," Dad added. "He's been complaining that the fractional distilling isn't doing a good job with the noble gases, and he'd like you to try tweaking the process you designed.

"Rob is going to handle finishing up the Kreuger project for me," Dad explained, "and, I'm going to have to let him handle the liquid air business without me. I don't want to draw attention to it if someone is scrutinizing my activities. He'll probably be happy to have me handle all the office work involved. He can run the compressor rig as well as I can with as much practice as he's been getting the last few months. Rob'll be short-handed out in the field without me. He can call in some of his buddies, though."

"I know some guys at school who might be interested in helping him out weekends and after school," I offered. I was thinking of the shop rats. A few of those guys were real go-getters and handy with tools.

"Put them in touch with your uncle," Dad suggested. "But he'll probably be looking for more full-time help. I'll run Amit's note on to Rob. Thank Amit for me, and remind him to be careful when you see him tomorrow. I don't want him taking any risks either."

The EVIL minions were already gone. They'd departed earlier that day in their white van, and they were staying at another hotel in the Berkshire family. Amit traced them to Meridian, Mississippi. They had reservations for Houston for several days following that. Amit could keep track of them through the Berkshire Inn guest database. Somehow, he'd rejiggered their Berkshire Club account so they'd made "Double Platinum." They were getting deluxe treatment from the chain, free upgrades to suites, and the like. If he could keep them coming back to Berkshire Inns, we'd know exactly where they were and have a good shot at figuring out what they were doing.

If they were working through Thanksgiving, they must be serious. I hoped Dad was right about our having some time. At the very least, if things went south, we'd have some warning.

* * *

After Grandpa Jack died, Grandma Tolliver began inviting us over to her house for Thanksgiving. I got the impression the rest of the Tollivers were not too happy about it. They were all courteous enough, but it was the courtesy of a superior earning virtue by deigning to socialize with their inferiors. I normally just kept my mouth shut, returned the required courtesies, ate the delicious food, and practiced my best behavior and manners.

Mom, Dad, and I arrived at the appointed time on a cold Thanksgiving morning. The Tollivers' maid opened the door for us. "Hello, Miss! So good to be seeing you!"

"Hi Cookie!" Mom smiled. "So good to be seeing you, too."

"Come right on in," Cookie said. "Yo' momma's busy in the kitchen and she won't hardly let me help," she said to Mom. "You might could talk some sense into her so's we both could lend her a hand." I followed as Cookie led us to the kitchen. "Where's that sweet little girl o' yours?" Cookie asked Mom.

"She's spending Thanksgiving with her boyfriend's family," Mom explained.

"Hard to imagine her all grown up like that," Cookie said. "Why, I remember when she was knee-high to a grasshopper."

We passed the living room, where I saw Abby deeply intent, studying some papers. I decided I might as well get my obligatory annual exchange of greetings with her out of the way.

I let Mom and Dad continue to the kitchen in Cookie's wake, went in to the living room – or was it a "parlor?" – and I sat down in the chair right next to Abby. I figured my refusal to await her formal permission to join her and my flagrant assumption of equality in helping myself to the chair next to her might annoy her enough to cut short our exchange. Amit was becoming a bad influence on me when it came to using social tricks on people.

"Hello, Abby," I said with as much warmth as I could muster. She jerked with surprise. Must not have seen me. "Sorry to startle you," I added.

She set her papers down as far away from me as she could reach and turned them face down. Now I was curious. "Hi," she said. "I didn't hear you arrive." She must have been focused. That gong they called a doorbell would wake the dead.

"How's your school year going?" I asked, politely.

"I'm going with Shawn to the winter dance," she said smugly. Ah yes, unscrupulous Shawn from the debate team. His father was a lawyer, so he was socially acceptable in a way that Amit could never have been. Besides, he was buddies and debate partner with our cousin, David, Uncle Mike's son. "Shawn and David were telling me about how you and Amit lost to Sharon and Emma in the pre-season debate tournament," Abby continued.

"You win some, you lose some," I observed indifferently. I refused to be baited by Abby. I continued looking calmly at her. I spoke; it's your turn, Abby. The silence stretched on. Finally she broke.

"Shawn is getting a Porsche for Christmas," Abby offered.

Heh. Nice try. "Kinda takes the fun out of it if you know in advance what Santa's bringing you, don't you think?" I asked. Abby paused, clearly frustrated by her inability to get a rise out of me.

"Shawn said you and Amit gave up on debate and did Student Congress instead at the last tournament," Abby said. My, that girl just wouldn't give up probing for a weakness.

"Why haven't you tried out for debate, Abby?" I asked. "You'd be good at it."

"Debate is for..." Probably for losers or geeks or something else suitably derogatory for the likes of me. Only her lawyer-wannabe boyfriend was in debate, too. She caught herself in time to avoid the trap. "Well, it's not for me," she finished weakly.

Best to quit while I was ahead and before she figured out a way to actually score on me. I figured I'd spoken with her enough to fulfill the demands of courtesy toward my hosts, so I excused myself. As I left, I saw her grab her papers and continue reading them. What was she studying so intently?

Everyone else was in the kitchen – my folks, Grandma, Cookie, Uncle Larry, and Aunt Nikki. Uncle Mike, Mom's other brother, and his family were off elsewhere this year. I could make a meal off the snacks and appetizers Grandma had laid out – sausage cheese balls, chips and nacho dip, and she had dinner rolls that had been sliced, filled with ham, cheese, and a spicy brown mustard, and then baked. Grandma popped a new tray of a dozen small rolls out of the oven. I helped myself to a couple, steaming hot.

Uncle Larry was bragging to Dad about how even in a down market, Tolliver Corporation was doing better than the rest of the businesses in the sector.

"A large part of the cost of construction materials comes from transportation," Dad was saying. "The Gore Tax is only going to make Tolliver lumber more expensive to your customers."

"We're doing our part to help preserve our planet's future," Uncle Larry observed self-righteously. Ah, yes. It was actually the "Preserving our Planet's Future Act." Only climate deniers like Dad referred to it as the Gore Tax.

"Besides," Uncle Larry added, "lumber naturally sequesters carbon out of the air. I have it on good authority that the EPA will soon be recommending that lumber producers, like Tolliver, get carbon credits that will more than make up for the carbon taxes on the fuel."

Dad was shaking his head. "All that red tape doesn't help either the planet, or your business. You pay their extortion with one hand and get their kickbacks and rebates with the other. It only breeds more bureaucrats and makes it more difficult to do business."

"It's hardly the government's fault if poorly-capitalized small businesses aren't able to do their fair share to help the environment," Uncle Larry opined piously. Uncle Larry may have had a point, but even I could see he was just trying to bait Dad.

Grandma Tolliver interrupted whatever retort Dad was about to make by handing him a cup of coffee. "Here you go, son," she said, "hot and black, just the way you like it." I always got the impression Grandma Tolliver liked Dad. "If y'all will accompany me to the dining room," Grandma added, "Cookie is ready to serve our Thanksgiving dinner."

I saw Abby come into the dining room empty-handed, so I excused myself as everyone was settling into their places at the table. I headed down the hall to the bathroom. I spied Abby's papers on the coffee table where she must have left them. Unable to resist my curiosity any further, I took a peek. It was a print out of a web page – "Explaining How to Preserve Our Planet's Future to Your Crazy Right-Wing Uncle." Oh my. This was going to be an interesting dinner.

I washed my hands and returned to the dining room as everyone was taking their seats.

At the head of the table, Uncle Larry said Grace. Then, Cookie rotated around the table, removing the plate covers. Grandma Tolliver picked up her fork and took the first bite of dinner. That was my cue to dig in, although with much tinier and more dignified bites than I would ever have eaten at home. Cut three bites, eat three bites, and cut three more. Mom had pounded proper table manners into me.

Abby piped up proudly, "Our turkey was raised free-range right here in Lee County. It's locally-sourced, so we're doing our part to avoid unnecessary greenhouse emissions and protect our planet's future."

I saw a hint of a smile on Dad's face. He turned to Mom, "Please pass the butter, dear." He was going to bite on a buttered roll, not on the political point Abby dangled in front of him.

Abby was undeterred. "The Preserving Our Planet's Future Act prevented global catastrophe by committing the U.S. to targeted reductions in greenhouse gas emissions. We've slowed the growth in temperature almost to a standstill, but carbon dioxide levels are still rising and more must be done to roll back the damage of our past recklessness." There was a long and pregnant pause. Finally, Dad broke the silence.

"What delicious gravy, Mrs. Tolliver," Dad said with a hint of amusement in his voice.

"Oh, bless your heart," Grandma Tolliver said, "but Cookie is actually responsible for the gravy."

"Oh," Dad turned to Cookie, "Thank you, Cookie for all your hard work. The gravy is particularly delicious."

"You're welcome, sir, thank you" Cookie said to Dad as she continued topping off water and wine glasses around the table.

I could tell Abby was getting frustrated at her inability to engage Dad in a political discussion about climate change. "We need to dismantle the capitalist system and make sure business takes its proper role as the servant to social needs, if we're going to protect our planet's future."

Dad studiously ignored her. I caught Uncle Larry glance at Abby in smug approval. The rules of etiquette are clear. The head of the table has a responsibility to steer conversation away from adversarial or controversial topics, but Uncle Larry was standing by, letting his daughter take pot shots at Dad. I had come to expect that kind of subtle yet contemptuous discourtesy from Uncle Larry. Much as I understood the danger of climate change and the importance of environmental concerns, I was finding Abby's harping to be tedious and annoying.

Exasperated with her lack of success, Abby gave up her indirect approach and engaged Dad directly. "What do you think, Uncle?" she asked him.

"You're too young to remember it," Dad observed mildly, "but socialism was tried over and over, again and again in the twentieth century. We had the "National Socialism" of the Nazis in Germany, and the "International Socialism" of the Communists in Russia. Both flavors of socialism left destruction and death tolls that would have been unimaginable to folks a century ago."

"Real socialism has never been tried," Abby asserted. "Those were unsuccessful and flawed attempts."

"Would you say the Aztecs never practiced real human sacrifice," Dad asked dryly, "because they never did get their crops to grow reliably no matter how much blood they shed?" I could tell Uncle Larry was getting angry at Dad's brutal directness. Mom had put her hand on Dad's arm. Dad continued quickly, "But, let's not spoil this lovely meal with any more politics. How 'bout them Vols? Think they'll take the SEC this year?"

Tolliver Corporation had a skybox at Neyland stadium on the University of Tennessee campus in Knoxville. Uncle Larry liked little better than to talk about the football team. He took Dad's bait, describing some of "our" best plays in the most recent games as if he were on the field with the team. That effectively ended Abby's attempt to indoctrinate her crazy right-wing uncle.

The rest of the meal passed without incident.

After Cookie cleared the table, Aunt Nikki insisted Mom and Dad needed to come out back with Grandma to see Grandma's chrysanthemums. Abby followed along leaving me with Uncle Larry. "So, how is school going?" he asked me.

"Fine," I said, neutrally.

"Abby was telling me about your women's suffrage debate a couple of months ago," he added.

Did he think I cared that deeply about winning every debate? "You win some, you lose some," I said philosophically, getting better at it with practice.

"Did you know that the Tollivers and other key players in the Civic Circle are deeply involved in the women's rights movement?" he asked.

"Oh?" I was genuinely curious. "No, I didn't." I wondered where he was going with this.

"Not with women's suffrage per se," he clarified, "but more recently. We're funding women's studies on campuses across the country and given grants to any number of activist groups. What do you suppose feminism is all about?"

"Women's rights?" Now I was confused. "Equal pay for equal work? No discrimination on the basis of gender?"

"Not really." He seemed smugly amused at my apparent ignorance. "That's not why we pushed it or why it was done. The women's rights movement had three goals. First, it got women into the workplace where their labor could be taxed. Have you studied economics at all?"

"Not formally," I said, "but I've read a bit."

"If you increase the supply of something, what happens to the price?"

"All other things being equal," I qualified my answer, "the price goes down."

"That's right," he said as proudly as if I were a puppy who had learned to perform a trick at his command. "So, with more women entering the work force the supply of labor increases and wages are depressed. It becomes a self-perpetuating sociological construct. There's a whole study of how to implement social changes that once implemented cannot be reversed – it's called a sociological ratchet. Things like women's suffrage, women's rights, Social Security, and many of the best, most progressive ideas are all policies that once implemented, can never be reversed. That's by design.

"Now couples need to have two careers to support a typical modern lifestyle. We can't tax the labor in a home-cooked meal. We can tax the labor in takeout food, or the higher cost of a microwave dinner. The economic potential of both halves of the adult population now largely flows into the government where it can serve noble social ends instead of petty private interests."

I wasn't sure whether to be appalled or amazed at the way he so casually considered commanding and controlling other peoples' lives. These were certainly some ideas I'd never considered before. "That's very interesting, sir." I decided to remain non-committal and see what else he might share. "You said there were three reasons for feminism?"

"Yes," he said, apparently interpreting my interest as approval. "The second reason is to get children out of the potentially anti-social environment of their homes and into educational settings where we can be sure they get the right values and learn the right lessons to be happy and productive members of society. Working mothers need to send their children to day care and after-school care where we can be sure they get exposed to the right lessons, or at least not to bad ideas."

"Many families homeschool, though," I pointed out, "and there are still many mothers, like mine, who stay at home. Mom put me and my sister, Kira, to work at chores around the house after school, made sure we picked up after ourselves and took care of ourselves, learned to do laundry and cook, and do dishes."

"Yes," Uncle Larry acknowledged. "That is a weakness. But, we're even now implementing a solution to it. It's going to be called "Common Core." We're going to tie together all the states and their educational systems to a single set of curricular standards, and we'll require homeschooled students meet the same standards. We're going to mandate testing to exactly quantify student performance to be sure no child gets left behind and identify problem schools and problem teachers."

I was confused. "That sounds like a good thing," I noted. "Quantify performance and hold public schools accountable for their failures."

Uncle Larry smiled smugly. "Oh, it is, but you should never consider a policy based only on its first-order effects. You have to look past that at the second-order consequences, too. Teachers will be evaluated on their performance based on how well their students do on their tests. So, what will happen?"

"They will be motivated to do their best to do a good job teaching their students." It still wasn't making sense to me.

"They will spend all their time teaching students how to optimize test scores to the exclusion of anything outside the officially approved curriculum, making sure they stay precisely focused on the officially sanctioned lessons," Uncle Larry clarified. "But, that's not the real benefit."

"I still don't get it," I confessed.

"What happens when they run out of time? When they are already teaching their poor little hearts out, and their students' test scores are still questionable, and the raise they were hoping for isn't going to happen unless their students become more proficient?"

I was still drawing a blank. Uncle Larry enlightened me. "They are going to assign homework to their students: enough homework to guarantee that even elementary school students are spending all their spare time doing homework. Their poor parents, eager to see that Junior stays up with the rest of the class, will be spending all their time helping their kids get incrementally more proficient on the tests we have designed. They'll be too busy doing homework to pick up on any anti-social messages at home."

"Homework in elementary school?" The notion seemed ridiculous to me. Except for the occasional project, I didn't even begin to get homework until I was in ninth grade or so. Even now, in high school, I was usually able to complete all my homework in spare moments while in other classes or during breaks.

"Of course it seems peculiar to you," Uncle Larry acknowledged. "You're not accustomed to it, but it's coming: slowly, gradually, bit by bit, until parents and children alike are used to the concept and take it for granted."

That sounded spooky. It reminded me of Dad's parable of the frogs in the slowly boiling water. I carefully kept my unease off my face and focused on looking interested and engaged.

"Children will be too busy to learn independence at home," Uncle Larry continued, "too busy to do chores, to learn how to take care of themselves, to be responsible for their own cooking, cleaning, and laundry. Their parents will have to cater to their little darlings' every need, and their little darlings will be utterly dependent on their parents. When the kids grow up, they will be used to having someone else take care of them. They will shift that spirit of dependence from their parents, to their university professors, and ultimately to their government. The next generation will be psychologically prepared to accept a government that would be intrusive even by today's relaxed standards – a government that will tell them exactly how to behave and what to think. Not a Big Brother government, but a Mommy-State."

Uncle Larry was getting on a roll now – animated and excited. I got the impression he didn't get to open up like this often. It was fascinating – albeit in a deeply disturbing sort of way. I didn't have trouble continuing to look interested and engaged. He continued taking my interest as an indication of receptiveness to his ideas, and he kept on describing his schemes.

"Eventually, we may even outlaw homeschooling as antisocial, like our more progressive cousins in Germany already do," he noted. "Everyone must know their place in society and work together for social good, not private profit."

"And, that brings us to the third and most important reason why the Tollivers in particular and other key players in the Civic Circle are big supporters of women's rights: sustainability.

"A free and rapidly-growing economy could be tolerated when we had a frontier to fill. But, the Earth can't accommodate many more people at a reasonable standard of living. We're running out of resources. We have to manage and control our population. That's the real motive behind the women's movement.

"Once a women's studies program convinces a gal she's a victim of patriarchal oppression, how likely is it she's going to overcome her indoctrination to be able to bond long enough with a guy to have a big family? If she does get careless with a guy, she'll probably just get an abortion.

"And even if she avoids anti-male indoctrination, there's plenty of social pressure to turn most gals into COGs." Uncle Larry looked expectantly at me.

Cogs? That made no sense. Uncle Larry was clearly waiting for me to take his bait, so I did. "Cogs?"

"Career-Oriented Gals," he explained, smugly. "COGs. All those COGs are too busy seeking social approval and status at the office to be out starting families and raising kids. They're encouraged to have fun, be free spirits, and experiment with any man who catches their fancy. Makes the office much more decorative too, if you get my meaning," he said with a smirking grin. I was creeped out, but kept a poker face.

"And by the time all those COGs are in their thirties and ready to try to settle down and have kids, they're past their prime. Their fertility peaks in their twenties. It's all downhill from there.

"Try starting a family in your mid-thirties, and you'll be lucky to crank out more than a couple kids, if that. Get a taste of what Common Core will require of you, and your enthusiasm for more kids will be completely sapped out.

"In another generation, we'll have implemented our own version of China's One-Child-Per-Couple policy without the nasty forced abortions and other hard repressive policies which people hate. What's more, there'll be fewer couples because so many young people will just be hedonistically screwing each other instead of settling down and making families. Makes me wish I were young again, like you, to take full advantage of it," he leered. "The net effect is we'll enter the great contraction and begin shrinking our population to more controllable levels. Already much of the Western world is at break-even or below. Our demographic trends would already be in decline if not for immigration.

"It's profoundly ironic," he observed with obvious amusement. "A strong, independent woman is now one who meekly obeys the media's and society's clamor to be a career girl and sleep around with whatever stud catches her fancy or with other girls, for that matter. A woman with the courage to defy that social pressure and devote herself from a young age to building a home and raising a family is an aberration, a weirdo, a traitor to her sex. There aren't many women with the balls to stand up against that kind of social pressure. It's not in their nature."

I was appalled and stunned in equal measure. I remained silent, trying to soak all this in, and make sense of it.

"I suppose you wonder why I would be telling you all this," he finally added.

"Well, yes, I am curious," I acknowledged.

"First off," he explained, "no one would believe you. And, if word got out that you had betrayed my trust, I would not only deny this conversation every took place, I'd also see to it that there were," he paused ominously, "consequences. If you are wise, you will keep everything I've told you to yourself. Don't even tell your parents.

"But more importantly, the reason I'm telling you this is that there's a new age beginning. The old ways of rapid growth are over. They have to end if we're to protect our planet's future and survive as a species. There's a new social order emerging: a more stable and sustainable society in which everyone will know their place.

"Your father is an admirable man in many ways," Uncle Larry generously acknowledged. "There aren't many men who could steal the heart of a Tolliver and have the balls to move right here to the center of our power and make it stick. Although he'd never have been successful without your mother's backing. It takes a Tolliver to beat a Tolliver. With her help, he did. I admit it. But, he's the last of a dying breed. The last of the great individualists. The last of the self-made men, pulling themselves up by their bootstraps.

"Your father may be a remarkable man, but he's hopelessly naïve. Conservatives like him think that progressives and liberals are too stupid to realize the consequences of our policies – how our policies perpetuate the very poverty and inequality we profess to despise. We're seventy years into Social Security for all, and we're forty years into a War on Poverty. We've taken trillions of dollars from the productive – money that could have been used to build new businesses and make new opportunities for the poor – and yet we have no less poverty to show for it than when we started. The great twentieth-century communist experiment failed miserably and left millions of corpses in its wake, yet we're taking our country down the same socialist path."

I was puzzled. "But, if socialism doesn't work, and you know socialism doesn't work, then why would you support it?"

"Why do most people support it?" he clarified. "Emotional reasons. It feels good to think you are helping people particularly if it's with other people's money. All gain, no pain. It feels comforting to have the approval of your herd. It feels good to be patted on the head by the media, the government, and the people in power and authority. It feels good to be told what a special little snowflake you are for being able to parrot back the progressive ideas we've force-fed into you.

"Most socialists support socialism for irrational and emotional reasons. In that sense, your father is right that they're stupid. Furthermore, because most socialists come to their political positions for emotional reasons, to feel good about themselves, that's precisely why socialists perceive conservatives as evil. Who is going to be the more motivated to triumph in a political battle: the side who thinks their opponents are mistaken, or the side that thinks their opponents are evil? But, I digress...

"Those aren't the real reasons the elite advocate socialism. The actual reason the Tollivers and the rest of the Civic Circle support socialism is because it will inevitably lead to a sustainable, low-growth or no-growth society with ourselves running the show. The Civic Circle wants stability and sustainability above all, in a controlled fashion, with us in charge, shepherding the ignorant masses, implementing our vision of social justice, and crushing any threat to our elite position in society. We're deeply conservative in our own way," he added wryly, "only what we want to conserve is ourselves and our positions in the elite without having to fight off every interloper with ambition and new ideas.

"A truly capitalist or free-market society is inherently unstable," Uncle Larry explained. "You can't have safety or stability when some upstart can put you out of business at any time by offering something better at a lower price, destroying the work of generations.

"That's precisely why we champion economic controls as the antidote for global warming. Maybe there's a crisis, maybe not, but never let a crisis go to waste. Of course, we know that carbon taxes and controls impose a huge drag and cost on the economy. Those negative impacts are precisely what our policies are designed to create: a low-growth, sustainable future with us in charge and no one to threaten our position." Uncle Larry seemed shockingly cynical about environmentalism. Maybe I should reconsider what Dad had been arguing all along?

"I'm getting off topic again," Uncle Larry confessed, with a smug smile. "The danger the Tolliver family and with all elites face is that we get inbred. It's called assortative mating. We and the rest of the elites send our elite children to our elite schools where elite ideas are pounded into their skulls and they become proficient at elite thinking. They meet other elites and eventually breed elite little babies to pick up the torch and continue upholding their family's position in the elite. It's self-defeating. Even within the Civic Circle there are cycles and currents and some elites are more elite than others. My grandfather, Ol' Tom Tolliver, got the family connected with the Civic Circle back during the Great Depression. He helped the Civic Circle and the New Deal Brain Trust bring prosperity to the hicks and hillbillies of eastern Tennessee through great public works projects like the Smoky Mountain National Park, the Tennessee Valley Authority, and the Oak Ridge Lab. Then, my father got us in the door as junior members in the Civic Circle. However, there's an inner circle that calls the shots. It can take generations to get in position, but a few careless heirs failing to live up to their responsibilities, and a family can slip out, without even realizing it. Oh, any family with the wealth and position to get in would still be comfortable enough for a good long while, but they'd no longer have the power to control events and look out for their interests.

"I'm thinking ahead to the next generation of Tollivers," Uncle Larry said with the conviction of a man on a mission. "I'm thinking of who will not only maintain our position in the elite but also push the family to the very top of the Civic Circle. Your mother is a Tolliver, and your father brought new blood, new energy into the family. Our family," he emphasized, "yours and mine.

"You can be a key player in pushing the family to the next level. You have a choice. You can be part of the problem, or you can be part of the solution," Uncle Larry offered with a hint of menace in his voice. I could hear the veiled threat.

I realized Uncle Larry must think my reticence was all about the fallout from Dad marrying Mom. He had no idea that the animosity on Dad's part stretched back to the loss of the Oak Ridge farm that ultimately broke Dad's grandfather, and to how the family homestead had been stolen for Great Smoky Mountain National Park. I'd just been made the proverbial offer I couldn't refuse. Or else. I decided I'd best be friendly, but non-committal.

"That's a very generous offer, sir," I said earnestly, "but I'm planning on going to Georgia Tech and majoring in either physics or electrical engineering. It's probably too late to get an application lined up for one of the top Eastern schools. Wouldn't I need to major in sociology or something like that?" He seemed to take my assent as a buy-in to his schemes.

"I know who to call. I could get you in most anywhere on my say-so. It pains a Harvard man to admit it," Uncle Larry acknowledged, "but you'll probably get a better education at Georgia Tech. Too many scions of the elite start to believe our own propaganda and can't see the truth behind the tales we tell the masses. You'll get a better, more demanding education studying at Georgia Tech. You'll learn logical thinking and analysis with less propaganda. Then you can finish off with a business degree, and take your place at Tolliver Corporation. You might even end up in my job someday.

"Besides, I think you'll find the times they are a-changing, even at Georgia Tech," he added cryptically. "I can't say any more. We shouldn't let one misunderstanding between our branches of the family so long ago stand between us." He offered his hand with apparent magnanimity as if we were about to seal a deal. I reflexively took his hand, and instantly regretted it, feeling as if he'd cornered me.

Jump in little froggy, Uncle Larry was telling me. The water's just fine. "You've given me a lot to think about, sir," I said. "I appreciate your openness and your offer."

"You can take your time," Uncle Larry said, "for now. Mull it over. Soon, though, you'll reach a point where you'll have to decide on which side you stand: on the right side of history with your family and the future, or on the side of a failed, archaic, and dying ideology."

Mom and Dad came in as Uncle Larry finished up. Only then did I realize that the chrysanthemums had been a ploy.

Uncle Larry had put Aunt Nikki up to distracting Mom and Dad so Uncle Larry could make his pitch to me in private. How devious of him.

We all engaged in the usual small talk before heading home.

So much of what Uncle Larry said made a lot of sense. I could see pieces falling into place. He had given me a glimpse of a structure, a pattern in human events that I had never perceived before. It was too big for me to keep to myself. I hadn't given my word to Uncle Larry to keep his secrets. I told Mom and Dad about the peculiar conversation on the way home. "I think I'm being recruited for the dark side," I said jokingly.

Mom was shocked, "Anyone who tells an underage boy to keep secrets from his parents is trying to take advantage of you – to cut you off from sources of support and security."

Dad was equally taken aback. "I'd never thought of it that way, before," he acknowledged. "I just assumed liberals were naïve and muddle-minded. It never occurred to me that there might be a deliberate method to their madness. But, it makes sense. In any socialist utopia, there's a 'nomenklatura,' a caste that occupies key positions and call the shots. And, it usually becomes hereditary as society becomes static and stratified. You have to have the advantage of parents in the nomenklatura to land positions in the right schools and to secure the right opportunities."

"That's got to be it," Mom added. "The claim that a no-growth/low-growth economy is necessary to save the planet is hogwash. I'm surprised a man as smart as Uncle Larry would truly believe that. I told you how the doomsayers of the 1970s were completely overtaken and overturned by events. In a free economy, people react to scarcity by devising ways to use less, to recycle, and to find substitutes," Mom noted.

"I must have missed that discussion," Dad noted.

"You were sleeping at the time, dear," Mom told him.

"Wouldn't that be a self-fulfilling prophesy, Mom?" I asked.

"How do you mean?," she asked me.

"What if you hobbled the free market? What if you kept it from devising clever solutions to resource shortages? Then you truly would have just the kind of economic malaise the doomsayers predict. Maybe that's exactly what they want to achieve with their social engineering." The thought was sobering.

Mom agreed. "It makes more sense to me that Larry sees socialism and environmentalism as excuses to control society for the family's benefit. He advocates regulations that keep interlopers from overthrowing the Tollivers' business with clever innovations and hard work," Mom explained.

By then we were home. Mom and Dad had been planning their second honeymoon in Nashville for a while, just the two of them. They hadn't taken a vacation like that since Kira was born. Uncle Rob showed up while they were changing into more casual clothes.

Mom looked thoughtful as she came down the stairs. "I have to wonder if the Civic Circle is tied into this physics business you've uncovered in some obscure way," Mom speculated. "Didn't you say that Xueshu Quan translated as Academic Circle?"

I hadn't made that connection before.

Then, Mom looked at me. "I'm uneasy about this. First, we have one 'circle' trying to hide the truth and threatening you for looking into it. Now, another 'circle' is trying to recruit you. Your father and I ought to stay," she said wistfully.

"We've already discussed this," Dad countered with a patient smile. "It's unlikely anything will happen. If it does, we should have a fair bit of warning. In any event, our son is far safer with Rob than with us here at home. Larry is just being Larry. Nothing to worry about. He's trying to avenge his family's loss of you by luring our son to the Tolliver cause.

"You've been talking about this trip for weeks," Dad continued. "We have the plans and reservations, and I'm not inclined to let myself get pushed around or spooked. When we get back, we'll figure out the next steps." He laughed, took Mom, and led her through some dance moves culminating in a spin and a deep dip.

"Very well," Mom agreed with a smile.

Dad turned to me. "We'll have to talk more when we get back," Dad said. "Until then, remember the lesson of the hypnotist. Be honest with yourself. Know your limits and the difference between right and wrong. Don't let yourself be a frog to be boiled up in Uncle Larry's pot."

Uncle Rob and I wished them well and said good bye. He backed his truck up into the garage. It appeared to be loaded – the bed was covered in a tarp.

"What's in the truck?" I asked, my curiosity getting the better of me.

"Nothing yet," Uncle Rob answered. After he closed the garage door, he pulled off the tarp exposing some boxes. They were all empty. "But, there will be something when we leave. Only, it won't be obvious to a casual observer since the truck looked loaded when I arrived." We gathered up a load of books and valuables from the house, filled the bed, and covered it with the tarp. I grabbed the bags I'd packed of my stuff in preparation for an extended stay. He had me ride on the passenger side floorboard of the truck "just in case anyone's watching." I was not looking forward to life as a fugitive, getting around like that.

When we got up to Robber Dell, he pulled the truck into his new barn – a steel-framed, steel-sided structure on the concrete pad where we'd eaten barbeque at the big Independence Day party. It was mostly empty except for a built-out section along one side, a couple of tractors and equipment, and now Uncle Rob's truck. The built-out section had two doors to the rest of the garage – one to a bathroom, and the other to a small living room. It made a small, but comfortable, living quarters. The bathroom actually had two entrances – one to the rest of the built-out living area, and the other to the garage. I assumed the idea was that anyone working in the barn could use the bathroom without trooping through the living room.

We unloaded the truck and stored the contents in the... bathroom? "No," Uncle Rob said at one point. "Nothing on the counter or in the tub. Put everything on the floor and make sure nothing's leaning against the wall." I followed his curious instructions. Apparently, I was allowed to stick some boxes on the toilet. Go figure.

There wasn't much empty space in the bathroom by the time we were done. Uncle Rob left to go to his trailer "for the benefit of anyone watching." I waited for him in the living room. A couple of minutes later he popped up from under a sofa cushion. "Tunnel," he explained.

Then we crowded into the little bit of open space left in the bathroom. He closed the door, and he flicked the lights on and off a few times. The walls and counters appeared to start rising before I realized that the floor was actually sinking. We came to rest about a dozen feet down. The toilet was still attached to the floor, but the bathtub now dangled up above us, along with the counter and sink.

"Does that toilet actually work?" I asked.

"Yup," he confirmed, proudly. "Flexible coupling."

We unloaded the boxes and Uncle Rob sent the bathroom back up on its hydraulic lift. The ingenious bathroom was the highlight of the refuge. The rest of the place was under construction and clearly needed lots of work to complete the build out. Uncle Rob set me up with a cot in one of the unfinished cargo containers. My new room had steel walls and a plywood floor. It was spacious, but long and skinny – not a very efficient layout for a room.

* * *

Friday morning, I got up early and worked on my scholarship essays, and on applications for a few schools with later deadlines. Maybe I was a sure thing to get into whatever school I wanted, with a little bit of help from Uncle Larry. Best not to take any chances, though. I had excellent test scores, but many of the top universities claimed not to weight them very heavily. They used "holistic" admissions criteria designed to yield "better-rounded candidates" and a "more diverse student body." Dad said admissions deans wouldn't want to unfairly deny the academically unqualified, but financially well-off, future alums a shot at filling the tuition coffers. He could be awfully sarcastic sometimes.

Uncle Rob gave me a tour of the refuge when he woke up. "Your mother will not want to share a bathroom with me," he said with a smile, "so our priority will be to finish the second bathroom for you and your folks." First, however, he had an errand he had to run. I'd been planning on hanging out with Amit this weekend, so Uncle Rob agreed to pass the word on to Amit that I'd be unavailable.

I stayed in the refuge working on my essays. It was almost spooky being by myself. The refuge was absolutely silent except for the occasional sound of the ventilation running. I turned on my music to mask the eerie silence. Clack click clack click. Clack clack click clack. Clack click clack click. Clack clack click clack. The static burst through the music in an insistent, rhythmic staccato pattern out of time with my music. Must have been noise on the electrical system. I gave up and turned it off.

Saturday, Rob and I worked on finishing the bathroom. I'd never done much plumbing, so it was interesting to see how it was done and to do some of it myself. Just after lunch, however, Rob's ham radio burst out into Morse code. I still hadn't learned Morse, but the real message lay in the time and the frequency. Uncle Rob checked against the code sheet. It was a message from Amit. "Imminent danger. Stay put. On the way." Great. Now what?

"Get ready to go," Uncle Rob told me. He dashed out of the room.

I grabbed my go-bag – a small duffle bag that Uncle Rob had insisted I have ready at all times. It had some essential outdoors gear, a change of clothes, some water, and a couple days of food. I heard the distinctive sound of a magazine being loaded into a pistol as I was lacing my hiking boots. He came back a minute later carrying the case for his AR-15 rifle and a black messenger bag. "Should I bring my pistol?" I asked.

"Bring it topside, just in case. If you haven't been directly implicated, though," Uncle Rob explained, "that pistol will only get you into more trouble, if not killed. Your best bet if you run into those EVIL feds is to keep quiet and play dumb, not try to fight it out.

"In any event, you're not coming with me," Uncle Rob insisted. "I promised your folks I'd keep you safe. You'll either stay here, or if this place has been compromised, I might send you with Amit to hide out at his hotel or take you someplace else myself."

"Your folks are probably in danger, and I may have to go get them from Nashville, or arrange a safe place for them to hide out there, until I can bring them back here. Let's see what Amit has to say."

We rode the bathroom elevator up to the barn. I followed Uncle Rob through the tunnel from the barn to the trailer where we waited for Amit. Uncle Rob didn't want Amit or anyone else to know about the refuge unless absolutely necessary.

Amit arrived. "Tolliver Library is sealed off. I passed by on my way here," he explained. "The sheriff and the state troopers have a perimeter around it already. On the radio, they're saying it's a chemical spill of some kind." He passed several sheets of paper to Uncle Rob and me.

"The EVIL minions in Houston," Amit explained. "They had a breakthrough, they're heading this way, and they're after your dad and Mr. Burleson." He passed Uncle Rob and me his intercept.

FLASH – CRITICAL REPORT:
Sherman Nexus (Category V)
Sherman, TN

Summary: *Category V Repeat Category V Nexus. Tolliver Library associated with supercritical outbreak of proscribed knowledge. We are securing Tolliver Library* *using local law enforcement. Technology Containment team dispatched to Tolliver Library, will arrive Sunday morning. Primary and Secondary Targets identified - vector between Xueshu Quan and Tolliver Library. Strike team dispatched to apprehend and interrogate targets.*

Details: *Tolliver Library in Sherman, TN, contains multiple examples of proscribed knowledge. See attached list.*

"I got their book list, too." Amit said quietly. "It's incredible. The physics books are only the tip of the iceberg." I continued reading. The report identified Mr. Burleson as the "Primary Target" and Dad as the "Secondary Target."

Primary Target purchased credit card associated with VOIP call to Xueshu Quan leak vector. Identification confirmed from sales clerk.

"It was the VOIP call," Amit explained. "That's how they got us. They traced the phone number to the credit card Mr. Burleson bought and gave to your dad. He paid cash, but they traced the credit card to the store, and someone remembered Mr. Burleson." Amit looked grim. "He must have been a regular customer."

IP address associated with Primary Target linked to online searches related to Heaviside suppression effort. Primary Target confirmed to be present in Houston at time of Xueshu Quan leak.

"Dad was planning on meeting Mr. Burleson at some big trade show there in Houston," I explained. "That's why they think Mr. Burleson must be the one who got the list from Nicole."

It was my fault. I may have killed Dad and Mr. Burleson. Because I didn't want to be rude to a girl, I inadvertently betrayed them both.

Secondary Target is owner of private residence at which a Nexus was previously identified. Secondary Target is a business associate of Primary Target.

Recommendations:

Arrest and Interrogate Targets Immediately: *the severity of the Nexus demands that the targets be arrested, interrogated, and terminated immediately to avoid any further risk or damage.*

Send Technology Containment Team to Tolliver Library: *Library should be secured immediately by local authorities until our Technology Containment Team can arrive Sunday morning to secure the Tolliver Library collection and assess the extent of the potential leak of proscribed knowledge.*

"We have to warn Mom and Dad and Mr. Burleson," I insisted.

"If we do it directly," Uncle Rob cautioned, "it will lead right back to us. Observe, orient, decide, and then act. Let's finish with observing and orienting, then we'll decide and act."

I looked over his shoulder as Rob scanned the list Amit had printed out of all the proscribed books from the Tolliver Library. It was nearly two pages long. A half dozen or so of the entries were the physics books with the anomalous edits Amit and I had already found. But the rest were a diverse lot of books from a seemingly random and unconnected set of subjects – like *Spring Heeled Jack: The Devil of Devonshire*. Another was *Suan Ming or the Art of Chinese Fortune Telling* by Angus McGuffin. There was *Mystery Airships of the Gilded Age*, and *A History of China from the Earliest Days to the Present* by John Macgowan. What possible connection could there be between all these books and bouncing waves? Tip of the iceberg, indeed. Amit and I had spent half a year working on physics books and missed ninety-five percent or more of the secrets hidden in the library. It was about way more than just physics.

Amit interrupted my train of thought. "EVIL got their panties in a wad about that "Xueshu Quan" list of physics books. This is easily twenty times more secrets," he said, grappling with the enormity of it. "They'd go nuclear over this, if they realized we had their list."

"Not only do we have the list, we have all those books, right there in town," Uncle Rob noted ruefully. "Only, the sheriff and the state troopers have them all locked up in the library behind a police barricade. We can't get through. And tomorrow morning, EVIL's going to grab all the secrets and make off with them."

"Maybe," I said thoughtfully. "Maybe not." I explained how the shop rats had shown me how to get into the steam tunnels under the campus, and how to avoid the alarms and sensors. "We went right past the library on one of our trips."

"You got in?" asked Uncle Rob, with a gleam in his eye.

"No, but there's a door labelled 'Library Building.' I didn't try it. It's probably locked, but if we got past the door, we'd be in the basement of the library. The first floor is likely where they'd have any motion sensors or security sensors. It's just the circulations desk, periodicals, journals, and some reading rooms. We could go up the stairs from the basement to the second and third floors and scan all these books. If they aren't going to be there until Sunday noon, we have plenty of time. We can get in on the far side of the quad behind the Physical Science Building. Even if they set up a perimeter, I bet that's far enough away that we can get in unseen."

"I can get us through a locked door," Rob assured us. He looked thoughtful for a moment and then gave us our orders. "Here's what we're going to do. First, I have to take care of getting your folks and Jim Burleson to safety. I'll have to run off, and make some calls and arrangements on a burner phone."

"A what?" I asked.

"A phone I purchased anonymously, so it can't be traced back to me," Uncle Rob explained. "You know where your scanner gear is in the barn?"

He meant in the refuge. "Yes," I said.

He looked as though he were weighing a decision. "Run on over there," he said, gesturing to the door. Ah! He didn't want Amit to know about the tunnel or the refuge. "Get your book scanner gear together," he directed me. "Amit, brew a pot of coffee and fill a thermos." He reached into a cupboard and pulled out a thermos for Amit. "Bring extra batteries for the laptop and flashlights – there might not be power. You two meet me by the science building near the Tolliver Library in about an hour." He looked at me again. "You'll need to ride on the passenger floorboard again, I'm afraid. I don't want anyone seeing you." I nodded in agreement.

"Plan A – we take our time, scan all the books on EVIL's list and replace them, with none the wiser," Uncle Rob explained. "It will be a late night, but we can be long gone before morning, with none the wiser. Plan B – if we don't have time for Plan A, we grab the books and run. Saddle up, boys; we're going on a raid."

Uncle Rob headed out the door and roared off in his truck. I left Amit brewing coffee in the trailer, grabbed the book scanner and my laptop from the refuge, and rejoined Amit in the trailer just as he was filling the thermos.

We made sure we had everything we would need. In my backpack, I had a laptop, batteries, the book scanner, and the wireless motion sensor. In addition to Amit's thermos of coffee, we filled a canteen of water, and gathered up some snacks. We were ready to pull an all-nighter to get the books all scanned before EVIL's "Technology Containment Team" could sweep in tomorrow and collect them all.

The science building was comfortably outside the perimeter the sheriff had set up. We met Uncle Rob parked around back of the science building. "Your folks are OK," he reassured me. "They've got Kira with them, and they're going to stay with a buddy of mine in Nashville. I'll figure out how to get them back in a couple of days." He paused, a cold, hard, look on his face. "But, Mr. Burleson is dead."

I froze. Amit and I took in the news. "How'd it happen?" I finally asked.

"It was all over the news on the radio," Uncle Rob explained. "'Cyber-terrorist shot while resisting arrest.'"

"They just shot him?" Amit looked horrified. "I thought they wanted to interrogate him first."

"Tough to say," Uncle Rob replied in a solemn, level voice. "Something like that goes down, adrenalin's running high, the suspect twitches or dodges in surprise, and it's interpreted as an attempt to draw a gun. Might never know exactly." He shouldered his messenger bag. "One thing's for sure – these books of yours better be worth the death toll they're leaving in their wake."

"My folks, and Kira? Are they going..." I began.

"They're safe," Uncle Rob assured me, "and if you want to keep the rest of us safe, you'll need to stay focused on getting us in, getting the job done, and getting out."

The three of us walked over to a metal panel on the sidewalk. Uncle Rob casually surveyed our surroundings. "We're clear," he pronounced. "Go!"

The shop rats had shown me how to construct a custom tool that grabbed on to the corner of the metal plate. The plates were supposed to be latched shut, but many of the access plates had latches – like this one – that were old and no longer worked properly. We'd used this particular entrance before, so I knew it was loose.

I slid my tool under the corner, pulled it up, and grabbed the sharp corner with my gloved hand. I gently opened the hatch on the sidewalk and climbed down the ladder into the dark tunnel. Amit handed the backpacks down to me, then crawled down the ladder, followed by Uncle Rob. Uncle Rob carefully shut the hatch behind us with a muted clank.

We switched on dim red LED lights to preserve our night vision, and we surveyed our surroundings. The low, distant hum of the ventilation gently pushed warm musty air past us. The ceiling of the concrete tunnel formed a familiar sidewalk on the surface. If you noticed the characteristic look of the steam tunnel sidewalks, it was easy to spot them from above ground. Many of the characteristic ventilation openings were disguised as brick benches alongside the sidewalk. The periodic metal access hatches in the middle of the sidewalks were dead giveaways. Once the shop rats had pointed it out to me, it was easy to see the pattern and the logic of the tunnel layout around campus. The tunnels converged at the steam plant, which sent steam coursing through the pipes and into radiators all over campus during the winter months. The tunnels also carried electrical, phone, and data lines throughout campus. One branch of the tunnel system next to the Administration Building had some kind of alarm sensor. If we blundered through the area, we'd set it off and have a couple of the sheriff's deputies converging on us. We'd be avoiding that branch today.

"Follow me," I said softly. I led Uncle Rob and Amit slowly, quietly, through the tunnel. At each intersection, Uncle Rob took the lead and peered around the corner with a small mirror. Once he confirmed it was clear, he'd motion me to take the lead again. A few twists and turns and the equivalent of several blocks later, I guided Amit and Uncle Rob to a yellow door labelled "Tolliver Library," secured by a deadbolt. Uncle Rob smiled. He snaked a fiber optic borescope under the door. "Room's clear," he pronounced. He pulled a string to bend the borescope back toward the door, and examined it carefully from the other side. "Sloppy," was his verdict. "No sensors on the door. They're not worried about anyone getting in this way. I think I can open it without setting off any alarms. It's looking like Plan A – we should have time to do the scanning and get everything back in place before EVIL arrives.

"Your dad told me all about your book scanner skills," Uncle Rob told us. "You guys gather up the books from EVIL's list on the second floor, and then get the rest of the books from the third floor. Set up on the third floor to scan them. They'll likely be coming up the elevators to check out the second floor first. Working on the third floor will give you the maximum time to escape. " He handed me a radio. "If you hear two clicks, the bad guys are coming. Signal back with two clicks to let me know you got my message. Then get your stuff together and haul ass down the stairs to the basement.

Take as many books as you can, particularly the unscanned ones, but don't delay – take only what you can carry quickly. I'll meet you here at the door to the steam tunnel. If you hear one click, all is well. Wait a minute and signal back with one click to let me know you are OK. I'm going to set up that wireless motion sensor, scout around the perimeter, and confirm we didn't set off any alarms. The deputies are right outside, so if they come in, we won't have much time. I also want to bypass the security system so we don't inadvertently trigger an alarm. When I'm done, I'll send you a single click on the radio, and I'll come check in to see how you're doing on the third floor."

Amit held a light in his gloved hand to illuminate the lock. Uncle Rob pulled out a set of fine picks and began to deftly manipulate the lock. I could read his progress and setbacks in his expressions as he dropped his poker face in complete concentration on his work. In just a couple of minutes, the deadbolt turned. "You really have to teach me how to do that," Amit said, the awe evident in his voice.

"Some other time," Uncle Rob acknowledged with a grin. "For now, we have work to do." He carefully examined the door to confirm no sensors were hiding in the frame. We were in. We navigated our way across an unfamiliar utility room. Emergency lights were on, so the sheriff and the state troopers must have disconnected the power because of the "chemical spill." Uncle Rob opened a utility box and unplugged a battery. "The security system is disabled," Uncle Rob said softly. "Everything looks clear. Plan A. Get going."

Amit and I went through the door into the public area of the basement, then the stairs and got to work. The books on EVIL's list weren't in catalog order, but they seemed to be mostly history and biography, with a smattering of folklore, science, and other subjects. It took us twenty minutes to collect our haul of books in a couple of big duffle bags and get them up to the third floor. Amit checked off the list to confirm we had everything, while I swiftly set up our scanner. I removed the bulky work gloves and got to work, flipping a page, taking an image. We were already on our third book when I heard the radio click. I figured it was Rob giving us the signal that all was well. "He's on his way," Amit concurred. He waited a moment and then sent a click in acknowledgement.

I broke out a couple of snacks for Amit and me, and I set one aside for Rob. At the rate we were going, we'd finish sometime early tomorrow morning – plenty of time to clear out before the morning arrival of the EVIL technology containment crew. Rob poked his head in the door. Amazing how quietly he moved – I never even heard him coming, and I'd forgotten to set up the motion sensor. His cocky grin evaporated as he saw our set up. "What's going on here?" he asked.

"We're busy scanning," I replied after swallowing my bite of granola bar. "I brought some snacks so we'd be ready to stay all night," I explained. "Want something to eat?"

Uncle Rob just stared – a grim look on his face. He opened his mouth to speak, then cut himself off. After a moment, he opened his mouth again and spoke. "Time for Plan B, boys," he said. "This isn't going to work. We need to gather up the books and clear on out of here. It's not safe to spend all night working here. The sheriff could change his mind and come in to secure the place at any moment. You know how curious he is about what's going on."

I was confused. "OK." I broke down the scanner while Amit gathered up the books.

"Let's grab the physics books too, while we're at it," Uncle Rob suggested. "How many of these books did you scan?"

"All the older books in the physics section," I explained. "Many of the older periodicals on the ground floor. Several hundred books, maybe a thousand including these. We can grab a few of the most important ones."

"We can't get them all," Uncle Rob said, levelly. I wasn't sure if he were making an observation or asking a question. "Take what you can easily tote," he said, decisively, "and let's get going." He hefted a couple of our duffle bags and followed me and Amit out to the stacks.

I grabbed the classic books. I knew them so well by now that they seemed like old friends – Maxwell, Hertz, and Heaviside. I also took the books whose subtle clues and defects had started everything: Franklin, Fleming, Whittaker, and Lodge. Fully loaded, down the stairs we went, right through the utility room to the tunnel door. "Go ahead," Uncle Rob said. "I'll secure the door." Amit and I pushed back the darkness with our dim red lights. We were followed by Uncle Rob a moment or two later. I navigated us the several blocks back to our entrance. Uncle Rob popped the hatch, pronounced the way clear, and helped us out.

"Your tool?" he asked.

I handed him my tool, and he carefully closed the hatch. "I'll run everything up to my place and hide it all," he explained. "Amit, can you take my nephew back to your hotel and hide him in a room, off the record, without anyone seeing him? They might come looking for him – or me for that matter – at my place. What with this Nexus business, I think it's safest to hide our purloined letter right under the noses of EVIL's minions. Get it?"

"Got it," Amit and I acknowledged.

"Good," Uncle Rob said authoritatively. "I'll join you at the hotel when I can." He handed me my go-bag, climbed into his truck, and drove off.

I got in Amit's car and we headed for the Berkshire Inn. "It's a good thing you already got everything incriminating out of your house," he noted.

Oh, no. I kept a flash drive hidden in the transformer block for my phone charger. I'd rebuilt it so it would come apart easily, and I could retrieve the flash drive if I wanted to look at any files on my other air-gapped laptop. "I just remembered something," I explained to Amit.

"It's not safe," Amit said. "They've already got Mr. Burleson, and they're looking for your dad, too. Your house is an obvious place to stake out."

"They've probably come and gone already," I reasoned. "I can sneak in the back, grab the transformer, and sneak back out without anyone noticing. Let's drive casually along the side of the block to check it out. If it looks clear, you can drop me off a couple of blocks away."

Amit reluctantly agreed.

I peeked out the window and looked down the street as we passed the turn to my house. The sun had already set, and the street seemed quiet and peaceful. "If there's any trouble, try to hang around a few minutes. If I don't show, go back to the hotel and wait for Uncle Rob."

He let me off a couple of blocks away. I casually walked along the street, then ducked into the bushes and made my way through the neighbor's yard on the back side of our block. I crawled up into the tree house at the back of our lot and watched. The house appeared empty. I saw no activity as I waited patiently. After about five minutes, I dropped down, made my way to the back door, and let myself in.

I quietly moved through the house to the stairs. I was about to go upstairs to my room to retrieve the cell phone charger when I heard breaking glass. BANG! A brilliant flash of light and an overpowering clap of sound stunned me. I dropped to the floor. The next thing I knew, I was being roughly manhandled. I was blinded and my ears were still ringing. Handcuffs bit into my wrists. I couldn't keep my balance. I was half-shoved, half-dragged to the front porch. I hoped Amit saw the commotion and was able to get away.

As my vision came back, a masked man in a black ninja outfit whacked me hard on the side of the head and screamed something else. I still couldn't hear, and my vision was clouded by an after image of the stairs, but I could see the ninja outfit had "FBI" emblazoned across the chest. I didn't have any trouble pretending to be even more dazed and confused than I already felt. He dragged me to a waiting SUV and shoved me in the back seat. My head hit the doorframe, hard, on the way in – thud! It certainly didn't help my feeling of confusion and disorientation. My hearing came back to me as I watched helplessly while the FBI ninjas ransacked the house.

Just then, more flashing lights pulled up. It was Sheriff Gunn. He caught the attention of one of the FBI agents. "I hear you boys done caught one of them cyber-terrorists. You really think it's the kid?"

I couldn't hear what the agent said to the sheriff but I gathered the answer was no – they had pegged my father as the cyber-terrorist they were after.

"I've been wanting to run that juvenile delinquent in for years," the sheriff said. "You sure you don't got no charges I could hold him on for you? Accessory to terrorism?"

Again, the agent said something I couldn't hear.

"Well, if you don't think accessory to terror will stick, I'm sure I could come up with something," the sheriff volunteered enthusiastically. "Disturbing the peace is always good. Lots of wiggle room. Judge most always sees it our way. Why not let me take him off your hands? I can hold him for twenty-four hours, easy. Probably lock him up for months if I put a word in to the judge."

I cringed as I heard the occasional crash, even from inside the car. They were systematically tearing apart the house. Agents were already carrying box upon box of stuff out of our house to a waiting truck. The agent seemed happy to be rid of me and the sheriff, so he could get back to looting our house. He held the door of the SUV open.

The sheriff dragged me out of the FBI SUV and transferred me to his cruiser. At least he stuck a hand on my head to make sure I didn't bang it on the doorframe when he shoved me into his back seat.

When we got to the sheriff's office, he took me in, removed the cuffs and deposited me in a cell. I was under arrest for "disturbing the peace." He read me my rights and asked if I had any questions. "No sir," I told him.

"This time, boy, you ain't free to go. You ready yet to fess up to what's been going on?" he asked.

"I won't answer any questions without a lawyer," I insisted.

"Figured as much," he said. "You can cool your heels in here a while. Think about it, but don't wait too long. Because if you don't talk to me, you'll be talking to the feds soon enough." He left me and went back to work.

My folks and Kira were safe in Nashville with Uncle Rob's friend. There was no sign of Amit, so he'd probably gotten away. I assumed Uncle Rob would be by to bail me out in the morning. It was getting late, and I was very tired. I decided I should try to get what sleep I could on the lumpy cot. I listened to the radio traffic floating in from the other room as I fell asleep. Tolliver Library secure. Federal search in progress... yes that was my address. I drifted off to an uneasy sleep.

Some time later, I was awakened by the urgent tone of a voice coming in over the radio. "Structural fire – structural fire at..." What? That was our address! Our house was on fire? I heard the dispatcher acknowledge the call and dispatch the fire department to our address. "Engine 1 copies, structural fire," the fireman added our address, "We're rolling!" Not long thereafter, I heard another call. "Dispatch, Engine 1. Federal agents on scene have ordered us to stand down, I repeat, federal agents have ordered us to stand down." I couldn't believe it. They were deliberately burning down our house? To destroy any possible evidence we might have hidden away? I felt sick to my stomach. Everything we owned was going up in flames. Well not everything. The feds had obviously cleared out some stuff – books, papers, and electronics, I figured. Also, Uncle Rob and I had taken out a load of books and some of the smaller, more portable antiques. That wasn't much consolation, though.

I thought about what Mom had said as she and Dad were leaving. The Civic Circle was a group of elite big shots who apparently engaged in social engineering on a wide scale. Xueshu Quan – Academic or Science Circle in Chinese – was a person, or more likely an organization, whose mission appeared to be seeking out and suppressing knowledge. It started out with just a few physics books, but the list of books we'd grabbed from the library showed that they had secrets to hide in history, biography, and even folklore. The more I thought about it, the more I convinced myself that Mom was right, and there had to be a connection. Uncle Larry and his Civic Circle elite wouldn't rest until they controlled everything, the way the Tollivers controlled the sheriff in particular and Sherman in general. My parents were on the run. Hopefully Uncle Rob's scheme had gotten them and Kira to a safe house, but our home and furniture were up in flames. Some of the pieces were antiques that had been in the family for generations. The more I thought about it, the angrier I got.

The radio chatter continued about some other incident, a 10-54 or some such out on the highway. I mentally tuned it out as I fumed about having been burned out of my home.

I must have drifted off again, because the next thing I knew, Sheriff Gunn was back.

"I've had enough of your nonsense, punk," he was saying. "I need to know the score, and I need to know it now."

"I said, I have nothing to tell you without my lawyer," I told him off. "But, next time you lick your master's boots, do tell Uncle Larry to go hell for me, will you?"

The sheriff glared at me. He spoke with a slow, cold, and deliberate intensity. "Son, you need to listen up and get your head on straight. Our nation was built on the rule of law. Last few generations of so-called statesmen we have, they liked the rule of law so much that they added more laws..., more regulations..., and more rules... and more... and topped it off with still more. Then, they dump their law books and their regulations on the likes of yours truly and tell us to go out and enforce 'em. It's too much, too complicated for a lawyer or anyone else to understand it all. They make it so you can hardly go a day without committing something they could call a felony. So, I got to make the call which laws to enforce and which miscreants are deserving of my attention. Smarter men than I might question the wisdom of a system where the law can be no better than the character of those who select what to enforce and what to ignore. They drown a country in laws and rules and leave it up to law enforcement to sort things out. It's a system ripe for abuse and corruption to leave so much discretion with me in particular, and law enforcement and prosecutors in general. The way the big shots see it, that ain't a problem, because they figure they can always bend the complexity in their favor. I don't much like it. But, them's the cards I been dealt and them's the cards I gotta play.

"The Tollivers made this here county what it is. They've kept it prosperous, more or less, at a time when other towns up and down Appalachia are falling into ruin. I respect that. My charge is to serve and protect the people of this county. That is my mission. Between them and theirs, the Tollivers, their employees, and the other folk who do business with them are more than half of this county. Frankly, son, it's the better half. I exercise the discretion I been given to drop the hammer on vagrants, troublemakers, and low-life scum. I lock 'em up or run 'em out of town. I make sure this town stays safe, and quiet, and peaceful.

"If young Miss Tolliver wants to cry on my shoulder about how you and your Hindoo sidekick have been mean to her, I'm going to listen and then I'm gonna have words with you two." He sounded almost paternal.

"If you deliberately provoke a response from Homeland Security and make me call out my SWAT Team, by God, I'm going to hold you accountable." The sheriff's demeanor had changed. Gone was the Dutch uncle with the friendly advice. His face flickered with barely controlled anger.

"You and your sidekick have been a couple of the biggest pains in the ass this town has seen in many years. One of the biggest regrets of my career is going to be that I didn't lock you both up and throw away the key when I had the chance. And now…

"You seriously don't have the least clue about the devastation you've caused and the shit storm you've dumped on Sherman, here."

I thought I'd seen the sheriff mad before. That was nothing. The man's fury was a primal force barely held in check by an ironclad will. He took a deep breath.

"There's someone here needs to speak with you," he said, coldly. His deputy moved to cuff me. "No, Steve. I got him. Open the door." The deputy looked puzzled. "If you say so, Sheriff," he said as he opened the cell door. The sheriff grabbed me by the shoulder and marched me ahead of him to his office. He opened the door. I saw Uncle Rob inside, waiting.

The sheriff closed the door from the other side and left me alone with him. Uncle Rob's face seemed hard and cold. Something was terribly wrong. He said, "Your folks... they're dead."

CHAPTER 10: FINALE

I was numb. I couldn't believe I heard Uncle Rob say what he'd just said. It wasn't a dream. It was real. Uncle Rob was speaking to me, his hand on my shoulder: "Focus," he said gently. "I need you to focus."

I was in shock. "How?" was all I could manage to say. "How did it happen?"

"Some kind of DUI is what they're saying. Drunk driver hit them," Uncle Rob explained. "A tragic accident. I don't believe it, of course. I think the sheriff's suspicious, too. He said he was about to head out to the scene. You're in shock. I understand. But, there's no time to grieve right now. You need to collect yourself. We have some time, at least a few minutes, maybe as much as an hour."

"Time for what?" I was confused.

"Time for you to get your story straight," Uncle Rob said insistently. "Before too much longer, that door is going to open, and you are going to be hauled in for an interrogation. They are going to go over and over and over your story with you, each time looking for inconsistencies, each time trying to trip you up. It'll be the same men who just burned down your house and probably killed your folks. If you give them any hint that you know anything about what was actually in those books or what it meant, the best you can hope for is that you'll be locked up under high security, with some trumped-up terrorism charge, for a very long time. And, that's a best-case scenario. Worst case, you're dead, and it won't be pleasant. If you're lucky, the sheriff may be in the interrogation room with the feds."

"Lucky? Sheriff Gunn has it in for me!" I exclaimed. "He's convinced I'm some kind of terrorist and swore I'd be locked up for a long time!"

"Let me guess," Uncle Rob said with a tired grin. "The sheriff shot his mouth off about this terrorism business and how he wanted to lock you up and throw away the key in front of these feds, didn't he?

"Yes…" I acknowledged tentatively, not following his reasoning.

"I see you're still in street clothes and not an orange jumpsuit, so you weren't processed and strip searched and anally probed for contraband and thrown in the Tri-County lock-up, right?" The look of horror on my face at that thought was answer enough. "That wasn't an arrest," Uncle Rob explained. "That was a rescue. He got you away from those feds and brought you straight here for safekeeping. The feds wanted to focus on tearing your house apart, and searching the library. They probably wanted the sheriff to quit bugging them – he can be annoying, particularly when he puts his mind to it. Those feds were happy to have the sheriff keep track of you until they had time to get back to you. Damn good thing the sheriff stepped in, or you might well have ended up like your folks. Sure, he's got some kind of nebulous charge against you. He can raise a jurisdictional stink about wanting to hold on to you, if the feds barge in here and try to take you and shut you up like they did to your folks. Mark my words, that was a rescue. You may well owe your life to the sheriff, and don't you forget it! But, we're getting off track. You need to be ready for the interrogation."

I took a deep breath and collected myself. "What do I need to do?"

"First off, you need to understand how the game is played," Uncle Rob explained. "One of the fundamental techniques is 'good cop, bad cop.'

"Yes, Mr. Burke, Dad's lawyer, he explained all that to me. But shouldn't I just refuse to say anything?" I asked.

"Normally, yes. But, these guys are playing hardball. If they think you know anything, you'll vanish. They will question you under torture, and you'll end up like your folks. I called Bill Burke," Uncle Rob explained. "He agreed you should be available for questioning. He'll be here in the morning to bail you out. You should insist that he be present for your questioning. The feds won't like that. The feds will be pushing the sheriff to just turn you over so they can rough you up as much as they like. The sheriff may be a pain, but at least he plays by the rules, and he's not about to let you get taken out somewhere to be tortured and killed by these guys. He may even call in your Uncle Larry to push the political angle on your behalf and try to get them to stand down."

"So, what should I say when I'm questioned?" I asked.

"When in doubt, your best bet is to play Sergeant Schultz with them." Uncle Rob explained cryptically. I didn't know who this Schultz was, so Uncle Rob clarified: "You saw nothing; you heard nothing; you know nothing."

"I can answer 'I don't know' to all their questions," I said confidently.

"It's not going to be that easy," Uncle Rob said. "They're going to want you to talk about what you do know. You have to give them innocuous answers to throw them off the track. Don't start rambling. Provide short, direct answers to their questions and then shut up. Make 'em dig for it. They'll latch onto every strand of your description and start pulling at it. They'll lie and make you think they know everything and all you have to do is confirm what they already know and the unpleasantness will be all over. They'll bluster and threaten you with years in prison, throwing you in to be gang raped by a pack of feral inmates. They will scare the living daylights out of you. You will have to let them see your fear and believe you are thoroughly broken and disclosing everything while maintaining a wall against them.

"I don't know about these feds or whatever they are. Maybe they aren't used to interrogations without shooting their suspects in the knee first. That could be an advantage. The sheriff, on the other hand, is a steely-eyed lawman who can smell a lie. Whether he's in on the interrogation or not, you need to tell the truth, but you need to tell it in a way that diverts the attention from you and focuses it on Mr. Burleson and your father."

"Aren't they going to be after you, too?" I asked him.

"They appear to have figured out that Jim Burleson was the central figure in all this," Uncle Rob said.

I opened my mouth to object, but Uncle Rob cut me off with a stern stare and finger over his mouth, gesturing for silence. Was Uncle Rob concerned someone was listening?

"Jim's obsession with Oliver Heaviside was the root cause of all this trouble," Uncle Rob insisted. "They're saying he may have murdered a girl in Houston. I know Jim well enough to know that's nonsense, but he may have gotten mixed up with the girl, somehow."

I kept my mouth shut and took in Uncle Rob's creative reconfiguration of the facts.

"The feds think maybe your father might have known something about it," Uncle Rob explained. "Since you lived with him, they want to talk with you, too. They haven't expressed an interest in taking it any further than that. Apparently Kira and I are both in the clear, for now at least."

"They're calling it cyber-terror," Uncle Rob explained. "How those old books Mr. Burleson was interested in could be mixed up in this cyber-terror business is beyond me."

"I certainly have no clue," I assured him.

"It's a shame you're getting dragged into all this," Uncle Rob opined. "You were distant from your dad, almost estranged. Not to speak ill of my brother, but he worked all the time. You hardly ever saw him. You met your dad's friend, Mr. Burleson, a time or two, and you knew he had this silly obsession with Oliver Heaviside. Wanted you to read some books about him. You looked at them, sure, but they were boring. The math went over your head. And, you didn't have time. Your dad was paying you to work for him, to study for your physics class, and do your debate research. That's what kept you busy this past summer. They'll have gone through your online search history, so be ready to tie most anything they come up with back to your alternative energy research."

Uncle Rob continued prepping me, running me through my story again and again, coaching me on details to add on successive passes through various descriptions. He told me to tune out the increasing noise and chaos, but it was hard to do. The hum of activity through the door became steadily louder and more chaotic, almost panicky at times. I heard them activating all the volunteer firefighters in the county. I caught a "send more units," and something about a "fourth alarm" and engines being dispatched from Knoxville and neighboring counties. The feds must have let the house fire get out of control. I hoped the neighbors were all right and none of the local and county firemen were injured. But, in a way, I also felt a deep satisfaction that in burning me out of my home, the feds were bringing more trouble down on their own heads. I pushed aside the chaos and the aching emptiness of my loss and continued to focus on Uncle Rob's prepping.

After the better part of an hour, Uncle Rob pronounced himself satisfied. "I'm going to ask them to take you back to your cell so you can try to get some sleep. No sense giving the feds the hint that we got our story straight."

Uncle Rob called the deputy, who escorted me back to the holding cell. It had all been too much for me. I felt overwhelmed by the stress and by my loss. I had gotten my parents killed. And Mr. Burleson. And Nicole. And her boss, whose name I didn't even remember. That only seemed to compound my guilt, that I got someone killed and didn't even remember his name. My mind whirled. There must have been a better way. Why couldn't I have avoided all this? Exhausted by my ordeal and spinning around in my futile recriminations, I finally fell asleep.

* * *

I was in the middle of the worst nightmare of my life. I dreamed my parents were dead and I was running through steam tunnels lined with dark and shadowy bookshelves. Demons reached through the shelves to grab at me.

"Did I hear you say you won't give us the boy?" croaked one demon to another. Now they were arguing over who was going to eat me. I woke up, heart pounding, with a burst of adrenaline. Only the nightmare was real.

"I didn't say I wouldn't. I said I cain't." Sheriff Gunn was arguing with Mr. Wilson and another EVIL fed. "I got him booked for disturbing the peace and the judge'll be seeing him later this morning. It's just like I said to your boys last night – I can hold him for 24 hours. I can speak to the judge and try to get him locked up longer. But, I cain't just turn him over to you without the judge's say so."

I felt exhausted as the adrenaline wore off. I just wanted to go back to sleep – to slip into oblivion and escape from it all. I was in danger, though. I forced myself to focus on what they were saying.

"It's been a long night, sheriff," the other EVIL fed observed. "Can you hold him until tomorrow so we can interrogate him then?"

"Why, ordinarily, sure," the sheriff seemed to be trying to oblige them. "All I'd have to do is convince the judge the punk needed to cool his heels a few days to learn his lesson. But, this here delinquent is an orphan now and you boys just burned him out of house and home."

"That's not our fault, sheriff," Wilson said hotly. "The suspect had a lot of electrical equipment, and the fire..."

"Don't matter whose fault." The sheriff cut him off. "What matters is the judge is a sucker for a hard-luck story. I bring in an orphan just lost his folks and his home burned down last night, and I try to hold him on a half-assed misdemeanor charge, the judge is going to release him to his kin. Probably won't even charge bail. Might even dismiss the case outright, no matter what I say. It's that simple. Ain't nothin' I can do about it."

"No reason why we can't pick him up as soon as you cut him loose, is there?" Wilson asked ominously.

"I think y'all don't appreciate the trouble you've caused hereabouts," the sheriff explained patiently. "I just got off the horn with the governor. He's had an earful from the state troopers 'bout you musclin' them off the scene of that DUI with the kid's parents last night, not to mention the fire. The governor can be a mite pissy when he gets awakened early on a Sunday morning with bad news. He reamed me up and down about why the remains of the boy's parents hadn't been released to the county coroner, and why all hell is breaking loose in my county. And, somehow, he heard about the punk and wanted to know why I had the juvie locked up in my office. He was mighty displeased with me when I explained I was doing a favor for you boys. 'Who's runnin' your county, sheriff, you or the feds?,' he says to me. I turn over the punk to you, and he's going to hold me responsible. No, sir."

"How'd the governor hear about the kid?" Wilson asked him.

"I have me a theory about that," the sheriff explained. "You heard of the Tollivers, right? Well this kid is kin to Laurence Tolliver his self. Some kind of nephew or somethin'. And, I already got me a call from Mr. Tolliver this morning, wantin' to know why I was holding his nephew. Now the governor and I have an understandin'. This county backed him by a comfortable margin in the last election, and he lets me run things as I see fit. But, if I piss off the Tollivers, and if the governor loses confidence in me, well, I'm out of a job come Election Day, guaranteed. I'm telling you, there's too much heat on the kid right now for me to just let you have him." The sheriff paused.

"And why're you so interested in a two-bit punk like him anyway?"

"His father may have been involved in this cyber-terror incident," Wilson explained. "We need to see if the kid is involved."

"That punk? Some kind of cyber-terrorist?" The sheriff snorted incredulously. "He's just a dumb juvie. He's undisciplined, emotional, impulsive, and cain't so much as steal a smoke without screwing it up and gettin' caught."

"We have to interrogate him to be sure," Wilson said. "We'll do it now, if you can't hold on to him, Sheriff. You don't have to be there if you don't have the stomach for it."

"You boys ain't listenin' to me," Sheriff Gunn was insistent. "The spotlight is on the kid. I got to do everythin' all nice and legal-like. And, he's got him a hot-shot lawyer on his way here from Knoxville."

I heard an expletive from one of the feds. "How the hell'd that happen?" Wilson said angrily.

"Probably the Tollivers again," the sheriff said. "I'm sure Mr. Tolliver has lots of lawyers among his Civic Circle friends. Everything's..."

"He's Civic Circle?" Wilson interrupted him. "The kid's uncle is Civic Circle?"

"That's what I'm tryin' to tell you," the sheriff reiterated. "Everything's got to be on the up and up because we're all of us under scrutiny. Go get yourselves coffee and a bite to eat, and come on back here at 8 am. I can give you an hour, ninety minutes, maybe, but then I got to take the kid to the judge."

* * *

A deputy escorted me to an interrogation room and brought me a cup of coffee and a breakfast biscuit. I ate the biscuit and sipped the coffee, wondering who might be watching me from the other side of the one-way mirror. The coffee made me feel a bit better. But I still felt numb. My thoughts were stuffed in cotton and it took effort to concentrate on the simplest things. I worked to remain calm. I focused on the confrontation to come. I ran through what Uncle Rob had told me last night. I needed to be the sheriff's dumb juvie. Miserable as my night had been, I at least got a few hours of sleep. That was probably more than either the sheriff or the EVIL feds could say. Every little advantage would help. The coffee and the food filled me with energy. I was ready. Just before 8 am, the deputy escorted Mr. Burke to the room.

"I'm very sorry about your parents," he began. "I didn't know your mother well, but I did know your father. He was a good man. He'll surely be missed."

"Thank you, sir." I replied.

He got down to business. "We don't have much time. I understand you want to talk?"

Was he hinting about Uncle Rob's visit and concerned someone was listening? "Yes," I answered.

"Good," he said with a warm smile. "You don't have to answer any questions," he advised. "It would not be surprising for you to be over-wrought with emotion at the death of your parents." He seemed to be hinting he'd back that excuse if I wanted to make it. "We can postpone this."

"Might be better to..." I tried to think how to phrase my thoughts for the benefit of any eavesdroppers, "...clear the air? Get it over with?" I needed to dispel any suspicions and get them off the case. If the EVIL feds didn't get a shot at me now, they'd come after me later under conditions of their choosing. This was my best chance of facing them in a fair fight.

"Very well," he said, "but defer to me. I'll screen their questions as best I can. And if you start answering something and I don't like the way things are heading, I'll say so and stop you. Listen to me, follow my lead, and do what I say."

"Yes, sir," I replied.

Sheriff Gunn came in, accompanied by Wilson and his partner.

"Sheriff," Mr. Burke shook his hand. Apparently, they knew each other. "Bill Burke," he introduced himself to Wilson and his partner.

"Special Agent Wilson, FBI." His partner remained silent.

"I understand you have some questions for my client regarding his arrest for – what was it again, disturbing the peace?" Mr. Burke began.

"Yes," said Wilson. He turned to me. "What do you know about your father's interest in physics books?"

"Physics books?" Mr. Burke seemed incredulous. "How exactly do you allege my client disturbed the peace with physics books?"

"We are investigating another matter involving your client's father," Wilson explained. "We would like to assure ourselves that your client was not involved."

"You believe my client is a party to some kind of conspiracy?" Mr. Burke seemed genuinely curious. "What overt act do you allege my client committed in furtherance of this conspiracy?"

"No, we believe your client's father may have been involved in an act of cyber-terrorism," Wilson explained.

"In what way do you allege my client agreed with his father to commit this act of cyber-terrorism?" Mr. Burke seemed so forthright and sincere, but I got the impression Wilson was annoyed at the need to have to explain and justify his actions.

"No," Wilson said. "We merely wish your client to answer a few simple questions regarding a potential crime involving his father."

"Oh," said Mr. Burke as if that clarified matters. "A potential crime involving his father. I see. You understand my client's father and mother were both victims of an automobile accident last night. You suspect there is some criminal involvement in the accident?"

Wilson clearly didn't like where this was going. "No, we have no reason to believe it was anything other than a tragic accident."

"I understand you took over the investigation from the state troopers. So, you found the driver responsible, and you established that he had no malicious intent?" Mr. Burke asked earnestly.

"No, the other driver is still at large," Wilson corrected him. Before Mr. Burke could butt in again, Wilson added, "I appreciate your client's interest in the unfortunate death of his parents. However, the matter we need to discuss with him pertains to some stolen property that may have been in the possession of your client and his father."

"What stolen property?" Mr. Burke asked.

"We believe your client's father came into possession of this book," Wilson passed a print out of an eBay listing over to Mr. Burke. He looked at it and passed it on to me. It was the listing for Oliver Lodge's *Modern Views of Electricity* from eBay. Amit had persuaded the seller to send a copy of the page with the bouncing waves text.

"The price of this book appears to be listed at $19.95," Mr. Burke observed. "Is that the price at which it sold? How is an allegedly stolen book with a value of $19.95 a matter for federal jurisdiction? The value doesn't exceed the threshold for..."

"It crossed interstate lines," Wilson interrupted haughtily. "By wire. And we have proof your client's father secured this page." He passed over a copy of the print out Amit had received from the eBay seller.

"If my client's father never actually purchased or possessed the book, only this print-out, what crime was committed?" Mr. Burke continued, "People buy things from eBay and other online sources all the time, and it's hardly a crime to ask a seller for additional information regarding the goods they offer for sale."

"The eBay seller was not authorized to share this information," Wilson insisted.

"This book was published when?" Mr. Burke asked.

"What does that matter?" Wilson asked.

Mr. Burke studied the print out. "Looks like 1907. Since it's published before 1924, it's in the public domain," Mr. Burke noted, "so there's no copyright issue involved. And a single page – that would be fair use, anyway, even if the book were under copyright. Hardly a matter for federal interest.

I'm still not clear exactly what crime my client or his father are alleged to have committed."

"This is a matter of national security," Wilson countered.

Burke paused a moment, studying the eBay listing. Then he observed, "But this is a book published in London in 1907?" He sounded earnestly befuddled. "How can the contents of this book be classified? How could my client be expected to know this is classified? I don't see any markings or labels that might have indicated the page was classified."

"All we want to know is what your client knows about this book," Wilson asked.

"Unfortunately, any records my client may have had pertaining to any of his or his father's property were destroyed in last night's fire or are in your possession as the result of your search." Burke pointed out. "Oh, that reminds me," he added, "my client was never provided a copy of the warrant you executed on his parent's house last night. Would you please provide me with, (1) a copy of the warrant as well as, (2) a receipt and list of any property you may have seized, and also (3) an itemized list of my client's property destroyed in the fire due to your negligence and, (4) your written acknowledgement of responsibility as well as the damages you intend to pay?"

I marveled at how Mr. Burke completely dominated the interrogation. I had to grit my teeth to avoid breaking out in a smile. I got the impression Special Agent Wilson wasn't used to tangling with an expert on a level playing ground.

"I will see to it that a warrant and list of seized property are delivered to your office, counselor" Wilson said. "The fire was an unfortunate accident – probably due to the negligence of your client's father and the excessive quantity of dangerous electronic hardware. Now, I would like your client to explain what he knows about this."

"I'm sorry, but I understand you seized my client's property in a civil forfeiture procedure. I'm still confused. What is the crime my client or his father are alleged to have committed?"

"Your client's father is a suspect in a cyber-terror investigation and his property was seized on that basis," Wilson argued.

"What does this eBay book have to do with an act of cyber-terror?" Mr. Burke asked in feigned confusion. He sounded amazingly sincere.

"This eBay seller was not authorized to have this book and may have colluded or conspired with your client's father," Wilson was becoming increasingly irritated and flustered.

It was like watching a magician at work. Mr. Burke deftly ran Wilson around in circles again regarding the alleged conspiracy between my father and the eBay seller, all the while trying hard to be ever so helpful, but just not understanding what legal justification Wilson had for asking me about the book. Dad used to say that an hour of a maestro's time is worth more than days of an amateur's. I could see how that worked with lawyers. The sheriff sat back quietly, sternly, and just watched, his expressionless face pierced by steely cold eyes. I could tell Wilson was getting exasperated. Finally, Mr. Burke deigned to pass on Wilson's question to me. "Son," he said to me. "Did your father own this Lodge book?"

"Dad had lots of books," I said flatly. 'Dumb juvie,' I told myself. 'Little words. Simple sentences.' "Or, he used to," I added sadly, with genuine emotion. "I don't know. I don't remember him owning that one." Which was true. I'd never laid my eyes on the original Lodge book with the bouncing waves language, only the edited version from the Tolliver Library – which was now in Uncle Rob's possession, not that I was going to add anything about that. We only had the scans from the eBay seller. I hoped he wasn't another victim of EVIL's cover up. Now, Mr. Burke was asking me another question and I needed to stay focused.

"What about this paper Special Agent Wilson has? Do you have any knowledge of your father communicating with this eBay seller?"

"No," I answered. Amit had communicated with the eBay seller, not Dad. "Dad had lots of papers," I added. "He kept most of them in his study," I offered earnestly, but unhelpfully.

Mr. Wilson didn't press me further. He added. "What about the fire? What do you know about the fire?"

"My house wasn't burning when you dragged me out of it," I noted in a level voice.

"No," said Mr. Wilson with frustration. "Not that fire. The library."

"What library?" I looked confused. Did he mean Dad's books in the study?

"The fire that burned down the Tolliver Library," Wilson clarified.

Now it was my turn to be dumbfounded. So, that was why there'd been all the extra chaos and alarms and fire engines coming in from Knoxville. "I was in jail," I explained. "I didn't know there was a fire."

"You didn't know the Library burned down?" Mr. Wilson was incredulous.

"I don't recall mentioning it to the kid," the sheriff noted, levelly. "And he's been locked up since I took him off your hands."

I got the impression Wilson was tired of the runaround. Maybe he figured pursuing me wasn't worth the hassle. Maybe he was simply biding his time until later. He gave up. That was about the end of the interrogation.

In an hour, I may have answered a handful of questions in total. For all the anxiety and worry and preparation, it was anticlimactic. Scratch that. It was a rout. Mr. Burke had stood his ground and dominated Special Agent Wilson. I didn't doubt the power of EVIL. Wilson was dangerous. He and his crew would stick a knife in my back in a heartbeat if they thought they could get away with it and if they saw some advantage in doing so. At this time and place, though, EVIL was defeated. For now.

After Mr. Wilson left, the sheriff cleared his throat. "So all of this," he said, fixing my gaze in his, "this is all about some old physics book?" He seemed incredulous. And really furious, although he was controlling himself with a noticeable effort. I didn't blame him.

"Yes, sir." I figured I owed the sheriff a direct answer for keeping me out of the clutches of EVIL.

The sheriff escorted me into the county courtroom with Mr. Burke following close behind. Uncle Rob was sitting there, and he gave me a subtle nod when our eyes caught. And there was... Uncle Larry? I was a bit surprised to see him, but there he was. He stood up, stopped the sheriff, put a hand on my shoulder, and said how sorry he was about my folks. He asked how I was holding up. I told him I was OK.

"Excuse me sir," the sheriff said to him. "I need to escort the boy to the judge."

Uncle Larry sat down, and I stood with Mr. Burke before the judge.

The hearing with the judge lasted just long enough for His Honor to express his regrets and condolences on the loss of my parents. Then he dismissed all charges. I was free to go. But where?

Uncle Larry, Mr. Burke, and Uncle Rob all wanted me to go with them. Both my uncles were strong-willed men used to getting their own way. And I'd just seen how ruthless and tenacious Mr. Burke could be when he put his mind toward it. I'd been coasting through the last day, letting Uncle Rob, Mr. Burke, and the Sheriff take care of me and tell me what to do. Not that I was complaining. Between the three of them, they'd gotten me out of the clutches of EVIL. Now, it was time for me to start taking back control of my own destiny.

I defused the argument. "Gentlemen," I said. "I appreciate all your help and support, and I'm sure I'll need more of it in the days to come. Let's go across the street to Kudzu Joe's and talk."

Once we all settled in with our coffee, the first order of business was where I was going to stay. "Your parents' last will and testament needs to be probated," Mr. Burke explained to me. "It is held at my firm, and I took the liberty of making copies. Your Uncle Rob is executor of their estate as well as your guardian." He passed copies to Rob and me.

"Your parents had life insurance, but the estate may be rather complicated to resolve," Mr. Burke advised. "The feds seized your and your parents' personal property and real estate in a civil forfeiture. Then it was mostly destroyed by fire. The government may argue that they exercised reasonable care and are not liable for any damages. They and the insurance company are likely going to have to fight that one out, and even if there's a settlement, the government might try to claim it under the terms of the forfeiture. It's not really my area, but I want to warn you it may be a long and complicated process."

"A trailer up in the hills is no place for a young man who has just lost his parents," Uncle Larry interrupted. He genuinely seemed to want the best for me. I could live in comfort and luxury with him, but I'd be always tense, always on edge around him and Aunt Nikki and Abby. Not to mention, his obvious interest in molding me into a future scion of the Tollivers completely creeped me out.

"That is a decision for the boy's guardian to make," Mr. Burke noted. I knew Uncle Rob was not about to let Uncle Larry have his way, but Uncle Larry was not used to being thwarted. I weighed in.

"I can stay with Uncle Rob for a while and see how it goes," I assured Uncle Larry. He wasn't happy, but he bowed to the inevitable. I was sure I'd be hearing more about this before too long, though.

"I understand the sheriff would like you to stay at the Berkshire Inn the next couple of nights," Uncle Rob explained. "Kira can stay there with you." She was on her way from Nashville. Uncle Rob and I would meet up with her, we'd have dinner with Uncle Larry, Aunt Nikki, and Abby, and then the three of us would head over to the hotel. I noticed a sheriff's deputy come in. Joe handed him a cup of coffee for free. The deputy took his coffee back to his patrol car parked outside.

I thanked Uncle Larry for his support. Larry clearly wasn't happy about leaving me with Rob, but there wasn't much he could do in the face of Mr. Burke's insistence that Rob was my guardian. He gave my hand a hearty shake, and he put his other hand on my shoulder. Then, he left.

"We'll need to talk more later, once things settle down a bit," Mr. Burke said, circumspectly. Ah, yes. He'd been working on the Xueshu Quan investigation. Rob and I thanked him, and he departed.

Finally, I was alone with Rob. "Amit sends his regards," Rob explained. "I told him to lay low and keep out of it all. No sense dragging him in publicly while EVIL lurks about."

The wall I had built to hold back the grief so I could carry on came crashing down.

"I as good as killed my parents," I looked Uncle Rob in the eye. "I know I didn't do it directly. I know EVIL is ultimately responsible. But still, I set it all in motion, and they died because of me."

"The only thing necessary for the triumph of EVIL is for good men to do nothing," my uncle observed wryly. "Don't think of your parents as passive victims. Don't you ever think of them that way," he insisted. "Your parents chose to do something. They turned their backs on safety and sanctuary. We call it 'running to the sound of the guns.' They had my friend drop them back at their car. Probably figured they could take the back roads in from Nashville and make it to my place. Maybe their car was found where they left it and EVIL put a trace on it. Maybe they were spotted by law enforcement somewhere along the way who called EVIL in. I don't know.

"Your folks' death probably saved you. It drew all the attention to your father and to Mr. Burleson. It made them the scapegoats and set up a firewall that kept you and the rest of us safe. If EVIL had captured and interrogated him and your mom... well let's not go there. Your folks did what they thought was right at the moment. They did the best they could with the information and resources they had. Even looking back now with the benefit of hindsight, I can't honestly say they made the wrong choice."

I was going to have to think on that.

We drove by Tolliver Library, or what was left of it. The deputy's patrol car tailed us. They still had the library site cordoned off, and a team was picking through the debris. The entire structure collapsed in on itself – only a few jagged fragments of wall thrust defiantly upward. EVIL was so determined to keep its secrets to itself that it wiped out an entire library. The wholesale destruction of knowledge seemed yet another horror, yet another abomination on this day that had already seen so much tragedy.

Then we went by the remains of my house – a few scorched walls, a chimney, a pile of debris. Dad's antenna hung limply, the transmission line severed where it melted. I got out and walked through the debris, recognizing small bits and pieces and fragments of my former life. I saw some tiles from the upstairs bathroom. I saw a shattered piece of my father's china lamp. No one knew exactly where it came from or how old it was. That lamp had burned whale oil, and later kerosene. It survived the Civil War and the confiscation of the family homestead up in the Cove. Carefully removed from the second farm near Oak Ridge before the final seizure, my great-grandfather converted it to electricity. It served three more generations of our family, illuminating countless meals and gatherings in our dining room, only to come to an end last night. I picked up and pocketed the shard.

The only place more or less intact was the old tree house. I climbed up. When I was a boy, my dad built the tree house and installed the control panel from an old washing machine. The tree house was my space ship, and the washing machine buttons and knobs were the controls. Someone had ripped it apart, looking for evidence I supposed, then decided it wasn't worth seizing. I put it back together, taking advantage of the first real privacy I'd had all day to cry. I hadn't been up there to play in years. I surveyed the ruins of my former home from the vantage point of my space ship's bridge. I set the controls – full speed ahead – warp 9. I hit the "engage" button. I gathered myself back together, wiped my tears away, and climbed down.

I pulled the shard of antique lamp from my pocket and looked at it. The lamp – and my former life – were no more. I had a new life to build now. I couldn't just cling to the broken fragments of the past. I threw the shard back into the rubble, and I walked to where Uncle Rob was waiting in his truck.

"That patrol car has been following us," I told him.

"I know," he acknowledged. "Sheriff's keeping an eye on you in case the feds make a move. Let's check in to the hotel and go meet Kira."

"Smuggling me in the back door to hide out is one thing, but is it a good idea for us all to stay in the same hotel a few days with the EVIL feds?"

"I checked with Amit," Uncle Rob explained. "The EVIL feds are enjoying their Double Platinum suite upgrades at a Berkshire Inn closer in to Knoxville. The investigation is centering on Jim Burleson, not on us here."

We went to meet Kira.

* * *

I skipped school on Monday. Uncle Rob took me to the store and bought me some new clothes. Kira was distant. I think she held me responsible for our parents' deaths. I couldn't blame her. She was spending most of her time catching up with friends. A deputy shadowed Rob and me wherever we went. There was even a deputy staying across the hall from us in the hotel. The sheriff wasn't taking any chances. The inquest into my parents' deaths was scheduled for Tuesday afternoon. Rob let me know that the sheriff had asked to meet with us. We met the sheriff at Kudzu Joe's Tuesday morning. Joe had a back room he sometimes closed off for private parties. Bill Burke drove from Knoxville to join us. The sheriff arrived not long thereafter. We got a round of coffee and settled in for our meeting.

"Thanks for coming," Sheriff Gunn said gruffly. Looked like he still hadn't seen much sleep. "This is one of the prettiest tangles of lies and half-truths I ever have seen," he explained. "But, I think the kid is in the clear, assuming y'all don't go poking around and making a fuss."

Mr. Burke began. "I have certain obligations as an officer of the court, as do you, Sheriff. Neither of us can go about suppressing evidence, let alone to a capital crime like the murder of my client's parents."

"Oh you don't have to worry yourself any on that score, counselor," the sheriff said. "This afternoon at the inquest, the duly appointed triers of fact will hear all the evidence from distinguished expert forensic analysts, brought in by the director's own most special FBI agents. I even wrote up most everything I'm about to tell you, only to have His Honor tell me it wasn't credible and my opinions didn't hold any weight against such distinguished outside experts."

"And mark my words," the sheriff predicted, "they will be concluding that your client and his wife suffered an accidental death in a collision of such extreme violence as to cause instant death at the hands of a drunk driver, who then hopped out of his car and has not yet been found. So what I am about to tell you are the amateur observations of a poorly qualified yokel, who just happened to be at the scene not long after the accident. Understand?"

"Very well," said Mr. Burke.

"I'll tell you what I know and what I think," the sheriff continued. "But, first I want the truth."

"You've seen these men won't hesitate to kill if they think you have a piece of their secret or even if they think you realize their secret exists," Rob cautioned. "If they knew we knew what we know, we'd be dead in a couple of days or less. You join our little club, and you'll be a marked man too. You have to keep this a secret."

"Your brother could have told you about the secrets I've kept," the sheriff said. "so talk."

Rob nodded at me.

"We call them EVIL – the Electromagnetic Villains International League," I began. What once seemed a whimsical joke was now devoid of any humor. I told the sheriff about the book with the bouncing waves language. I described the disturbingly high mortality rate among the pioneers of electromagnetics. I discussed meeting Nicole, getting the Xueshu Quan list from her and how we presumed that EVIL had strangled her and killed her co-worker from the bookstore in a hit-and-run. I relegated Amit to a very minor role, and left out his ability to keep track of them and tap into EVIL's communications. The sheriff probed all the while, asking questions.

"You still don't know why this bouncing waves stuff is so important?" the sheriff asked.

"No, sir," I said. "I think I understand it. The concept seems very simple. It's a bit counter-intuitive, maybe, but apparently EVIL will do whatever it takes to suppress the truth and kill anyone who comes near it."

"All this death and destruction," the sheriff was shaking his head. "For hardly any good reason as I can see."

"There's a hidden truth, Sheriff," I explained. "We don't know exactly what it is yet. The bouncing waves are part of it. We only have a few pieces so far, so we don't understand the big picture. But, we do know the most important truth EVIL is trying to hide."

"What?" the sheriff asked.

"That there is a hidden truth," I pointed out, recalling Mr. Patel's words, "and that they are trying to hide it."

There was a long pause around the table as that sunk in. Rob spoke up. "There you have it, Sheriff," he said. "Our cards are on the table. I wish we knew more, but that's what we have. What can you tell us about my brother's death?"

"Fair enough," the sheriff said, gathering his thoughts. "Bottom line is, it was an arrest gone bad – plain and simple. A few details don't make much sense, but I've enough of the big picture to tell it wasn't no accident."

"The feds were already out there when one of my deputies spotted the accident and called it in. No one wants to work traffic control when there's an incident scene, so I volunteered my deputies to free up the feds.

"When I got to the scene, I played junior G-Man, following them around like I couldn't get enough sniffing of their manly jock straps. They ordered me back out on the perimeter to keep me and everyone else out, but damn if those orders weren't real tough for a dumb redneck like me to understand. I just had to keep coming to them for one clarification or another, each time taking a different route through the area. I got a good look at most everything and, well son, it wasn't pretty.

"Someone ran them off the road," he explained. "Your dad was driving. Hit a tree and took the impact on his side. I don't think he made it. That side of the car was stove-in. Your mom's side wasn't that bad off. I think she survived, initially."

I stood up, turned my back to them and faced the wall. The sheriff stopped. I could feel their eyes on my back. If they saw how upset I was, they'd want to stop and spare my feelings. I couldn't have that. I had to be a part of figuring this out. I took a deep breath, calmed myself, and said, "Please continue, Sheriff."

The sheriff continued. "They had a team nearby waiting to arrest them. Probably following in another vehicle. Your mom never made it out of the car – may have been hurt too bad to move, may have been staying with your dad."

I focused on a burlap coffee bag, hanging on the wall as a decoration. I tried to distance myself from the painful words.

"I didn't get close enough to see inside the car," Sheriff Gunn continued, "but there was a gun fight. There were bullet holes in her car door."

I looked more intently at the burlap bag. "Greenwell Farms" was printed on the rough fabric.

"I saw some brass where the G-Men took cover," the sheriff continued explaining. "There were two dark spots not far from the car where it looked like a couple guys might have bled out. That much blood, those two are dead."

"Kealakekua, HI," said the burlap bag that was failing to distract me from my pain. Hawaii? Must be. It wasn't helping me feel much better.

"The way I figure it," the sheriff reasoned, "those two came up to arrest them, she saw them coming, and decided to shoot it out at close range."

I wasn't the only one upset. I could hear the sheriff take a breath and collect himself before he continued. "She got two of the bastards, alright. The rest of them got behind cover and filled her with lead. She may have nicked one, judging by the blood I saw on one of the trees, but I doubt she got a second magazine loaded. That was it."

"Two isn't enough, Sheriff," Rob was saying in a harsh voice thick with fury. "It was a good start under the circumstances, but it's not nearly enough. I want the rest of their carcasses strung up."

"You are not going off..." the sheriff began.

I heard Rob's chair push back as he stood up and cut him off, "Those bastards killed my brother and his wife and so help me, they're going to pay for it."

I turned around in time to see Sheriff Gunn stand up, too. He was uncomfortably close to Rob. The two of them had their arms at their sides but it looked as if either could strike the other at any moment. Neither was backing down. The tension in the air was palpable.

"'To everything there is a season, and a time to every purpose under the heaven,'" the sheriff said calmly, stepping back. He'd blinked first, wow. "You need to understand. This is my county. These are my people. No one comes into my county, kills my people, orphans their children, burns them out of house and home, and gets away with it. No one, no matter how high and mighty. No one. To act now, though, means they get you and the kid, too. I think he's in the clear, but he won't be, if you go play vigilante on me. This is a time to mourn, a time to build, a time for silence. I will move in my own time and I will get the job done."

"No," said Mr. Burke. "None of us can be taking the law into our own hands. We will gather up what evidence we have, and I can make sure it gets before a grand jury. We'll bring charges against them in a state court where the feds won't be able to push the judge around."

"No," I said. They all looked at me in surprise. "No. Those men who killed my parents – they are tools," I explained. "Instruments for evil in the hands of evil men. Don't get me wrong. I want them, too, but more than that, I want the hand the wielded the tool. I want the men who called the shots and gave the orders." Rob had an intent look on his face – one I couldn't decipher. I continued. "I don't want them warned that we're coming for them by going after their minions and pawns."

"All of you need to calm down," the sheriff said, "and let me finish before you run off half-cocked on your various crusades.

"Any chance we can take a closer look at the wreckage?" Rob asked.

"Nope. They wouldn't even let the troopers look at it. Though I managed to walk the troopers' sergeant in and out past the wreckage, so they could tell him in person. They impounded both vehicles and they've both been crushed by now. Also," he turned to me, "your parents' remains were cremated."

Rob blew up at that, "I told you! I insisted that they be released..."

"You don't have to yell at me, Rob," the sheriff interrupted him. "Horrible mistake. Unpardonable mix up. Ever so sorry they are."

"Sorry, Sheriff," Rob apologized. "I know it's not your fault."

"They truly are running roughshod over this case, aren't they?" Mr. Burke observed.

"Like I was telling you," the sheriff confirmed. "The arrest went south. There was a shoot-out. For some reason, they didn't want to own up to the fact they lost a couple agents, so they staged it as an accident. Still haven't acknowledged a couple of their own were killed. The fix is in. This afternoon, the inquest will convene and rule that the deaths were accidental. The reason I'm telling you all this is I need you to leave it alone."

The sheriff cut off Rob before he could object. "I know it sticks in your craw, Rob. But, I got the kid away from those phony feds by convincing them if they pushed any further, the attention and the publicity wouldn't be worth it. They came close to a public exposure of their cover-up, and they lost a couple of agents. Must be real sensitive about that loss to want to stage an accident, instead of trumpeting a heroic gunfight trying to bring in a dangerous cyber-terror suspect. Means they don't want no scrutiny. Price they paid makes it easy for them to convince themselves they got the job done, and the case is closed. Raise a stink, and they no longer have the incentive to go away and let matters slide."

We chewed on that a moment in silence.

Rob changed the subject. "I understand Larry took a personal interest in his nephew's welfare."

"I did notify Mr. Tolliver of his sister's demise, just as I notified you regarding your brother," Sheriff Gunn acknowledged. "He offered straight up to bail him out and take him home, and, well, you know how that all turned out. Mr. Tolliver may well have placed a call or two. I did get a call from the governor expressing his displeasure at the way I aided those phony feds to bypass the troopers' investigation of the accident. Of course, I figured I had to since they would have covered it up anyway, and at least I got a good look at what they were covering up out of it. I'll need to visit Nashville to square things with the governor after the funeral."

"I'm going to piss you off, Sheriff," Rob predicted, "but I have to ask it. Did Larry appear to have any foreknowledge of his sister's demise?"

"Now that's going too far, Rob." Sheriff Gunn was indignant. "I know your family has cause to be upset with Mr. Tolliver, but that was a long time ago. I've never seen any indication Mr. Tolliver would cause trouble for your brother, let alone be the sort to sanction the murder of his sister and your brother."

"I had to ask, Sheriff. I do believe you," Rob assured him. "I wouldn't be sharing this additional information with you if I didn't trust you." He turned to Mr. Burke. "Bob?"

"My original client is dead, Sheriff," Mr. Burke began, "but before he died, he tasked me to get to the bottom of these cyber-terror allegations. I've shared the results of my investigation with his executor," he gestured to Rob. "I advised him to keep the results confidential. He disagreed with my counsel, and on his recommendation, I'll share it with you."

"Sheriff, you and the Tollivers are real close," Rob explained. "I'm taking a big chance telling you this. I need your word that this goes no further."

The sheriff nodded his head. "Very well. Y'all have my word on it."

"My client," Mr. Burke explained, "was able to give me an important clue – that someone or something named Xueshu Quan had an interest in these bouncing waves physics books. Xueshu Quan has a mailbox in Arlington, Virginia, so my firm engaged a private investigator to learn more. Our investigator spotted a woman who retrieves the mail from Xueshu Quan's box in Arlington on a daily basis, apparently on her lunch hour." Mr. Burke shared a couple of photos of the woman. "She gets the mail, grabs some lunch, and heads back to the office. They're awfully cagey. She takes different, circuitous routes each day. They have a couple of their own, watching her. They're looking for tails. Took a week to actually trace her back to her office without anyone realizing our investigator was following her. Our investigator hasn't been able to confirm exactly which office she works in because security on her building is tight, and I cautioned him not to take any risks. But she works in the same building as the Civic Circle."

"So there is a connection," I said.

"Appears so," Mr. Burke concluded.

"But, that means Uncle Larry..." I began.

"May be tied into this," Rob observed.

"I don't believe it," the sheriff insisted. "You spend so many years knowing a man, you take his measure. Mr. Tolliver can be ambitious and ruthless at times in his personal and business dealings, but I do not believe he would ever condone, let alone participate in, the murder of his sister and brother-in-law."

I saw the light bulb turn on for the sheriff. "When I told those phony feds Mr. Tolliver was Civic Circle, they backed down and stopped trying to fight me over the boy. I figured they realized with the governor interested and a lawyer on the way, it was too late to simply make the boy quietly disappear. Maybe it was the tie-in to the Civic Circle on our end that did it."

"The Civic Circle might well be involved," I observed, "without my uncle knowing the details. They've kept this bouncing wave physics secret for a century. I doubt it's common knowledge among the members. It could be a case of one branch of the group not knowing the details of what another is doing."

"And laying off when they realize they might be stepping on their associates' toes," the sheriff added, thoughtfully. Now it was making sense to me why EVIL had been far more ruthless with Nicole than with me. Not only were they confident I had no knowledge of their secrets, but also they were deterred by my connection to the Civic Circle through Uncle Larry.

"You called them phony feds, Sheriff. Why?" I asked.

"My first tip-off was Mr. Patel out at the Berkshire Inn. He picked up there was something off about those guys. So, I called down to the Knoxville FBI office. They told me there weren't any FBI agents operating in my county. I went to confront Special Agent Wilson, and he insisted the Knoxville office call Washington. The director's office vouched for them, so I apologized for the misunderstanding and let them go on their way. But, I didn't give up there.

"I called some friends in the FBI and had them do some digging," the sheriff explained. "Near as they can tell, those phony feds never attended, let alone graduated from, the FBI academy. They are not nor have they ever been on the FBI payroll. The director's office may vouch for them, but they are not 'real' feds."

"Who are these contacts of yours, Sheriff?" Rob asked.

"Need to know, Rob," he said with a thin grin. "Need to know. My contacts are in a position to be able to tell me such things, though, and I trust them."

"What about the Tolliver Library fire?" I asked.

"The investigators can find no sign of arson, but the timing and the intensity of the fire are both suspicious," the sheriff concluded. "The fire suppression failed, too – someone must have cut off the water, somehow. Maybe it was our phony feds trying to destroy more evidence or protect their secrets. Maybe not. They've shown much more interest in looking into the Tolliver Library fire than they did the burning of your home.

"Any other questions?" the sheriff asked. There were none. "For the boy's sake," the sheriff reiterated, "there can be no suggestion that we suspect his parents' deaths were anything other than an accident."

"I also want to make sure it's absolutely clear all around," Rob insisted. "There can be no word or hint of what we believe – that the Civic Circle is tied into these murders."

"I know better than to ask you all not to look into this further," the sheriff added, "but for God's sake, be careful, and be discreet."

"Some shadowy cabal in the government – or worse, outside the government yet able to control it," Mr. Burke ruminated. "I think we're all agreed this cannot be allowed to stand. We need to figure out what's actually going on. We need to work together to unmask these conspirators and expose them. We need to assemble a unified front, rally allies and supporters, and take them on."

"That dog won't hunt," Sheriff Gunn countered, shaking his head ruefully. "They are the system – or at least they control or influence large parts of it. You can't take them down within the system. A centralized effort like the one you describe would be easily detected and crushed. They'd get a whiff of your communications, take a closer look, and suddenly you'd be awakened in the early morning by a heroic SWAT team and 'found out' as a terrorist. Just look at what they did to the boy's parents if you don't believe me."

"We have to do something," Mr. Burke insisted.

"You have the right idea," Rob acknowledged. "We need to expose them. We can, and we will. But, the sheriff's right. A centralized response? No way. We're operating from a position of weakness. David versus Goliath.

"They believe themselves all powerful. They believe themselves above the law. They believe they are the elite and they run the show. They aim to construct a New World Order: some kind of neo-feudalist society with themselves firmly at the helm and the rest of us in our places as their peasants. Make no mistake, they are powerful, and they will use that power to crush any obvious opposition.

"They look strong, but they have weaknesses, too," Rob explained. "There are only a very few who actually know the score and call the shots. The rest join in for prestige or status or to secure some advantage in their New World Order. They can be attacked on a moral level. Expose them, somehow, carefully. Unmask their brutality. Reveal their schemes. As we've seen, they are very, very sensitive to having their secrets revealed. So let's figure out more of their secrets, and reveal them. But, we have to do it in ways that don't directly lead back to us.

"Any stone that any of us can throw is a mere pinprick. But even a pinprick at the Circle's pretensions to omnipotence is a start. The smallest victory discomforts them and shatters the myth of their inevitability. The pinpricks we all can inflict will embolden others to throw stones of their own, to question the Circle's plans, to resist and to rebel, in ways that none of us can possibly imagine.

"In this kind of decentralized and distributed struggle there are no leaders nor followers, yet everyone is a leader and everyone is a follower. There is no centralized plan of battle, and yet we can observe and learn from each other's success and failures. That way there's no hierarchy, no head to lop off. This is not a conventional war of force versus force, at least not yet, but a battle of words and ideas on the moral and mental level.

"Go forth," Rob advised. "Learn more about our enemy. Pick a stone wisely. Take cover. Avoid detection. Aim carefully. Let fly."

As we were leaving, Rob cornered the sheriff. "You're confident Larry Tolliver had nothing to do with this?" Rob asked.

"I am," the sheriff replied. "And keep in mind," he said with a thin grin, "I'm a steely-eyed lawman who can smell a lie, remember?"

* * *

The inquest was anti-climactic. The EVIL agents didn't even make an appearance. They'd already prearranged the desired outcome: vehicular manslaughter by party or parties unknown.

My folks' remains had been cremated against our expressed instructions to hide the evidence of their murder. Grandma Tolliver wanted the cremains buried in two coffins in the Tolliver family plot. Uncle Larry agreed and informed the funeral home and church of their decision. This being Sherman, the Tollivers got what they wanted, and no one consulted us, despite Rob being my parents' executor and holding their power of attorney. Kira was particularly furious when she learned of the plans. Rob and I had to calm her down.

What sense it made for the urns to be placed in the open coffins for a viewing was beyond me. When we learned about the arrangements, Rob secured identical urns and filled them with some wood ash to withstand a superficial inspection. When we had a private moment with the coffins, Kira pulled out the duplicate urns from her unusually large purse, and we swapped them out for the urns in the coffins. Rob said the three of us could figure out what to do with Mom's and Dad's remains later.

Rob, Kira, and I stood as the line of mourners flowed into the church for the funeral. I'd wondered if Uncle Larry would want to stand in the reception line with Rob as brother to one of the deceased. That would have been awkward. Instead, he elected to lead off the line of mourners coming to pay their respects.

A few of my high school teachers came by. Coach Warner insisted I'd done enough for the semester to get A's, and not to bother coming back to school until after the Christmas holidays. The principal was with him and backed him up. I thanked them all.

Amit and his family came up to me in line. "I'm sorry I haven't been able to be there for you," he said simply.

"I understand." I assured him. "It's for the best."

Dr. Kreuger was next in the line of mourners. "I'm so very sorry, my young friend," he said.

"Thank you, sir." I cut him off before he could say more. "I wasn't privy to the details of my father's arrangements with you, sir, but I imagine there's a good bit more that needs to be done on your project. I'm handy with things like that. If you'll call me later this week, I'll see what I can be doing to fulfill my father's promises."

"You would..." he began. "At this time?" He looked overwhelmed. There was a lot of that going around. "You are good...," he cut himself off. "No, sir," he said. "Good man you are. You stand on two feet." He paused. "You don't need anything right now. But, sometime in future you need help. Only you don't ask. You are too proud and too strong. But, is not help. Is debt I owe your father. Is more than just his work for me. Your uncle he already square that up with me." I saw Rob exchange a look with him and nod before returning to his own conversation. "Your father he make me and my family safe. Ingenious what he did." He glanced around, clearly not wanting to elaborate where he could be overheard. "I owe your father. Debt I cannot pay now, except to you. You understand?"

"Yes, sir," I said. "I think so."

"I owe your father," he insisted again. "There will come a time when you need some money to get started, a down payment for a house, a job at my factory, maybe just a place to stay when you are in town. When you need, you will ask me, so I can pay down the debt I owe your father. You understand? You promise?"

"Yes, sir," I said. "Thank you, sir."

"Thank you, sir," he said.

Frau Kreuger and all three children gave me hugs.

I got enough offers of jobs or money that I honestly lost count of them all. There must have been a couple dozen contractors there with the same story. Dad had given them their start as apprentices. They'd take me on tomorrow or any time I wanted. And, if I ever needed anything, I should let them know. I was overwhelmed by the intensity of feeling.

The church was packed to overflowing. Grandma had insisted on orchestrating the services, and I didn't have the energy or inclination to deny her. We sang a hymn.

"We gather here today to lay to rest our brother Roy, and our sister, Amanda," the preacher began. Roy and Amanda. Amanda and Roy. The names still seem foreign, awkward, to me. They were always just Mom and Dad. And so they remain in my memories of them.

The preacher led us in prayer and presented a sermon. The service all blurred together. But I remember the end. Kira spoke toward the end. She related some of her favorite stories and recollections of Mom and Dad. She concluded with one last anecdote. "Mom used to tell me how Dad swept her off her feet with his dancing when they first met. My folks spent so many years raising my brother and me. They hardly had any time for themselves. This past weekend, they traveled to Nashville, just the two of them, for a couple of nights out on the town. They had breakfast with me before they left. I've never seen them happier – Mom was almost glowing with excitement about how she and Dad had danced the night away. That was the last time I saw them. They never made it home. But I'm so glad Mom and Dad got to have a last dance together before they left us."

Rob and I led up the pallbearers for my father's coffin. Uncle Larry and the Sheriff, looking sleek and deadly in his dress uniform, led the pallbearers for my mother's coffin. Kira had insisted on lending a hand, too. There must have been a quarter-mile worth of contractors' vehicles and pickup trucks in the procession to the cemetery. And so we laid their coffins and the duplicate urns to rest.

Sheriff Gunn had asked Rob and me to stay at the Berkshire Inn one last night. "I think you're both in the clear, but if they're going to try anything, this would be the time." Amit's Dad refused to accept any payment. Rob and I had adjoining rooms up on the third floor.

I was exhausted, but I couldn't sleep. My actions had consequences. I would be living with them for the rest of my life. I kept replaying my choices, wondering what I could and should have done differently. I was interrupted by a soft knock on my door. I grabbed my .45, rolled out of bed, and crawled to the door of Rob's adjoining room.

"I heard it," Rob said as he came through the door, short-barrel shotgun in hand. "You stay back, I'll check."

It was Amit. Rob let him in.

"I thought you should see this," he said, handing me a sheet of paper. "EVIL finished their investigation."

Chapter 11: The Enemy Reports

Amit handed us the intercept and took a seat. Rob sat next to me on the sofa, and we read the report.

> ***Final Report – Sherman Nexus (Category V), Sherman, TN***
>
> **Summary:** *A Category V Nexus arose in Sherman, TN due to a supercritical outbreak of proscribed knowledge. Targets terminated and illicit publications recovered or destroyed. Situation now under control. Details follow.*
>
> **Details:** *We recovered illicit publications describing fundamental electromagnetics outside safe paradigms. Recovered contraband included unredacted works of Oliver Lodge, Edmund Taylor Whittaker, John Ambrose Fleming, and William Suddards Franklin.*

"I thought you and your dad scrubbed the house of any incriminating documents," Rob said to me.

"I left a flash drive hidden in a cell phone charger," I explained. "That's why I went back home. They may have found it."

"I don't know," Amit cautioned. "Apparently Mr. Burleson had lots of the books and scans printed out. There've been a few other mentions."

> *Evidence strongly suggests Primary Target became aware of suppressed Heaviside analysis on wave interaction. Both Primary and Secondary Targets were skilled electrical*

contractors. Secondary Target had background in electrical engineering. Neither Target had experience in fundamental or applied research. No evidence Targets realized implications or succeeded in reducing to practice. Additional non-proscribed but related works (by Nahin, Hunt, Searle, Carr) found that, taken together, suggest Primary Target was researching Heaviside containment effort. Practice and certain methods of technology control may have been compromised to the Target. No evidence Targets connected the Circle to these actions.

"'Reduction to practice,'" Rob said. "There's something in those bouncing waves of Heaviside's. Something with serious implications. Something that concerns them."

"It's complicated enough that they're convinced neither Dad nor Mr. Burleson could have figured it out," I observed. "But, they recognize Mr. Burleson and Dad were wise to the effort to suppress the Heaviside paper."

"Do you have any idea what this Circle is they're talking about?" Amit asked.

I filled him in on Uncle Larry's attempt to recruit me, and the apparent tie-in between the Civic Circle and Xueshu Quan. "I figure the Civic Circle is a kind of public face to the organization and Xueshu Quan is a group within the Circle whose goal is to keep undesirable truths hidden."

"That's huge," Amit said. "The Civic Circle has members everywhere. They're tied into everything: business, media, finance, government."

"There must be an 'Inner Circle,' if you will," Uncle Rob speculated. "They're behind the Civic Circle and run the Circle's direct action arm that we've been calling 'EVIL.' I doubt very few Civic Circle members are actually clued in to what's going on. The rest are just useful idiots, like Larry Tolliver, who are in it for the prestige, the connections, and to look out for their own interests."

"The Circle is convinced no one has seen their hand behind all these events," I noted. "They don't know that we know."

"If they even suspected we knew, we'd be dead," Rob said soberly. "Keep that in mind."

Unauthorized release of proscribed knowledge traced to Tolliver Library in Sherman, TN. Once the principal library of now-defunct Tolliver Technical Institute, Tolliver Library was a top-tier research library before WWII. It subsequently fell into obscurity and thus failed to receive appropriate scrutiny from Xueshu Quan. Recommend a detailed review and investigation to confirm that similar threats are identified and neutralized. A fire consumed the library and its collection, however an external digital catalog shows significant amounts of proscribed knowledge much greater than that confirmed as having been in possession of Primary Target. See details in the attached file. All proscribed publications are believed destroyed in fire. Fire appears to have been accidental as no evidence of accelerants or arson was recovered from the scene. Timing, failure of fire suppression infrastructure, and extremely destructive nature of fire are highly suspicious, however. Unable to ascertain specific cause of fire or identify responsible party, if any.

"They didn't start the Tolliver Library fire?" I was incredulous. "I was convinced that fire was them hiding their tracks like they did at my house."

"It can't have been an accident," Amit insisted. "And that means..."

"There's someone else out there," I concluded. "Some third party that wanted to prevent the library from falling into their hands."

"A potential ally," Amit agreed.

"Keep in mind that the enemy of your enemy is not necessarily your friend," Rob cautioned. "Read that next part."

Primary Target also obtained proscribed knowledge through online inquiries to sellers of used books. Found unredacted copy of pp. 301-302 Lodge Modern Views of Electricity with fingerprints of both Primary Target and

> *Secondary Target. Microdot analysis ties printout to the serial number of a color printer purchased by Secondary Target. Secondary Target also purchased toner for printer about time a potentially dangerous pattern of online searches began (see previous report). Initial investigation failed to identify potentially hazardous synergy between online searches and proscribed knowledge available from Tolliver Library.*

"That must be the hardcopy Dad took to Mr. Burleson," I concluded. "But what's a microdot analysis?"

"Apparently color printers place a pattern of yellow dots that provide a serial number and time and date stamp on everything they print," Amit explained. "It was implemented to trace counterfeiting of currency with color printers, but now it's routinely used to trace printouts back to printers."

"We need to dispose of that printer," Rob observed.

Amit nodded his head. "I know. This is the last time I intend to use it."

"The takeaway here is your tradecraft sucks," Rob insisted bluntly. "You boys were amateurs. You were playing games and going through the motions of maintaining security. You did do some things right with your wardriving and anonymous Internet searching, but you can't just do it right most of the time. You have to do everything right, all the time, and every time. Or, it will kill you and those around you.

"Your interception of this was a masterful piece of hacking," Rob told Amit, holding up the printout we were reading. I could see a smug grin on Amit's face. "But you still screwed up big time and almost got caught at that truck stop. In fact you did get caught. The sheriff saw right through you two guys, and the only reason that didn't end your schemes right then and there was because the sheriff was even more suspicious of the phony feds and their cyber-terror lies than he was of you. You cannot count on such a lucky break next time."

I could see Amit was as sobered by Rob's after-action review as I was.

"I want to sit down with you, Amit," Rob insisted. "I want to review your methods, and your procedures, before you undertake any more initiatives. I want you to assume the Circle figures out the vulnerabilities you're exploiting. If they know someone is doing what you are doing, how could they go about tracing it back to you? Let's not add to the death toll. I don't want you to lose your parents and your life because of an avoidable mistake. We need a secure firewall around your hacking, so it doesn't lead back to you or to any of us.

"Yes, sir," Amit said softly.

"You boys were sloppy," Rob continued. "And you were only saved by a huge element of luck and by the fact that Jim Burleson was even more sloppy and inept than you were. It got him killed. It got your parents killed. We can't afford to do that again. Never again."

"I'm sorry," Amit said simply. "I'm so very sorry I screwed up, and I'm sorry you had to take the brunt of this – losing your parents, losing your house, getting arrested. I wish I could have done a better job of being there for you when you needed me. I never should have let you go back into your house. I knew it was a dumb idea, and I let you go anyway." There was no trace of the usual cocky and arrogant Amit who alternately amused and annoyed me.

"There's plenty of blame to go around, Amit," I consoled him. "We all made mistakes, and yours were no worse than mine. There was no reason to pull you in while I was under scrutiny. It might have jeopardized our window into the Circle's communications and put you and your parents at risk, too."

"I will work with you both on our processes and our procedures, so we can all keep each other safe," Rob insisted. "Above all, I do not want you boys trying to investigate or to reach out to any secret group capable of burning Tolliver Library to the ground right under the Circle's noses until I say you're ready. You hear me?"

"Yes, sir," we both replied.

In addition, proximity to Oak Ridge National Laboratory led earlier investigation to conclude detection of a Category III Nexus was a measurement error due to artificially induced neutrino flux. We recommend enhanced scrutiny and more frequent surveys for potential Nexus formation in the vicinity of nuclear labs and power generation facilities. Also, our program to suppress and eliminate nuclear power generation should be accelerated to reduce the likelihood of further false positive detections.

"Neutrino flux?" Rob asked. "Sounds like a bad Star Trek episode."

"No, this is science, not science fiction," I insisted. "Neutrinos are subatomic particles that are the byproduct of certain nuclear reactions. Somehow, artificially generated neutrinos generate a kind of noise that makes it tough to detect the signature of a Nexus."

"They had a Nexus scanner in that white van of theirs," Amit noted. "So you think they were detecting neutrinos with it?"

"Neutrino detectors are huge," I explained, "like vast tanks buried deep underground in mines. Neutrinos' interactions are so weak, there's no way we know of they could be detected reliably with anything compact enough to fit in a cargo van."

"With technology we know about," Amit corrected. "They may have some ideas that aren't public knowledge."

"This also tells us they have their fingers in the anti-nuclear movement," Rob noted. "There's another potential pressure point."

Caution: *Supercritical concentration of proscribed knowledge identified in Sherman Nexus would account for a Category III Nexus but is insufficient to account for a Category V Nexus. At times, Nexus magnitude exceeded that of September 11, 2001. These extreme readings cannot be accounted for by any known or foreseeable consequence of uncovered events.*

"You realize what this means?" I asked, gravely.

"We've somehow unleashed another 9/11?" Rob asked.

"Something like that," I explained. "A Nexus is an inflection point, a change in the course of history. What happened here in Sherman is a change that's somehow even bigger than 9/11."

We pondered that point in silence.

"Then EVIL's ruthless attempt to crush the agents of that change..." Amit began.

"...which led them to kill Nicole, and her boss, and Mr. Burleson, and your folks..." Rob continued.

"...has given rise to a brand new future." I concluded. "A brand new future in which we now know about the Circle and their plans. A new future in which we can move against them, expose them, and crush their schemes." I paused, looking at Rob and Amit. "Understand. This hasn't ended. It's only just beginning. What the Circle started here in Sherman is going to change the world in a way more profound and more significant than 9/11 did. Their brutality and their ruthlessness had consequences, will have further consequences. We are the agents of those consequences."

"They tried to bury the truth. But, 'they have sown the wind, and they shall reap the whirlwind,'" Rob quoted. The thought gave me a cold satisfaction.

Attempts to interrogate Targets failed. Primary Target shot while resisting arrest. Secondary Target and wife shot and killed two agents and wounded another before successful termination. Intelligence grossly underestimated tactical threat of Targets and did not assess Secondary Target's wife as a tactical threat at all, so Operations should not be held responsible for these losses.

"So, the sheriff was right," Rob was grim. We brought Amit up to speed on what the sheriff thought had happened.

"But I still don't understand why they decided to cover their tracks by calling it an accident instead of a heroic shoot-out with the cyber-terrorists." Amit looked puzzled.

"They're not real feds," Rob explained. "Line-of-duty deaths mean inquiries and inquests and after-action reviews and questions about what they were doing and why they were doing it. Bill Burke filled me in on your 'interrogation.' Can you imagine the Circle's minions saying 'we found a page from a 1907 physics book with the suspect's fingerprints on it that tied him to 'cyber-terror?'"

"I'm surprised they weren't suspicious that your folks shot it out with them," Amit said. "That should have indicated to them that your folks knew the stakes."

"Damn peckerwoods," Rob commented. "Trying to shift the blame from their own incompetence. Your mom was a wicked good shot," Rob explained, "a real natural. But, there's no way she could have shot and killed two agents who were the least bit competent. Those guys were mercenaries. Maybe ex-military or ex-law enforcement. They had some kind of training, but they clearly didn't keep up with it. Good training is expensive and time-consuming. You need the right facilities and resources. It leaves a footprint that might be seen by other people. The Circle either doesn't have those resources or doesn't want to risk the potential exposure. Real feds have better training. Usually, at least. They practice together as a unit. These guys? They were sloppy, they were cocky, and they were killed. Let that be a lesson to us all."

> *Performed assessment of tertiary threat: son of Secondary Target. Secondary Target's son lacks technical expertise to derive implications of proscribed knowledge or to reduce it to practice. Local law enforcement assesses Secondary Target's son as typical delinquent, poor self-control, emotional, undisciplined. In addition, Secondary Target's son is nephew of Civic Circle Initiate. Unlikely Secondary Target's son is an active threat, however recommend Target's son be placed on Homeland Security Watch List and tagged for reinvestigation in five years.*

> *Latest measurements consistent with a Category I Nexus rapidly approaching background levels. We conclude that*

we have successfully contained the Nexus by termination of Targets.

"Looks like you're off the hook for now," Amit assured me.

"They'll be back to check on you again," Rob cautioned. "I have a feeling that whatever you do with your life these next five years, you won't look like a delinquent to them the next time around."

"I'll have 'reformed' a bit from my wild high school days, I'm sure," I agreed, dryly. "Whatever I do, I'll make sure I look squeaky clean. The bottom line is the Circle is convinced they've solved their problem."

"We need to do nothing to disabuse them of that notion," Rob insisted.

Specific Actions:

1. *Investigate similar formerly significant research institutions, libraries, and facilities to ensure that proscribed knowledge is properly contained.*

2. *Review monitoring of online book sales for earlier identification of potentially criminal search or buying patterns. In the future, such investigations should specifically search for additional vectors of proscribed knowledge available to suspects.*

3. *Review the need for enhanced scrutiny and more frequent surveys for potential Nexus developments in the vicinity of nuclear labs and power generation facilities where Nexus signatures may be obscured by background neutrino flux. Continue efforts to suppress and reduce nuclear power generation.*

4. *Review tactical investigation process and threat assessments by Intelligence to reduce the risk of future such incidents of tactical surprise.*

5. *Place Secondary Target's son on Homeland Security Watch List and reinvestigate in five years.*

It had been a long day. I yawned.

"You're tired," Amit said. "We can discuss it more in the morning." He left.

"We have a lot of work ahead of us," Uncle Rob said. "We'll start in the morning. Get a good night's sleep."

I went to bed.

I did not go to sleep.

Chapter 12: My Manifesto

They say the greatest trick the devil ever pulled was convincing the world he didn't exist. My enemy's greatest strength was his anonymity. For a century or longer, my enemy has worked tirelessly to hide, not only the truth, but also the very fact that the truth was hidden, and the identity of those doing the hiding.

The Circle failed.

Now, their mask was off.

Now, I knew their name.

Now, I knew their methods.

Now, I knew a part of the truth they struggled so diligently to hide.

And now, I was the one in possession of the hidden truth: I knew the Circle existed. They had a public face – the Civic Circle. They had a private side – Xueshu Quan – involved in hiding technical and other secrets. They had a direct action arm that killed anyone who got in their way. What they did not have was any idea how much I knew, or how much their secrecy had been compromised.

I knew they were not responsible for the library fire. Did they themselves have an enemy with whom I might make common cause? The Circle was extremely dangerous because they possessed an irresistible power. They had an amazing technology that could literally tell them whenever the course of history was changing or when a threat to their power arose.

That incredible power made the Circle complacent. Their complacency made them vulnerable.

The Circle could detect a Nexus – a point of change where possibilities abound and a new future is born. They could and would intervene violently with overwhelming force to control the potential change, to guide the future toward their ends, and to further their own interests. In exercising that awesome power against my parents, they had just made themselves the very instrument of their own eventual demise. The more I thought about it, the angrier I got. They took and razed my great-grandfather's farm, the work of generations, then wiped out my great-grandfather a second time and drove him to drink. They crushed and stunted my grandfather through hardship and privation, driving him to an early grave. Now, they had killed my parents and Mr. Burleson, and Nicole, and her boss. But, it was more than just them. The death toll was staggering. Some of the best among us: scientists like Maxwell, Hertz, and FitzGerald, maybe even political leaders like Kaiser Frederick III. The Circle exterminated anyone who might expose their secrets, and killed remarkable men who were making a difference: a difference that for some unfathomable reason the Circle was unwilling to tolerate.

The "Category V" Sherman Nexus, indeed! The Circle had detected a major turning point in history. They thought Mr. Burleson and my father were the threats, so they killed them both, along with my mother. They thought that by killing the agents of change they could keep society running smoothly along their preferred trajectory. But, none of their victims was the true threat.

I was.

I knew it.

In some strange way, I could feel the certainty of it in the core of my being.

By their actions the Circle had made a determined and ruthless enemy out of me, unleashing a tsunami that would utterly wipe them out. They had no idea it was coming. That was an incredible weakness I could and would exploit. I vowed I would be their downfall.

The Circle was immensely powerful, supremely arrogant, confidently complacent…

…and so utterly and completely doomed.

True, I was feeble by comparison.

For now.

The vicious bastards killed my parents like they had so many others. The Circle had not the slightest compunction or mercy, and there was nothing I could have done to stop them. In their assessment, I lacked "technical expertise to derive implications of proscribed knowledge or to reduce them to practice." I was "emotional" and "undisciplined," a "delinquent" with "poor self-control." Thank you Sheriff Gunn! The Circle had dismissed me as not worth the trouble to kill. I was quite confident I would soon be demonstrating the error of their assessment. While they might have underestimated me, in all honesty, their fundamental assessment was probably correct.

For now.

But I would not be feeble for long.

I would acquire and cultivate allies. Already I had friends, like Amit, who would help me penetrate the Circle's communications. I had family like Uncle Rob who would help me strike when the time came to act. I had other allies like Sheriff Gunn and Mr. Burke who knew part of the truth and would shield me and support me when called upon. And my father's friends and associates would stand ready to aid me, particularly if I disclosed the circumstances of my parent's murder: men like Doktor Krueger, and Greg Parsons. Despite how creeped out I was by Uncle Larry, his efforts to 'entice' me to the Tollivers and propel the family further into the Civic Circle might well pay dividends.

I would acquire intelligence.

I would develop technical expertise.

I would discover the rest of the Circle's hidden truths.

I would derive the implications of this "proscribed knowledge."

I would "reduce them to practice."

I would seek out opportunities to confound and confuse the Circle.

I would move in secret, applying my capabilities and my resources to thwart their schemes, to expose their secrets, and to weaken their power.

And when I was ready, I would move with my allies to utterly crush the Circle, showing them no more mercy than they showed my parents.

There would be a reckoning.

And when that day of reckoning came, so help me, I would look them in the eye, and I would say:

"My name is Peter Burdell.

"You killed my parents.

"Prepare to die."

There was much to do.

I would start tomorrow.

Tonight I slept.

Soundly.

The End.

Look for Pete's continuing adventure of in
A Rambling Wreck: Book 2 of The Hidden Truth.

ABOUT *THE HIDDEN TRUTH*

This is a work of fiction.

Obviously.

Gore did not defeat Bush in the 2000 election. The September 11, 2001 attacks did not successfully target the White House and Capitol Building, nor did they spare the World Trade Center. The Government did not create an Internet monopoly like Omnitia as part of the Patriot Act. There was no "Preserving Our Planet's Future Act," although global temperatures have actually been remarkably stable since the beginning of the twenty-first century.

And, alas, there was no second season of *Firefly*.

On the other hand, many elements of *The Hidden Truth* do appear to have parallels in our reality. Three of the five great pioneers of electromagnetics, James Clerk Maxwell, Heinrich Hertz, and George Francis FitzGerald, really did die prematurely at the peak of their respective careers. Bruce J. Hunt's *The Maxwellians* provides a great overview. William Suddards Franklin's 1909 *Electric Waves* does curiously omit the mention of Oliver Heaviside on page 115 from the index. Oliver Lodge's *Modern Views of Electricity* (third edition, 1907) actually does have a rather puzzling figure (number 65 on page 302) that displaces nearly an entire page with no mention whatsoever in the text.

The scientific conspiracy depicted in *The Hidden Truth* draws on the real-life drama of the discovery of electromagnetics. Paul J. Nahin's *Oliver Heaviside: Sage in*

Solitude: The Life, Work, and Times of an Electrical Genius of the Victorian Age and his later *Oliver Heaviside: The Life, Work, and Times of an Electrical Genius of the Victorian Age* (same story, but revised and extended a bit) go into Heaviside's life and work in excellent detail. Did Heaviside really discover the concept of electromagnetic waves bouncing from each other? It's a natural extension of the work he described in his 1912 *Electromagnetic Theory*, volume 3. By a remarkable coincidence, the supposed paper by Heaviside on wave interactions sounds suspiciously like some of my own electromagnetic discoveries. See my paper at http://arxiv.org/abs/1407.1800 for details.

Winners write the textbooks in science as well as history, and too often we forget that there are multiple plausible models of physical phenomena. *The Hidden Truth* explores how and why an alternate physical model might have been shunted aside in a deliberate attempt to cripple progress in science and technology.

The story of the Radio Corporation of America (RCA) and in particular how David Sarnoff crushed Edwin Howard Armstrong's FM radio technology may be read in Tom Lewis' excellent *Empire of the Air*, or viewed in a great documentary of the same name by Ken Burns (see episode 7). The geopolitics of RCA in the context of American efforts to overthrow the Marconi monopoly and British dominance of the worldwide telegraphy system are well described in Peter J. Hugill's *Global Communications Since 1844: Geopolitics and Technology*.

The Simon-Ehrlich bet really happened with the outcome described. I suspect the narrator's mother must have read Simon's *The Ultimate Resource* as well as *The Doomsday Myth: 10,000 Years of Economic Crisis*. Norman Borlaug did fend off the starvation of a billion or more people with his high-yield crops. And, as Ronald Regan observed, "Some years ago, the federal government declared war on poverty, and poverty won."

Great Smoky Mountain National Park really was created by eminent domain from the property of many small landowners in the fashion described. Durwood Dunn documents the history of this disgraceful expropriation in *Cades Cove: The Life and Death of a Southern Appalachian Community 1818-1937*.

The Venona Project was a secret effort to decrypt the messages of Soviet spies. Only declassified in 1995, the program identified espionage targeting the Manhattan Project as well as spies throughout the U.S. government.

Was the women's rights movement actually a callous ploy to get women into the workplace so they could be taxed and their children indoctrinated by the state? Aaron Russo argued so, claiming that a Rockefeller family member disclosed their role in the plot. See his documentary, "America: From Freedom to Fascism," for details.

But how could the Circle know the future path of technology well enough to control it? Who founded the Circle? What is the Circle's ultimate goal? How can the Circle possibly be defeated? For answers to those questions, you will have to await future installments of my tale.

ABOUT THE AUTHOR

I'm Hans G. Schantz. Thanks for reading my book. As a small business owner, successful inventor, and scientist, I reduce theory to practice, I figure out and show how things work, and I apply science to solve real-world problems. I appreciate fiction that shows how ordinary people with extraordinary courage and determination can accomplish remarkable achievements. That's why I wrote *The Hidden Truth*.

Will there be a sequel? That, dear reader, is up to you. If *The Hidden Truth* does well enough to make it worth my while, you may, before too long, see the continuing adventures of Pete, his friend Amit, and Uncle Rob along with new friends and allies (and a few new enemies) in *The Brave and the Bold*, *A Rambling Wreck*, and *A Hell of an Engineer*. And that's just the beginning. I have a loose outline for about a dozen novels set in the current timeline along with ample opportunity for crossover and interaction with alternate timelines.

How long will you have to wait to see our heroes test their wits against EVIL Amit complete with his EVIL goatee from an alternate EVIL timeline? Again that depends on you. I have many demands on my time. My wife, Barbara, and I make our home in Huntsville, Alabama with our four children - twin girls and twin boys. When I'm not busy perfecting NFER indoor location products, improving SafeSpot proximity detection, inventing new wireless technologies for The Q-Track Corporation, or relaxing with my family, I like to write fiction. How much fiction I write depends on the reception for *The Hidden Truth*. More sales make it more likely there will be a sequel and will encourage me to complete a sequel more quickly.

Here's how you can help.

Write a review: Readers love feedback from other readers. If you're enthusiastic about *The Hidden Truth*, write a review on Amazon or Goodreads. Share it with your friends through Twitter, Facebook, and other social media. Post it on your blog.

Tell a Friend: Know a friend who might enjoy *The Hidden Truth*? Ask them to buy a copy, or better yet, buy them a copy as a gift. If they like the story, encourage them to write their own review and tell their friends.

Follow ÆtherCzar: I'll keep readers posted on the latest plans for sequels, discounts, and any special promotions on my Twitter feed: @aetherczar, through my blog at: http://www.aetherczar.com/blog, and through my Amazon Author Page: http://www.amazon.com/Hans-G.-Schantz/e/B001K8EGEW. You may sign up on my mail list at http://www.aetherczar.com/HiddenTruth.

May I suggest some other books to keep you entertained while you wait for the next installment of *The Hidden Truth*?

C.S. Forrester's Horatio Hornblower is the classic coming-of-age series, following the titular hero from his beginnings as a midshipman, through his service as captain of a "ship of the line" in the Napoleonic wars, to his final adventure as a retired admiral.

David Weber's Honor Harrington series (start with *On Basilisk Station*), Lois Bujold's Miles Vorkosigan Saga (*The Warrior's Apprentice* is a good place to start), and Peter Grant's Maxwell saga are all excellent examples of this kind of story-telling. A good series of this genre starts with a young and naive hero who through strength of character and hard work gradually acquires the experience and skills that lead to ultimate success.

Many fine science fiction authors write outstanding military science fiction depicting combat and conflict in a futuristic, yet credible, way. Michael Z. Williamson's *Freehold* is a good example.

Unfortunately, there's not much science fiction written from the perspective of an entrepreneur or businessman. Writing is a notoriously poorly paid line of work, and a truly successful entrepreneur, inventor, or businessman is unlikely to make as much from writing as from a successful start-up. Further, the demands of entrepreneurship and family responsibilities leave little time for writing. Still, a few science fiction works I've come across do touch on the inherent drama and excitement of business and technical entrepreneurship.

Heinlein's *Citizen of the Galaxy* has its moments, portraying the business dealings of interstellar Free Traders and the inner machinations of a large corporation. Leo Frankowski did an excellent job working realistic cash flow issues in a dramatic and engaging way in *The Fata Morgana*, but it was all just background to launch him into his "real" story, which I didn't find as compelling. More recently, Vin Suprynowicz has begun a series of books involving book-collector heroes who find and solve science-fiction mysteries involving rare books and old documents: *The Testament of James* and *The Miskatonic Manuscript* are his first two installments. Drawing on his own experience as a collector and dealer of used books, Suprynowicz does an excellent job of depicting the challenges his heroes face in distinguishing book club editions from more valuable printings and managing to make a living in a difficult business.

Some of my favorite stories, like Jim Butcher's Dresden Files (Book 1: *Storm Front*) or Larry Correia's *Grimnoir Chronicles* take place in alternate worlds very much like our own. Butcher's hero, Larry Dresden, is a modern-day wizard/private investigator who keeps the streets of Chicago safe from any number of supernatural threats largely unseen by the city's more mundane inhabitants. I like Butcher's depiction of mystery and adventure and epic battles against the supernatural lurking unseen all around us. Correia's *Grimnoir Chronicles* work from the assumption that magic began slowly popping up in a small number of talented individuals since the mid-nineteenth century. Set in an alternate 1930s, Correia draws heavily on an extensive knowledge of history, science, and culture to craft an alternate world with enough parallels to our own to keep a reader oriented and enough marvelously creative twists to entertain and thrill. Story telling in a universe very much – but not quite – like our own lets me focus on plot and characterization in an everyday context, avoiding complicated world building. In *The Hidden Truth*, I have endeavored to follow the fine example of these gentlemen.

At the same time, I also enjoy historical and technical mysteries: something like Dan Brown's *DaVinci Code* or *Angels and Demons*, but with more plausible history and more credible science. Another book somewhat similar in spirit to *The Hidden Truth* is Arturo Perez-Reverte's *The Club Dumas*, a literary mystery-thriller that pays homage to Dumas's *The Three Musketeers*. John C. Wright's does a remarkable job blending Christian stories and the remarkable real-life history of the Island of Sark in *Iron Chamber of Memory*. His *Somewither* also presents a beautifully crafted coming-of-age tale that blends science and ancient legend together in a most satisfying manner.

My greatest inspiration is the work of philosopher and novelist, Ayn Rand. I'm partial to *The Fountainhead*, but *Atlas Shrugged* is also a favorite of mine. In fact, I wrote a detailed timeline of the events of *Atlas Shrugged* and compiled an extended Table of Contents. You'll find them on my Atlas Shrugged page.

Thanks again for your interest in *The Hidden Truth*.

Acknowledgements

I'm delighted to acknowledge the contributions and assistance of my alpha readers. Brandy Harvey provided detailed proof reading and excellent suggestions to improve plot and characterization. Retired Brigadier General John R. Scales provided outstanding feedback on the logistics and operations of EVIL's direct action team, as well as additional helpful suggestions and corrections. National Instruments IT guru, Jay Garing, confirmed that Amit's scheme to tap into EVIL communications appears plausible. Jerry Gabig verified the credibility of the interrogation scene. Stan Evans provided useful insights on small-town law enforcement. Additional contributors, reviewers, and proofreaders included Barbara McNew Schantz, June Coker McNew, USAF Major Dan Travers, Dean Cook, Phil Oliver, Angie Storz, and Alex Storz.

Made in the USA
Middletown, DE
06 June 2025